Louisa Young was born in London. She was for many years a freelance journalist, working mostly for the motorcycle press, for *Marie Claire* and for the *Guardian*. She has travelled widely and published ten books. She lives in London and Italy with her daughter and the composer Robert Lockhart. She is the adult half of Zizou Corder, authors of the best-selling *Lionboy* trilogy, which is published in thirty-six languages.

Praise for *My Dear, I Wanted To Tell You*:

'Every once in a while comes a novel that generates its own success, simply by being loved. Louisa Young's *My Dear I Wanted to Tell You* inspires the kind of devotion among its readers not seen since David Nicholls' *One Day*'

The Times

'*Birdsong* for the new millennium'

Tatler

'Powerful, sometimes shocking, boldly conceived, it fixes on war's lingering trauma to show how people adapt – or not – and is irradiated by anger and pity'

The Sunday Times

'[A] tender, elegiac novel. Others have been here before, of course, from Sebastian Faulks to Pat Barker, but Young belongs in their company'

Mail on Sunday

'A love story built on rich, strange details of the first world war'   *Guardian*

'Beautifully realised'   *Daily Express*

'Masterfully conveyed'   *Woman & Home*

'Full of drama, betrayal and addictive real-life detail'   *Red*

'This is a moving and powerful novel, one you're not likely to forget'   *Choice*

'A book that should be read by everyone'   *New Books*

Also by Louisa Young

FICTION
Baby Love
Desiring Cairo
Tree of Pearls

NON-FICTION
The Book of the Heart
A Great Task of Happiness: The Life of Kathleen Scott

LOUISA YOUNG

My Dear, I Wanted to Tell You

HARPER

HARPER

An imprint of HarperCollins*Publishers*
77–85 Fulham Palace Road,
Hammersmith, London W6 8JB

www.harpercollins.co.uk

First published by HarperCollins*Publishers* 2011
This paperback edition 2012

1

ISBN: 978 0 00 736144 1

This novel is entirely a work of fiction.
Some characters (or names) and incidents portrayed in it,
while based on real historical figures, are the work of the
author's imagination.

Printed and bound in Great Britain by
Clays Ltd, St Ives plc

For Robert Lockhart

Prologue

France, 7 June 1917, 3.10 a.m.
It had been a warm night. Summery. Quiet, as such nights go.

The shattering roar of the explosions was so very sudden, cracking through the physicality of air and earth, that every battered skull, and every baffled brain within those skulls, was shaken by it, and every surviving thought was shaken out. It shuddered eardrums and set livers quivering; it ran under skin, set up counter-waves of blood in veins and arteries, pierced rocking into the tiny canals of the sponge of the bone marrow. It clenched hearts, broke teeth, and reverberated in synapses and the spaces between cells. The men became a part of the noise, drowned in it, dismembered by it, saturated. They were of it. It was of them.

They were all used to that.

In London, Nadine Waveney, startled from dull pre-dawn somnolence at the night desk, heard the distance-shrouded crumps and thought, for a stark, confused moment, *Is it here? Zeppelins?* She looked up, her face the same low pale colour as the flame of the oil lamp beside her.

Jean scampered in from next door. 'Did you hear that?' she hissed.

'I did,' said Nadine, eyes wide.

'*France!*' hissed Jean. '*A big 'un!*' And she slid away from the doorway again.

Nadine thought, *Sweet Jesus, let Riley not be in that.*

In Kent, Julia Locke sat bolt upright in her bed before she was even half awake, saw the cupboard door hanging open and thought, foolishly: *Oh . . . thunder . . .* but she was sound asleep again when Rose, in her dressing-gown, looked in on her.

In the Channel, the waters wandered suddenly this way and that, in denial of the natural movements of tide and wind.

At Calais, a handful of late-carousing sailors paused and turned.

At Étaples, a sentry woke with a sharp nod that he felt certain would crack his head backwards off his neck. 'Crikey,' someone murmured, 'hope that's us, not them.' Two ruins away, a sixteen-year-old whore paused and shrank, her heart battering and shaking. Her thirty-five-year-old punter fell away from her, unmanned as his blood hurtled elsewhere in his body.

Beyond Paris, a displaced peasant sleeping on a sack didn't bother to wake. Sheep, less well-informed, panicked and ran to and fro. Their shepherds couldn't be bothered to.

An upright piano stood in a field, gaping and rotting, where it had been since October 1914.

In the Reserve Line those who slept leapt awake; those who sat by dampened braziers jumped; those who leapt and jumped were pulled down by their comrades, with profanities and muffled cries of 'Fuck sake, man.' The Aussie sappers who had dug the tunnels under the German line, and laid the six hundred thousand pounds of mines, grinned and smoked. Ungentlemanly it might be, as warfare goes, but *they* had started *that*, with their filthy illegal gas – and, anyway, it's effective. Which is all anyone cares about by now.

Up the line, the Allied men in their trenches reeled with the earth around them, and kept reeling until the earth around them let them stop. Above, a flock of starlings launched and circled, a counter-nebula of black on blue. Below, the fat rats scattered.

Across no man's land, the soldiers flew up in the air, and fell, and the earth flew up in the air, and fell, and buried them whether they were dead or not.

And the German artillery responded, and it all doubled, redoubled, an exponential vastness, and in Berlin wives and girlfriends sat up at night desks and in beds.

Locke and Purefoy had been ready for it. That edge was on the night, the edge that leaked something coming . . . something else, beyond the ordinary filth. Everyone wore a dulled alertness, so when they started, though it was a shock, well, it was always a shock.

Locke was by the sack-flap entrance to the dugout, smoking, humming softly a song he was composing, about bats.

Purefoy was staring out through a periscope from the fire-step, thinking about Ainsworth, Couch, Ferdinand and Dowland, and Dowland's brother, and Bloom, Atkins, Burdock, Taylor, Wester . . . and the rest. He was reciting their names, all the names he could remember, and their qualities, and trying to remember their faces, and their voices, their Christian names, and their little ways, and how they had died, and when, and where.

As the string of mines went monumentally up across the way, little landslides of earth trickled down from the ratty timber-and-sandbag ceiling on to their tea-chest desk. Locke grabbed his head, elbows round his ears. He barked, loudly, wordlessly – then flung his arms out, and strode into the body of the trench. Purefoy was already moving along the line, joking, clapping the men on their shoulders.

In the answering barrage of shells, one took the edge off the parados twenty feet along. Purefoy and Locke and their companions flung themselves down in the homely mud of their trench, that six-feet-deep poisoned haven with which they were so familiar and, crouched under the parapet, shared the peculiar safety of knowing that the worst was already happening.

Chapter One

London, towards Christmas, 1907

On a beautiful day of perfect white snow, cut-blue sky and hysterical childhood excitement, Nadine Waveney's cousin Noel threw a snowball in Kensington Gardens. It hit a smaller boy they didn't know, smack on the side of the face, causing him to gasp and shout and lose his footing, and knocking him on to the uncertain icy surface of the Round Pond. Still shouting, the boy, whose name was Riley Purefoy, crashed through the filmy frozen layers – and shot out again, gasping, shaking slush and icy water off himself until his hair stood on end, and laughing uproariously. Noel, who was bigger, stared at him, unsure. Nadine, standing back, smiled. She liked that the smaller boy was laughing. She'd seen him before in the park. He was always scrambling about, climbing things, collecting things. Once they'd come face to face halfway up a conker tree, deep in the green leaves. He'd had a pigeon feather in his hair, like an Indian warrior. He'd laughed then as well.

Jacqueline Waveney, well dressed, high-cheekboned, self-consciously verging on Bohemian, insisted on bringing Riley home to warm and dry him. They lived close: just across the Bayswater Road from the park gate. 'Everyone comes here when they fall in,' she told him, as they scurried along the path to the gate. 'Or if they get rained on. We're the first stop for people in trouble in the park.' Her smile was warm and her accent strange – French, though Riley didn't know that then.

The house was huge to him, though quite small to them. He was taken through a hall to the drawing room: 'droing room', Jacqueline said. Riley looked at the tall ceiling, the creamy panelling, the velvet sofas, the warm fire, the glossy peacock-green tiling around it. Inside, Mrs Waveney had him wrapped in a towel, and his clothing taken away to be hung on the boiler. He was given hot chocolate to drink, and some dry clothes to wear, too big for him. The people stood around him, noticing, but not seeming to mind, that he was really quite a common little boy.

Noel was jolly sorry, and said so gallantly.

Mrs Waveney thought: *Look at him, poor thing. We could probably spare those clothes.*

Her husband Robert, the well-known orchestral conductor, looked in. 'Hello there,' he said, or something like that. 'What's all this, then?' Riley knew who he was. He'd seen him crossing the park often enough to the Albert Hall. He'd seen his picture in the *Illustrated News*.

Nadine, whose honey-yellow eyes slanted like a naughty fairy's, glanced and smiled.

Riley took in the well-known dad, the friendly family, the cuddly maid, the paintings on the wall, the grand piano, the books on the shelves, the smiling girl. It was not like

14

his house – though his house was very snug, and contained his parents and his little sisters, whom he loved and ignored, except his dad, who had given him a clockwork grasshopper for Christmas, and could still throw him up in the air. He was a fireman, and he said, 'Don't look to the fire brigade, Riley, it's a good job but you can do better.'

Riley was neither shy nor ashamed to be there. He did not feel that he was in the wrong place. He tasted the hot sweet chocolate, and he looked around boldly, and he knew that this was what his dad was talking about. Better.

His clothes did not dry, and Jacqueline, who thought him sweet, with his bright eyes and curly hair, suggested he come the next day for them. His mother Bethan, a devoted woman of Welsh extraction and firm ideas, baked a batch of tarts that he was to offer as a thank-you, and remember to bring the tin back.

'Don't know why,' said his dad, John, in his undershirt in the kitchen chair, braces slung over his wide shoulders, looking at the paper. 'It was their boy knocked Riley into the pond.'

'It shows manners,' said Bethan. 'Go to the back door, won't you, Riley love? And watch out for 'em!' she called. The middle classes were always after something from the working man. *As if they didn't have enough. Not that I'd want it. Fancy ways.* Bethan had been known to laugh out loud in the street at extremes of fashion among the better classes. She watched keenly, fearfully, as her only boy went down the street to visit the other world. *He won't fall for it, will he? He won't get ideas and resentments? We don't want it – he won't. We've brought him up right . . .* She found

15

herself murmuring a blessing for him as he disappeared round the corner.

John rolled his eyes. Bethan was stuck and strung up about the middle classes. Scared of them, wanting what they had, pretending she didn't, resenting them for having it, and on top of all that, there was her furious head-tossing pride in being a working woman with no need for any of *that*, thank you very much.

~

Riley didn't think there was a back door, unless he went down the side alley. He went to the front door. He arrived at the same time as another visitor, an older man with a beard and an alluring turpentine smell, in a black velvet coat smoothed and shining with age. For a moment Riley held back, thinking of his mother, wondering, but the man said: 'Hello there, young fella!' and they went in together.

Riley, having been led to believe that posh people were standoffish, was surprised.

'Hello, Riley!' called Mrs Waveney. 'Are those for us? Mmm – how lovely of you. Noel, darling, Riley is here! Ring for Barnes, would you, and ask for some tea?'

Riley soon worked it out. It is because they are not just posh, they are artists. On Sunday strolls in Kensington Gardens Bethan took pleasure in pointing out to him different types of posh, and how ridiculous they were. Johnno the Thief would do a similar thing, judging whose pocket was worth picking at Paddington station. Riley surveyed the old man's velvet coat, the beautiful woman's dark red curls, the taking a common-as-muck boy back to their very

16

comfortable beautiful house, with the paintings and the strange items . . . a curved and shining dagger hanging on the wall, tiny ivory elephants in a glass-fronted cabinet. Artistic, definitely. Bethan would sneer, because her dad hadn't let her sing when she was a girl, and Johnno would let them pass, because ones like that never had much cash on them.

'Top bruise!' Noel said enviously, and poked Riley's cheek-bone. The silent girl smiled at him again, and Riley smiled back. They were in the middle of decorating a fir tree with ribbons and shining orange fruit and glass balls. Riley had seen such things in the extraordinary windows of Selfridges, the new palace of splendours from which he had been chased two days before. This one was not so big but its colours sparked his eye.

'Come and help us,' said Mrs Waveney. 'Can your little fingers tie these on?' She passed him a clear round glass ball, light as sunlight, pure as a bubble.

'Where should I put it?' he asked.

'Wherever you want, darling,' she said.

He stared at the tree. Glass balls dangled on the sprigs of dark fir, hanging, gleaming. Pink like a rose petal in the sunken garden near the Orangery, pale green like the lime-walk leaves in spring, blue like the flash under a mallard's wing on the Round Pond. There were too many bunched up at the top. He checked how many were still in the box. Plenty to cover the whole tree. Carefully, he fed the gold wire fixing of the clear ball round a sprig on a branch in the middle, quite deep in. It would reflect the light and balance the coloured baubles. Without thinking, he undid a couple of the coloured ones and redistributed them lower down.

The older man watched Riley, smiling, enjoying the care he took, noting his flat, broad-cheeked face, his scruffy curly hair, his dark eyes, his wounded look.

They drank tea, ate the jam tarts. Jacqueline was amused by the way Riley tucked in. Many boys would feel obliged to hold back, under the circumstances.

When the time came for Riley to leave, Robert Waveney said courteously, 'Well, now, Riley, Sir Alfred likes your face. He wants to put it in a painting, on top of a goaty-legged faun. What do you think? Could you sit still long enough for him to paint you? He'd probably give you a shilling.'

Riley saw the gates of opportunity swinging open before his eyes. Beyond, he could see Better, shining in the distance like the lilies of heaven. 'Course I can, Mr Waveney,' he said.

Chapter Two

London, 1907–14

Riley, the Waveneys and Sir Alfred lived in a part of London that, from one street to another, couldn't make up its mind. Riley's home was a little house up by the canal, a working man's cottage, in a row, damp, with a yard with a privy in it. Two minutes away was Paddington station, through which the whole empire passed, observed for pickpocketing purposes by Johnno and by Riley out of pure human curiosity. (Riley did not pick pockets. He'd promised his mum.) Five minutes from there was Kensington Gardens, where the trees were tall and the grass was smooth and children in white petticoats dashed after hoops, and nannies in uniform dashed after them. If Riley went with Johnno, the park-keeper chased them out. If he went alone, and was clever about it, he could play there all day, watching ducks, climbing trees, diving and dipping in the Serpentine, spying on gardeners, learning statues by heart, hiding.

Beautiful houses lay along the north side of the park: Georgian villas with magnolias in their wide gardens; high white stucco-fronted mansions, mad fairy-tale apartment

buildings six storeys high, with curved balconies and con-
servatories, and ornate bay windows at unlikely angles. The
Waveneys' was the first Riley had been into. Sir Alfred's, in
Orme Square, was the second. At the Waveneys' he had fallen
for the comfort; at Sir Alfred's, it was first Messalina, the great
dane, big enough to pull a cart, with her ebony satin jowls
and quivering legs, and second the paint: the colours, and the
smell, and the rich oily shining magnificence. And then the
paintings: heroines and beggar maids, knights in gleaming
silver-grey armour, coiling strings of flowers and loops of
braided hair, emerald weeds floating under water, gauzy drapes
of cloth you could see through to the wax-white glowing flesh
beneath, glimpses of cavernous blue skies . . . all made of
paint, and light seeming to come from inside the canvas. It
looked like the real world, so real, but much, much better. It
was a kind of miracle to Riley that such things could be created out of thick coloured oils squeezed from lead tubes.

And there was Mrs Briggs, purse-lipped and holy-minded,
who gave him cake and hot tea.

Riley knew perfectly well that this was not his world. He
recognised that if he did not act swiftly it might be whisked
away from him as quickly as he had been whisked into it.
If someone were to look closely at the expression on the
face of the young faun garlanded with vine leaves standing
to the left of Bacchus in Sir Alfred's famous painting
Maenads at the Bacchanale, they might detect in it a badly
concealed combination of desperate desire, cheerful delight
and devious determination.

'What are you painting next, sir?' he asked, with bright,
transparent disingenuousness.

'*The Childhood of the Knights of the Round Table*,' Sir Alfred said, amused.

'Any of 'em look like me at all, sir?' Riley said, putting on a noble expression, and turning a little towards the light.

He almost wept with joy when Sir Alfred agreed that his face was just right for the young Sir Gawaine fighting his way through a thorn bush (representing the Green Knight he was to face in years to come), which would require another few weeks of his presence.

Riley applied his mind to ways of making himself useful to Sir Alfred, his various pupils, and to Mrs Briggs. There were plenty: errands, tidying up, fetching, copying, sharpening, lining up, climbing to the upper shelves, which neither Sir Alfred nor Mrs Briggs could reach. Every day, modelling or not, he turned up after school 'in case Sir Alfred needs anything, Mrs Briggs' – and he always did: someone to run to the art suppliers, someone to take Messalina to run and play and leap about in the park, someone to clean up the studio without actually moving anything the way Mrs Briggs always did, someone to sit for an anonymous young shoulder or a foot, someone who didn't mind being bossed, who loved being told things by an old man with many, many stories to tell, who was young and strong and delighted to learn how to prepare a canvas and had none of the vanities of an art student. After some months of this, Mrs Briggs, who liked everything in its place, pointed out that the position was unregulated, and the boy should be paid for his work. After a burglar stole Sir Alfred's late mother's jewellery, it was decided the boy should live in, as extra security. (Riley was aware of the irony.)

Bethan and John were invited to tea in the kitchen by Mrs Briggs because, after all, it was not as if they were hiring a servant. Riley, only half aware that this was improper, dragged them upstairs to meet Sir Alfred, and to see his studio, and his paintings. John thought the paintings beautiful, and Sir Alfred very gentlemanly, and said cautiously: 'As long as he's going to school . . .'

Sir Alfred said: 'Of course, Mr Purefoy. He's an intelligent lad.'

Bethan said very little, and that night she cried because she knew she was outnumbered.

From the beginning, Riley wrote down every word he heard that was unfamiliar to him. On Sundays, when he took his wages home, he would ask his parents what these new words meant. If they didn't know, he would ask Miss Crage at school. If she didn't know, he would go through the tall, feather-leaved volumes of Sir Alfred's *Encyclopedia Britannica*. Or ask Mrs Briggs. Or Nadine, who came every Saturday morning for her drawing lesson. Or he would ask Nadine's mum and dad, when she invited him back there – like that day when she dragged him to see the new statue of Peter Pan, which had appeared overnight in the shrubbery by the Serpentine, gleaming bronze among the heavy leaves, and afterwards they went to her house, and Sir James Barrie himself was there, drinking tea and laughing about the big secret and surprise of the statue, laughing such a wicked little laugh, and Riley had imitated it so well, and Sir James had said he wished he'd known Riley before because he would have modelled a Lost Boy on him, and Riley felt a momentary pang of unfaithfulness to Sir Alfred and Art, in favour of Sir James and Literature.

But, best of all, he could ask Sir Alfred.

'Come on, you little sponge,' he would say. 'I only wanted a boy to clean my brushes, and now I've got a miniature Roger Fry on my hands.'

'What's a Roger Fry, sir?' said Riley.

'Pour me a whisky and I'll tell you.'

'Well, he's bettering himself, isn't he?' said Mrs Briggs to Mrs Purefoy, when she called at the house one day to take him to buy a shirt, he was growing so fast. Mrs Briggs had bought him a shirt only two months before, but she didn't want to make anything of it.

Bethan was glad he wasn't running around with those boys at the station any more, but she wasn't happy. It wasn't just that the son of a free working man was – sort of – in service, because he wasn't in service, quite. If he was in service, how come he was going to school each day, and how come he and the girl Miss Waveney were down Portobello together that time with that giant black dog as if it was theirs, gawking at the Snake Lady and sharing a bag of humbugs? And it wasn't that he was getting educated beyond his station, because she knew that education meant a lot to John, though, herself, she didn't see the point as he wasn't so much learning a trade, was he? It wasn't even that she didn't see enough of him – who would expect to see a big working schoolboy of fourteen, except to feed him and make him wash if you were lucky? Many women didn't see their working boy from one year's end to the next. What bothered her was that he didn't talk the same. He tried to hide it from her, when he came home, but she knew. He was learning to talk proper. They might not have done it on purpose but they had transformed him, from a blob of a boy into – well, it wasn't clear what.

~

Robert Waveney and Sir Alfred were about to go to the Queen's Hall to hear the marvellous Russian, Rachmaninoff, playing his new piano concerto, under Mengelberg. Riley, it turned out, was coming too.

'He'll appreciate it more than I will,' Sir Alfred said truthfully. 'In fact – actually, Robert, what do you think of this – his school chucks them all out at the end of the year – what shall we do with him? I was thinking more school.'

'He wouldn't get into Eton, surely,' Waveney said. 'He's hardly educated at all, is he?'

'Well, now, selfishly, I don't want to send him away. And one doesn't want to encourage any . . . illusions . . . or any sense of injustice. About money and so on. Resentments. I thought perhaps Marylebone Grammar . . .'

Waveney agreed that that would be more appropriate, and knew one of the governors. Riley, whose dad had told him, 'You're lucky if you even get one opportunity in your entire life, and when you do, I advise you to recognise it and grab it by the bollocks, and don't let go,' swelled with joy. A school where everybody wanted to be there was a revelation to him; the teachers spread panoplies of glorious knowledge before him, and when the other lads mocked him for this or that he hit them. All was as it should be, and he strode the territory fearlessly.

24

It was hard walking past the end of his parents' street each day without having time to stop in and say hello, but he had so much to do, working like a demon at his studies, and at his duties, not to let Sir Alfred down. As well he always wanted to see what his mentor had been painting each day, and he couldn't bear to miss any visitors – men of the world, blasé young students, knights of this and that, Nadine – or interesting outings where he could carry Sir Alfred's sketching things and hear what he had to say about ancient Egypt or Sebastiano del Piombo or whatever turned up. And he needed time to draw, himself, because it seemed he wasn't bad, actually . . . not good, but not bad . . .

Patterns and habits grew up, and it all seemed very normal. Time passed, and it was normal. Even for Bethan, the sudden lurches of maternal loss subsided after a year or two. They were lucky. Placing a boy was like marrying off a daughter – the good parents' first responsibility. And Riley was, it seemed, placed, and happily. The years of Riley's late child-hood were, by any standard, long and nourishing and golden; blessed, not riven, by the double life he was able to lead. The weeks belonged to school and Sir Alfred, and Sundays to his family, when he would eat, and let the little girls climb all over him and use him as a seesaw and make him throw them up in the air. Loads of older brothers and sisters lived away, after all, and came back slightly too big for the little house they'd been born in. It only made them more glamorous.

~

Early one mild spring Saturday morning, seven years after he had first come to Orme Square, Riley, now eighteen, took the long, unwieldy pole that Sir Alfred could no longer manage and unwound the bolts on all the skylights and high windows in the studio. A beautiful soft air slipped in off the park and the squares, limpid, blossomy, dancing with cherry and lilac. Riley was thinking, *How would you paint that? Who could paint that clean lightness?* Even the horses' hooves outside on the Bayswater Road sounded lighter. What a day!

Nadine arrived as usual about nine for her drawing lesson, though it wasn't till ten, and as usual Sir Alfred was still at his coffee, talking to the newspaper. So, as usual, Nadine perched herself on the old workbench up in the studio, wearing her dark blue pinafore, swinging her legs, and watching as Riley laid out brushes, checked supplies, made a list. When he had done he stopped and sketched her instead, light pencil, just a quick thing. He didn't think it was very good. She was much better than him at getting a likeness. There was a bunch of hyacinths in a glass jar beside her on the dark wood, also blue, the blue of the Madonna's cloaks in Sir Alfred's books of Renaissance paintings. He would have liked to paint them, and her. He was fascinated by the variability of colour, by the adjustability of oils. He longed for an excuse to stare at her for hours.

'I came on my bicycle today,' she said, testing him out.

'Can I have a go?' He had been idly trying to persuade her to come swimming in the Serpentine; she was resisting. She would never come swimming any more. The thought interested him. Maybe he could use the testing of the bicycle to get her into the park, at least.

'It's a girl's bicycle,' she said.

'All bicycles are boys' bicycles,' he said.

She gave him an evil look. She had long ago persuaded him that the suffragettes were right, but he still liked to torment her. 'That's too nearly true to be funny,' she said. 'I shall have a motorcycle when I'm older. I'll go abroad on it, all over the world, drawing and painting everything I see, and paying my way in portraits. No one will stop me.'

'They wouldn't dare,' he said. *Why do I keep saying stupid things? Mean things?*

'You mean *you* wouldn't dare . . .' she said, but she said it fondly.

'I'd dare anything where you're concerned,' he said boldly.

'Oh, you won't have to. After I've been all over the world on my motorcycle I'll want to come back and be a famous artist and have a lovely house and babies. I'll bring a kangaroo to be my pet. You can share it.'

'The kangaroo? Or the house?' He had a sudden quick vision of an adult life: two easels at opposite ends of a sunny studio.

'Everything,' she said. 'You can even share my motorcycle, so long as you don't pretend to everyone that it's yours.'

She said it so easily, he thought she must not have any idea what she was saying. Of course he let the delightfulness of the image dazzle its impossibility into invisibility. Her future, after all, was planned and certain: marriage. His was more . . . open – which allowed him to think impossible thoughts.

Don't get attached to the girl, Riley. They're not like us. His mother's voice.

Change the subject.

27

They talked about who could paint a spring morning like this one.

'Samuel Palmer,' he suggested. She was of the opinion that Palmer was more June, heavier and more lush. He liked to hear her say the word, 'lush'.

'Well, Botticelli, of course,' she said.

'Perhaps there are springs like that in Italy, but that's no English spring.'

Then she exclaimed, 'I know! Van Gogh. Like the almond blossoms.'

They took out the large folder of reproductions that Sir Alfred kept purely, Riley sometimes thought, to sneer at – or perhaps out of fear of such a different way of doing it. They laid out the picture on the long, pale, rough trestle desk under the window, and stood side by side, falling into the picture, the moss and sunlight on the branches, the eternal deep sky behind, the lovely light-catching little blossoms twisted this way and that, the darts of tiny red buds, the one small broken-off branch with its sharp remnant blade pointing up like a thorn in Paradise.

'I wonder where it is now,' she said. 'The actual painting.' They had seen it in an exhibition at the Grafton Gallery to which Sir Alfred had taken them. The paintings, to Nadine and to Riley, had been perfect, wonderful, naturally beautiful, right, somehow, and they hadn't understood at all why people were laughing, and expostulating, and leaving.

Riley, who had often taken this picture out and had read the back of the print, said: 'It's in Amsterdam.'

'Let's go and see it,' she said.

There, with the pressure of her arm against his, in the

morning sun, under the window, smell of oils and turpentine and hyacinth, her voice: 'Let's go and see it.'

'On your motorcycle?' he said, with a laugh.

'Yes! Or – in some real way. Let's *do* things, Riley. I'm going a little mad, you know. We'll be grown-ups soon. Let's DO things. Like when you took me to look at the Snake Lady in Portobello Market, and all those people were singing.' They'd only been thirteen when they'd done that, and they'd got into terrible trouble. 'Let's go to Brighton and paddle and eat shrimps and see the Pavilion! Let's go to Amsterdam . . .'

'Let's run away together to Paris and go to art school,' he said. 'Let's rob a bank and live like kings and go to Rodin's open weekends at his studio, and wear gypsy robes and eat figs.'

'Stop it,' she said. 'We could do *some*thing . . .'

Footsteps on the stairs shut them up. It was one of Sir Alfred's students, Terence, turning up to work on his big oil of Kensington Palace. Riley felt a strong urge to push him down the stairs. Instead he revelled in a beautiful look of complicity with Nadine, which made his blood run warmer and his heart light and brave.

He glanced at Terence's painting emerging from its dustsheet. Why Terence bothered, he hadn't the slightest idea. It might as well have been painted in 1860. Plus he was doing it from east of the Round Pond, looking west with a sunset behind the palace, so for all he called it *Queen Victoria Over the Water*, the statue in front of the palace was all wrong because in reality it would be in shade. In fact everything would be in shade, as his light was completely wrong . . . He should be doing it in morning light, but he was too lazy to get up early. Sir Alfred was indulgent with him, Riley thought. *But then Sir Alfred is indulgent with me too, so . . .*

Oh, go away, Terence.

It was *all* he wanted now. All he ever wanted. Alone with Nadine. The very words gave him a frisson.

Why should it be impossible? Surely in this big new twentieth century he could find a way to make it possible. After all, his mother would have thought it impossible for him even to *know* a girl like Nadine . . . Things change. You can make things change. And the Waveneys weren't like normal upper-class people. They were half French and well-travelled and open-minded. They had noisy parties and played charades and hugged each other, and Mrs Waveney didn't always get up in the morning. Mr Waveney had told him that champagne glasses were modelled on the Empress Josephine's breast. There'd been a Russian round there once, and a German with *anarchist leanings*. Riley had looked that up too.

'I say, Purefoy,' said Terence, fumbling around with his canvas. He was a tall, slender young man, with corn-coloured hair, who dropped things. 'Don't suppose you'd sit for me a couple of afternoons next week? If Sir Alf can spare you? I'll pay you . . . There'll be no . . .'

'No what?' said Riley, amused.

Terence glanced at Nadine. 'Nothing you might not want to do,' he said delicately. 'I'll give you sixpence a session.'

'How very grand he is,' giggled Nadine, as Terence left to see if Mrs Briggs would make him a cup of tea.

'Why does he want to draw *me*?' asked Riley.

'Because you're handsome,' Nadine said. She was sitting on the table under the window, looking out, her legs drawn up, pale and studious now with her sketchbook, her black hair wild.

He was surprised by that. 'Am I?' he said, and he turned to her, feeling a little bit suddenly furious. '*You*'re beautiful,' he said, and even as he said it, he couldn't believe that he had.

She turned to look at him. And she froze, and then he froze, and at the same time the blood was running very hot beneath his skin, and he terribly wanted to kiss her.

She jumped up from the table and stood looking at him.

He was not going to kiss her. He must not kiss her.

He reached out his hand and, very gently, he laid it at the side of her waist, on the curve. This seemed to him less bad than a kiss, and almost as good. His hand settled there: strong, white, paint-stained. She felt its weight, felt how right it felt, felt its possibilities.

The hand relaxed.

They stood there for a moment of unutterable perfection.

Oh, God, but the hand wanted more – to snake round to the back of her waist, to strengthen on the small of her back and pull her in; the other one wanted to dive under the wild black hair to the back of her neck, to spread, to pull her in.

He locked the hand in position, to save the moment, to prolong it, to protect it, to not destroy it: it was a miracle.

He had to take the hand away.

She looked at him. She looked at his hand. She looked up at him again, questioning. Every drop of blood in her was standing to attention. And she laughed, and she ran from the studio, clunking down the stairs, singing a kind of joyful *toot ti toot* song, a fanfare.

Sir Alfred, coming upstairs, noticed it. He recognised it, and glanced upstairs. Terence? He didn't think so.

Mrs Briggs, crossing the hall, caught Sir Alfred's glance for a second, and raised her eyebrows.

~

Someone had shot an archduke. It was in all the papers. Everybody was talking about it.

'What's it about?' Nadine asked Riley.

'A Serbian shot the Austrian archduke so the Austrians want to bash the Serbians but the Russians have to protect the Serbians so the Germans have to bash France so they won't help the Russians against the Austrians and once they've bashed France we're next so we have to stop them in Belgium,' said Riley, who read Sir Alfred's paper in the evening.

'Oh,' she said. 'What does that mean?'

'There's going to be a war, apparently.'

'Oh,' she said.

Well, it would be over by the time they were old enough to go to Amsterdam, where he would put his hand on her waist again, and she would laugh and sing but not run away downstairs.

She hadn't said anything. Neither had he. But when they talked about everything else, and caught eyes when the same thing amused them both and nobody else, or when the orchestra was particularly thrilling, there was a new electric layer to the pleasure they had always taken in these things. Sometimes they looked at each other, and her blood sprang up every time. Sometimes he had to go into another room. He was dying. He didn't think girls died in the same way. He felt her smile on him, all the time.

~

'Papa,' she said easily, happily, walking across the park with him to the Albert Hall. 'What is it like to be in love?' She was happier asking him than her mother. Her mother would ask questions, practical ones. It wouldn't occur to Papa to ask questions about practical things.

'Oh, it's marvellous,' he said. 'Or terrible. Or both. The Romans saw it as a fit of madness that you wouldn't wish on anybody. But there's nothing you can do about it, that's the main thing.'

She grinned, but he was already thinking again about bar seventy-eight in the slow movement.

~

Sitting for Terence was money for old rope. All that uncertain summer Riley turned up at the tall dark-red house in a row of tall, dark-red houses in South Kensington. He ran up the many flights of stairs to Terence's studio where, on entering, he marvelled briefly at how messily rich people could live, and he sat. Terence drew him, sketched him, pen pencil watercolour, this angle or that, under the window, by the plant, catching the light, standing sitting lying across that chair.

'What do you think of the war, then?' asked Terence, one late August morning. 'Pretty bad, isn't it? Everyone's getting very het up. '

'Are you?' asked Riley.

'I'm not the type,' said Terence.

It turned out that 'not doing anything he might not want to do' meant not taking his clothes off.

'I'll take my clothes off,' said Riley, mildly. 'If there's more money in it.' Whatever happened, he was going to need money.

There was more money. Riley thought it was funny.

But he quite liked Terence. He observed his manners, copied his nonchalance, stole words off him, and then dropped them again, mostly. The public-school languidity and slang seemed to him unmanly. Riley was looking around for the kind of man he might be going to be, and having trouble finding one. He wasn't ever going to deny what he was. But he needed to do better. How to reconcile that? He was eighteen now. School was finished, and no one had suggested any possible future activities. How long would he be Sir Alfred's boy? What could he be, a boy like him? But there was a problem. The first step in every direction was Nadine, and the shadow of Nadine not being permitted overhung . . . everything. Every possible step into every possible future: impossible. Impermissible.

Perhaps if I made lots of money . . . the City? But you need money to start. Art? Not talented enough. And how would you pay for art school?

Crime?

He laughed.

34

But sitting naked in front of Terence wasn't going to do it . . .

While Terence drew him, he thought about what he read in the papers: angels appearing on the battlefield, the evil demon Hun, and the boys Over There. He wondered. Boys from Paddington were going, his mother had told him. 'But don't you go joining up,' she said. 'The army's just another trick they play on us.' Her dad, Riley knew, had been killed somewhere in Africa, in the army. 'You don't want to go getting involved with abroad,' Bethan said.

France, to Riley, meant the golden sunflowers Van Gogh had painted in Arles, the bright skies, the lines of trees, the colours of Matisse, the sea, Renoir's girls in bars, David's dramatic half-naked heroes, Fragonard's girls with their petticoats flying, Ingres' society ladies with their white skin, black hair and melting fingers . . . He thought of Olympia, naked on her *chaise-longue*, with the little black ribbon round her neck and that look on her face. He thought about Nadine. He thought that, as he was naked, perhaps he had better think about something else.

It was only natural that Terence should stare at Riley's body, given that he was drawing it. He stared at Riley standing, sitting, lying across the chair. Riley was what they call 'not too tall but well-knit', cleanly muscled, and his skin was particularly white like an Ingres lady's.

'I don't suppose . . .' said Terence, that afternoon. 'No, of course not.'

'What?' said Riley, but Terence wouldn't say, and suggested they pack up as the light was going, which it wasn't.

Chapter Three

There was a recruiting party up by Paddington station. On the Sunday, coming back from his mum and dad's, Riley had seen them marching around in their red coats, the sergeant pointing at men in the crowd, telling them they had to go to France because gallant little Belgium needed them. He'd seen gallant little Belgium on a poster: she was a beautiful woman in a nightie, apparently, being chased by a red-eyed Hun demon in a helmet with a point on it. She became, slightly, in his mind, Nadine's mother, Jacqueline.

You had to be five foot eight, the sign said. Riley saw a fair number of lads turned away for being too little and skinny. The rest were piling in, and everyone around was cheering them along, and they were grinning sheepishly. Happy and excited. Going to France! Shiny buttons and boots and, Jesus Christ, square meals and a different life!

Once again Riley thanked God, who had so completely blessed him. In his mind he ran through: Sir Alfred, his kindness and generosity; Mum and Dad, their love – except when Dad said art was all very well but a bit nancy, wasn't it, for a man?; the education he was getting. Though he needed more.

Always more. Perhaps in the evenings. There was a Working Men's Institute . . . history, science, philosophy, maths . . .

And Nadine, that bloody girl. Whom he had to kiss. *I will die if I don't kiss her. But how on earth can I kiss her?*

I am a lucky, lucky boy, he thought, *and I will do better, I will do whatever it takes*, and he swore to himself once again that he would not squander what he had been given.

One Saturday Nadine did not turn up.

'Miss Waveney ill, sir?' Riley enquired of Sir Alfred, at the ewer in the studio.

Sir Alfred, without looking up, said: 'Miss Waveney's well-being is not your concern, Riley.'

Oh!

'Is it not, sir?' Riley said carefully, after a moment.

'No,' said Sir Alfred.

Riley let that settle a moment. He tried to. It wouldn't. It grew tumultuous in his belly.

Riley's fingers moved over the silken tip of the brush he was cleaning, a hollow feeling threading through him.

'Is she not coming again, sir?' he said, giving a last opportunity for what was happening not to be true.

'That's not your business either, Riley,' said Sir Alfred.

Oh.

Brush. Fingers. Turpentine.

Damn it, ask outright. He's implying it.

'Would she continue to come, sir, if I wasn't here?'

Sir Alfred almost snapped: 'Don't flatter yourself.' Then he thought for a moment and said precisely: 'Changes are not made to my household to accommodate the parents of my pupils.' He looked a warning at Riley: *Don't pursue this. I am not going to discuss it.*

Riley had to think about that.

What does he mean? What – what has happened?

Have Mr and Mrs Waveney asked him to get rid of me? Because of Nadine? . . . And has he refused?

He couldn't read it any other way.

But it's not fair . . .

'Miss Waveney is talented, sir,' he said. 'More than . . . most.' He didn't want to say, 'more than me'. He knew he couldn't set himself up against her. *Why not? Because she is posh and you are not?*

Sir Alfred took his time answering. Eventually he said, 'Miss Waveney is a girl. She will be happiest and most fulfilled in the bosom of her family, making a good marriage.'

Inside, Riley reeled.

But you knew that all along! a voice inside told him. *You've always known! You didn't really hope!*

This is not fair. They've taken her away. I won't see her. She won't learn any more. I won't see her.

Actually, he had really hoped. *And it's not fair on her! She wants to be an artist, and she could be!*

'I'm going to Terence's studio this afternoon, sir,' he said. His voice was small and tight. 'I shouldn't be too late.'

He was furious, furious, furious.

❧

Rain was gushing down so hard the drainpipes were rattling and overflowing on the back of Terence's building, and the sky was bruise-coloured at five in the afternoon. Riley bought a newspaper. Over there, men of many nations were fighting the battle of the Marne. The light was bad and Terence couldn't draw.

He said, 'Would you like a cup of tea or a beer or something? Wait till it blows over?'

Riley said he'd have a cup of tea, and proceeded to make it on Terence's little gas ring. The milk jug he kept on the window ledge for the cool (not that it was much warmer inside) had filled up and overflowed already with rainwater. They couldn't be bothered to go all the way down to get more, so they drank their tea black. Terence brought out some buns, and tried to start up a discussion on proportion and perspective, using the raisins as examples. Riley was not responsive. He was staring round the studio, at the kit, the space, the myriad signs of relaxed independence and creativity. Why should talentless Terence have all this, and Nadine not?

Terence lit a small cigar. 'What do you think about how the war is going?' he asked.

'If we had female succession,' said Riley, containing his restlessness in a sort of vicious languor, 'we'd be on the other side. Think about it.' (He was copying Terence's quiet confidence. He was mastering it) 'If Queen Victoria had been succeeded by her eldest daughter, who was . . . ?'

'Can't remember,' said Terence. 'She had so bally many.'

'Princess Victoria,' said Riley, noting that it was not necessary to be well up on the entire royal family to pass, 'and bearing in mind that Princess Victoria was married to . . . ?'

'The Pope?' drawled Terence.

'Emperor Frederick the Third. She's Kaiser Bill's mother. So, Kaiser Bill would be King of England, and we'd all be fighting alongside the Hun.'

'I say,' said Terence. 'Isn't that treason?'

'No,' said Riley. 'It's just another truth that people don't care to look at.'

'Will you go, do you think?' Terence asked. 'I mean, do you think you could? I hope I wouldn't have to be in it because, to be honest, I've been reading the papers, you know, about what went on at Mons and so on, and the Marne now, and of course it will be over by Christmas but, you know, even for a few weeks, I don't think I could face it – I'm a bit of a coward.' He looked up, almost shyly. 'Don't you think that's often the case, though, when a man has an artistic temperament? Sir Alf, for example. Of course he's too old, but could you imagine Sir Alf ever having been the kind of man who could be a soldier? Of course not. Men like him – like us – aren't the type. But you – you're different but I do think that you also have an artistic temperament. No, I do. Considering you've had no proper training you're bloody talented. Which some people might be surprised by, you being, as it were, working class . . . but I *really* don't see,' said Terence, aware that he was conveying a great favour, 'that that's any barrier to sensitivity. And what is an artistic temperament other than sensitivity? Really?'

Riley reached forward to help himself to another bun, and then lay back in his chair, arranging his legs in a stylishly negligent fashion. Sometimes he completely understood his mother's view of the posh. *I am, after all, as it were, working class. I should, no doubt, after all, bally well accept that I am, after all, as it were, working class.*

Ah, but I fucking well don't accept . . .

Am I perhaps developing anarchist leanings?

Would Nadine want a man with anarchist leanings?

I know she cares about me.

The rain battered the windows.

'You might as well stay for supper, you know,' Terence continued. 'Such a filthy night. Probably clear up later. Mrs Jones will bring up a stew and dumplings in a while. There'll be plenty to go round – she's good that way.' Riley was glad to hear that people of his type were capable of generosity as well as sensitivity. *Oh, stop it. Terence is all right. It's not him you're angry with.*

'People are saying it's awfully romantic and noble,' Terence was going on, 'to fight for your country, for something you really believe in, and it is, of course it is . . . but of course the real joy and breakthrough of the romantic movement was that it means it's no longer necessary to be hidebound by the rules of classicism, and tradition, which means, it seems to me, that *all* rules are there to be questioned, and all kinds of behaviour should now be considered on their own merits, not simply in the light of traditional rules and models . . .'

Riley took one of Terence's cigars, and said: 'I've always thought that one should do exactly what one wants, as long as it doesn't hurt people.' At this Terence smiled his very wide blond smile, and pressed Riley to another glass of smoky red wine, which Riley accepted. *Hark at me! One!*

'The problem is, it does hurt people,' he went on. 'There's

always someone who is going to be hurt by one not doing what *they* want. Or by one doing what they don't want one to do, like—' and he had had no intention of using this example, but it leapt out, as the things uppermost in our minds tend to, unexpectedly and unwelcomely '—loving someone they don't want you to love . . .'

Terence understood com*plete*ly. Riley was glad to be understood. His fury and hurt about Nadine's removal were beginning to surge and shovel around inside him now, fuelled no doubt by the wine, so he accepted another glass, as a result of which he accepted some whisky – quite a lot – as a result of which he found himself an hour or so later spreadeagled across a green chenille blanket on Terence's single bed with Terence's mouth around his tumescent dick.

He liked it. Oh, God, it was magnificent, the wonderful warmth, and surging . . .

At least, his dick liked it. His dick absolutely loved it.

Riley lurched from the bed, pushing the blond head aside. Terence called out to him but already Riley was staggering like a clown in his falling-down trousers; with his shirt-tails flying he was down the many flights of whirling stairs, out into the storm, hurtling up Exhibition Road, making distance, his heart battering, his chest tight, clambering the black railings into the park. He flung himself breathless on the turf on his back. The rain was pouring down, punching his face.

A big girl's blouse, a posh man's plaything with a fake posh accent, nancy boy to a nancy posh artist in nancy fucking Kensington smoking fucking cigars. Sensitivity, my arse. Artistic temperament and fucking sensitivity.

Fucking posh fucking

But they're not all . . . said a sane little voice beneath his fury.

Was it all based on that? Bloody Terence – and Sir Alfred? He'd never even noticed Sir Alfred wasn't married – it had never . . .

Nadine –

Nadine . . .

Bloody Waveneys, bloody bloody posh bastards all the fucking same.

Not good enough for their girl, only fit to be used by their boy.

I should just go round there and . . .

Fury was consuming him. The first person – other than himself – to touch it had been a man. The first time he came off – other than by his own hand – a man. A man he liked. A coming off he liked.

Do I go to hell now? To prison, certainly, if anybody found out. Or I've got some horrible disease . . .

And now he would have to lie to her all his life.

What life? What life, exactly, was he imagining anyway? How could he imagine any life with her? How would that ever come to be? *Nadine will spend her life with a gentleman. You are not a gentleman. It's been made perfectly clear.*

Maybe, but I'm not like Terence either . . .

Yes, you are. You did it, you liked it – you're one of them. You always said you didn't mind what people did but look at you now . . . You're ashamed because you're one of them.

I'm ashamed because I'm *not* one of them. If I was I wouldn't mind . . .

Really?

43

I'd be up there still with Terence . . . well, maybe not
Terence . . .

Oh? Who, then? What handsome man do you yearn for?
Nobody! Nobody! My mother was right, they just want
something from you . . .

He lay until the rain was pooling in his coat, his limbs
gradually seizing up with the cold and the wet. Finally he
rolled over and slept a little in the short light night, his nose
in the short brown and ivory-white stalks of the cropped
grass.

Within hours the day dawned, cool and clear. He scraped
himself up, brushing the grass from his coat and trousers,
tucking in his shirt, rubbing at his face as if that would
make it look better. He didn't want to go up to Bayswater
Road, or to Orme Square. He didn't want to run into anyone.
He didn't know what to do. He had been out all night – Sir
Alfred . . . Mrs Briggs . . . what could he say to them? What
are you meant to say?

He walked the other way, trying to ease his stiff legs,
down towards High Street Kensington. Kensington Palace
looked beautiful, floating on the morning mist, illuminated
as if from within by the early sun, and the statue of Victoria
– the Bun Penny – glowed like a pearl. *This is how Terence
should have painted it*, he thought. *Damn Terence.*

He stopped in at the Lyons Tea House, and ordered tea.
He stared at the thick white cup until the waitress suggested
he buy another or move on, would you, because there's
others need the table, and then buying another, and another.
I should go to Sir Alfred's, he thought. *Apologise, at least, for*

staying out, even though I can't explain. He'll think the worse of me . . . but then I think the worse of him . . .

Oh, it's not his fault.

I should go home, he thought. But he knew he wasn't going home. *What – talk to Mum about it? Or Dad?* This was not a situation a young man took home.

Where does a young man take this situation? he thought, and he laughed, a sleepless, angry, hungry, lonely, embarrassed, humiliated laugh. He knew perfectly well where this was leading. It was inexorable.

His seventh cup of tea stood cold in front of him.

He was still damp through from the park when he went up to the recruiting station. He had calmed down a little, but not much. He was going to do it. He bloody was. With him gone, Nadine could go back to Sir Alfred's. He'd prove himself a man, in the army. Hard work. Proper work. No nancy stuff – no art. Make Nadine proud. Or knock her out of his system.

'Here I am,' he said to the recruiting sergeant. 'You can have me.' He gave him a big grin. Change. Big and total change.

You only had to be five foot five now. He was sent in the back to be looked at. He stripped off and flung his shoulders back, coughing in the cold back room while another posh man held his balls. Was he eyeing him up? *Stop it, Riley, they're not all like that.* Next behind him was a tough and scrawny Cockney youth who said, apropos the balls situation: 'They've always got you by the bollocks one way or

45

another, ain't they? The women and the money and the fuckin' upper classes . . .'

Riley grinned again. Here we go. That's more like it.

He went next door to fill in forms. Name, address (he put Sir Alfred's); next of kin (Mum and Dad); DoB (26 March 1896), height and weight (5 ft 9 ins, 10 st 11 lbs), eyes hair complexion (grey black pale). Wages – half to Mum and Dad. Regiment: no idea – you tell me. Length of service: one year or duration of war. Duration of war, of course. He didn't want to spend a whole year in the army.

~

Riley had one day before reporting for training. They wanted to get them out there quickly.

Mum and Dad, Sir Alfred, Nadine.

He went round to his parents' that night. He stood in the street by the front door, and he leant against it, and he recalled his mother's face when she talked about her dad, and abroad, and the first wave of soldier's cowardice came over him. He did not want to see her look like that at him. She'd think she was losing him. (Riley hadn't noticed that she already knew she had already lost him, not to the Hun or the army, but to people who spoke nice, and knew the point of things of which she had never heard.)

He peeled himself off the door and ran up Praed Street towards the Waveneys'.

He looked up at the windows. The drawing-room lights were off, upstairs' were on. *It's too late to call now.*

He thought of Nadine in her nightgown, brushing her Mesopotamian hair. He thought of the curve of her waist

46

under his hand, and he ran across the road, back over the railings into the park, and he hardly had to touch himself to the thought of all the parts of her before he came.

Oh, God, I am so . . .

He didn't fall for the one that it made you go blind, and the palms of your hands hairy. *But it was hardly . . . Still, no signs of disease yet. How would it show?*

Oh, God, how can I even think of her? That clean and beautiful girl?

Her parents are right, Sir Alfred is right. A good marriage, not to me. Leave her alone, Riley. Know your place. If she likes you (she likes me), all the more reason to leave her be.

He wiped his hands on the grass, and on his trousers, and walked on up to Sir Alfred's. Mrs Briggs opened the door – and fell on him, hugging and scolding. Messalina stood behind, and crooned at the sight of him.

'I've joined up, Mrs Briggs,' he said.

She fell away from him, saying: 'Oh dear me. Oh dear me, Oh, you good brave boy.' And she ran, almost, her skirts swaying, to call for Sir Alfred.

'I've joined up, Sir Alfred,' he called, one hand on the dog's head, as the old man was still on the stairs, coming down through the dim light, one hand on the polished banisters. 'I hope you don't mind . . .' It sounded so pathetic. But he did hope Sir Alfred didn't mind. He was aware he was being precipitous.

Sir Alfred emerged into the light of the hallway. 'No,' he said mildly. 'No, I'm . . . proud of you.'

Mrs Briggs was crying, and talking about underwear. Mrs Briggs had no children of her own.

Sir Alfred took Riley by the hand, and held it firm. 'Congratulations, Riley,' he said. 'When do you leave?'

'Tomorrow, for training,' Riley replied, conscious of remnant spunkiness. *I've lived six years in this house, with these two*, he thought. *One third of my life.*

'Mrs Briggs, give him something nice for dinner,' Sir Alfred said. 'And, Riley, come up and say goodbye in the morning.'

'I'll lay out your studio, sir, before I go,' said Riley. 'And I'm sorry about last night and today, sir . . . and what we were talking about.' He felt suddenly and desperately sad.

'Well,' said the old man. 'Well. Just as well. I know these are big decisions.'

'Yes, sir,' Riley said. He was proud of that.

～

The next morning he went early to the Waveneys' house.

He couldn't go in. He couldn't do it. Be sneered at by those people he had thought liked him.

He stood across the road, under the trees of the park, by the bus stop. He didn't have long, if he was to drop off the letter at his parents' house, and be in time to report at the station.

He prayed for her to come out.

Go to the door, you fool!

He couldn't.

His legs did it without him – hurtled him across the road, up the path to the door. Quick and fumbling, he started to stuff the letter he had written the night before

48

through the letterbox – and the door moved before his hand. Opened. Jacqueline – Mrs Waveney – stood there.

'Oh, hello, Riley,' she said, her head drawn up and back on its long neck, and he looked at her and saw that he had understood the situation perfectly.

He shoved the letter at her, and he said, 'There's no need to worry, Mrs Waveney. I've joined up. If you're lucky, I'll get killed. Nothing to worry about then, eh?'

He grinned at her boldly, then turned and sauntered away. *That's done it. If I ever could of, I couldn't ever now.*

Could have, *Riley.*

He posted the letter to his parents as there wasn't time to get up there.

~

Dear Nat,

I've gone to join in the war. I am taking a Tale of Two Cities with me to put me in the mood for France and fighting but I don't know if there will be much reading. I'll write to you again.

With love from your foolish boy

Riley Purefoy

He didn't put, *when I'm a soldier back from the war I'll be a proper man, not the type to enjoy the touch of another man after four tots of whisky.*

He didn't know you weren't meant to put 'love'.

~

Dear Mum and Dad,

I've been thinking and I think you are right about art being a bit nancy, so I am joining the army and will be in France soon, Doing my Bit as they say in the papers. I am sorry not to say goodbye but they are sending us off for training (I think I am going to need quite a lot of that) immediately so there's no time really. Tell the little 'uns they had better be good while I'm gone and I'll bring you back something nice from France for Christmas, from your very loving son who hopes you'll be proud of him, yours faithfully, Riley Purefoy

Now is it 'faithfully' or 'sincerely'? Sir Alfred had told him once – 'faithfully' if you're using the name, 'sincerely' if you're saying 'Dear Sir'. . . *or is it the other way around?*

He couldn't remember. He put 'yours faithfully', because he felt more faithful than sincere.

Chapter Four

Flanders, October 1914

'Where are we, then?' Purefoy asked Ainsworth, as they clambered off the train.

'Not a fucking clue, son,' said Ainsworth. Ainsworth was from Lancashire, not a big man, steady. He was older. He had a wife and kids at home, and if you pressed him, which Purefoy had, once, he'd admit that he'd joined up because it seemed the right thing to do. He didn't say it in a tough way. He built railway carriages for a living and had been sent to the wrong regiment by clerical error. He didn't mind. Purefoy liked him. He liked his moustache, his accent, his deep voice, and his imperturbability.

The existence of Ainsworth in some way made up for the unexpected appearance of Johnno the Thief, or Private Burgess, as he was now called. He had caught Purefoy at once with his playful, knowing eyes, and said: 'Aye aye. What you running away from, then? Upper classes spat you out again, did they?' His head was thrust forward, as if everything were done on purpose, by his design.

Tall trees lined the road. Grey slates clad the roofs of the town. Horses ambled by. All around them soldiers like themselves were assembling, standing about, clunking through the rain, heading east. The Paddingtons took their turn in the formation, waited, smoked, and finally hitched their packs on to the bus to set off over flat ground, past square-built farms round courtyards full of muddy ducks, houses with their long wet thatched roofs sagging down, as it were, to their knees, like the muddy hems of drooping petticoats. 'I'm tired already,' remarked Ainsworth, cheerfully. 'Don't know how we're meant to get through a whole war.'

Several of the men laughed. The sergeant major yelled at them.

Ainsworth started humming a little tune.

Then they were there: Pop. Getting off, the boys clanged softly with kit, and stared. Most hadn't seen the country before. A boy called Bowells pretended to faint at the lush smell of pigs. Narrow-eyed Couch made – as usual – a point of not being surprised. The others had made a game of his professed cynicism. Only a few of them knew it was because he was under age. His devotion to soldiering was exemplary.

'Smells like Ferdinand,' said Bowells. Ferdinand was from Wiltshire. He'd come up on the train to join up in London because – well, he hadn't told anyone why. There were a few like that in the Paddingtons. 'Comes of being named after a station,' Ainsworth had said. 'You'll get all sorts.'

'Oink oink,' said Ferdinand, who was a bit fat.

Purefoy was happy. His feet felt big and tender in his boots. He liked his pack; the webbing, the gun. He liked the fresh cold air. He liked the blokes.

The fields around the little town were dug and mangled. Flatness rolled out before them: wintry and covered, as far as Purefoy could see, with the activity of men. He saw tents, big ones, many. Tracks and roads, metalled or not. Piles of boxes, piles of planks, piles of coal, piles of trunks, piles of sacks, groups of men, carts and limbers, horses, dogs, field kitchens, latrines behind flapping canvases, earth and sky. Graves.

'It's all quite simple,' Captain Harper told them. 'The Hun is over there. He's been racing north to the sea, trying to get past us into France. King Leopold – jolly clever move, this – opened the floodgates up there, so that rather than fight to the sea, he brought twenty miles of sea to the fight, so now we see what brave little Belgium is made of . . . All along the line, each side has dug trenches up as far as the coast. So. We've stopped the Hun for the moment. However, he's taken Antwerp, but we have Nieuport, so now we have retreated to Ypres, the regulars . . .' the real army, as Riley thought of them '. . . have been holding them off since the Hun cavalry took the Messine Ridge . . .'

None of the names meant anything to Purefoy. Captain Harper sketched them a map.

'So the gate-as-it-were, now it's slammed shut, has been dug in, and we're going to hold that line . . .'

It took very little time to be used to it all.

'When do we fight?' wondered Purefoy, shovel in blistered hand. The digging was heavy, claggy, but soft. He was getting to see exactly what Belgium was made of.

~

He received a letter.

She wrote:

... I dare say it's rather complicated getting your letters
over there, and sending letters out – not as bad as it was
for Captain and Lady Scott and the Antarctic explorers, of
course, being on the other side of the world plus being
frozen in six months at a time; but even so I don't know
where you are or when you'll get this – so I'll write and
hope for the best. I hope the army is everything a boy could
wish – I have to say it sounds like hell to me, but I'm a girl
and things seem different to us – no, to be honest I hope
they've discovered you have terrible flat feet or something
and can't really go. Chin up, old bean – is that the sort of
thing to say? Really I haven't the least idea how to be a
soldier's correspondent. But then I really can't imagine that
you have the slightest idea how to be a soldier. I suppose
they teach you – but nobody is going to teach me. So if my
letters are all wrong please forgive your dear old friend
– Nadine

He put it with the letters he had received at the training
camp. The first one read: 'Golly Riley that was a very sudden
absquatulation. What happened? Did your dad disown you?
Have you got Sir Alfred's jewellery under your cloak? When
will you come back through London? I had to go to Sir
Alfred to find your mother's address to ask for your address,
and your regiment and so on. Imagine you having a regiment! Well at least there's no hun where you are now,
wherever you are . . .' The next, a picture postcard of the

Peter Pan statue, said: 'Your Park Misses You – sorry is that too facetious? Let me know how you are and if you need anything.' And so on, in the same vein. Chatty. Sweet.

He would have written back. He would have found a way. He fully meant to.

~

They fought on 11 November. The Prussian Guard, that morning, were taking Hooge, just north of the Menin Road. They'd broken through. The real army was fully occupied already. So everyone else there was – cooks, orderlies, clerks, servants, engineers, Riley – had to go in, kill them, force them back to their own line.

He fought. Hurtling towards each other, undodgeable, across a field. Clumps, scraps of turf, just a dark field under the pale sky, cold air, light rain. As he ran, breathless and terrified, his heart clenched, a big sudden clench, and from it radiated surges of . . . something, something strong, shuddering . . . *It is fear*, he thought. *It is fear, concentric fear. Fear is strength: direct it.* He shot. The man spun. He bayoneted him.

He had to pull the bayonet out again, which was strange. And that wasn't an end: it was just a moment on a long line of moments, and time went on, and they went on. He stepped away in a mist of red, a numbness spread across him, a sense of capacity. He smelt the blood, and took on the mantle of it. He ran on, screaming, till he found himself alongside Ainsworth, and felt safer. Ainsworth's body was warm during the night, against the rim of a shell-hole, packing an old jam tin with greasy mud and bitter shell

55

fragments. Lid on, make a hole, position fuse. Strike your light on the striker-pad strapped to your wrist . . . light the fuse. Wait, with it fizzing in your hand – wait just long enough so that it won't land unexploded, allowing Fritz to pick it up and throw it back, but not so long that it blows your hand off. Or your head.

It is not clear how long this wait should be.

Hurl.

They hurled all they had, then things were being hurled at them so they took off.

During First Ypres, as that period came to be known, every second man fighting was killed or wounded, though Purefoy didn't know that.

~

The first time he was aware of coming back to himself, there was straw beneath him, men around him, barn roof above him, smell of animals – what had happened?

Someone was talking. Johnno the – Burgess.

'Should've been at Mons,' he was saying. 'You think this was bad? Mons was bad. Ten days going in the wrong direction, then six thousand French reservists turned up from Paris in six hundred taxis – What? I thought. Taxis? From Paris? If I only talked *français* I'd hail me one and get a lift back there . . .' Burgess had been transferred from the remains of another platoon, and liked to be sure that everyone knew.

Purefoy was trying to remember things: arriving in Belgium, long, looping rivers, peasants, farms, steeples, markets, the bus driver when they arrived at Poperinghe saying: 'All right, boys, this is Pop.' Flanders meant Drowned Lands in Flemish. *Like flounder*, he thought. Amsterdam was not so far. Just over there. The other side.

I killed a man.

He had thought killing a man you could look in the face would seem more honourable, but no. He would be happy not to get that red feeling again, those concentric waves from his heart. He hadn't seen his face anyway.

I knew a German once. Knife-grinder, used to come to the house. And the anarchist. What was his name? Franz.

He stared and started, and sat up again. Just had to get the Hun to go home, then they could go home, let the politicians sort it out. They couldn't really mean us to be doing this.

In the corner, someone was weeping and shaking, like a Spartan after battle. There was a word for it, he'd read it – what was it? The Shedding. Shedding the fear and the horror of what you have just seen and done. They had it all organised. Captain Harper was patting his shoulder and looking a bit lost.

Some others were playing cards. A Second Lieutenant was writing a letter. He lay down again. Sat up again. What the fuck? What the fucking fuck? What was he *doing*?

He couldn't stand the quiet so he went outside: the moon was looking at him and the stars were rolling around. So he went back into the barn. There was snow on his hat.

Burgess was telling Ferdinand he'd met a bloke who'd seen Sir Lancelot on his white horse with his golden hair and armour, leading ghostly troops against the Hun, and the Hun had turned and fled in fear and terror. For a moment Purefoy saw the whole scene, clear in his mind, a huge canvas by Sir Alfred.

Ainsworth said, 'I heard it was St George.'

'It was Father Christmas,' said Burgess.

Ferdinand lay, white, eyes staring. Purefoy gave him a cigarette and he took it wordlessly. Purefoy pressed his mind and thought about Sir Lancelot, Sir Gawaine, and Sir Alfred Pleasant, RA, FSA, of Orme Square, Bayswater Road. He thought of Sir Henry Irving who his dad had seen as Shylock at the Lyceum. He thought of Sir James Barrie, and the knights of olden times, and the knights of peaceful times, painters and writers and reciters of Shakespeare, nibs and brushes, greasepaint and burnt sienna, stage-fighting and struggling with a metaphor, have-at-thee and stains of carmine on a smock and *The Childhood of the Arthurian Knights*. He thought of Sir James and Sir Alfred strolling in Kensington Gardens, discussing the latest exhibition at the Grafton Gallery. He thought of the Hun in Kensington Gardens. *Keep that image*, he thought. The Hun bashing into London, bashing his mum, bashing Nadine's door in. *We've stopped them for the time being; that's good. That's what I'm here for. I'm here for a reason. There is a reason for all of this. That is the reason.*

After a while Ainsworth came and sat by him.

His mind would not be quiet. He thought: *How come men such as us, kind, humorous Ainsworth, young Ferdinand, who really cares only for food, young Bowells, who only wants to fit in – well, that's part of it, isn't it? – how have we slipped so easily, apparently so easily, into this bayoneting, murderous, foul-blooded maelstrom?* Burgess was different: Burgess had been born fighting. Purefoy knew many Burgesses on the streets of Paddington: the violent, scurvy blood royal of the British criminal class. Understood them, avoided them, loved them, was them, dreamt of living a life where people didn't have to be like that. That was, after all, his life's ambition. Or had been. Not to have to be like that.

But the rest of us?

Just keep a hold. You've signed on for the duration. Be as good a soldier as you can and it'll be over soon.

He lit a cigarette, and sat on his bale with his big hands dangling between his knees. He fell asleep where he sat, and his cigarette rolled away on the damp straw, and set nothing alight.

~

And then it was winter, and Christmas, and it did not seem to be over.

Purefoy sent a card to Nadine. He couldn't help himself. He knew he had abandoned her, but from the letters she sent she didn't feel abandoned. He had not known how to reply.

Their normal routine was four days in the front line and four in the reserve, which was quieter in the way of not being shot at or shelled, but no less busy. He had sat, in one or two rare moments of quiet, at a wonky wooden table in the local *estaminet*, drinking odd Belgian coffee and staring at a small oblong of blank army-issue writing paper, trying to remember what he thought about during the long nights on the fire-step, when he had imaginary conversations with her. But there was no time for mental clarity, to allow him to connect the blank piece of paper with the imaginary conversations and work out a relationship between them, and her, back in London. He could not tell the truth, because it was disgusting. He could not lie, because that was fatal. So he sent her a delicate envelope of silk, with green and pink embroidery, wishing her a peaceful day of joy, 1914, and a quick-scrawled letter: '. . . I am beginning to find the star shells beautiful, so long as they don't land on me. Do you remember the painting Starry Starry Night? In a peculiar way they remind me of that. It seems a long way from home, but we all know we are doing what has to be done and we are glad to be able to do it. The boys are a great lot, cheerful and . . .'

One little Christmas card couldn't hurt. It would be rude not to.

She sent a card back. 'So glad you're having such fun.'

Is she joking?

Is that all she has to say?

All around him sprang the black protective gaiety of the Tommy. He didn't realise that he, too, was becoming wrapped in it, because knowing it would have stopped it working, and it did work, for a while. *Two Austrian aristos get shot, and to sort that out millions of us have to get shot – Fate is playing a brilliant trick on us, and getting away with it: what else do you do but howl with laughter?* He sang along, loud and jolly: 'Tipperary', Marie Lloyd songs, 'Hanging On The Old Barbed Wire'. He caroused cheerfully in the communal baths on their days behind the lines. He nicknamed their trench Platform One, and noted how similar a trench was to a grave: you could just pour more mud in and none of us would need a funeral, he'd cracked, or a shell might do it for you. He manned the fire-step gamely; he stood to and stood down and complained about the food; he drank like a fish when it was required; he stared out over no man's land, listening to the blackbirds in the middle of the night, or the Hun singing 'Stille Nacht', which they did beautifully, requiring a harsh chorus of 'We're here because we're here because we're here because we're here' to the tune of 'Auld Lang Syne', to drown them out, lest sentiment rise. He did not let sentiment rise. He *was*, it turned out, a good soldier: strong, loyal, friendly, brutal.

He laughed with everyone at how Ferdinand's main aim in trench life turned out to be being present whenever anyone got a tuck parcel from home, just in case, you know, and he noticed how Ainsworth always gave him a handful of the fiendish northern sweets his wife sent him, to which Ferdinand had taken a liking. 'Uncle Joe's Mint Balls, they keep you all aglow.' Ferdinand was young, and cried sometimes at night. 'You just keep sucking on Uncle Joe's balls, lad, you'll be all right,' Ainsworth said, seemingly in all innocence, and gamely laughed himself silly when he realised, which cheered Ferdinand right up.

Purefoy found the boys tragic. Bowells, for example, fair and scrubbed, desperate to achieve the worn look of the seasoned soldiers, to use the argot, stain up his uniform. Bowells had wept his first five nights, because there was a dog making a noise out there in no man's land, and he had feared for its safety. Burgess had been going to tell Bowells not to worry about the damn dog, the damn dog was eating corpses, but Ainsworth had kicked him, and made a laconic cut-throat gesture.

Am I tragic like them? Purefoy thought. *And if not, why not? I'm as young as them* . . . Sometimes when Ainsworth gave him his granite-faced smile with the little twist of the mouth, Purefoy felt that to Ainsworth at least he was less a soldier and more a boy. 'Courage for the big troubles in life, lad,' he'd say, 'and patience for the small. Be of good cheer. God is awake.'

The dog was beautiful: massively furry, big and clever. A Bouvier des Flandres, the girl at the *estaminet* said. A Flemish cow dog. He wouldn't mind a dog like that when he got home. A life with a dog. Him and a dog, going on their adventures. He had a sudden memory of Messalina, her heavy head, the beautiful gambolling movements she made when she ran.

Winter was so cold. So cold. And wrong – they weren't meant to be still there. Flanders had become mud beneath their feet. The trenches they had dug looked to Purefoy like one great long unhealing wound, splitting the land. The railways ran towards it, feeding it with fuel and men and ammunition. The camps and hospitals and tents and tunnels alongside were parasites, and then down the middle lay no man's land, mined and festooned with barbed wire, a long, suppurating ulcer. The wound, like a perpetual-motion machine, seemed to be taking on a life of its own, and there it was, and there was he, and that was it: a system.

He was sitting one morning early, waiting for the dixie containing breakfast to come down the line, a silvery blueshot dawn, a day that, he realised, would be as limpid as the one a year ago, *God, was it a year ago*, if you looked up, not out, and just saw the blue sky, and the birds flying across it as if nothing was happening, if you blocked out all the rest . . .

Purefoy kept throwing; kept throwing. He threw for weeks, for months. At some stage he was given proper grenades and a helmet, though they all learnt to piss on a handkerchief to breathe through long before gas masks came around. One night he saw Captain Harper flying across the sky like a whirling starfish before shattering into a flaming shell crater, and he put the sight in that special part of his brain he would never go to again, fed it through the greedy slot in the forever unopenable door. His thoughts jumped like fleas, like drops of water on a hotplate, uncatchable, inexplicable.

The new CO was a Captain Locke, tall and pale with a swooping body, like a heron's, and a nose like an eagle's beak. His long thin legs crossed round and round themselves when he sat; Purefoy could tell that out of uniform he would wear tweeds, and they would flap around his long ankles.

With him, in the summer, they were moved along the line, south towards the River Somme. Their new trench system extended out of the cellar of what had been a handsome old stone farmhouse, where beautiful wallpaper hung, sooted and flapping, from the last shards of upright wall. The cellar had been dug out for the officers, and someone had put a piano down there.

'Anyone play at all?' asked Locke, hopefully, sticking his head out.

Ainsworth, it turned out, had played the organ at Wigan Parish Church. He hesitantly entered the officers' glamorous cave, and smiled a little at the sight of the piano. 'Little rusty,' he murmured, but when he sat down an air of authority arose from him, and when he sang, a beautiful, manly rendition of an aria from a Bach cantata, silence dropped like blossoms, churchlike. Locke closed his eyes. Riley could only suppose everyone was feeling the same lurch of loss and love and beauty and alienation from everything that they were losing hold of by the very acts of trying to protect it.

'Ain't that German?' said Burgess, when Ainsworth had finished.

'Well spotted, soldier,' said Locke. 'However, it is Bach, and Bach was a citizen of heaven sent down to enlighten and delight men of all nations. The Kaiser has no monopoly on the genius of his country's sons.'

'What's the name of the piece?' Purefoy asked.

'"*Ich habe genug*",' said Ainsworth.

Locke barked with laughter. 'Which means,' he said cheerfully, '"I have had enough." More or less. Ainsworth, thank you, that was splendid. The rest of you, lads, back to work. Er – you – stay and give me a hand with this . . .'

'You' was Purefoy. 'This' was Captain Locke's gramophone, which needed unpacking and setting up.

'You know what Comrade Lenin says, sir?' said Purefoy, as they attached the horn.

'Comrade Lenin!' exclaimed Locke. 'Good Lord, man, what do you know about Lenin?'

'Not a lot, sir,' said Purefoy, mildly.

'Are you a Communist, Private?'

'Would I tell you if I was, sir?' said Purefoy. It popped out. Locke gave him a look. It struck Purefoy because it was a human look in a military world, and it was those looks, those flashes of the other reality, which kept him alive even

64

as they made him want to weep. He desperately wanted them, but he had to avoid them. Bowells, for example. He couldn't look Bowells in the eye any more. It was too naked and pathetic.

'So, what does Lenin say?' asked Locke.

Purefoy grinned. 'Along the lines of music softens the heart and brain, sir, and disinclines a man from his purpose . . .' Robert Waveney had quoted this to his wife one afternoon, playing her a recording of a new Russian pianist.

'Just lay off the Chopin, Private.'

'Don't know any Chopin, sir,' Purefoy lied. He'd been along to the Albert Hall often enough to rehearsals with Nadine, a world away, a world ago.

'Well, don't learn any, then.'

'Yes, sir,' said Purefoy.

Captain Locke did, one afternoon, play some Chopin on his gramophone. Purefoy recognised it, all right, and as he passed, the melody clutching at him with soft little tearing claws, he caught sight of Locke, inside, listening. The look on Locke's face was so very lonely that Purefoy called out to him: 'Now, now, sir, we agreed no Chopin!' Locke looked up, shocked, startled – pleased.

Purefoy scurried on, away from the captain's look. *I really don't know my place, do I?* But – *Oh, yes, I was going to improve myself, wasn't I?* The thought burnt up like all the others, in the grimy, unpleasant duties of the day.

≈

Captain Locke was a pure man, with pure and pleasurable tastes. As a boy he had liked to follow the gardener around the old greenhouses at Locke Hill, to smell the earth and help pick the grapes. Latin verse had amused him. When he played cricket he had reminded his cousin Rose of an actual cricket, with his terribly long legs and his cheerful disposition. Even playing his cello, plaintively and not very well, he had looked like a soulful insect, all elbows and knees.

He had noticed a surviving patch of gooseberry bushes on the parados, remnant of some long-gone Frenchman's garden, and one evening crawled under them, froglike, on his back, to prune them. The new leaves were a golden, melting, greenish colour, and the sun shining through them put him in mind of a chandelier he had come to know during his honeymoon: burnt-sugar Murano glass, eighteenth century. He had seen it often, lying on his back in the big white bed at the Cipriani, while his beautiful soft creamy-rosy-marble wife Julia lay in his arms, or crawled across him, wrapped around him, delighting and enchanting him, as they came to realise that there was really nobody there – no parents, no schoolmasters, no vicars – to tell them they couldn't or shouldn't just take off all their clothes in that paid-for foreign room and do anything they wanted. And they did. Things neither of them had ever thought of; things that made them blush. Her beautiful, beautiful flesh, and her sweetness, her kindness to him, and the lovely way she always seemed to be on his side, even when he was being a bit of a twerp, not knowing things about what a woman wants . . . Well, how could he? Sisterless, a schoolboy, a university man . . . Apart from Rose, he hardly knew any women at all. Rose had a phrase about English public schoolboys: physically over-developed, intellectually semi-developed, emotionally not developed at all. Good old Rose . . .

He and Julia had begun, in their Venetian privacy, to develop that emotional side. When his father had died so suddenly, Julia had been everything a man could wish for. When he was obliged to take over Locke Hill, she had glided into her role as chatelaine with the grace of a woman twice her age. She knew how to talk to servants. She took care. On their return to Locke Hill, after Mother had moved out – said she'd much rather be in the little flat in Chester Square – Julia had made Locke Hill, with its warm red bricks and polished wood and slanting sunshine, into a kind of heaven. She knew how to choose the colours to paint things; she needlepointed charming cushions, her lovely mouth instructed Millie how to plump and place them just so, and called Max the red setter in from the frosty lawn. He quite fell in love again with the crook of her fragrant elbow holding the trug, as she took the lavender from the stone-flagged terrace to the piles of smooth-ironed sheets in the big linen press. Every night he had raced home from Locke and Locke (he'd been promoted – a married man now) to try to get her pregnant.

He hadn't, during the honeymoon, paid much attention to the chandelier, but the colour, the melting light, had stayed in his mind. Now it was a brutal little shaft of memory, pricking and stalling him, and when thus stalled and sabotaged he had to stop a moment to put the memory away.

'Gooseberries, lovely gooseberries,' he said, out loud, but softly. 'Someone might be grateful, in a few months, if they survive. Not much chance of a mackerel to go with it, I suppose, but a gooseberry is always a lovely thing.'

Purefoy was touched by Locke's apparent belief that some kind of future, the time it took for a gooseberry to ripen, was a possibility. He found Locke a decent bloke.

~

The new trench had been in French hands before, and quite a hotspot. Rebuilding the communication lines after a hit, the Paddingtons found corpses in the walls, scraps of uniform, the smell, a hand. When a shell hit, thundering your head and splitting your eyes, it was not only fresh limbs and organs that showered you. There was a French lad under the floor of the trench too: he appeared between the duckboards. They had been walking on him. They dug him up and buried him again, and Purefoy got sick: puking and crapping like a dog, too weak to walk. Burgess dragged him along to the MO's dugout, which was in itself unusual, for Burgess never did anything helpful.

He murmured to Purefoy as they went, confidentially, under the arm slung over his shoulder for support: 'We could do each other a favour, you know, Riley . . .'

Purefoy heaved, his stomach wrenching.

'Make it worth your while,' Burgess was saying. 'It'd be no trouble to *you* . . .' He eyed Purefoy sideways. *Honest Riley. Worth a punt, for old times' sake. Too good an opportunity, really.* 'Give us some of your puke, Riley, and I'll make us both rich. There's knackered men round here who'd pay good money for a couple of days in hospital.'

Purefoy turned his hanging head to look at him, and Burgess gave a little I-didn't-invent-the-system shrug, and a straight look back. 'You can't say they don't deserve a rest,' he said meekly.

Purefoy's stomach heaved; he puked on Burgess. Burgess laughed, his dimples pitting his cheeks. 'Thanks, old pal,' he said.

The MO sent Purefoy to a field hospital towards Amiens for two days' rest and anti-laxatives. Over the next few days seven men from the Paddingtons turned up with the same condition. But, then, it was the kind of bug that got around, and most of them had been digging alongside Purefoy and the dead French boy.

~

When Purefoy returned, Captain Locke called him in. Purefoy thought Locke didn't look that well either.

'Purefoy,' Locke said, shuffling papers. 'Er. Yes. You're to be promoted.'

What?

'Experience, courage, attitude on the field and in the trenches – hasn't gone unnoticed. Some concern that you aren't quite a gentleman, but – well – beggars and choosers, rather, no reflection on you. You're a fine soldier. The men respect you.'

Purefoy, who had seen braver men and better attitudes, Ainsworth for example, said so, in the accent his mother disliked, which he couldn't help using in the company of the class he'd learnt it from, the accent that had made it possible for him to be promoted from the ranks. 'And I can't afford it,' he said.

'You won't have to keep a horse,' Locke said. 'And the regiment's had some donations. One from – someone who knows you.'

A silence.

Another silence, of a slightly different quality.

'Sir Alfred,' Purefoy said. He glanced at the floor. 'I shall be sorry to have to disappoint him.'

'Your name was on the list before Sir Alfred made his donation. It's coincidence, Purefoy.'

It's bribery.

'Well, then, Fate is conspiring to benefit me, sir,' said Purefoy, 'but I can't possibly accept it. I cannot have the regiment . . . um . . . for my advancement.'

'The regiment requires your obedience, Purefoy. The regiment is promoting you, the financial circumstances allow. You have no choice.'

Was it bribery? He didn't think Locke was lying about the coincidence.

'Is that an order, sir?'

'It can be. I'd rather it didn't have to be. Listen – perhaps your benefactor thought you wouldn't accept if he offered to support you directly. But the idea of this promotion came from the regiment, as it should, and it impugns the regiment's honour to suggest otherwise. Do you want to impugn the regiment's honour, Purefoy?'

Purefoy did not want to impugn the regiment's honour.

'No, I didn't think so. So stop making me do a moral dance for you, Purefoy. Accept your good fortune, and don't be so surprised,' said Locke. 'Seems to me the men like someone leading them who has an idea what they've been through. If the top brass have finally noticed that, then good.'

'Isn't that a bit, ah, Communist, sir?' asked Purefoy, and Locke said, 'Watch it. You're still a private for now.'

'I just don't see why me, sir,' said Purefoy.

'Don't be disingenuous, Purefoy,' said Locke, and Purefoy raised an eyebrow. 'Exactly. How many of the men know what disingenuous means? The army needs your type.'

I've heard of Chopin, I've got a vocabulary, therefore I'm fit to lead, he thought. *Oh, God, you want me to lead them.*

Locke drummed his long fingers on the tea chest and gave Purefoy a frank look. 'Purefoy, old man,' he said, 'I would much rather have you than a nineteen-year-old direct from the school OTC.'

And Purefoy thought, *Well, you'll have to promote me now – you can't say incendiary things like that to a man in the ranks.*

~

'Where you off to, then?' said Burgess, darning his socks on a tree stump, not looking up, as Purefoy rattled past with his kitbag.

'I'm going to Amiens,' said Purefoy. 'To be trained in natural superiority and talking posh. And not taking care of my own kit, eating well and sending other men to their deaths. Do you want to come?'

Burgess looked up then. 'Oh, are you,' he said. 'Are you. Well, good luck, Private Purefoy. Don't forget us. We won't forget you.'

'It's all the same when a shell lands on you,' said Purefoy.

'Ah, but a shell doesn't land on you, does it?' said Burgess. 'Because you're in a nice little dugout, listening to opera. Aren't you?'

Purefoy paused a moment. 'Yeah,' he said. 'You're right. No officer has ever been killed in this or any other war.'

Captain Harper's shining body flew again across his mind.

Burgess waggled his fingers. 'Bye-bye!' he said, in a sing-song voice.

'Piss off, Johnno,' said Purefoy, as he shouldered his bag, and went.

~

As the train taking him away clanked and shuddered into movement, Purefoy felt a sharp stomach-tug of a harsh and guilty joy. Clanking and shuddering away from death, away from corpses, away from damp, away from mud, away from groans, away from rats, away from the miasma of pure and constant fear . . . For several weeks he would not have to kill anyone, and no one would try to kill him. *Thank you, Sir Alfred, thank you thank you thank you thank you.*

He prayed that officer training would teach him to hate the Hun individually. He had been having trouble maintaining the idea that the boys the other side of no man's land were in themselves any different from the boys over this side, and the faces of the old knife-grinder and the anarchist popped up in his mind with disconcerting regularity. The gas wasn't their choice. Kaiser Bill was Queen Victoria's grandson. *Franz Dahrendorf! That was his name. The anarchist.*

The land now outside the window was green. *Oh, God, it does all still exist. Sheep. Leaves.*

You will, at some stage, if you live, have to go back, Purefoy, where there are sheep and leaves and Sunday lunches. You will have to go back into it and not be brutal.

Can you bear that in mind? Is there any room for that?

When he reached his billet in Amiens, the stairs confused

him, and the sheets on the bed seemed alien. He wrote a letter to Sir Alfred: short, and to the point. Then he lay down on top of the alien sheets, carefully, his boots still on, and stared up at the ceiling, following the line of its moulding round and round.

~

It seemed the rush of enthusiasm that had rendered Purefoy a Second Lieutenant had been premature. Recruitment had not, after all, declined quite as had been feared, and there was, after all, no shortage of young men of education who could be called Second Lieutenants and released to the Western Front. Also, someone, somewhere, had decided that in the interests of social stability officers promoted from the ranks should not go back to the men they had served alongside. 'In other words,' he wrote to his parents, 'they don't know what to do with me.' So he was given leave.

Second Lieutenant Purefoy sat on a single bed in a room above a pub in Dover. He was going to London. He would visit his mother and father and his sisters . . . God, his sweet little sisters. He wanted to send them a picture postcard right now, a funny dog in a tartan costume, with a monocle, or something, but then they'd know he was in Blighty . . . *oh, I can't go home . . . but I've got to . . . and I'll see Sir Alfred and Mrs Briggs.* For a split second, before memory caught up and kicked him, he found himself thinking that he might visit Terence.

He tried to picture his family and friends in London. He assumed they still existed. After all, here was a single bed in a room above a pub in Dover.

What the fuck could he say to any of them?

Well, there'll be none of that swearing for a start.

He went down to the bar. Drinking would be one way of dealing with this detachment, this disbelief. He stared at the bottles, the beer barrels, the little taps: crimson wine, black and ivory stout, oily invisible gin. He stared at the drunken soldiers around him, and the blowsy girls. Sex. He recalled the feeling of the curve of a hip under his hand. Would *any* hip feel like that? Send the frisson, the glow, the shot of warmth and possibility up his veins, under his skin, to his heart and his belly and the back of his eyes?

Now was the time to change the mood. How was he to do it?

He went upstairs, and finally wrote his will, on the pages labelled for the purpose in the back of his Soldier's Small Book (paybook, military service record, instructions on how to avoid bad feet – rub soap into socks). He left everything to his mother. He'd get the train as soon as he had worked out what to say.

The food was bloody brilliant. Oxtail, dumplings, steamed pudding for dinner. Fish and chips and chocolate for tea. He bought a box of twenty-four bars of Fry's Chocolate Cream, and ate them sitting on the narrow bed. He bought two more boxes, made a parcel and sent one to Ferdinand with a note: 'You're to eat all of these yourself: NO SHARING', and the other to Ainsworth: 'PLEASE HAND THESE OUT TO DESERVING CASES.'

He had a second bath some nights, and had to pay extra for the hot water. He noticed he had given himself a little pot belly with all the food.

He couldn't go and not talk to them. He couldn't talk to them.

He lay on his back with his new officer shoes off and one by one ran through the people he might talk to, and what he could or couldn't say to them. Everything he had to say: *I love you, it's hell, I walk on corpses and breathe death, it's only a matter of time before I prove a coward, and I don't want to be a coward, but I don't understand, either I kill people, or I'm a coward, that's the choice, someone somewhere set it up and I get no vote, I can't say, 'I don't accept that' – and I have accepted it, for a year I've accepted it, this is the situation but I don't understand how I got here, how it is just going on and on, and nobody mentions it, and if you don't like it they think you're mad, and you get shot, for cowardice, desertion . . . and your own men, your companions, your brothers, have to shoot you . . . and I'm so fucking scared out there every day, every night—*

and now they've made me a fucking officer—

STOP IT.

You're a soldier, Riley, a good soldier and a decent bloke. For a bleak second he desperately wanted to go back to the front, where there was no time or space in a man's mind to think about anything beyond good soldier, decent bloke. *No – officer. It's different. I will have responsibility.*

Yes, but no actual authority.

They were proud he was an officer now. That was the kind of thing people at home wanted to hear.

He didn't want to think of Nadine as 'people at home'. He wanted Nadine to know and share every single damn thing he ever knew or did on this earth, and to understand,

75

and to share hers too . . . and he would rather get a shell tonight than have Nadine even hear of the possibility of the things he had known in this past year . . . and how do you get round that one?

And you're leaving her alone, remember? He hadn't answered her letter in response to his Christmas card.

Yes, but I . . .

He looked out at the sea. Many nights he could hear the guns. On the seafront, some philanthropist had put up an iron sign on an iron leg, pointing out what was where across the sea: Calais, Dieppe, Dunkirk . . . Rome, Amsterdam, Moscow. He held his hand out in front of his face, like a divider. *This side, to the right, ours. That side, to the left, theirs. Down the middle in the sump, us lot.*

Amsterdam, where she wanted to go, was on the other side. Van Eyck and Rembrandt and Franz Hals and . . . a furry peach, a silver-bloomed plum, striped roses and streaked tulips, vanilla and raspberry, arched stems and green beetles gleaming and one little wormhole . . . bright sunflowers whirling . . . a branch of almond blossom.

What a pompous, self-important, sententious, over-imaginative young man I was. What a thoughtless, useless, unkind . . . to leave without seeing Mum. To make all those decisions about what people were and what that meant – that Sir Alfred was a queer, and would not forgive me for staying out the night, that the Waveneys would never let me marry Nadine, that because Terence did a queer's thing to me I had to . . . Well, I didn't know, did I, what I was going into.

So now, now that that world was so distant, and that attitude even more so, how could he pop back into it for tea and a chat? How could he write to that world, saying: 'I hope this finds you in the pink as I am . . . It's all pretty quiet here . . . Please send any kind of tobacco, and socks.'

He went back to his room, went back to bed. Turned his pillow over.

He slept all right, though. Dreams, obviously. Not very nice ones. But nothing compared to some of the lads.

~

Captain Locke had said, in that charming way of his, 'If you pass through Sidcup on your way to town, pop in and see Mrs Locke, would you? It's not far from the town. Tell her I'm all right? You won't have time, of course, but . . .'

Purefoy was reminded of how the posher someone was, the less they seemed to care about class – those educated, wealthy, dreaming men who don't have a simple clue what is not possible when you are poor. He both loved and hated them for their genuine ignorance. How marvellous, how ridiculous, that it should be possible. He allowed himself to wonder what Mrs Captain Locke would think of him, Purefoy, turning up. The trenches were in some ways a leveller, to those who took it that way. But the advances Purefoy had craved were only cultural and matrimonial, wherein the Flanders mud had offered no progress, other than the odd burst from Captain Locke's gramophone, and the occasional expression in Captain Locke's amiable blue eye that showed he, too, knew of the existence of Better.

But Private – whoops – Second Lieutenant Purefoy calling on Mrs Captain Locke of Locke Hill? Dear God, no.

Chapter Five

Sidcup, June 1915

Julia stood in the hall at Locke Hill, little feet firm on the black and white tiles. The doormat was crooked. She straightened it.

It was rather a beautiful morning outside. She could – she should – be out on the lawn, admiring the sun in the lilac and smelling the early roses. A cup of tea, perhaps, in the little *Sitzplatz* Peter had arranged beyond the hornbeam. She *must* find another name for it. Or a stroll by the stream. Max would want a walk.

She had heard the phone go, and she heard Rose deal with it. Rose was so good – such a blessing to have such a sister-in-law. Cousin. Peter's cousin. Cousin-in-law. It was a shame she was away so much with her hospital, and lovely when she came back for a visit.

Julia went into the sitting room, hoping to find some tiny aesthetic job that needed doing. All through the war, since Peter had left – five months now! – she had kept it looking nice, in case he should come, because you can't rely on communications, and he might, you never know, just turn up unannounced, and a woman has to do *something*. He never *had* turned up unannounced, but his leaves had been erratic . . .

She went over to admire their wedding photo, silver-framed on the piano. Pretty her, at twenty-four: heavy satin, family lace, and the wide, deep-bosomed neckline of before the war, which suited her so well. Already it looked dreadfully old-fashioned. Her hair was as pale as her dress. She glowed, truly. Like the inside of a seashell. And handsome him, at twenty-seven, tall and happy, trousers flapping round his long legs, in morning dress among his myrmidons in morning dress. No idea of war on their sweet faces. St George's Hanover Square had been filled with white lilac and orange-blossom and roses – Madame Alfred Carrière – sent up from Locke Hill in baskets. The people in overcoats and caps who had gathered to observe and admire had not been disappointed by Peter and Julia.

They had had no *idea* that he would be called upon . . . Well.

He hadn't been called upon. They hadn't *had* to call him. He had been only too eager to leave.

Yes, well, we've been over that, and agreed to disagree.

Don't go over it again, Julia – what can you hope to achieve?

But even that thought was by now part of her pointless spiral of punishment, herald to the stupid parade.

You said it was necessary, but it was selfish! True, there had been talk of conscription, but only talk! And no one believed they would dare actually bring it in! And certainly not for married men . . . fathers . . . as you might have been by then . . .

And you said it wouldn't count if you waited to be conscripted. You wanted to give of your own free will.

And I did understand, darling. I understood that when we married we made a bond, and that what you wanted to give was no longer only yours to give – and I had almost expressed it in a perfect, beautiful, wounding sentence, but it had turned ungraceful at the end . . . and so had I, weeping, snivelling, begging.

Why did you want to leave me?

I didn't want to leave you. This is not about you and me, darling, it's about the country. If men are going to fight to defend our country, then it is wrong for me to sit here safely, accepting their protection. I should be with them. That is all.

It had sounded terribly manly. She'd liked it, for a moment. But then the waiting started, and with it the fantasising. He left her alone, and gave her nothing to go on, and in her ear the constant gremlin whispered incessantly: How can you possibly be so ungrateful, so selfish, so wicked? That poor man – think what he is suffering and risking for your sake. How dare you mind?

'Julia? Darling?' It was Rose, dark, bright, thin, looking round the door. 'I'm going into Sidcup. Anything you need?'

My husband, thought Julia, but she said nothing because it would be unkind to say such a thing to a woman like Rose.

Rose knew perfectly well that nobody had ever really expected her to be a wife. She'd only been sent to live with Peter's family in the hope that someone in Kent might marry her, as no one in Wiltshire would, but the hope was only ever mild. She might have been a little in love with Peter when she was young, but everyone – including Rose herself – recognised her now as a woman without marital or romantic needs. Those who bothered to think about her – including, again, herself – thought her lucky to be so, in this depleting landscape where many girls were likely to be left bereft of their expectations.

Rose had scorned the role circumstances offered her: china-mender, correspondence maintainer, ageing wallflower. Instead, back in 1913, she had joined the Kent VAD. At the first training camp in the summer of 1914, when 170 of them had been available to tend a dragoon who had fallen off his bicycle, and the Herne Common local paper had sent a photographer, Rose had identified a different type of woman that she was able to be. She had enjoyed the cricket matches. She liked sleeping in the round tents, learning how to use a biscuit tin as an oven. She liked her grey cotton dress, her army regulation lawn cap, her linen cuffs and collar, county badge and epaulettes, her white gloves for field work. She had looked at Miss Latham, who had served in the Balkans, and the Marchioness Camden, who visited and spoke so encouragingly. She was touched when the Dragoons' band appeared to play for them, in gratitude for their kindness to the boy on the bicycle. She liked that when the cadets from New College took part in an 'engagement', playing the parts of both the invading Hun and the defending Englishmen, she was capable of putting her training into action so efficiently. She liked the slightly bemused looks Julia gave her.

Rose was quite aware that the real thing would be very different. Mrs Blanchard, who had served as matron to an ambulance column in the Franco-Prussian war, had made that perfectly clear. Despite that – no, because of it – *I can do this*, Rose had thought. By September 1914 she had been attached to a hospital near Folkestone, and had taken up smoking.

Now, in the doorway, she looked at beautiful Julia in the morning light and pitied her. Though beauty was not Julia's only quality; it could only be the first thing about her. When she entered a room, nobody thought: *There is a generous, determined, kind-looking woman.* Her kindness, her determination and her flashes of wit were, in everyday life, dazzled out of view by her rich pale hair, her tiny waist, her glowing skin, the surprise of her dark blue eyes, and the slight dip at the bridge of her straight nose, 'the imperfection which makes you perfect', as Peter called it. Few people cared about her better virtues. And as she was an adoring wife, not the type to exploit the male response, what was she supposed to do with it? It was only for Peter, and Peter wasn't there. In a world increasingly made up of women and old, or sick, or juvenile men, unmanned men, it was of no benefit to her. Indeed, it must be a disadvantage. There are always women ready to hate another woman for her beauty, Rose knew that. She had been included – unwillingly – in enough nasty little conversations behind the backs of pretty women by other plain women who assumed, wrongly, that Rose would share their jealousy as she shared their dull looks.

So Rose pitied Julia for her beauty, or thought she did. But Julia had learnt to love her own beauty, because beauty was her currency, and other people valued it so highly. Each day since Peter had left, after breakfast, she sat on the needle-point stool by the French windows, morning sun streaming in, and tuned his cello. She made a lovely picture. She had thought about it, and she had laughed at herself for having thought about it. She had considered how most charmingly to cast the cello aside (without causing it damage) in order to run into her husband's arms when he appeared in the doorway. She had laughed at herself about that too.

She missed him *so* much. What was the point of doing *anything* without your husband to do it for? She had tried more public-spirited ways of helping out. She'd launched straight in at Elliman's when they went over to munitions, gamely pulling on a hideous pair of overalls ('I honestly, genuinely look like that elephant your uncle Kit sent the pictures of from India,' she said to Rose) and packing explosives into long, tubular shell cases. She couldn't stick it. 'The girls are terribly coarse and vulgar, and they don't like me, and anyway Peter wouldn't want me all chemical and yellow.' She couldn't be a VAD because 'Well, my hands . . .' she said, but she was doing herself a disservice there. It wasn't vanity. It was a horror of blood, an abrupt, puking horror, which helped nobody, and which she was ashamed to admit to. It was easier to confess to vanity. People expected it of her, anyway. She knew that.

A stint at the Department of Pensions in London ended with a kind reprimand from an elderly civil servant driven to distraction by some truly shambolic filing. Only after these false starts had Julia discovered that her real war work was exactly the same as her peace work: Peter.

It started with making nice things for Peter: sandbags,

for example. Beautiful sandbags, of quality canvas, or even linen, and she embroidered his regimental crest in the corner: a wild boar's head with a crown on, the motto '*Sic Petit Arcadia*' – 'thus he reaches heaven'. She saw no irony in it at that early stage. Mostly they were used as pillow cases, and for one general, as a shoebag for his dress shoes.

After that hand-knitted socks, scarves, vests, long-johns; cakes, letters, parcels of cigarettes and chocolate with loving messages on the back of amusing picture postcards, selections of the new gramophone records . . . that lovely recording of *E lucevan le stelle*, by Leo Szilard, that he loved . . . But she grew bored with doing that because she couldn't see the results, though his thank-you letters were charming. More importantly, she felt, or perhaps more controllably, things should be nice for Peter *when he came home*.

Rose did not notice Julia's inability to be satisfied. 'You don't really need to . . . I'm sure he'll write and let us know when he's coming,' Rose would say, from time to time, but really she had more important things on her mind – so what if, after the sandbags, Julia had no faith in the wartime post? (So many letters and telegrams flying this way and that! Who knew where they might not end up? He was *perfectly* likely to turn up unannounced.) And, anyway, Julia had no faith in anyone else's understanding of what Peter needed, and Julia had nothing else to do.

And when he had come back after training, his farewell few days before leaving for France, Julia's joy had been so extreme that there was no room for anything else in the house: for anyone else's emotions, or for silence, conversation, mutual enquiry, rest, forgiving each other the fights there had been about him joining up in the first place . . . and then he had gone again, and she had returned to plumping the cushions. It took her fifty-three minutes to plump every cushion in the house, if she didn't hurry.

What Rose didn't know was that Julia spent every night with the same phrases and memories and resentments and ancient conversations lining up at the end of the bed, waiting to take their turn in tormenting her, and woke every morning in howling loneliness for her husband, her sheets too smooth and her bed too tidy, with a hunger for things to be right just as strong, desperate and justified as that of any scared soldier, any exhausted ambulance driver, any battle-weary medic.

Rose thought Julia appallingly self-conscious, the kind who never got anything done. *If she applied half the energy she applies to herself and the house to something useful, think what she'd achieve! She's just going to disappear in a cloud of lavender water one of these days* . . . But Rose wasn't being entirely fair. Considering that Julia had been bred and trained to be a beautiful wife, and nothing else, she wasn't doing too badly.

'No, thank you, darling,' Julia said. 'I don't need anything.'

∽

Purefoy didn't get up to town. He lay on his bed in his room above the pub, trying not to think about Nadine. Then, when he returned to France, he felt a new fear: that of not be able to do what was required of him. He was willing enough to go back to the front – keen, even, for duty to blast thought from his mind. He just wasn't sure that he could walk, button his jacket, say good morning. The week in Dover, the officer training, and the look in Burgess's eye before he left had all uprooted him.

A good officer. A good Second Lieutenant. A good soldier. The machine of which he was part deftly slotted him back. Even at the dock, he felt the required state of mind begin to descend upon him, inexorably, as on every man there. It seemed to him a mass state of mind, like gas, or the all-pervading stale-biscuit smell of damp khaki. It's there; there's nothing you can do about it. It's somehow natural. Now that he had identified it, he found that he could look at it from arm's length before letting the familiar sick comfort of it sweep over him again. He wanted to approach all of it with clean senses: the trains, the pristine uniforms going out, the dirty ones coming in, the land-scapes streaming past the carriage windows, the rattle of window frames, the smooth slopes and low curves of the heavy countryside towards the Somme valley, the con-tained anxiety of the station at Amiens, the smells of soot and paraffin, the ever-increasing destruction, the lackening trees, the cling of the muddy road to the sole of the boot, the camp, the dark damp culvert that was the entrance to the trench system.

They hadn't found somewhere else to send him so he was, after all, back with the Paddingtons in the support lines behind Hébuterne. He found Locke in the wallpapered rabbit hole, and sat on a box, and accepted a glass of whisky. Dinner was about to be served. Locke was stepping out to see how the fellows were doing. Purefoy, accompanying him in his faultless new khaki, polished and presented, whistle and revolver, felt an utter fraud.

Ferdinand and Bowells grinned at him like lunatics. Burgess said nothing, gave nothing away. Ainsworth said, 'Aye, lad, sir', and shook his hand. Purefoy felt it quite absurd.

That night, hunched over Locke's small desk, he wrote a letter:

My dear Nadine,

I am sorry that I had leave just now and I could not visit you. I am sorry that I joined up and left without speaking to you and left only that silly letter telling you I was going. I am sorry I sent you that stupid Christmas card. I am sorry I have not been able to write to you, about my life here, so that you could see how I am, and how I do. There's no excuses, but there's reasons, and I will try this once to explain it, because very soon I will be back in the thick of it, and unable again to communicate. This is why: out here, I do not exist. That is my protection against all this. The gigantic upheaval, the all-encompassing immensity of what goes on out here, dwarfs the individual to nothingness. There is no room for private welfare, because the common welfare overtakes all. And the horrors? Nat, we have horrors, and the worst horror is that before I came away on leave I no longer saw them. I stopped looking, because seeing doesn't help, and I didn't like what I was seeing. Instead, I concentrate, an almost hypnotic state of concentration. It's as if I am running past everything at a jog, thinking only of where I am going. My self retreats, my focus is narrow. My body does what has to be done.

While I was at Dover last week that condition of mind receded a little, and I thought clearly, as a human being. But such luxuries are not for the Front. This is the last evening when my mind and heart are engaged. I have kept them open in order to be able to say this to you. To tell the truth, I don't want you to know about this kind of thing. But not telling you seems like a form of death, a death of the heart, or the mind, or the spirit. There are more ways than the physical to die, which I never knew before. I have learnt it this year. I do not care to think what else I shall learn as the war continues. As clearly it must.

We return to the Front Line tomorrow. I am going back under and I will not write again. Pray that I come up again, and my darling be there to help haul me out at the end, if I make it –

Oh, dear I shouldn't have written that.
Well, fuck it. Fuck it. That's how I feel.

Chapter Six

London, August 1915

The letter, the first since the Christmas card, was sent on by her mother, with a note on the back in swirling, elegant writing: 'Have you an admirer? Tell all!'

Not likely. Not after the look on your face when you gave me the first letter, the oh-Nat-I'm-just-going-to-war-'bye-then letter. The stupid stupid stupid unkind letter. Not after you said: 'It's probably for the best, darling. I know you liked him but you know he's not the sort of boy . . .'

Oh yes he is the sort of boy, he is EXACTLY the sort of boy. He is THE boy.

Liked. In the past. Thanks for that little extra, Mother.

Followed by the Christmas card which might as well have been from someone's uncle they hardly knew . . .

Nadine was not able to say, either to her mother or to herself, that her mother was wrong and she was right and Riley was everything, everything he should be. Because he wasn't. He was – he had somehow turned into – someone to whom she could only write those stupidly cheerful notes. If she could write at all. Was it distance? Was it the fact of words on paper, uncomfortable, unchangeable? Was it whatever had happened that had made him leave so suddenly? Was it whatever was happening out there, which she couldn't ask about, which he wasn't writing to her about?

But that moment, in the studio, when he had turned to her, and she had turned, and there was that moment when she had thought, for a second of absolute bewildering thrill, that he was going to kiss her, and he hadn't but he had put his hand . . . and that moment when they had looked at each other, and then, just then, for that moment . . . wasn't he everything? Wasn't it all true, just true, and possible, and true?

Like the Donne . . . eye beams twisting . . .

And Papa had said, *There's nothing you can do about it* . . .

And the heart was true, and the heat, in that moment, with his hand on her waist and that big old pinafore, the hyacinth smell, that morning, was a promise. They had made a promise then. They had. They had. That touch, that surge, that look.

The entire autumn, no one mentioned him to her. She had wanted to ask. She had lain in bed wondering who best to ask, going round in circles. And when she had asked, she learnt nothing. Her family had heard nothing from him. Sir Alfred had had only a card when Riley was in training. She had asked Terence, who had rather embarrassedly said, no, he hadn't heard from the old boy. She had been tempted to visit Mrs Purefoy – she had even got her coat on to go to their house – but having already written for his address she grew embarrassed; overcoming the embarrassment she couldn't find the street; having found the house she grew

90

embarrassed again at its smallness, so she decided to write after all; and having written she received no reply; and thus ignored she retreated into humiliated confusion and did not know what to do.

During a drawing lesson in the studio she had braved the topic again with Sir Alfred. (Thank God her parents had got over their moment of concern about her studying art, for now at least.) 'I wonder if there is any news of Riley,' she said. 'I suppose he would have written to you. Or his mother.'

'The Paddingtons are in France, I believe,' said Sir Alfred. 'Or perhaps Flanders. If he'd talked to me, I would have put in a word for him with the Artists' Rifles.' He turned away, and the broad old back said clearly: Enough. Don't ask.

So instead she had grown paler and thinner, and began swarming inside, as every possibility, every nightmare, every story in every newspaper, every bad thing that could happen was happening, in her mind, to him. Every single bad thing.

Jacqueline, as Christmas passed and the war was not over, noticed her daughter's decline. 'Go to Scotland, darling,' she said. 'Stay with Uncle George. Get some fresh air.'

'I'd much rather go to art school, Mother. To the Slade.'

Jacqueline closed her eyes for a moment, annoyed. 'We've talked about this,' she said.

'It's what I would like to do,' Nadine said politely. 'It's what I am good at.'

'It's not suitable,' said Jacqueline, with a little tightening in her face, annoying Nadine, who knew that her mother had sat for plenty of artists in her youth. Jacqueline glanced at her daughter, saw the retort in her eyes, and cut it off. 'And you're not good enough,' she said.

'Who says?' Nadine replied, stung. This was a new tack from her mother. She *was* good.

'Sir Alfred,' lied Jacqueline. *A girl needs a good reputation, these days more than ever. Art school is for times of peace and plenty, not for unmarried girls in wartime.*

Nadine held her head very high, and blinked. She didn't believe it. Sir Alfred knew she had enough talent to invest in. He didn't think a girl could have a career as an artist, but he didn't deny talent when he saw it . . .

For a moment Jacqueline wavered, looking at her proud daughter, then steeled herself. *It's for her own good.*

Nadine looked at her arms, thinner than ever, and her narrow feet. What was the point of a female? Even at the best of times, let alone during war? All she wanted was art and love . . . *Like Tosca*, she thought, with a little laugh. And love was – well, denied. And art too. Her cousin Noel had said to her, on his most recent visit, that he felt less than a man because his asthma prevented him being Over There. Well, she felt less than a woman. At least a man knew he was meant to be a soldier, and a boy knew he was meant to be a man. But she – she was too young to have found out the point of herself anyway, and now she was shipwrecked, stranded in time. Not a woman, not a girl any more, and not, apparently, an artist.

Scotland?

No.

'Then I'm going to join the VAD,' she said blandly. 'I'm going rather mad here, knowing there is so much to do and not doing anything. I have been reading all about it. I shall take all my frustration out on sheets.'

'No,' said Jacqueline, immediately, instinctively.

'Well, I must do something, Mama. I think that's a fair choice, the Slade or the VAD.'

But Jacqueline could only see it as men, or more men. Artistic, immoral men, with attractively long hair and no prospects, or broken, heroic, half-naked men in desperate need ... Getting Riley out of the way was one thing, but there were always more men: wrong ones, new ones, ones outside the systems of safety ... *Lord*, she thought, *it used to be so much fun playing with fire, back when everything was safe.*

The wounded, she decided, would be less attractive to her daughter than the artists.

While scrubbing, boiling, lugging, hanging, pouring, twisting and folding made up most of Nadine's duties at London General Number 2, Chelsea, the reality of blood and flesh was also available to her, and she saw it. It was a shock, and she was by no means sure at the beginning that she would be able to stay in the hospital. To strengthen her nerve, she blackmailed herself, imagining that each boy was Riley, and she was some French or Belgian girl. Each shattered leg she saw became his leg; each twisted arm was his arm; each pale and sweaty brow was his handsome brow; each gunshot wound settled itself into his flesh. It both brought her closer to them and protected her from them. But what started as a spur and a naturally arising technique of self-protection developed with pandemic haste into a morbid, almost-constant fantasy about the terrible things that might be happening to him.

Jean, older and wiser, with reddened knuckles and a pot of rouge number two in her bag, said to Nadine, over biscuits and Bovril, one carbolic-scented night-shift, 'You're ill-wishing him. Don't. God didn't give you an imagination so you could use it to worry all the time.'

So Nadine saved Riley's letter till Jean was not there. It burnt in her apron pocket. But, oh, the circumstances of the letter faded into nothingness at its contents. He might as well have leapt out of the envelope in person, telling her everything as clearly as he always had, which now were these impossible things, these things that swept her every previous concern to the eight winds. He hadn't written? Oh, diddums. He had gone away? Poor little you.

I don't exist.

How can that be? She read it again.

Is it so bad that there is no room in the same dimension of creation for both it and him, and that as *it* is all-powerful, *he* must cease to exist?

That's the wrong way round, surely. Surely *it* must cease to exist, because he, palpably, *does* . . . It. It. A gigantic amorphous It, and a little speck of warm flesh and blood standing in front of It, in the middle of It, fading away.

She thought of his eyes and his mouth, his jokes and his intensity. She remembered him up the tree, popping out from among the sun-spattered chestnut leaves, their sharp folds. She thought of that first snowball, and his black curly hair, like hers but different, and how even then she had liked how he was like her but different. She pictured a little brain and a little heart buffeted to and fro inside a cloud of smoke and flash and shrapnel. She remembered the hardness of the wood of the trestle table under her thighs, bare legs for the spring day, the moment like lightning, when a link had flashed awake, body mind heart, and for the first time she had felt herself connected to herself.

~

My dear Riley,

What can I say to you now? I only want to say what will help to make you stronger and perhaps happy, but at the same time, if you don't exist, then you won't want to hear from me at all, as I will only remind you that you *do* exist, with a past and a future and people who love you, but then you know at heart that you do – but if you find it better for now to put away that knowledge then perhaps this isn't the moment to mention it, so I won't . . . but I WON'T send you a letter of 'hope this finds you as it leaves us and Mother and Father send their regards' . . . not to scorn the people who do that . . . and of course Mother and Father *do* send their regards, or at least I'm sure they would if I ever saw them, at least, Father would, though Mother would say – actually not say, just *look*, that I shouldn't be writing to you at all – she has become more and more proper since the War began, unlike everybody else who does exactly the opposite – she lives in fear of chaos and freedom, which she thinks are the same thing, and much more dangerous than the Hun. She is hardly artistic at all any more and has taken to wearing stays again, just when everybody else is giving them up – goodness, how she would disapprove of my mentioning that – but I only see them once a week now if that and I'm not waiting till next week to write back to you just to be able to send their regards. Reading back, that doesn't quite make sense but I think you will see what I mean.

Riley, I was so happy to hear from you, so utterly happy that I sang on the ward, and Sister gave me such a look and asked, so I had to tell her that I had had good news, that someone I feared might be lost was not lost after all – because for all you say you don't exist and for all I respect that and your reasons for having to think it, Riley, you do! Riley exists! And that alone, dear Riley, makes me so happy that I sing. Oh, now I've done it –

But surely it is the really existing which will keep you sane for after it's all over? We've had some shell-shock cases in here and oh, Lord, Riley, I don't know how anyone can decide which needs to be fixed first, their broken limbs and wounds or their broken minds. I can tell you what I do: an awful lot of washing and cleaning. Piles of sheets that would stretch to Paree, dreams of wading through Keatings and Lysol . . . But I have two special talents: first, I speak French. So sometimes I am called from cleaning to speak French or translate something, though more often it's talent number two: I don't faint at blood. So I am called on to help clean up in the operating theatre, and I have seen such sights – my God, Riley – well, you will have seen them too, and at closer quarters. Why do I tell you this? Because I want you to feel a bit less alone. And it can't go on much longer. Governments will just have to take a look at the hospitals and see straight, at what is happening, and they'll stop.

But, Riley, while talking of feeling alone: I'm going to say this now and then I won't mention it again – don't you don't you don't you ever, *ever ever* again take it on yourself unilaterally to decide that you won't let me know how things are doing with you. We were worried stupid about you. If it were allowed to be furious with a Brave Young Man Giving His All at the Front then, Riley, I am furious with you. *Furious.*

Yours *furiously* – Nadine

~

The letter was waiting on his return from the front line. It was Ferdinand, on his usual look-out for food parcels, who saw that the normally taciturn Purefoy, who got few communications and those short and from his mother, had flushed and put a letter in his pocket.

'Got a girl, Purefoy?' he crowed. 'Where d'you find her? Have her send out something nice, would you?'

Locke coughed.

Ferdinand giggled, and said: 'Oh, sorry, sir. Sir.'

'Smarten up, Private,' Locke said. *Oh, they'll get used to it.*

'Sir,' said Ferdinand, and lowered his lids with a happy little gleam. He was so proud, so delighted for Purefoy he still couldn't hide it.

Burgess was smirking.

Purefoy thought, *Ah, well, that's it for me. I am no longer what I once was.*

~

He read the letter later, during a saved five minutes with a fag, knees up leaning against a trench wall leading from the pink and grey and gold dug-out with the piano. Above, on the level he associated with the past and the other world that he had found himself incapable of approaching, beyond the rim of trench life, the evening summer sun was sloping and glowing over the great flatness. In the lull before the uproar of the night, it gilded the flooded shell-holes with sudden hot, brazen surfaces, dazzling to the eye and mind. Captain Locke had something very juicy and operatic playing on his gramophone inside, a passionate aria of squeezing, rising, squeezing, rising . . . and then always the final falling away, the falling note . . . It was not the soundtrack Purefoy would have chosen.

Purefoy read the letter carefully, several times, and every now and then he closed his eyes for a moment. He thought about her hand moving across the paper, holding the pen, about whether she licked the nib still, the press of her hand on the words, her mouth, her inky hair like a Mesopotamian goddess's, about unfinished business and the curve of her waist and how he would perfectly likely never see her again.

Her pen, he noticed, had jabbed through the paper on the last *furious*.

Chapter Seven

Locke Hill, Kent, December 1915

When Peter's letter arrived, Julia was sitting in his library chair, re-reading the bulb catalogue, holding the fort. (She laughed a little at her military imagery.) Now, frost stiffened the lawn and only three icy pale roses lingered along the veranda – but she had planted next spring's bulbs herself, wearing gloves, of course, and treating her hands afterwards with warm oil, for her hands, too, would have to be lovely for him, and, after all, Harker did the heavy work in the border. So – snowdrops for January, aconites and the astonishing miniature irises for February, daffodils, hyacinths, tulips, anemones and so on till July . . . the roses and shrubs would carry through . . . autumn crocuses; November would be a problem, unless the rudbeckia lasted, but there would be the wintersweet and holly and the Christmas roses . . . next Christmas! Well, it would *certainly* be over by then. And, anyway, there was this Christmas to think about . . . The image played across her mind . . . a wreath (made by her) . . . the red-berried holly, of course, and ivy; the iridescent coins of honesty seed heads, rubbed free of the little dry veily bit, to shine like pearl lustre; a little yew – or is that too funereal? He wouldn't want that . . . rosemary, perhaps . . . and the fire crackling, the smell of the goose roasting, and champagne excoriatingly cold in the gold Viennese coupes, and the tall figure in his trenchcoat, tired and hungry, so glad to be home . . . Whatever time of year he might get leave, however long this terrible thing dragged on, the garden would be beautiful for him.

She read it swiftly, and telephoned at once to Rose to apply for leave from the hospital.

Four days later, two days late, Peter arrived. Julia had been standing on the doorstep patting her hair since the letter arrived – patting her hair, pinching her cheeks, and turning to check in the ormolu mirror how much older she looked since June.

'You look beautiful,' Rose said pityingly.

'But I do look older,' Julia said, with a little smile.

'So will he,' Rose reminded her.

It had been only ten months – they knew ten months was not very long, compared with some others. It wasn't so simple that he had left a boy and returned a man, or left in the bloom of youth and returned a ruin, or that he had left a gentleman and returned a soldier. He was still twenty-seven, still six foot three, with his fine hair, and his slight stoop, his apologetic smile, his bony jaw, his blue eyes. He looked a little thin and pale – he always did. But there was a new papery tiredness on his fine skin, a new parched quality to his slenderness. Rose had to remind herself not to run to him to be the first to be embraced.

And then she had to remind herself not to look as Julia
hurled herself into his arms, melted herself inside his greatcoat, her pale wool dress a streak against the darkness of
his uniform like a headlight beam through night. It was as
much their reunion as his return that brought a tear of
relief to Rose's eye.

∽

Peter was affable, quiet, busy. He played with Max, the red
setter, in the garden. He read the newspapers. He arranged
to go to town for a meeting to do with Locke and Locke.
He went to bed directly after dinner, and slept late in the
morning.

'That's good, I think,' said Rose, who had had some of
the wounded from Loos in the hospital, and had listened
to their nightmares and their midnight weeping. She had
seen – God, hadn't she seen! – how strange men could be
when they came back from Over There.

'What is?' said Julia.

'His sleeping so much.'

'Oh, yes,' she said.

Julia was angry, and Rose knew why. Peter was not being
affectionate with her. There was no warmth in his eye.
During the night Rose had heard none of the little creaks
and muffled gasps that she now knew betrayed what Matron
chose to call the Full Expression of Married Love.

The following morning Julia was wearing the cream dress
again, which looked to Rose sacrificial.

Rose hoped things would improve after she left them
alone together. 'Be gentle with him,' she had whispered to

Julia, kissing her goodbye when she left to return to Folkestone. Julia had given her a rather amazed look. Was *Rose* really telling *her* how to behave towards a husband? *Too* funny.

Rose recognised the look from visiting wives at the hospital, kind, good, ignorant women with no idea what they were up against. *Poor Peter*, she thought.

~

Peter sat in his chair, his father's old chair, feeling the support of familiar old cushions, the shape of them formed by the backsides of generations of Lockes of Locke Hill. His grandfather's books stood dark on the shelves, a little gold tooling gleaming dimly here and there in the firelight. His great-grandfather's dress sword, in its glass case, lay on the table behind the chintz sofa. Here he was, in the arms of his ancestors.

The newspaper, whose versions and analyses of the battle of Loos he did not recognise, stood as it were of its own accord, hardly needing the support of his heedless hands. He found he was blinking fast, trying to chase away images he could not live with.

'Darling,' said Julia. She crossed the drawing room to his chair, and made to creep into his arms, inside the newspaper. 'Darling, we've hardly had a moment. How are you, my love?'

He did not know how he was. How could she expect him to know? How could she expect him to answer?

He had lost fifteen men at Loos: Burdock, Knightley, Atkins, Jones, Bloom, Bruce, Lovall, Hall, Green, Wester,

Johnson, Taylor, Moles, Twyford and Merritt. The Allies had been seven to one against the Hun, and fifteen men had died under his command.

And then he had been sent home. Before he could – could what? Could be with the other survivors: huddle in a pile with them, smoking in silence, sharing air, sleeve to sleeve, being not alone. And before he could find out if fifteen was many or few – well, God, of course it was fifteen too many, but by war logic, by the bitter standards of Over There, he didn't know if it was many or few; he didn't know if he had done well or badly in comparison with others; he didn't know if it was all right to ask himself that question, and he didn't know who to ask if it was or not. He didn't know how the boys were now. The paper told him none of this. But he saw Ainsworth's muddied face over the rim of a shell-hole, asking him for something that he couldn't make out, and he saw some limbs, just limbs, lying there, and Burdock, Knightley, Atkins, Jones, Bloom, Bruce, Lovall, Hall, Green, Wester, Johnson, Taylor, Moles, Twyford and Merritt were dead. His men. He thanked God for Purefoy, who turned out to have the knack as well as the guts: he knew whether or not to put a hand on a shoulder, at which moment to offer a smoke. Purefoy knew that when you had to say something, and there was absolutely nothing a man *could* say, it didn't much matter what you said. Purefoy had the tone of voice. Whenever any bloody fool carped on about promotion from the ranks diluting the quality of officer stock and all that idiocy, Locke would point out Purefoy.

Julia was sitting on his lap, nestling a little, moving her lovely bottom. His arms closed around her and he dropped the paper, as she wanted. He held her. Such a little woman. She could just break. It was for *her*, really, all of it. To keep her safe. Not to let the Hun do to her what they'd done to Belgium.

He'd carried the boys back in bits. An armful of Atkins; Bloom's head on his shoulder and his arm round his neck, resting like a woman's or a tired child's. His own long-fingered hand white against Bloom's hair, embracing the dead head to keep it from flopping.

She was looking at him in that shy way, the up-and-under the eyelashes look. He knew what it offered.

God, he wanted to want to –

The weight of her body on him. Her arm round his neck, clinging. The flesh . . .

Something dug and bit in his stomach.

He managed to kiss the top of her head, as you would a child come to say goodnight. It was as much of a 'no' as a slap in the face.

With a tart little blink she pretended that hadn't been the question. After a moment she got up, and went to the window, and came back and sat herself down mermaid-style at his feet, looking up at him. She said gently, 'What can I do for you, Peter? How can I make you happy?' At which he let out a bark of laughter, which sounded much crueller than he had intended, even to his own ears, but which he could not pull back. She winced.

Do you even read the version in the papers? he thought. *Do you have the slightest idea what's going on out there?* And then stopped himself. It wasn't her fault.

'I only want you to be happy, darling,' she said boldly, flinging caution to the winds.

He blinked. 'Well, I'm afraid that's not in your power, my dear,' he said mildly. 'So you'd best put it out of your mind.'

Slap, slap, slap.

She turned and went upstairs. He pushed himself out of the chair, like an old man, and poured himself a brandy from the sparkling clean, perfectly positioned decanter on the deeply polished sideboard.

~

The following morning Julia went up to London on the train. She proceeded smartly to Selfridges, where she bought herself a dim green wool dress with a wide collar and a soft V-neck, belted at the waist, and the new war-crinoline shape, flaring to her calves. It showed her narrow ankles, and it showed her throat. She bought a pair of new shoes, dainty black, almost practical, with a heel. She looked at the underwear – every time she looked in a shop they had brought out new designs. Goodness, they were pretty. Blue figured silk ... but Peter had never liked the thigh-restricting corsets. She blushed, and banished the blush. That was what she was here for.

'What's that?' she asked, gesturing to an unfamiliar item.

The girl gave a delicate smile. 'It is a bust-improver, madam. The, em, moulded area increases the generosity of the form. It's entirely invisible, of course, when worn. But not, em, something madam would be requiring.'

Goodness.

Most of the new styles were so soft and free-moving. That was all right – her breasts were still good. Weren't they? Yes. She chose a nice light corset – no stays or any of that old-fashioned nonsense. *Vogue* disapproved of women wearing the new knitted-silk dancing corsets for the day. She'd read it was daring. She felt daring. Perhaps Peter would like daring.

Then the girl showed her some beautiful silk chiffon drawers and chemises in the Oriental style. Pale green like a pistachio nut, bias cut, with a dusty pink trim. The sort of thing *Vogue* called: 'Those blushing trifles that are born to blush unseen.'

So much had been unseen of late. Well. Perhaps he would look at these.

'*So* pretty,' she murmured. The drawers were tiny. They wouldn't be the least use for everyday wear.

'We also have this,' said the girl, modestly. With a little flourish of her neat hands a delicate slip appeared along the counter, the same silk chiffon, with fine satin ribbons for the straps. 'And, er . . .' It was a deep-sleeved wafting boudoir gown, the same silk chiffon with *devoré* velvet, and a soft sash to tie it.

The girl actually stared at Julia in the changing room, her peony skin, the exquisite scraps of lingerie. Like a present wrapped only in ribbons.

Julia bought them all. *And* new stockings.

Christmas Eve, by the cruel requirements of the regiment, was his last night. After their delicious, elegant, slightly formal dinner, over which Julia had taken considerable trouble, she said she would go to bed early, and she kissed Peter sweetly as she went, not saying she was tired, or had a headache, or anything.

She had a bath: not too hot, to make her flesh red. Not too much jasmine oil. She had hoped he would come up while she was in it, shoulders emerging prettily from the water, but never mind, because after drying herself, perched on the edge of the bed, she put on the lovely new things. She had never worn anything so racy. Did they look too dreadful, in this country bedroom? Did they look ridiculous on her?

A horrible thought struck her – it was her. *Her.*

I'm losing it. Bloom.

Old. Fat. Wrinkles.

No-o-o, she told herself. *He loves you. The . . . marital side . . . has always been . . . a joyous . . . and it will be again. You're doing the right thing.*

Julia had been brought up ignorant of . . . the marital side, until at the last minute her mother had said: 'There is something unpleasant to which a wife has to submit.' But her mother had been wrong about it, so wrong.

Julia was quite cold when Peter finally came upstairs.

He'd brought his book.

He didn't go and shave.

In the middle of the night he groaned, and rolled over, and clutched her wildly, scarily. For a moment she was glad, and tried to return what she hoped was his embrace – but it wasn't. It was more like a kind of fit – horrible, quick, desperate, violent. She found herself stiff with shock beneath him, suffocated by his chest on her face, her breasts painfully squashed, almost twisted. He didn't seem to be either awake or asleep and, for the first time, she understood what her mother had meant.

She lay rigid and furious at the edge of her bed, the white-sheeted side of the mattress like a cliff falling away beneath her. His hot body spread across the whole territory; she couldn't bear to let it touch her. She could feel its heat, and quivered.

You were not meant to be angry with a serving soldier (but she was) . . .

She had wanted him to make love to her (but not like that) . . .

His leave was so short (and so horrible) . . .

They'd been awfully lucky to get leave over actual Christmas (and, to be brutal, she wished he hadn't come) . . .

They had been so happy, before he had gone away to protect her. Well, that was pretty damn ironic, wasn't it?

He left the next afternoon.

'Well,' Julia said, pale in the frosty air, 'Happy Christmas!' She kissed him sharply on each cheek, and turned away, clicking her heels on the black and white floor to go and sit by the fire.

'Goodbye, my dear,' he said, very quietly. He was so very tall.

~

Rose, who had been unable to get away from the hospital again, came the following week on her afternoon off. Julia told her, fussing over tea in the little sitting room at Locke Hill, that she was thinking of training as an ambulance driver and going to France.

'They only take ladies of good family,' she said. 'It was in the paper.' She patted around her on the sofa, searching ineffectually. 'Look, here it is . . . and I *really can't*,' she said, 'just keep on hanging around. I really want to be *in it*, doing my *bit*.'

Rose smiled. Hamlet's line, 'Nothing is good or bad but thinking makes it so', came to mind. Julia seemed to have a natural talent for deciding, unilaterally, that something was or was not the case. She could, by changing her emotional lighting, block out a disquieting incident and ignore lines or passages of dialogue. She could, by approaching from a different angle, translate and transmute until history was rewritten and maps redrawn. It was not conscious. Filters roamed her mind, and memory slid this way and that, like stage flats, not so much at her bidding but at the call of her emotional necessity. A bad cake could be lathered with whipped cream and raspberries, and called the latest French Fancy, a recipe from Lady Panton. A moth-eaten jacket became a reason for a lovely shopping spree. Peter had told Rose once that he saw this as an optimistic knack, useful in times of minor difficulty. It was one of the things which made him think that despite her great beauty she would be a good wife.

'I could do that, couldn't I?'

Rose wondered if Julia's mother had been in touch. Mrs Orris was a flag-waving committee-running powerhouse, a mistress of getting other people Over There, a firm believer in *one big push* and embarrassed, Rose felt, by the lack of sacrificial instinct in her own daughter. The daughter of a friend of hers had actually been killed by a shell on a field hospital, and she wouldn't shut up about it. Rose saw that Mrs Orris, having no son to offer up to glory, would rather thrill to an equivalent sacrifice.

'Other girls are Over There,' Julia continued. 'My mother . . .'

Ah, yes.

'. . . she would much *prefer* it if I were . . . and I would be nearer him . . .' She tailed off. She still loved him. Why was she even thinking that insidious word 'still'? It had been a bad leave. These things happen. Mrs Bax had been quite vocal about how dreadful things had been with her son Freddie. Julia knew it was her duty to make the leave, and Peter's behaviour, acceptable. She tried, very hard, recasting it this way and that in her mind. She terribly wanted to do her duty. But when her only desire was to do all that was required of a wife, he had rejected her over and over. She couldn't do anything for him. He didn't want her. And then he insulted her.

The situation was irreconcilable. But she had to reconcile it. It was her duty. He was her husband. He was protecting them.

She turned to Rose. 'I need to do something,' she said. It was a genuine plea.

Rose assumed this was a display of wishful thinking from Julia.

'You faint at the sight of a steering wheel,' she pointed out. She didn't care to enter into the many other reasons why this was a ludicrous idea. Nothing would come of it anyway. Sometimes it seemed as if Julia had somewhere acquired vouchers for extra attention. As if they had come free with the silver-blonde hair and the rosy mouth. And when nobody else was there, Rose was meant to redeem them, once a week over tea. Rose, being single, a foreigner to marital complexity and of independent cast, had no idea what war – or society – required of a wife. She thought Julia was being banal.

'Well, I'm sure you think it's time I toughened up,' Julia said. 'I know my mother does.'

Rose thought it was time Julia's mother shut up. Julia's mother had never, to Rose's knowledge, uttered a single opinion that she hadn't received from elsewhere, had never said a single thing that she hadn't read in the paper that week or heard over some cup of self-important tea. And irritating though Julia could be, Rose held that she was sweet-natured and pretty-faced and that one of the many injustices of the war – a small one, in the big scheme, but still – was how the sweet-natured pretty-faced daughters of England were required to toughen up. A girl like Julia wasn't made for it. Why *should* she have to?

How do we learn it? Rose wondered. *If I knew, I could save people the trouble of having to learn it directly – but I only know that one day you wake without weeping, and you look the unbearable in the eye and you bear it, but hold on to the compassion. Without actual feeling. Can you do that? And remain useful?*

Then could you clear away those amputated limbs?

Rose had seen girls – nurses, VADs, ambulance drivers – working in France, existing in what she now saw was a state of constant shock. She had briefly shared the long, cruel hours and the vehicles awash with gangrenous blood and bits of limb and coughed-up scraps of greyish-yellow gassed lung, which had to be hosed out every morning. She had both envied and feared the girls who dealt with that, and when she caught a fever two months in she had come home thankfully, and taken up her duties again at the milder level of the hospitals on this side of the Channel. And that had been a year ago . . . What state were those girls in now?

'I'm not sure ambulance-driving would be right for you,' said Rose.

'You don't think I could do it, do you?' Julia said tightly.

Rose tried to produce, at the drop of the hat, some kind of expression that would not be interpreted as patronising. It wasn't possible, of course, because she was being patronising. She had patronised Julia for years. It was her compensation for Julia's beauty and good marriage.

'I think,' Rose said, 'there are better uses for your talents.'

'What talents?' said Julia. 'The only talent I have is for looking nice and there are no men here to look at me and I'm getting old!'

'You're younger than me,' said Rose, mildly.

'You know what I mean,' said Julia.

Rose did know what she meant. She meant Rose was not a beauty, so it didn't matter for her.

Rose kept a mental list of the tiny changes the war was making, which no one was bothering to record because of the hugeness of everything:

1) That the shame of her not being married was dissolving and disappearing as if it had never existed.
2) That she was no longer required to make herself available as a potential wife, and she was liberated from

112

the discomforts, hypocrisies and embarrassments which that had caused.

3) *Ambition*. The fact that she could have it at all. Just that.

She added this one:

4) Before the war, what Julia had just said would have been a great insult. Now it had to be seen as a trifle.

Peter returned to France in a state of layered horror at himself, each layer leaping in turns over the other to occupy the front of his mind. One layer was fifteen dead men, two of them still in his arms, their dead limbs heavier every night. The other was that he had allowed those fleshly ghosts to cause such filthy behaviour to his wife, the woman he was meant to cherish; that he had upset her, then leapt on her like an animal; that she had been unable to look at him the following morning, only turning to him long enough to show a pale, puffy face and blaming eyes. He had been unable to find enough love or energy within himself to put this right in the time available and had left her waving at the door, her hand automatic, her eyes hideous with confusion and loss. He had been filled with useless pain about the horrible realisation that flesh, all flesh, even her flesh, was bloody meat, as cold and hideous as Atkins's heavy cold leg and Bloom's damp white brow and the French boy under the duckboards. All the way to Dover her thigh and young Atkins's made an irresistible flickering exchange of images, like a magic lantern, a film show gone wrong, a dismembered can-can.

113

Crossing the Channel, the *froideur* with Julia began to diffuse in the roar of responsibility, in the grand shared mentality of soldiers. By the time he was back with the regiment it had frozen and slipped down the back, suspended like those little creatures that live in ice, waiting for the sun and the thaw before they can grow, or feed, or blossom.

And then Julia sent him a letter, at the beginning of February, quite different in tone both from the repetitive lines of wilful cheer to which he had grown accustomed, and from anything he felt he deserved to receive.

My darling Peter –
We have such a lovely Valentine's surprise! So little, I think, my love, have we expected such a blessing that it seems we had forgotten all about it, and so strange it must seem to you – it seems so strange to me, even here, so how it will sound to you, so far away from anything to do with— Oh, my darling husband, I never thought I would have to write such news in a letter and now that I do have to I almost don't know how to phrase it. Well – here goes! I am to have a baby. We are to have a baby. Dr Tayle has been, and it is quite definite, and everything is as it should be, so – ! So what do you think of that? He – I am quite sure he is a boy, though I haven't a clue why! – is due at the end of September, so I am now thinking, Oh, let him be a child of peace, let everything be over by then, and let him enter into a new and better world, with his papa right by to welcome him and love him every day of his little life, and no more separation. My darling, won't that be grand? Won't

114

we be the most wonderful parents? And if by some unholy bad fortune everything is not over by then, well, the moment the world looks on our lovely baby she will realise the error of her ways, and *make* peace happen just for the sake of his lovely blue eyes – for he will have blue eyes, and he will be lovely, and can we call him Harry? My darling, I am going to post this *now* so that I know you have the news, at least, and I will write you more and longer soon, this evening probably, as Dr Tayle says I am to rest, which I read as meaning I do not have to go and play bridge with Mrs Bax – hurrah! – but must stay home and write to dear you instead. So please, my darling, write back to me as soon as you can and tell me all that you think, and if you like the name – Harry Locke – Harold Locke – I feel it sounds very English and good, a son to be proud of. I feel completely fine by the way, only a <u>tiny</u> bit sick in the mornings and Millie – who knows all about it as the oldest of eight! – provides me with an arrowroot biscuit the night before, the secret is to eat it <u>while you are still lying down</u> and there will be no sickness. And it works. So I must rush to give this to Harker to put in the post and please please write to me by return. I shall wait for your letter, longing to know how you feel and wishing so much we could be together for this <u>special wonderful blessed</u> moment!

My darling – all the love in the world is coming to you, from your loving wife, your <u>Julia</u>

The letter made no sense to him. For a moment he thought it a mistake, somebody else's letter delivered in error. Then he thought there must have been a biological mistake: surely such relations as he had inflicted on his wife that night were not – could not – well, of course they could. Why should they not? The emotions involved had no role in biological efficacy.

It was a punishment. He would look at his firstborn son, and see his own behaviour.

And his wife! Her utter sweetness! To overlook the circumstances of conception, and come forwards with such loving, loyal, forgiving . . .

Either that or she was mad.

'Anything wrong, sir?' said the young adjutant, lurking in the doorway of the dug-out.

'Apparently I'm to be a father,' said Locke, confused, the words sticky in his mouth. He had seen animals being born. Blood, slime, split flesh.

'Congratulations, sir!' said the adjutant, who was nineteen and a virgin, and to whom the words meant very little.

Chapter Eight

London, April 1916

Riley Purefoy was walking across Kensington Gardens in the sun, coming up from Victoria station, going home. He hadn't been in London for two years. It seemed very peculiar to him. There were no shells going off. No one was shooting. No gas-gong. No sergeants shouting. Firm clean ground underfoot. No corpses, no wounds, no huddled smoking men, no sweet stink of blood, no star shells waving beautifully through the sky. It was quiet. There were women. He was clean and dry in the flea-free uniform he had had pressed and steamed at the hotel in Dover. God, how shamelessly he appreciated the advantages of being an officer. It was worth all the little sneers in the mess, the sideways glances from etiolated toff twats, the dumb attempts at mockery from chinless boys whose pubescent moustaches and public-school slang did not, it turned out, make them natural leaders of men. He fully intended to buy himself some decent-quality puttees, now that he was allowed such freedoms, and to have done for ever with the annoying little thin ones.

Coming up towards the Round Pond, the centre of the

world, he stared at it for a moment, banished the image of sunset-flooded shell-holes, and lay down on his back on the grass. He'd heard there were show trenches in Kensington Gardens, so people at home could share their boys' experience. Burgess had laughed like a drain, reading out their beauties as described in the paper.

He stared at the sky. No one told him to do anything, or needed him to tell them what to do. Some children came and giggled at him and very quietly he asked himself, in the quiet, *Are you there? Riley? Are you still there?*

He knew that to lure himself from the protected depths back into the light of day was a dangerous idea, because he would have to dismiss himself again, send it back, in only six days. He didn't know if it would be a route to mental safety or to madness. Too much of that damn word. The papers going on about shell-shock – was it physical, was it mental, were only naturally degenerate characters susceptible to it? – how the ranks got hysteria but officers got neurasthenia . . . *even the madness is divided by class* . . . Men who'd gone off shell-shocked or neurasthenic reappearing at the front, cured . . . talking, one or two of them, of psychiatrists, electric treatment, hypnosis . . . *Patch 'em up and send 'em back* . . .

Riley thought it a miracle that *everybody* hadn't gone mad.

Ainsworth said they should count how many northerners were shell-shocked versus the southerners, because the front was not that different from home for the northerners. Slag heaps, explosions, screaming metal, fire and iron, digging, being ordered about. Ainsworth had had leave. Three days.

It took two days just to get from Ypres to Wigan. He left the moment he was dismissed, didn't stop to change or bathe, might even have made it in time only the conductor on the tram in Manchester had put him off, saying: 'I'm not having you on my tram, covered in fleas.' So Ainsworth had got off and walked, and taken the liberty of spending one evening with his children and one night with Sybil, and then he'd gone back and been marked AWOL, and Riley had been able by the judicious use of silence to lose the procedures of the incident.

Riley lay. Some birds were singing. Pigeons cooing: *poo poo, poo poo, poo.* Always five. It was just about here that he had lain the night before he joined up, in the English rain, all night, after running out on Terence, and his coat still sodden at the recruiting station the next evening . . . and not telling Nadine he was going. Just leaving that note.

What a fool he had been about Terence. Of all the things that can happen to a man's body, to make such a fuss about someone putting their mouth on part of it . . .

No, that wasn't quite right.

What if it had been a woman? That would have been wrong too . . . for him. As wrong? No. He knew lots of the boys pleasured each other, preferred on some un-thought-out level to be . . . physically affectionate . . . with their fellow soldiers than with grubby whores. Because there is love there, with your brothers, and loyalty, and the same desperation. Every man wants something, but plenty don't want to want what they want. Plenty more desperately want to want, but they can't get it up. And thinking they'll go to Hell for any of it . . . He recalled Ainsworth laughing at that: 'We're in Hell now! And you're right – doubtless it's because we've had a wank or two.'

Thoughts of a wank. Thoughts of Nadine.

He rolled over on to his front, nose in the grass. Stop it.

I am going to do all the right things for that woman from now on.

Really? asked a little voice. *What, leave her be to marry someone of her own sort? Get yourself killed so she never has to face the fact that prole and posh ne'er the twain shall meet, what with the rich girl being in her pretty Georgian villa and the poor man at the gate of the park across the road, staring up in his war-granted finery, bought with the blood of the men who died.*

Riley stared that stream of thought down, stopped it, picked it up by the tail like a dead rat and dropped it in the forbidden zone of his mind, alongside First Ypres, Second Ypres, the spiralling death of Captain Harper, whose face he could no longer recall, and a few other things. *Just shut up.*

God, so many things he can't think of . . .

It was Sunday. Would he go to the Waveneys' first, or to his mum's? He pushed himself to his feet and walked on under the spreading trees, tiny green buds sprouting along the black branches, brown shiny sticky-buds erupting with pale, feathery claws. At the park's iron gates he paused, looking out across Bayswater Road. He glanced over at Sir James Barrie's house, next door on the corner, and thought about Nadine telling him the story of *Peter Pan*, and about the first time he had met Sir James in the Waveneys' drawing room, and been surprised that he had no armour or sword and was just a funny-looking little Scotsman. And how he had been glad that Sir James did not speak in the same quick, clipped yet somehow drawling voice that everybody else in the Waveney house had. Except Barnes, of course, and Mrs Barnes, who glared at him as if he were a cuckoo. An armed cuckoo. An armed anarchist Communist cuckoo with a swag bag and a stripy shirt. *Oh, Mrs Barnes, how are you now?*

As Riley walked up the short path and knocked on the door, he felt a sudden sharp yank of nerves at his insides.

Barnes opened it. 'You!' he said, and clocked Riley's height, his uniform, and the badge on his sleeve. A little battle of emotions passed over his face. 'I've signed up, you know,' he said, a little defensively.

'I'll see you out there,' said Riley, with half a smile, as he slipped into the hall. Barnes took his cap and his case. 'Are they in?'

'Mrs Waveney's in the drawing room, sir,' said Barnes, and Riley felt the man's little wince of surprise at finding himself calling Riley 'sir'.

When Mrs Waveney turned from the fireplace to greet him he was for a moment floored by her beauty. She was clean. Her hair was coiffed and lovely. She was so very smooth and female. And like her daughter.

Second Lieutenant Purefoy pulled himself up. Mrs Waveney was formal with him, he noticed immediately. Not cold – just uncomfortable. He recalled what Nadine had written: it was as if the free-and-easy, self-indulgent self she had allowed herself to be before the war no longer fitted her, and she did not know what else to wear, in these straitened times. She enquired after his health, and seemed nervous. It was strange to him, after all those years of warm – illogically warm, looking back on it – welcome he had had from this family, all the generosity, the vast amount he owed them. Riley had no idea what Mrs Waveney saw when she looked at him. He thought perhaps she was angry. The sudden going, his nasty valedictory comment, the equally sudden return – she had a right to be angry. Or she might be embarrassed, knowing that he knew she had tried to separate Nadine from him. Or sad, even, to have lost the rather sweet relationship they used to have, the loving respect of the boy he used to be.

Valid though these points were, none of them, in fact, informed her current expression.

She had last seen a grateful, hard-working boy who knew his own good fortune, a pet, a safe little thing only just beginning to outgrow the nice slot they'd so kindly and carelessly given him. The last thing he'd said to her, 'If you're lucky, I'll get killed', had been childish and cruel but under-standable, under the circumstances.

Now, two years later, she saw something so very different: an officer, a tough, broad-shouldered young man with a thin slice of scar on one high cheekbone, and a wound stripe; a battle-hardened warrior, a hero of the Western Front, the human sacrifice for all of them, and up to *here* with what people were beginning to call Sex Appeal.

She'd taught him his alphabet, for goodness' sake, and even she . . .

My God, she thought, *is Riley Purefoy to be something after all?*

No. It's just war glamour.

It was late, but she offered him tea.

'How is Mr – er . . . Waveney?' Riley enquired. *Am I*

flustering her? The thought of it made him smile, and the smile looked a little cruel to her, and that flustered her more.

'Mr Waveney is well,' she said, and she glanced at his sleeve. 'He's very involved, you know, with the Patriotic Concerts at the Albert Hall. They're raising lots of money! A great success . . .'

Am I to be embarrassed about being an officer on active service, when he isn't? Riley thought. *Well, I'm not.*

'Congratulations,' she said. 'I'm not surprised *at all.*' And for a moment the old warmth was there. He held her gaze steadily, saying nothing, half the smile still at the corner of his mouth.

It is extremely important, Jacqueline realised, *that Nadine does not see him.*

'And Nadine?' he said.

Where did he get that tone of authority?

'Nadine's not here,' she said.

He waited.

'She's at the hospital.' *Let's hope he doesn't know which one.*

'When is her time off?' he said.

Jacqueline gave a little laugh. 'Well, we never know, really, it's all terribly irregular . . .'

The message was clear in her apologetic tone.

He watched her. So beautiful. So like her daughter.

He hadn't told her he was coming. He hadn't known he was coming. He hadn't known what he could say, to what he could invite her. The fits and starts with which they half declared themselves in letters . . . He had not seen her in two years. Since they were children.

I should go on to Mum and Dad's, he thought. *Give the girls their presents. I should go on to Sir Alfred's.*

He waited outside, standing on the Bayswater Road outside Sir James Barrie's house – was he in there, in the firelight flickering behind the curtains? He and his boy who would never grow up? An image glanced by: boys he had seen who would never grow up, flying, landing on the wire, bits of them—

It's only an idea, a memory. It's not a hallucination. Just a memory. Can't be avoided, can't hurt. You're still sane, Purefoy. Look how beautiful the green lawns of the park are in the misty evening light, unmuddied, smooth, alive, no holes, no bodies, no barbed wire, no explosions. Such a simple thing to be grateful for. No wrongness. Can no wrongness be enough to make rightness?

God, no wrongness. No wrongness would be fucking marvellous.

He had been told that at times of particularly heavy barrage the guns could be heard in London. He had been told that picnics on the South Downs had been silenced by the distant echoing, and that sometimes, at night, you could look out of your window in Kent, across that tiny little arm of water, and see the burnt glow of the long and random wound not far away. It seemed wrong for him, a soldier, to know this. Under the unwritten, unspoken laws of the great mute conspiracy that all of this was all right and not against the laws of nature, certain things had to be not known. Soldiers, for instance, did not mention over tea at home the corpses of young boys floating down flooded trenches, half eaten by rats. Equivalently, those at home should not be telling those of us Over There that they can hear the guns and see the Zeppelins burning. Because if England is not calm and golden and peaceful, what are we fighting for?

He stared up the road, and down.

She came, in the end, from the bus stop. He turned and saw her because he noticed the suddenness of her stopping when she saw him, thought it was him, thought it couldn't be. They looked at each other for a long moment, across the road. A bus passed between them (double decker, Marmite advertisement on the side) and their eyes were still linked as it went on by.

Finally he threw himself across the road. The most astounding effort of will stopped him folding his arms, his coat, his body, his legs, his heart around her. He could feel her quivering as he stood an electric two feet away from her.

'Hello,' he said. He took his hat off. Put it on again.

'Hello,' she said.

'How are you?' he said politely, and she started laughing, so he said, 'Shall we walk?'

She nodded. His curls were shorn and his neck was strong. He was taller. He was a soldier.

They went in through the gate to the park.

He took her hand, and a layer of tension shook itself off him in a great shiver. They walked to the Round Pond, of course, because that was where the path led. There was no one there, just water-birds in soft piles, roosting. The evening had turned damp and melting, cold, insidious, dreamy. Each of them thought only of the warmth and solidity of the other's hand, the presence of it, the solidity.

'How have you been?' he murmured, after a while.

'Cold and lonely,' she said, with a little laugh.

They walked on.

'Well,' said Riley.

Then, 'How have you been?' she said.

'In Hell,' he replied. Their steps matched, muffled, as they turned towards the Broad Walk. 'Only we're not allowed to say.'

They walked.

Warm hands.

'Who would have thought,' she said, 'that this is what we would be?'

He suddenly recalled a postcard he had received as a child, from a friend whose family had gone to Canada: 'I am six now. Are you any older?'

He smiled, looking down. They walked on.

'Cup of tea?' he said. 'Lyons? Or have you turned into one of those beer-drinking war girls? Do you need a sharp one at the Ram? Or a pink gin at the Kensington Close?'

She laughed a little. 'Cup of tea,' she said, and began to cry.

'So what kind of war girl are you, Nadine?' he asked her, sitting at a table with a thick white cup each and two buns, the window steaming up behind him, the mirror glittering behind her so he could see how completely gorgeous she was from two angles.

'Don't you know?' she said.

Their eyebeams were twisting.

'Not a beer-drinking VAD of loose morals . . . not a saucy munitionette with yellow cheeks and a boyfriend heading for management . . . You don't look the kind to lift morphine and cocaine from the stores and flog it to shell-shocked soldiers in nightclubs . . .'

'They do that in France too, do they?' she said.

'All the time. The streets are running with them. Glorious women in uniform, dripping with stolen omnipom and ration packs, heading for the highlife in Paris . . . There are some clubs, the smartest of all, where you can't even get in without a red cross on your sleeve and a Poiret evening bag packed with menthol snuff . . .'

'What do you know about Poiret?' She laughed. 'What on earth is going on out there? I thought there was a war on.'

'Oh, we have our amateur theatricals. Private Johnson is a lady most of the time. Even the colonels kiss his hand. Sorry, *her* hand. I don't want to talk about there. Talk about you. What war girl are you, if you're not a drug-runner?'

'Oh, I'm much more mundane,' she said. Her hair was fluffing up in the steam.

He raised his eyebrows at her. 'Tell me,' he said, and the request was so simple it blind-sided her, and she couldn't not.

'I'm the girl who tends every soldier as if he were one soldier in particular, and thinks all the time of French or Belgian girls who at that very moment might be tending *him*,' she said, and stopped as suddenly as she had started. She found she was holding her face very tight because actually, as she had realised halfway through, did she have any right to say this to him?

127

She stared at him. Stared at his scar. *His beautiful grey eyes, sparkly half-moons when he grins, really sparkly, like diamonds. He's not smiling now . . . What has he been through? What has he done?*

He was looking at the table, stirring his tea. He tasted it, and put in a little more sugar. Then he put his hand over his mouth for a second, and then he took out a cigarette and tapped it.

Does she mean . . .?

He couldn't assume. Time had passed. They were not children any more. Had her life raced on – after all, why shouldn't it? *Are you any older?*

One touch, for God's sake. For two years he'd been faithful to one touch of her waist. Almost faithful. Emotionally faithful. He looked at her hand on the table. He couldn't assume.

I am capable of bravery. He smiled to himself. 'So who's the lucky fellow?' he blurted, grinning stupidly, and dropping his teaspoon.

Her mouth fell open. She'd told him, and he hadn't heard. Or had he heard all too well – was he sparing her? 'Riley,' she said.

'Mmm?'

Her face was stricken.

'Riley, don't be a complete idiot,' she said. 'We don't have long.'

'Of course . . . your mother . . .'

'I couldn't care less about my mother,' she said. 'Your *leave* is not very long. I am working all hours at the hospital. I want to make your every moment here . . . perfect, so that you know what you're missing and you don't forget and

128

you don't lose faith and you come back. Remember, you asked me to be there to pull you—'

'I love you,' he interrupted, and was astonished to find the words on his lips, in the air, on their way to her.

She lifted her chin, gave him a sideways look. What was the look? Surprise? No – wariness? Perhaps. Distrust? No. Ah – no. It was – *aha*!

'I love you,' he said. 'I always have done. I always will. Nothing to offer, not a chance your family would accept me, even if you—'

'I do,' she said.

'Do you?'

'You know perfectly well.'

They looked at each other in silence. Then Riley stood, and moved round the table, and sat down again, next to her. Their sleeves touched, the length of their upper arms. They sat like that for a moment. Then he breathed out, long and slow, and turned his head slightly so that her wild Mesopotamian hair was just there, touching his cheek.

The nippy was coughing. Her face was indulgent, though. Soldier and his gal in a romantic dream! She wished she had a handsome officer to lean her head against. All right for some . . .

Riley started, and ordered more tea and more buns. Nadine blushed very slightly. He wanted to mention that she was blushing, so she would blush more. He wanted – oh, God, what he wanted.

He was incredibly happy to find that he wanted. He had been afraid that he wouldn't want again.

He stuffed himself with a bun instead. For the moment.

She felt the need to change the subject. More talk of love would lead to the difficulties surrounding . . . Oh, God, he loved her, he did, she did, they did, it was.

It was.

She was smiling like a fool, glowing.

His beautiful face, which she would kiss. Fury that someone, someone they didn't even know, had damaged his beautiful face, given him that little scar. Proud of his courage. *He's a man*, she thought, and the very word gave her a frisson, a lurch inside.

'How did you get that?' she said quickly.

'Shrapnel,' he said.

'Is that why you were promoted?' she asked. 'Were you terribly brave?'

'It's what happens,' he said brusquely. *Damn I'm being just how they are – I'm doing what I don't want to do. Stiff upper lip, don't alarm our people at home—*

'So are you a gentleman now?' It just leapt out. Stupid thing to say! But he laughed.

'Mmm, yes. Gentleman Second Lieutenant with nothing extra behind him. It occurred to me it might be one of the advantages. Along with the servant and the extra socks and two leaves a year and evening shift at the brothel – oh, God, Nadine, I'm so—'

She was smiling painfully. 'Really?' she said. 'And is that something you terribly need to tell me about?'

'It – oh, Nadine. Soldier talk. I'm sorry. I'm not fit for decent company – I've never used the brothels – oh, God, I shouldn't even be—'

'Riley,' she said, 'I work in a hospital. I know about these things now.'

He blinked. He didn't want her knowing about these things. He wanted her . . . *What? Pure and happy and symbolic? Grow up, Purefoy.*

'Girls do now,' she said.

'Oh,' he said.

'Why?' she said. 'If you've never – have you never? Riley, you're a man, have you . . .? Never?'

It was inconceivable, this conversation. His parents would never have talked of these things, even after twenty years of marriage. He didn't think hers would have either. And neither would he and Nadine, had it not been for the It, the great It, which had metamorphosed girl and boy into Nurse and Soldier, Nurse and Soldier. What might they have been, if . . .?

No ifs.

And now she was asking him . . .

'No – I have. I have.'

'You have.'

'I . . . have.'

'What was it, then?'

'It – what, the circumstances? Or the – doing?'

'Both,' she said, and she tried to smile, and her beauty radiated through him, so that for a second his blood fled and he wanted her so much, to fold her in his arms, to love her and do all the unspeakable things to *her*, so much, that he had to close his eyes for a moment.

'Circumstances,' he said. 'Right.' *Dear God, am I really telling her this?* 'Not a brothel. Billet, farm family, little kids, fat old mum, dad at the front. Um . . .' *Dear God, yes, I am.*

'The eldest daughter. Soldier's widow, name of Mireille, very sweet . . .'

He looked up at her. *Fuck, I should have lied.* '. . . came and sat on my bunk one night and asked me.' *I should have lied.* 'Er . . . Physical incident. A thing bodies do, very nice – sweet girl. Affection, I suppose. Ah – warmth. Not a lot to it. Not a bad thing . . .' *till now* '. . . not the greatest sin of all time. Can't see God minding that much, what with everything else He's letting go on . . . Only regret is . . .'

He couldn't say it. There are limits.

'Physical incident,' Nadine said softly.

'Mmm,' he said.

Silence.

'And you did it without me.'

He was shaking. 'My one regret,' he said very quietly, to the sugar bowl. *Did she really say that? Did she . . .? Am I hearing things? Is it starting now . . .?*

Silence.

It was real.

'Well,' she said. Embarrassed.

The noisy café shifted around them. *Oh, fuck it. We've come this far.*

'I couldn't exactly do it *with* you,' he said softly, leaning forward.

Her head shot up. She stared at him. 'I'll tell you something, Riley,' she said, very precisely, very softly, very clearly. 'I'm not losing my virginity to a Hun rapist. And I'm not giving it to anybody, *anybody*, ever, if . . . I'm damned if I . . .'

132

He started to apologise and she stopped him. He paused, and he swallowed. 'Nadine,' he said. 'We're here, we're alive, we love each other. Let's be happy.'

She started crying.

He slammed a handful of change on the table and led her out, through the bustling, nosy stares of the waitress and the ladies and the old men, and walked with his arm held close round her waist back towards the park, and on the dark corner where the horse-chestnut trees overhung the road leading up through the park to Kensington Palace they kissed, mouths and skin and warmth and, oh, sweet Jesus.

It was Riley who pulled away.

'You don't know what you're provoking,' he said, with a tight little smile, stepping back, taking out a cigarette to do something, anything, to keep his hands from sliding around inside her coat to encase the beautiful curve of her hip and pull her damn skirt up.

'I do,' she replied.

'And how could you?' he asked. 'You—'

She shot him a look. 'Girls *do* talk,' she said.

'What kind of girls have you been talking to?' he asked suddenly, fearfully.

At that she laughed, such a bright and lovely sound, a girl laughing, this girl laughing. *Like music to my ears*, he thought, and it was like music to his ears, but better – like a waterfall washing through his filthy memories, his corrupted eyes; like – like a girl laughing.

'My mother!' she said happily, and her voice, her innocence, her everything, just undid him, that she was *here*, with him . . . 'She said she knew it wasn't the English way

133

to tell a girl anything at all, but she thought it would make things easier for me. It made sense, anyway.'

'Made sense of what?' asked Riley, who was reeling.

She glanced up at him. 'Are you going to be English about this?'

'About what!' he said helplessly.

'Well,' she said. 'Feelings.' She blinked. 'Sex feelings.'

'You have sex feelings?' he asked. He had gone scarlet in the face.

'Mmm.'

He stared for at least four seconds before throwing himself at her, holding her, wrapping her as he had resisted doing before.

'Sit down with me,' he said after a while. 'There's a bench. There's the park. We could go in there,' he said. 'For a while.'

'Riley,' she said, 'is that the kind of dishonourable suggestion I've been warned about?'

'No!' he said. 'Or yes. God, yes. But no . . .' His face was disappearing in the dusk and she was glad, because she didn't know if she could bear it.

'So what's it like, Riley?'

'No!' he cried.

'Why not? You must have liked it – you said you did. Don't all men do it, whenever they can, because they like it so much? Isn't that the big secret?'

'Jesus, Nadine, what has your mother been telling you?'

'That wasn't my mother, that was Jean. She's a VAD. She's twenty-five.'

'Ah,' said Riley. 'Is she.'

134

There was a moment.

'So why haven't you been doing it all the time?' she said softly.

He sighed, and a flash of light from a window high up caught his eyes as he looked up. 'Fear,' he said, 'diseases . . . and . . . the idea that there was something better . . .'

Silence.

'Go on,' she murmured.

'Not that interested in the physical incident itself,' he said. 'I mean, yes, of course I am, but, er . . . more thinking about the love part.'

'The love part,' she repeated, and he choked on a low laugh.

'Sorry,' he said. 'It – um—'

She was suppressing a laugh too. 'Yes,' she said. 'Suddenly it's all a bit music hall . . .'

'And I was just saying something so romantic.'

'Yes.'

'About love,' he said. He was terrified. Pit-of-the-belly terrified. Going over the top . . . *Oh, God, leave me alone* . . . This is more than that. Love is strong as death. Where was that from? Set me as a seal on thy heart . . .

'Is love allowed, in these times?' she said. 'Is it recommended?'

I don't give a damn if it's recommended: it's all there is.

'I will never make love to you,' he said suddenly. 'I won't corrupt you, and leave you with a taste for it, tainted goods, so if I'm killed no one will have you. I'm not like Burgess . . .' The rigidity in his body as he said it was harsh and familiar to him: the result of the constant stand-off between a man's

135

instinct and what is required by those around him whom he respects and on whom he depends. Instinct – to make love to the girl you love, to survive, to go home. What is required – to tear yourself away from the girl and throw yourself in the path of bullets shells mortars bombs and poison gas.

'Who's Burgess?' she said, but that was not what she meant.

He stared at her. 'I want to do everything right,' he said, just standing there in the dark, in his coat, his arms hanging by his sides.

Tread carefully, she thought.

'No one can expect that of you when the entire world is doing everything wrong,' she said. 'Anyway, your coat is covered in bits of grass.'

'I expect it of myself,' he said. 'It's not a free-for-all. Good and evil still exist, don't they?'

'It means we have to work things out for ourselves, doesn't it?' she said. 'Find our own route through the chaos.'

'Well, that's my pattern,' he said. 'My attempt. Even if you were to . . . I won't. Listen, you're the only woman I want to do it with, and I can't do it with you – it's too strange even talking about it with you, and you wouldn't do it anyway, and I can't ask you to marry me, yet, because – everything – and I can't make you promise me anything, and I . . . but unless we're married, if we can marry, and that would be after the – if it ever ends . . . but I'm not going to do it with anyone else . . .'

She wrapped herself very gently around him, slid her arms inside his heavy coat, put her face by his, breathed very gently. *Here, alive, love.*

Chapter Nine

Near Hébuterne, France, June 1916

Here, alive, love
Be of good cheer
We're very proud of you, Riley

Purefoy was pretending not to notice Private Burgess, at the corner of the reserve line of Edgware Road, as they had christened this one, in conversation with a boy called Dowland, one of the new conscripts, a useless, terrified little creature. Purefoy was hoping that what he was seeing was not what he was seeing. He saw Burgess see him, see that he might be being seen. He saw Burgess, carefully casual, not break off from the conversation. He saw Dowland move away. Five minutes later, he saw Dowland heading for the latrines. Ten minutes after that, a figure approached them from the far side, against the evening light.

Purefoy hoped that it was not Burgess.

It was.

What am I meant to do about this?

No question: report them both.

And then what? Reporting these things puts the men at risk of death by firing squad. They're at risk of death every day and night anyway. Hun bullet; British bullet. So what?

But come on, there's no proof.

That's because you've avoided looking for proof. Or looking at it, when it was in front of your nose.

No, you can't leap to conclusions on something like this.

No, you ignored it because you didn't want to face it. You ignored it because the moral dilemma it presented was unanswerable.

How very rational you're being today, Riley. 'The moral dilemma it presented was unanswerable.' Honh hee honh hee honh hee honh – how the men would laugh in their cod French accent at that. It's because you don't want to see the look of disgust, the accusation of treachery in Burgess's eyes. You don't want to hear him say, 'Your dad must be so proud of you, Riley.' It's because of some old Paddington-boy loyalty; it's because Burgess's dad was your dad's mate.

A big cheese had sent round a memo: 'We face enormous challenges. In the weeks and months to come, every man will be required to do his utmost. With the dedication, courage and self-sacrifice of the British soldier and his colonial allies we will overcome all obstacles . . . There has been a tendency among a very small minority to attempt to avoid the patriotic duty of every man. This cannot and must not be allowed to continue. Any attempt to "Swing the Lead", or to put oneself at risk on the battlefield in hope of injury, must and shall be punished to the limit of the law . . .' Or words to that effect.

Purefoy could not, as he wished to, release his anger at this by saluting and saying, 'None of my business, SIR, if the poor fuckers have lost their mind to such a degree that they do handstands on the fire-step hoping some friendly sniper from the enemy lines will shoot them through the foot, or that their right hand of its own accord shoots a bullet through their left, and they can't find their mind to stop it doing so, because in my opinion the whole damned war is Suicide by Hun, SIR, and if the men are individually taking it on themselves to imitate unilaterally the multilateral action of the policy-makers, then who am I, SIR, to stand in judgement upon them?' He was astounded, sometimes, by the fluid articulacy of his own fury. In his mind, at least. He did not ever *speak* like that.

Suicide by Hun: if he could interpret the internal motive of every private in the dark of the morass as the bullets whistled and the artillery rained down and the thunder burst your ears and the star shells flew so beautifully overhead, like Tinkerbell at the Christmas matinée . . . interpret their motives? He couldn't even remember their names. Bloom, Burdock, Lovall, Bruce, Wester, Atkins . . . um . . . Merritt . . .

And what was my motive? Oh, yes – to escape the great shame of having enjoyed a French lesson from a boy. To let Mr and Mrs Waveney succeed in denying their daughter the man she loves. To prove I was a man when I clearly wasn't. Jesus Christ, what reasons to pile yourself in blood and misery. And what is my motive now? To do my bit to help the lads to not go mad and to win the war . . .

Being a good soldier was harder to hold on to now his conscience was disoriented.

Dowland left the latrines first. Purefoy wondered what Burgess had given him. A cup of petrol? Tobacco or pepper, to give a convincing performance of conjunctivitis? Dowland was green enough that he would probably pay for the information and the technique. Or something more esoteric? A lad called Baker had been sent back a few weeks ago with a kind of cancerous seeping blob in his neck, a swelling with some kind of life of its own. He'd admitted injecting paraffin wax ten months before.

There went Burgess, back the way he had come.

Poor little Dowland was scurrying like a rabbit, down this way. Jesus, he deserved better. Burgess was gone, out of view. Riley tipped his helmet back and put his leg out to park his boot on the opposite wall of the trench, blocking the way.

Dowland shuddered to a halt. Pulled himself together, saluted.

'What did he give you, Dowland?'

Dowland started to shake.

Purefoy looked at him kindly.

Dowland couldn't speak.

These boys are no use out here. Why send them? Why not recognise that cowardice is a fact and most cowards wish they weren't, and it's not their fault and it's not under their control, and keep them the hell out of our way while we get on with it?

'Come on, lad, it's not the end of the world.'

'Don'tknowwhatyou'retalkingaboutsir,' Dowland said. 'Sir.'

'Did he tell you to open a .303 cartridge and chew the cordite? The MOs know about that one. If you turn up with a temperature and an erratic heartbeat, that'll be their first assumption. Puric acid? They're on to that too. Everyone knows puric acid is easier to get hold of out here than real jaundice. Or was it caustic black on a needle, to put through the back of your knee? What was it? Tell me.'

The boy was blinking madly. No courage in him at all. No strength. He crumpled. 'He can get me tuberculosis, sir, if the big push holds off. He's got a friend at the CCS. Or an injection of paraffin wax. Or condensed milk, sir – excuse me, to put up my thing and it looks like VD. I can choose.'

He couldn't pronounce it properly. Ta-berckle-osis.

Well. Tuberculosis was a new one. And if it were true, unanswerable. Real tuberculosis would indeed get you off duty. Paraffin wax would give you an abscess – and quite possibly a cancer. But VD? That baby?

'Well, don't go for the condensed milk, lad. No one will believe you,' Purefoy said.

'Sir?'

'They won't believe you've had relations with a woman, Dowland,' said Purefoy, clearly.

'Sir?' Dowland repeated.

Purefoy took hold of him by his skinny shoulder, and leant in close. 'Soldier,' he said quietly, in his ear. 'Do not take or do anything Burgess tells you to take or do. If you want to half kill yourself, let the Hun do it for you, for free. And don't ask Burgess for your money back.'

Dowland stepped back and looked at him. His nose was red. 'I can't stay out here, sir. I can't. I can't.'

Purefoy said: 'Yes, you can.' He sighed, and smiled. 'Yes, you can, Dowland. It's easy. Just do as you're told.'

~

Burgess had been doing well with his sideline in the past weeks. Something big was coming up. Hordes of conscripted men were being shipped in. Streams of experienced soldiers were arriving from up and down the line. They lay around in the sun in piles, smoking, wearing their patience like regal gowns. It put the wind up everyone. The cavalry was there, utterly grand. After the barrage, the men would tear holes in the German front lines, and then the cavalry would gallop through them and finish the war.

God knew how the word spread, but men – seasoned soldiers, mainly – had started to appear on Edgware Road, looking nonchalant, happening to run into Burgess, happening to take a little stroll. It was far too late, as Burgess had whispered, regretfully.

Look at him now, tucked down on the fire-step rolling a cigarette in the dark, hissing sideways to a lad called Yellerton, who had a ribcage like a ladder and had been in a complete funk since that animated equestrian statue had made his speech.

'Tomorrow,' Burgess was saying, 'I bet you I get back alive.'

'Cocky,' said Ainsworth, who was staring through the periscope, watching rolling clouds of light and dark chase each other to and fro over the German line.

'I bet you,' said Burgess. 'How much?'

'Tempting Fate,' said Ferdinand, who had himself been breathing shallow for a week now. Purefoy wondered if it was just terror, or if Ferdinand had been chewing cordite.

'Five bob?' said Burgess to Yellerton. 'Five quid?'

Purefoy smoked quietly. A low wind was teasing the glowing ember of his fag, smoking it for him and carrying away the frail twist of grey.

'Five bob!' said Yellerton, gamely, because – just like Couch and Bowells in the early days – he wanted to smother his innocence and fit in.

Couch, now an old-timer, rolled his eyes, and Burgess yelped: 'You're on!' before Yellerton had a chance to back down.

'How're you going to get your money, Yellerton, if he does go west?' Purefoy murmured, and everyone started laughing at Yellerton, and Burgess looked Purefoy straight in the eye, then pretended he hadn't. For Burgess, Purefoy was a danger: dormant, evidently, but a danger. That Purefoy had done nothing about him yet did not mean that Purefoy would never do anything about him.

But what can I do? Purefoy could find no logic in punishing a man for enabling other men to make desperate stupid attempts to save their own lives by endangering their own lives, when their lives were in greater danger all the time, from the very people who would seek to punish them. There was no logic.

But tuberculosis?

A burst of action: Yellerton, humiliated, awash with fear of the morrow and a toxic admiration for the soldiers he found himself among, punched Burgess hard in the face, as if to give him his own ticket out, a tidy little broken jaw.

'Yellerton!' Purefoy barked. 'Burgess!'

Yellerton, little-boy tears on his soft scarlet cheek, restrained himself, settled, stood to attention. Burgess touched his chin, and tried to look as if he had hardly felt it.

Purefoy said. 'Report to Major Locke at dawn.'

'We'll be otherwise engaged at dawn,' said Burgess. 'Sir.'

'Then report to him now,' said Purefoy, who had long before learnt not to rise to Burgess's insolence. *I'm not going back to the ranks for you two. Burgess, Burgess, you fool – if I don't, someone else will, and then they'll want to know why I didn't . . . After this is over, after this offensive, I'll face up to this, and I'll deal with you. I have to. I have to.*

'He's otherwise engaged now,' said Burgess. 'Sir.'

'Then go and wait for him,' said Purefoy.

Burgess smiled. Waiting outside the officers' dug-out was a lot cosier than waiting here.

And then the Allied shells, as if they had taken their deep breath now, started again. Yellerton shrieked, against the wall like a dog, his legs quivering.

'But they're nearly at breaking point, aren't they, sir?' he shouted.

They've been nearly at breaking point for about a year and a half now, Yellerton, Purefoy didn't say. There had been eight days of this bombardment: three thousand guns along twenty miles of front would do it, destroy everything, and tomorrow we go over the top . . . *Well, well. I've done it before; I'll do it again. I'll do my best. It's all I can do.*

⁓

144

The next morning the sky was high and pale and blue, the rain light, the air cold. For a moment, Purefoy thought: *It's only countryside.*

The whistle went for the first wave.

Purefoy didn't see the first wave going over. He was praying, and when the whistle went for the second wave, *us*, he stopped praying, and he looked to his own men.

Locke shouted.

Burgess spat.

Couch said, 'Thank you, Mother.'

Ferdinand tried to say something about unto something we commend but forgot the words.

Dowland and Yellerton both had their eyes closed.

Purefoy and Locke and Ainsworth scrambled over side by side, which created a bond between them that could never be broken, and a wall around them that would probably never be breached. Walk, they had been ordered. Follow the first wave and back them up. The enemy has been destroyed by the barrage of the past days. Approach slowly and steadily.

They walked.

Gunfire.

There wasn't meant to be gunfire.

The gunners were supposed to be dead, and their guns blown up.

It poured, like horizontal rain. A storm; a deluge.

Walk? Into gunfire?

Dowland looked to Purefoy. Purefoy looked to Locke. Locke looked for a signal.

There was no other signal.

Orders were orders. What was held to be the case was not the case, but the men had to proceed as if it were.

They proceeded.

It was very soon apparent that eight days of bombardment had stirred up old corpses and mud, reburnt old burnt trees, reshaped existing craters in new and more cavernous forms – but the barbed wire was fine. As were the bunkers. And the machine-guns. And the artillery.

Couch fell, into the mud, three feet out from the parapet, face down, among others.

Ferdinand collapsed into the German wire that wasn't meant to be there: landed on his knees and fell no further because the wire held him up. He looked as if he was praying, his head falling forward, his knees on a hassock of mud. He was not praying alone.

Do we assume there's a plan? Do we just . . .?

Proceed.

The word 'attrition' entered Riley's mind, like a quick little worm, and ran round and round. He hadn't known what it meant. It meant going on grinding them down until they had to give up. Grinding down by pure manpower and steelpower and explosive power. *Grinding who?* Purefoy thought. *Grinding us? Why aren't we all dead? Or are we dead?* And then in a single psychic movement his entire self curled up and retreated, swift as a bird flying over a copsed hill into the sunset, and he was in the very small place at the back of his skull. Outside passed along, like underwater. He heard his breathing in his head, felt his heartbeat fill out the empty space, racketing, roaring.

Couch lying down.

A poor head, all alone in a shell-hole.

Locke, gesturing.

Dowland, running back to the English line – falling. An officer behind him. Pistol up. Jessop?

The first wave was dead at their feet; the third wave rolling through them.

Ferdinand, praying.

The German wire, and his own hand cutting through it with clippers, metal biting through metal – there he is, he can see himself.

Himself, in a German trench. *Nice revetting!*

A Prussian, shooting.

Breath.

So many soldiers.

His bayonet in a bloodied tunic. Feel the resistance. Stink of blood and cordite. Noise, bare or shrieking, muffled, coming in waves. His own heartbeat. The concentric circles and the rising red.

Oh, the tall brave one, oh—

Where is everybody?

Twelve German prisoners and an ambulance.

A tangle of brambles, harsh and bleak, with, *ah*, dead men hanging off them like rags, poor fuckers.

Locke again, howling: 'Where are the others?'

The fourth wave . . .

Shelling. Shrapnel flying around, dropping, hissing, whizzing, floating, no, surely not, all around. He paused to watch it.

The *noise*, blurred and wavy, coming and going . . .

Time passing. Presumably.

He was in woods. Locke and Ainsworth were there. So was Captain Jessop but he was dead. They were fighting alongside – he wasn't sure who. They were tripping on the roots of trees that no longer existed. He had no breath and his eyes started in his head. His arms flew to automatic actions. Metal and blood.

Locke wasn't there any more. He was—

Ohhhh – ohhhh, Major Locke, that don't look good.

Major Locke was smiling at him.

Take the major home, Riley.

Purefoy was glad to have a clear and definite opportunity to do the right thing, and he took the major home: lifted him over his shoulder, ran low and zigzag, held fast as lockjaw to the major's leg and his arm, shouted at him all the way – a mile and a half, he was told later. Blood all over his face, looked a right fright. He did remember handing him over to the stretcher-bearer with incredibly black eyebrows, and not knowing what to do, and Locke, his leg at a very strange angle, shouting, 'Carry on, Purefoy! Back to the lads. Jessop's in charge!' and him saying, 'Jessop's a goner, sir,' and Locke saying, 'Damn, so he is – then you're in charge, old boy.'

So he gathered some other wild-eyed stragglers and shouted to them, and they turned back, shuddering, staggering, past Ferdinand, Couch, Dowland, Jessop, Bloom, Wester, Lovall, Green, Atkins – *God, what are their names? I'm forgetting their names* – and proceeded on back up the tiny hill.

~

He was spun – what? He was aware of mud and blood and noise, of the taste of his collar in his mouth, stink, racket, a great bucket of mud, alone. Poor Ferdinand, fond even of trees, sad that the country should be mashed up and poisoned.

He was staring up. Stars and flowers and bodies whirled across his sky.

～

Someone was tugging him. He seemed to have no shirt on.
Voice: Come on. Come on, Purefoy.
He let himself be lugged, low, dropping.
I'm all right, he said.
No you're not, said someone.
Was it night? Or was that just him?

～

Nadine read about it two days later, from a newspaper-seller yelling outside the station.

Daily Chronicle
3 July 1916

At about 7.30 o'clock this morning a vigorous attack was launched by the British army. The front extends over some 20 miles north of the Somme. The assault was preceded by a tremendous bombardment, lasting about an hour and a half. It is too early as yet to give anything but the barest particulars, as the fighting is developing in intensity, but the British Troops have already occupied the German front line. Many prisoners have already fallen into our hands, and as far as can be ascertained our casualties have not been heavy.

Chapter Ten

France, July 1916

Major Locke was talking to him.

'. . . so you see,' he was saying, 'we kept the Hun off the French at Verdun, and that was, um, valuable, as it doesn't do to let a Frenchman feel alone . . .' and for a while Purefoy, half consciously grateful for any scrap of logic or policy, considered hating the French.

He opened his eyes to chandeliers and mirrored walls, a sparkling, dripping, doubling and tripling of reflecting glamour. He closed them again. There was a smell of rotting swamp. Gas gangrene. Your flesh goes green. Opened them again. Still seemed to be in a giant nightclub. Not that he'd ever been in a nightclub. He'd thought, when he woke earlier, that he was hallucinating. Now he realised he must be at Le Touquet, in what had been the casino in the parallel universe of Before, when it was possible to be something other than a new circle of hell.

'You're looking better, Purefoy,' said Locke. 'Nearly up to scratch?'

'Fine, sir,' he replied. He stopped to check. Pain in his

shoulder and the feeling of loss in his head, a kind of reeling emptiness that seemed to have replaced his . . . his something. 'How about you?'

Locke waved a crutch, and said, 'Mustn't grumble.'

'Blighty one, is it, sir?' asked Purefoy.

'Neither yours nor mine, I'm afraid,' Locke said. 'You should have left me out there longer. Might have had to have it off – then I'd be all right. That's the kind of detail you tend to forget when you're out there praying for a Blighty one. The reason it is a Blighty is the very reason you wouldn't want it.'

'Sir?' said Purefoy.

'Do you remember, Purefoy?'

Purefoy was silent for a second. Then, before he could control himself, he blurted: 'Ferdinand Couch Dowland Jessop . . .'

'And many others,' said Locke. 'But not me, thanks to you.'

Purefoy said nothing.

'You saved my life. And apparently I promoted you to captain.'

What? Purefoy blinked, suddenly very aware. *Not again . . . they must be desperate . . .*

'Because of your courage and discipline under fire beyond the call of duty, your experience, intelligence and leadership abilities, and, of course, your rapport with the men.'

'Thank you, Major, I do know that you've noticed I'm common as muck . . .'

'Do you want it or not?' Locke said, with half a smile.

'I haven't been lieutenant yet.'

'Details, Purefoy. We need captains: all the old ones are dead. But don't go on about it – someone might notice.'

'I'd be honoured, sir,' Purefoy said. More training, more money for Mum, more leave. Half his brain was racing, half seemed . . . as dead as the captains.

'Soon as you're fit,' said Locke. 'Sort out the details and so on.' He stared down at Purefoy, bandaged in the bed. 'Ainsworth bought it,' he said. 'Died of wounds. They buried him at Hébuterne. Apparently he wanted you to have this.' He held out a scrap of paper, folded, worn.

For a flash it was unbearable. Then control descended. 'I'll write to his widow,' Purefoy said. 'Sybil.'

'Sybil?' said Locke.

'Sybil,' said Purefoy. 'It's her name. Wives have names. Sybil.'

'Julia,' said Locke, thoughtfully.

'Nadine,' said Purefoy. 'If she'll have me.'

Locke remembered the letter to her, the one from a year ago, about not existing. A year more war on top of that. How can a man feel now, if that was how he felt then?

'You know Julia is expecting a child,' said Locke.

'You told me, sir. Congratulations,' said Purefoy.

'I'm feeling very odd about it,' said Locke.

'I should imagine you are, sir,' said Purefoy.

'Well, yes, I am.' Locke stood for a moment, balanced on his crutch, then picked it up and looked at the bottom of it. 'I thought I might get drunk, one of these nights,' he said.

'Good idea, sir,' said Purefoy.

'Yes, I thought so. Perhaps you'd join me.'

'Soon as I can lift a glass, sir.'

~

I'll be given a platoon – oh, God, a company – of conscripts, bank clerks, farmers and lowlives and God knows what. Don't want to waste a proper officer on them, so they drag me out of the mud to lead them slowly into gunfire.

Orders are, don't run.

Morality no longer exists: no guidelines, no natural law, no common sense.

Love thy neighbour.

Wasn't the Hun our neighbour? Our old queen's cousin? Christian nations slaughtering each other?

Who, then – who let this happen? British men marching British men slowly into gunfire?

There is nothing redeemable here at all.

Unless it's just, you know, necessary. To stop the badness.

From what they overheard, it was still going on.

~

A casino full of men mewing like baby pigeons: the sound of men dying. He didn't care where he was. They'd marched them into gunfire and shellfire, and told them to walk slowly. He'd lain in a shell-hole and four men had asked him to say something, to someone, and he'd promised, and he didn't know who they were, or what he'd promised to say, and he'd gone back and gathered up another load of men *and taken them out again.* And Ainsworth, Couch, Ferdinand, Dowland and Jessop. *And many others.*

They were saying it had been a success.

Dowland's brother was in the next ward, a vast room which had been a skating rink. A skating rink – full of beds full of one-legged and no-legged men. *What extraordinary nonsense.* Dowland's brother had no legs. Purefoy went to see him, and looked about, and thought: *When did this become possible? When did this become normal? This should be full of children with red velvet collars, and laughing women with elegant furs saying, 'Oh, no, no, you go. I'll stay and have a tisane . . .'*

Dowland's brother wept all day. He had been told about his brother, the coward, who had been shot in the back in the field by his commanding officer. The doctors here had a big new enemy: collapse of the will to live. Captain – as he now was – Purefoy lay quietly. Gunshot wound to the upper arm. Right as rain in no time.

Memory came to him in waves, and left him again. He held no memory of the journey north from the battlefield to Étaples, and the passing of time was eluding him. He hadn't known his mind could hide things from him. He considered the deaths of Ainsworth, Dowland, Couch, Ferdinand and Jessop (*and many others*), and the survival of Burgess, and read nothing into anything. Too many of every type of man had been left fluttering in bloody shreds on the wire for any idea of logic to survive any better than their ragged bodies. Only a fool thought only the good died young. But in the quiet moments he considered the virtues lost: the kindness of Ainsworth, his battered gentleness, his singing voice, and the un-cluttered pleasure he had taken in simple things; Ferdinand's childish delight in food and company; Couch's vulnerability – the honest desire he had to be a proper man, perverted though it was into a soldierly fetishism, the same as had made a murderer of Jessop. It seemed a shame that these admirable qualities should disappear from this fast-depleting world. If there was to be a world at all after what they had seen and been through on 1 July, these qualities would have been useful. It would be a shame if a new world contained nothing but, on the one hand, Burgesses and, on the other, those who followed discipline and obedience to the death.

His put-away silent self reached out quietly for the characters of Ainsworth and Couch and Ferdinand and Dowland and Jessop, and took them to the protected secret area of his mind. He hadn't really known Dowland. Only that he was young, and didn't smoke, and that his nerve had given out.

∼

Did they not think? Did they just think we were too stupid to do anything more complicated than walk out in lines, slowly? Too dumb to follow a creeping barrage, perhaps, or dodge from cover to cover? Did they not consider making a feint: stop the barrage, wait and see if the Germans still had their guns and were going to use them; then, when they did, our artillery could have picked up the barrage again . . .

We thought they knew what they were doing.

∼

Some started screaming. Some were struck dumb. *What is happening*, Purefoy wondered, *inside me? I've surrendered to bloodlust, I've waved the flag of insane cheerfulness, I've wept, I've lied, I've analysed my thoughts for hallucination . . . How do I know I'm not going mad? Why wouldn't I? The strain of trying to hold on to sanity would drive you mad.*

A shaker passed through his ward: he had started to shake and hadn't stopped, legs flinging, arms wriggling, unstoppable, day and night, couldn't walk, couldn't sleep, couldn't stop. He had been removed to their own area before he drove down morale.

Purefoy lay back in his hospital bed and considered the parts of a man. *Because my shoulder is wounded, they do not look at my mental state.* He thought about Dowland and his brother. It seemed to Purefoy that if your legs are shot to pieces no one expects you to keep going, but if your nerve, the machinery of your self-control, is shot to pieces, they do. It's not your will, your desire, your willingness to fight on – it's a separate part of you, but it's one they don't understand yet, because they never yet put this much on a soldier. Ainsworth had talked about that – how they had never before given heavy industry to war.

They. It.

And what did I do? During the attack, during any attack, I felt . . . callous. I thought of nothing but pushing on. I don't believe I felt or thought anything at all – like a dog that you couldn't call away from chasing a cat; or like a creature with the scent up . . . a yob still tearing at a girl's clothes when she's crying no. Remember – those boys in the shell-hole, and he wanted water, and all I felt was impatient. As far as I remember. Remember carrying Locke. Remember the men you can't remember. Remember the red concentric circles. Remember

Ainsworth. Remember Ferdinand Dowland Couch and Jessop (and many others). Remember everything.

Dismember: to take to bits. Remember: to put back together.

There was one lad, a deserter, he'd forgotten his name, and he'd said to Purefoy: 'I didn't run away, sir. It was my legs. I couldn't stop them, and they took me with them.'

Is that cowardice?

Remember him.

~

Last year we had many smallish hopes, made many smallish attempts, suffered many smallish failures, and we died one by one. This year a change of plan! One big hope, one big push, one big fuck-up, and we all die at once.

~

It was days later that he woke up in the glittering, glamorous room thinking: Captain Purefoy. Captain Purefoy. With three pips, perhaps – perhaps . . . Could he present himself with three pips?

Captain Purefoy to see Miss Waveney on a personal matter . . .

When will we have our life back?

Will we have our life back?

What life can we have, now? What would 'back' mean, exactly, now?

He rolled over, and a dart of pain shot through his shoulder. With rest and quiet, enough of his life force had returned for him to realise how much of it he had lost, and that was a godforsaken moment.

My blood, my time, my youth, my friends, my strength, my sanity.

Come on, Purefoy. Buck up. You're alive. You're young. Sort of. You're alive. Here. Now.

～

If no one won that, after all that, that – if neither side won that, then neither side can win. The war won, and goes on winning.

～

Captain Purefoy rejoined the shattered Paddingtons with a shining, puckered scar in his upper arm and a second wound stripe. The battle was still going on at the Somme. He wished they were down there but someone had noticed their depletion and put them back in the Salient, which was, for once, quiet. What the men called 'peacetime' – no actual battle going on right there.

He was happy to be back, even behind the lines, stuck in Pop, on light duties. No time for thinking, out here.

Locke took him aside just as he arrived. 'Thought you ought to know, in case you didn't,' he said.

'What?' asked Purefoy.

'It was Burgess who brought you back.'

Oh, thought Purefoy. *Old times' sake? Paddington station? My dad and his dad?*

Surely not.

'Thank you,' he said.

Burgess himself came up behind Purefoy, later, and coughed. 'Sir,' he said, with his innocent face and his habitual insolent little intonation of disrespect.

'Burgess,' said Purefoy. 'I hear I owe you—' he said, and stopped, because he didn't want to owe Burgess. 'I hear you pulled me out. Thank you.'

Burgess looked at him steadily. The fresh bloom that had disguised him so well back then was completely gone. His eyes were dull, his teeth rotten, his demeanour exhausted. 'I'd do the same for anyone,' he said. 'I know you'll be a bit . . . *surprised* by my sudden attack of better nature but, despite what *you* think, I'm only human.' He stared Purefoy in the eyes – a challenge. He lowered his voice, and said wearily, 'And if you want to turn me in, *sir*, then fucking turn me in. I'd rather know, one way or the other. Sir.'

And that did surprise Purefoy. He grasped at himself within the haze. 'I won't turn you in,' he said, 'because you're going to stop doing it. There's going to be nothing to turn you in for. And don't try to use that against me because, *Burgess*' – and here he used the same insolent emphasis that Burgess used – 'if you do, I *will*, and the hell with the lot of us.'

Chapter Eleven

Sidcup and France, September 1916

It looks like the moon, Julia thought, not for the first time, sitting back on her bed, her dressing-gown falling. It was so very round and white and . . . *full* . . . *sort of waxy and gleaming* . . . Her legs poked out, beyond it, beyond her reach. She lifted her left foot, and waved at herself with it over the mound of her belly. *Quite extraordinary.* But, even more extraordinary, it was perfectly normal. Perfectly normal. To have a tiny baby growing inside your own body – just in there, with fingernails and a bottom and everything. She laughed – and felt a responding wriggle from the creature within, tight under the marbly moonish skin. It was rather disgusting.

In there.

Soon to be out here.

Extraordinary.

But the nobility of her situation pleased her. The smiles everybody gave her, grateful for the promise of an actual christening rather than news of a distant funeral; for a baby not a corpse. Brave, fecund wife; brave, wounded husband.

The war would end. He would come back. They would have their child and everything would be as it should be. The pain and loneliness would be redeemed in domestic bliss. It was quite easy, actually, when a man was not there, to make him, in your mind, all that you wanted him to be.

A letter lay on her nightstand. It was one of several, all very similar, formulaic, comforting but somehow distant, separated from her by a film of something, a wafting, inscrutable chasm that she dutifully ignored.

My dear Julia,

Sorry to have been quiet for a while. I'm pretty well; I am still considerably north of where we were and my leg, if anything, is better than it was before. Loss of blood was the worst of it, and apparently I have had enough time now to make pints more, so with the rest and good food and so on I am an improved model, apart from the headaches. I wanted you to know that I am thinking of you, my dear, as your time draws near. To think, out here, of a little baby is almost impossible. I just hope and pray that it is not too hard a time for you, and that our child is brought into the world swiftly and safely. I am hoping to have some leave, of course, and will let you know as soon as anything comes through.

Your Peter

Why not take such things at face value, if face value works, and between-the-lines makes unsettling reading?

~

Mrs Orris, sitting on Peter's chair in the drawing room, had been talking for nearly an hour. Nothing interrupted her flow. Julia, sitting back on the pale chintz sofa, uncomfortable and huge among the cushions, did not find it strange. Her mother had always done it, was doing it now, would always do it. Early on in life Julia had noticed that her father never listened to her mother. She assumed her mother had acquired the habit as a result. Perhaps she hoped that if she went on long enough someone, somewhere, someday, would take notice of her. Julia had always taken notice of her. She had no choice. But Julia's attention didn't count for anything with Mrs Orris.

The powdery white jowl bobbed and fluttered. She had recently replaced her former favourite subject, 'Get Julia to do some war work', with a new one, 'Get Julia to move closer to home now she is having a baby'. Or, more precisely, and though neither Mrs Orris nor her daughter would ever put it this way, she had moved from 'make Julia feel bad about being unable to stick at any war work' to 'make Julia feel bad about being unwilling to move closer to what her mother persisted in calling home although Julia had left there several years ago as an adult to live with her husband'.

'You see, it's really not safe,' she was saying, not for the first time. 'You're right in the path of the Hun if – God forbid! – they were to invade, but, even if they don't, with these airships they come straight up to London to drop their horrible bombs and you're right in the way, which is bad enough when it's just you but with a little one, you have to learn to be a bit responsible, with Peter away, and of course you can't just turn around and ask him, as he's not here . . .'

Yes, Mother, I know . . .

'. . . so you really have to grow up a little and buckle down and do your bit, because it really is irresponsible to try to live in this big place all on your own, when you could just come home and Margaret can mind the baby and you can have a good rest to get you back on your feet and you'll be safe, which must be what Peter wants most of all . . .'

Julia wondered briefly why her mother thought she had a direct line to what Peter was thinking, when she, Julia, hadn't, if she was honest, had the slightest idea what he was thinking since 1914.

'. . . and when that awful hospital opens, I mean obviously it's not awful but one wants to be able to go for a walk without . . . and I do hope, darling, that you've been sensible because, really, a shock like that is the kind of thing which can bring on a baby at a bad moment. I'm sure that you won't walk up that way but, you know, there's nothing wrong with their legs, and you can't avoid everyone in a blue suit – I mean, why would you? They are heroes, obviously, but we have to be realistic so, really, I do think it was silly of you not to come up to Berkshire earlier, and now it really is too late for you to travel but as *soon . . .*'

Julia was not worried about the new hospital. She'd read the article in the paper. Facial injuries did sound awful but, as the journalist had said, if you've got trenches . . . She quite often found herself imagining the scene: a moonlit night, a British helmet, a lifted chin, a cigarette, a Hun sniper . . . *oh, don't be disgusting . . .* No, surgery to rebuild a face sounded

163

marvellous to her – like a miracle. The surgeon sounded quite heroic, and was very nice-looking in the photos.

'I'm going to have a rest, Mother,' she said, and tried to push herself up out of the sofa with both arms, elbows akimbo like a great grasshopper.

Her mother, fussing around her, still talking, made her stay put.

Julia conceded.

In her dozing dream a man in a blue suit with no face was holding her tight round her hips, squeezing her with his strong arms, letting go, squeezing her again. His arms were very warm.

Her mother was still talking as Julia felt a single great blow inside her, a donkey kick, a shock.

She called out, a great gasp of surprise. The moon was shivering. The floodgates opened. Her thighs, the sofa, were suddenly awash – not blood: clear, like seawater.

Now it begins. Thank God. Get this vastness out of me, and give me back my body.

She wished to God her mother would go away, and Rose come.

～

Locke Hill, Kent,
September 1916

My dear Son in Law,
Well, it has certainly been a very exciting day here, and you will be delighted to hear that you are now a father. I won't

164

bore you with the details, but you should know Julia is a bit under the weather with it all. I will of course stay and look after her. I know you were thinking Harry for a boy, by which of course you mean Henry, so should we go ahead with that?

In haste –
your very affectionate mother in law,

Jane Orris

∽

France
My dear Julia,
I just received your mother's letter. I am thinking of you all now, tucked up at home. A baby is such an alien idea to me here, surrounded only by men and warfare. Take care of him well, and of yourself, dear girl, and when I return let us take things up again as a happy family. I am happy to think of a new little creature, in the middle of so much that is destructive. That said, life goes along pretty ordinarily out here. Don't worry about me.

He screwed up the letter in order to copy it out again, leaving out the last sentence. She didn't worry about him. She hated him – with good reason. He couldn't begin to address this in letters. He couldn't, whatever she said in her letters, pretend it wasn't so. Every word had been game but brittle, with the gay clarity of 'Oh, that doesn't matter at all!' as if it were up to her alone to decide whether, or understand if, it mattered or not. He was damned if he was going to accept this hollow, unsubstantiated, rubber-stamp forgiveness. He didn't deserve any kind of forgiveness.

But with a baby in the scales, didn't everything now have to rebalance?

He glanced up. His lamp was guttering and he happened to know the billet was short of oil. If his wound had been worse, he could have been with them now, talking, proving, earning, building, loving, being . . . *Don't think about it. You're here. Because you're here because you're here because you're here – NO – you're here to make sure your child has a future as an English boy in an English England.*

'I don't like Henry,' he wrote.

The name just jumped into his mind. 'Please name him Thomas.'

Tom Locke, my baby son.

'Purefoy,' he yelled. He signed off: 'Send me a picture. It would be a nice thing to have.'

Then he wished he hadn't written it, because it sounded as if he wanted to see the child before he was killed. He read it through again. Everything in the letter sounded all wrong. Should he write that? No. That would be even worse. 'Your loving husband, Peter'.

'Purefoy,' he yelled again, and Purefoy stuck his head in through the door.

'Purefoy, read my letter, would you?' Locke disappeared behind the screen in the corner, and the sound of splashing came through.

Purefoy read the letter.

Locke came out shirtless, scrubbing at his head with a thin white towel. 'Is it all right?' he said.

'What – you having a son, sir? It's bloody marvellous.'

Locke grinned a little, and raised his eyebrows. 'Mmm,' he said, and pulled out a new shirt. 'Umm. The letter.'

'It's fine, sir,' said Purefoy. It wasn't. This rather unusual man presented a shallow version of himself . . . *but not everyone can express themselves well on paper. And perhaps that's what she wants from him.*

Purefoy had in his pocket his most recent letter from Nadine:

My dear dear boy,
This shyness is crippling my letters – I have so little time to write, so much I could say, and I am all the time thinking of not saying things which will make you unhappy, like not talking about the war, because I don't want to remind you of it – as if you had forgotten. But people here do forget it, and it makes me furious, as I'm sure it would you – there, you see, something else I should not say. So what is safe to say? Only the most dangerous thing of all. How much I love you. I completely love you. Is it just because I need something to love? NO – it is because of you, from your first grin up that tree, to every funny or intelligent or beautiful thing you have ever said to me, your courage and strength, and your weakness too – I'm sure you must have some weakness – well, yes, I know you do – but, do you know, my love for you is like a living thing I keep in my pocket and late at night, or in the middle of some hard dull task, I think of it, or take it out. I can last a day with that

in my pocket, and a day is all there is. And in the morning, it is still there. I am so proud to be loved by you.

Now I have to go and wash some sheets. Ever more, ever more, more sheets, more love, ever more,

your Nat

In his other pocket was a letter he was about to post to her:

Dearest Nadine, girl of my heart

Yesterday I imagined that your father was standing over my shoulder as I wrote you that last letter – the rather warm letter – or perhaps over your shoulder as you read it. I know there is NO POINT in thinking about all the troubles which may come. I told you, I think, about my friend Ainsworth – before July the First of cursed memory he showed me a kind of prayer he carried with him, a gift from his wife, along the lines of Courage for the big troubles, Patience for the small ones and when you have done your duty sleep peacefully and be of good cheer . . . Major Locke brought it to me in the hospital. Ainsworth had asked that I should have it. So I sit, when I have a chance to sit, and think that the end of the day is the end of the day . . . though of course here the end of the day is not the end of the day, it is the beginning of the night, and the night has its own livelinesses. Am I making sense? You would think that compared with here the idea of your father would not be so frightening, wouldn't you?

Do you see Sir Alfred at all? If you can, please go to him and tell him of my affection and respect. I have such kind letters from him – he seems not to mind at all when I am silent for long periods. I owe him so much, and God only knows how I can ever repay him – of course he thinks I am repaying him by being here, and of course I think that I was here anyway, so that hardly counts. I have told him a little of the madness that sent me away so rudely in the first place, and a little of the madness here – though you know, my darling, I think I am not going mad after all. I feared I was – but now I see, I have seen since July 1st, that to go mad would be the only sane response so I need not. Does that make sense?

Accept some little seeds and crumbs of chocolate for the small creature in your pocket. Stroke it from me, tell it to hold on. I am back now in the harness and we go up the line in a few days. I'll write to you again before we do. My love, my love – all my love. Do you know – today, I am happy. I am happy because we love each other. That, perhaps, is madness.

I am not scared. I have – well, you know – only one regret.

Only yours,
Riley

Locke was combing his damp hair. Purefoy knew what he would say next.

'Fancy a drink, old man? Wet the baby's head?'

~

They went first to the Golden Goose, pushing through a disconsolate queue of men waiting for the brothel just round the corner, and sat by the window. The pretty red-haired girl, who swore her name was 'Gingaire', gave Purefoy a kiss on the cheek for his new third pip. The female breath made him shudder; she noticed, and called him *mon capitaine*, before going to get their bottle of champagne. Carefully she unwrapped the foil, released the cage and eased the cork. Even so it popped wildly and foamily, and Purefoy smiled. Locke gave him a look, and poured the beautiful bittersweet wine.

'Ah, the reliability of wine,' he murmured, taking his glass. 'To wives and sweethearts. And babies.'

Outside, a wave of grumbling had started among the men in the queue.

'After eight o'clock!' a voice was calling. 'Officers only now! On your way, on your way.'

'Not very happy about it,' observed Purefoy, glancing out, tipping his glass this way and that. Ginger's father had acquired some fine crystal coupes from somewhere, which he kept on a linen runner in a mahogany cupboard for those he called 'his' officers.

'None of us are, are we?' said Locke, and Riley saw his eyes were glassy, with grief, with previously taken drink, with . . . he couldn't tell with what.

Purefoy longed to talk, to be able to talk, to talk to this man he liked, but this was not the conversation he wanted.

Some of the men were bustling into the Goose. Frustration bubbled in them, and they smelt of it. There was an animal quality in killing, which Purefoy had seen and felt and recognised, and now he saw and smelt something similar in this frustrated queue. He found it disgusting, pitiable, touching. All that masculinity, in the wrong place, nothing to do with it. *If things were different, scientists would be discovering and labelling whatever it is in us that stinks when we are lustful, or violent, and whatever it is that coats our tongues in metal when we're frightened, why a shuddering heart sends a voice into a squawk, and releases our bowels and the strings that hold our skeletons together. Or perhaps there are scientists – greybeards – doing that, in Edinburgh and London and Berlin. Or perhaps they are all too busy inventing better faster quicker bigger bombs and rockets and aeroplanes and poisonous gases. How would we know? We know nothing. We are just here.*

'Do you love her, Purefoy?' asked Locke. Purefoy looked up. Locke seemed shy to be asking it. Purefoy liked this delicacy, a fastidious sweetness, like an intellectual vicar. If Locke had to name the female part, thought Purefoy, he'd pronounce it like Sir Alfred, in Latin, in some ancient form belonging to some special college they'd been to. Purefoy had once had to take Messalina to the vet. There was something wrong, Sir Alfred had said elegantly, with her *waggeeenah*.

Poor fucking Locke.

'I love and adore her, sir,' he said.

Locke gazed at him softly. How can he love and adore her? How does he manage to do that, now? He wanted to ask him, but didn't dare. 'Sit down and get drunk, Purefoy,' he said. The desperation was beginning to creep up around the edges of himself, dark stains seeping. His heartbeat was increasing. Soon it would take on the wild pattering and then how could he silence it?

'And let's go next door,' he said. 'Let's go next door, and love and adore.' Or, at least . . .

'Not for me, sir,' Purefoy said, as kindly as he could. But when Locke jumped up, Purefoy went with him. He didn't like to leave Locke alone.

The brothel had been the doctor's house. The remains of red-hot-pokers sprouted among the shaggy ornamental grasses in the front garden, and a big bed of golden-orange day lilies shone madly against grey stone in the evening sunlight. The river ran alongside it, giving it a wildly over-grown damp green lushness shocking to the men coming from the front. It was really quite charming. Purefoy waited inside, among the tall, heavy cupboards filled with bottles of protargol and potassium permanganate and *preservatifs*, next to the hunting-scene prints and a view of the Cloth Hall at Ypres from the south. He couldn't help reading the notices about Lysol and Vaseline and foreskins, signed off from the morality section of the police. *The sooner we win the war*, he thought, *the sooner Nadine will not have to look at other men's parts.*

He sat down on one of the doctor's wife's handsome chintz chairs and closed his eyes. It was important to him that he should take Major Locke back to the billet all right. He dozed, and dreamt he was hurling sunflowers, sending them spinning into a green and gaseous night.

~

Upstairs, Locke was with the usual girl. He was on familiar terms now with most of the patchouli- and chemical-scented *putes*, in the course of trying out a new proposition:

that if there were a living girl in his arms, the corpses of Bloom and Atkins could not come and take up their place. It didn't work.

⁓

Purefoy was waiting for him. They picked up another bottle and went back together against the hurtling glow of the bombardment, like a great and perpetual and abominable dancing sunset in the east, in the wrong direction. They spent the evening listening to the scratchy, ghostly music of Locke's Victrola. After Purefoy left, Locke put on Leo Szilak singing '*E lucevan le stelle*', and was able, for a minute or two, two-thirds of the way down his second bottle, to think about how sweet, how beautiful, how soft to the touch his wife was, and how she knew in so many different areas exactly what he liked, and about how he could make her mew by starting in, and then stopping, and starting in again. Then the wounds of the flesh became conflated again in his mind, and he took a whisky or two, just to settle himself.

Chapter Twelve

Sidcup, January 1917

The baby was beautiful. Clean pink soft little thing. She loved him the moment she came round, with a desirous, hungry, laughing love. It wasn't that. The first luxurious, voluptuous, sleepy two weeks, she simply would not physically let go of him, just fed him day and night, watching his ecstatic rolling eyes, his cheeks getting visibly plumper by the day . . . When her mother or Mrs Joyce tried to take him, she just sent them away. But when she got ill, and neither of them could stop crying, it was probably all for the best to have let her mother take him back to Froxfield. She was right about the airships. She was right that Margaret would be better than Mrs Joyce. And of course it would have been wrong to keep another girl from war work by trying to hire a nurse. And of course Julia couldn't cope with the baby on her own. And if Dr Tayle said that Julia wasn't well enough to travel, well, she wasn't well enough to travel. Everyone agreed it was quite selfish of Julia to want to keep the child with her, under the circumstances. Sentimental, even. Sacrifices had to be made and, really, when mothers all around were sending their sons to the front without complaint, it was quite ridiculous for Julia to kick up a fuss about her baby. Boys have to go away sooner or later anyway, don't they? Julia, Mrs Orris made clear, should pull herself together.

So when Julia emerged from her fever, weak, swollen-breasted and alone, it was to find that it was her own fault for being so useless, helpless, sentimental and stupid. Her mother was surprised, too, at how she managed to look both fat and haggard, and how her eyebrows had gone pale. In their last conversation before Mrs Orris left with Tom, she had said: 'It's astonishing, really, when you've been so ill, how you can still be so fat. You still look pregnant!' Julia could see for herself her poor belly, huge and flaccid, dimpled white, like uncooked dough, streaked with stretch marks. *But it was for Tom – it's all right, it was for Tom . . .*

At least the milk had dried up now. The pain! It was worse than giving birth. And apparently it takes longer to dry if the baby is there, wanting it. So that was one good thing. She had liked the pain, though. The thrill of involvement and deserving suffering had, she felt, united her with Peter. She, too, had had a bloodbath, a dreadful wound in a good cause. Her body had been ripped like a soldier's. The scars were a different matter. The recovery . . . She was beginning not to feel like an animal any more, 'like a milch cow', her mother had said distastefully. But she had liked being sucked at and pummelled. It was so real and intense and useful. She had loved it – being loved, and eaten alive, by her beautiful son. Her breasts, dry as they were now, ached for him. Her arms were empty.

'What do I feel like now?' she whispered, peering into the mirror. *What am I? Apart from fat and haggard.*

When she was well enough to come downstairs, she tuned the cello, and thought about when she would be well enough to go to Froxfield. Then she plumped the cushions. Then Mrs Joyce came in and told her not to exert herself.

She stared out of the window.

She fell back on the cushions and stared at the ceiling.

She picked up a copy of *Vogue* her mother had sent, and read: 'It is lamentable that the far-famed beauty of the Englishwoman must suffer from the terrible strain her country is under-going.'

She let it fall.

She picked it up again, and read: 'It is her duty to use every means in her power to prevent the effect on her beauty . . .' She turned the page: a picture of Countess Bathurst looking absolutely gorgeous in her Red Cross uniform.

Her clothes didn't fit any more. She couldn't even get into the green wool dress, let alone do it up. Her mother had written to Peter, and they'd got a letter back. Her mother had read it to her, and then put it somewhere, and had gone off before remembering where. Julia couldn't find it.

Her body missed its child, in sweeping flurries of ferocity. As soon as the doctor said she was well enough she'd go to Froxfield and she'd bring him home. Her mother couldn't just *keep* the baby, if Julia made clear her position. Margaret could come here!

She knew her mother would never let Margaret go.

'Stupid stupid selfish stupid,' she muttered.

~

'I'm going to London,' she told Dr Tayle, some weeks later. 'Rose needs to go up and I can go with her. We shall have some fun! I feel quite up to it.'

She looked in the shop windows and felt depressed. She sat in the foyer at VAD Headquarters reading her *Vogue* (longer lines, a straighter profile, younger models, shorter hair and an ever-more-slender shape) while inside Rose was interviewed for her transfer to the new hospital, which was to be called the Queen's Hospital. Darling Rose.

'Have you come to volunteer?' said a languid girl, with a boyish crop and a pile of files, passing by.

'No!' squeaked Julia. 'I can't! I have a baby!'

The languid girl looked around, vaguely, as if to see where the baby was, and moved on.

Even a girl like that is useful, Julia thought. She pulled herself up. 'Tell Miss Locke I've gone on, would you?' she said to the receptionist, who was at least fifty and ugly. *But of some use, unlike me.*

In the first shop, she bought two lip rouges.

In the second, she looked at corsets, but could not bring herself to try anything on, to ask, even, what size she was now.

In the third, she bought a hat, a low, close-fitting thing, in which she felt she could hide, while still looking slightly chic.

In the fourth, she considered having her hair cut short.

In the fifth, which was upstairs from the fourth and part of the same establishment, she read the list of aesthetic treatments and, encouraged by an elegant and very slender European woman in a white coat, decided to have a clay facial to tighten and brighten her complexion. It felt so nice to be touched that she decided to have a massage, 'to refine the figure,' said the European woman. Her name appeared to be Madame Louise.

For perhaps the first time in her life Julia's nakedness embarrassed her. But the masseuse said nothing, just pummelled and twisted her body rhythmically, almost lovingly, up and down, lifting and placing her limbs, sweeping off ripples of tension. *Perhaps*, Julia thought, *I don't look that bad, or how could she bear to touch me?*

Madame Louise smiled at Julia when she came out of the little massage room, pink in her clean white dressing-gown, the uniform of beauty therapy. 'You look so relaxed!' she said. 'Really beautiful. What else can we do for you today?'

Julia looked at the list. Oh, why not?

Eyebrows.

'We can do it now,' Madame Louise said. 'You won't need to stay in. But a low-brimmed hat will be necessary if you are planning to go out and about.'

Well! Julia had the hat right there. It felt like an omen, a benediction.

She wrapped her dressing-gown around her and lay back on the hard bed and the clean white pillow, and had her eyebrows plucked out completely and replaced by fine, sweeping arches of tiny fluttered black dashes, tattooed in on either side. Madame Louise did it herself, and Julia felt as if she had been promoted from the mere masseuse. The needles prickled her skin like electricity. It hurt. She liked it. She felt professional.

Madame Louise suggested she might prefer not to look, immediately afterwards – but she did. She wanted to, and she was glad when she did. Blood and ink were wiped from her forehead; and two long black streaks flared like wounds across her white brow. Madame Louise showed her how to apply the special oil, how to dress them to keep them clean.

'The little scabs should appear in the next day or so, and they'll be healed in a week. It is very important not to pick.'

Julia appreciated her serious tone. There was after all blood, and permanence, pain for perfection, recovery. Julia was suffering for what she was good at. She was serious.

'Well, that is a good start!' announced Madame Louise. 'And . . .' she gestured delicately around Julia's jawline '. . . when Madam is interested in something for the slight . . .'

'What?' asked Julia, turning round, flashing.

Madame Louise made a little apologetic *moue* with her painted mouth. 'There's just a little . . . slackness . . .' she murmured.

'Oh!' cried Julia, as if embarrassed to be so caught out.

Madame Louise passed her the magnifying mirror.

'Oh,' said Julia again.

Their eyes caught. The woman looked awfully sorry to have to be the one to bear the bad news.

'Do you . . .?' asked Julia.

179

'Oh, yes,' said Madame Louise, reassuringly, as if relieved to be on safer ground. 'Dr Lamer . . . some wonderful techniques . . . would you . . .?'

She would. She went in to see Dr Lamer right then. He had a few minutes before his next client. He was a discreet, serious little man, well dressed, kindly. He had studied in Berlin. He had been in America. Many advances had been made and were being made all the time, so ladies were able to feel completely safe now, knowing that procedures had been tried and tested . . . Yes, he *had* met Major Gillies, at the hospital in Aldershot, a very different line, of course, but some marvellous work being done there, he had heard, great advances.

Julia thought of Rose, and blushed a little, and corrected herself: *What I am doing is valid! It's just as valid as Rose. Not everybody can do the same things, and Rose can't be pretty and keep a man happy and I can, so I'll do it to the best of my ability. Wife and mother.*

She came out of the beauty studio feeling light and strong, her new hat and fringe positioned carefully to cover the bandaged blazon of her patriotic new brows.

How wonderful, to know such things could be done. How wonderful.

Dr Lamer had said she was to think about it. About her jawline, which, of course, she had thought about often before, particularly with reference to the fear that it might end up like her mother's. About the things which could be done to avoid that. And there were other things, more urgent, such as (1) her figure! *Well, a steamed-fish reducing diet would see to that – or I could get one of those rubber*

*corsets. You just wear it, and perspire, and become slim . . .
or take up dancing like Isadora Duncan in a Poiret gown.*
And (2) her poor breasts – or did they count as part of her
figure? *Dr Lamer could probably do something about them
too. Peter need never know . . .* And her nose! Her imperfection! *After all, Gladys Deacon had her nose done with paraffin
wax, years ago, and whatever they say about her she is SO
beautiful – that portrait by Boldoni.* She'd read somewhere
that Miss Deacon had had the statues at the Louvre mea-
sured by a professor of aesthetics to find the perfect classical
proportion because she wanted the straight, classical Greek
line, no dent at all from the forehead to the bridge . . . *Peter
admires her, I know . . .*

There are all kinds of things I can do, she thought. *I will
turn thirty more beautiful than I was at twenty, and that will
be my gift to Peter, when he comes home.*

She strode busily past Liberty, without even glancing in
the window of the houseware section, despite the presence
there of some really quite alluring peacock blue glass. A
vast new territory of improvability was opening up before
her eyes as she swung back up the road.

Chapter Thirteen

London, April 1917

'Take him dancing,' said Jean. 'He'll just want a bit of fun. That's all they want. Fun and a drink and whatever they can get. Tell him to get some preservatives, or I'll get some for you off my Georgie. I'll do that anyway.'

She shoved the sacrilegious packet at Nadine surreptitiously in Chapel. Nadine had to take it or it would drop. She blushed scarlet and stuffed it into her apron pocket and sang loudly: 'There is a green hill FAR a-a-way without a city wall.' *Why would a green hill have a city wall anyway? And if it meant outside the city wall, why not just say so? It still scanned.*

She didn't for one moment deny to any soldier or anyone else the right to fun and a drink and whatever they could get. It made *her* feel ill, that was all. All of London was dancing now – dancing like lunatics, lunch hour, after work, nightclubs, hotels, tea dances, church halls – to jazz bands and gramophones. Dixieland! There were Americans and black men on the streets of Soho, with trumpets and saxophones. A new edict went out from the ministry: wounded men were to stay in convalescent homes until they were fit for service again. They'd been having too much fun in the West End, and not getting better quickly enough.

So if all Jean wanted was a drink and a dance and whatever she could get then good for her, but all Nadine wanted after a shift with the dead and the dying and the damaged was to bury her head in Riley or, failing that, the thought of Riley.

His letters were mostly short and useless, but she knew why, and she knew what to do about it. *Hold on.* She wrote back full of jokes and affection, descriptions of the daffodils, a jolly meal, a bicycle trip, a training course. Nothing about the blood and the death. He knew she knew. She knew he knew. It was people who didn't know, or who had blocked it out, that she couldn't deal with. Her *mother* . . .

Last time she had gone home her father had been out and her mother had been lying on her *chaise-longue* wrapped in cashmere, reading a potboiler of modern psychological theory by Addington Bruce. She was on chapter twenty-three, 'Sigmund Freud and Psychoanalysis'.

Jacqueline was determined to do something nice for Nadine, who deserved it. 'I've been thinking,' she said. 'How are you for underwear?'

'I'm fine, thank you, Mama. I had those nice combinations at Christmas.'

'No, darling, I meant real underwear. Something pretty and nice.'

Nadine saw it moving in, like rain from the distance, and tensed in preparation. *It's my afternoon away from the hospital, why must I spend it tense?*

You know why. Because your mother is afraid you'll never get married, because all the men are being killed – and I am growing coarse and unattractive in my habits.

'You need cheering up,' said Jacqueline. 'And you need a little help – I know it is hard in wartime, but the things which were all right before the war, being a little relaxed and that could be beautiful, if we were a little lazy, you know, *laxitée* . . .' she smiled at the memory of how Robert used to chide her for it, indulgently '. . . but you know that *laxitée* was born out of beauty and art and creating, not from, you know, neglecting a little the joys of being a woman . . .'

Apparently, it was better to lie around all day drinking champagne and talking about art in your peignoir than not to care about frilly drawers because you were on your feet nursing all day.

'When we were relaxed, darling, we were always elegant.'

Whereas I'm letting standards slip, and should go to a hairdresser . . .

Gradually what actually concerned Jacqueline emerged from the clouds of her amorphous, slightly insulting goodwill. She paused, regrouped, and advanced again.

'Darling,' she said. 'I have been reading, and thinking.'

Nadine almost spat. *How lovely for you, Mother.*

'Darling, let me tell you. Don't be angry. I think you have become *fixated* on Riley – no, listen. Because it is impossible to find a young man, it being wartime, you have fixated on the impossibility itself and chosen Riley, because he is the most impossible young man of all.'

Nadine stared. *Fixated! My dear, fixated!*

'Because you love your father so much, you are scared of the possibility of any young man dethroning your father in your eyes. *Therefore* you have fixated on an inferior young man, who never could.'

Really.

'So, in order to grow up, you must cast off your fixation with the inferior, impossible young man, and find a possible, superior young man . . .'

Nadine's lips had pursed themselves. *Mother, Mother, why are you always telling yourself that things are good or bad when every human experience tells us that everything is both?*

'And do you have a superior young man in mind, Mama?' she said eventually.

'Oh, darling . . .' For months Jacqueline had trailed superior young men through the drawing room on Sunday afternoons: polite, bewildered boys who had been Over There, self-satisfied little charmers with cushy posts at the ministry, bearing that peculiar news which was no news, those stock phrases. Nadine would run into the house and straight upstairs to see her father, and hide with him, talking of their own dear familiar nothings. Sometimes she sent nice VADs from the hospital (she didn't dare send Jean) in her place, and indeed a couple of romances emerged, while she lured her father out to the pictures.

This had been her first visit home for weeks.

Nadine would love to flirt with them, dance with them, go to the new Harold Lloyd with them. She knew they needed it. But she could only give them morphine and lay damp cloths on their foreheads when they started plucking

185

the sheets and talking to people who were not there. She had told her mother before that she had nothing else to give. She told her again.

'You get time off, darling.'

'I spend my hours off asleep.'

Jacqueline said: 'Of course we all know the value of beauty sleep, but there is a limit to how much a girl needs.'

Nadine, who had been working double shifts for several weeks due to a nasty digestive bug that had been doing the rounds of both patients and nursing staff, and was sleeping on average five hours a night and only three for the past three nights, gave up the struggle. In tones as weary as her body, she said, 'Sorry, Mother, but do you know I think I'd rather have a little nap now, instead of this conversation?' and stood up, shaking a little, to leave.

'Nadine,' her mother snapped. 'My husband – my *husband* – may be called up and sent to the front at any time. You might have a little respect for the fact that I am being *positive* and not just *moping*.'

Nadine turned back, and the shaking increased and 'I am NOT moping!' she screamed. 'I am WORKING every hour God sends with men who DIE – so STOP TELLING ME TO HAVE FUN.'

Jacqueline was blinking. She looked as if she had been assaulted. 'A little *respect*, Nadine,' she said quietly.

'Yes, Mother. That would be lovely.'

The words plopped like pebbles into mud.

The moment sat between them when they both realised they should and no doubt would apologise – but the urge to make it worse was strong in Nadine, itching at her fingers, her articulacy, her frustration. Unissued retorts lined up restlessly along her tongue.

Respect? For what? Your idiocy?

I could have slept this afternoon, instead of coming here for this. I wish I had.

No one is going to send Papa to the front, Mother. Oh, and by the way, he is my father as well as your husband, or hadn't you noticed? Is he only your husband now?

And one of the retorts barged to the front and burst out: 'The inferior young man, Mother, is fighting in France – *your* parents' country. I'm *sorry*, Mother,' she snapped. It was not the meant sorry: it was the nasty little sorry followed always by 'but' – *but I really can't be expected to . . .*; *but this has gone on long enough*; *but I'm going to have to . . .* She couldn't be bothered to find a but. She didn't want to hurt her mother. She wanted to fall on her and weep.

'I'll see you soon,' she said, and pecked Jacqueline on her still-shocked cheek, and left, the words of the flare-up circling her, like rooks above a nesting site.

'Go away,' she said to them.

She could go back to the Chelsea, and just lie on her little hard narrow bed in her little dark shared room and try to sleep . . . or she could lie in the park, to feel the grassy earth beneath her back and the air on her face . . . though then soldiers on leave would come and talk to her, with their desperate hunger. Sometimes she wished she *was* a trollop, so she could give those boys a moment of some kind of joy.

She'd just have to go to the cinema. There might be a Charlie Chaplin on at the Coronet. And at least they had stopped showing those horrible topicals, cheering Tommies setting off, grinning like loons and waving, fun fun fun at the recruiting station, and the Roll of Honour flicks, where floating head after floating head appeared, like decapitated ghosts, each labelled with – at the beginning – the name of his regiment and where he was serving, but now more likely what he had had shot off him and how he had died. And that bloody patriotic music . . . They *had* been fun at the start: waiting to see if someone you knew came on, and cheering when they did. But it seemed no one could stomach them any more. Either they knew about Over There, and were appalled, or they were doing that thing, that thing, behaving as if there was nothing special going on, two hundred miles south and across some water, no further than Birmingham, or Manchester, pretending it wasn't real, unable to bear having the truth of it displayed in front of them. The fury flared up in her again. *If you really are so interested in the human psychological theories, Mama, instead of picking me apart, why don't you study the lengths to which people are prepared to go not to see what is before their eyes? 'My husband may have to go to the front.' Really, Mama, we all know they're desperate for men but I really don't think they'll be taking a fifty-five-year-old conductor who's up for a knighthood for his patriotic fund-raising, and sending him out to the Salient.*

And, Mother, though we never mention it and you pretend it isn't true, my true love is there, he is there, he is there . . .

An idea sparked. Perhaps the reason her mother pretended Riley wasn't Nadine's true love was because she couldn't bear her daughter to have a true love at the front, and Riley's being at the front was something she couldn't change, so instead she changed him being Nadine's true love . . . Really she was just trying to protect Nadine. No. That was too convoluted to be true.

She crossed over into the park and turned west, glanced over to the Round Pond, and to where the pale green branches of the trees overhung the road behind Kensington Palace. 'One little boot in front of the other, girl,' she murmured to herself.

It was hard, sometimes, to imagine that so much time had passed. Exactly three years hanging on little more than one touch, one meeting, one kiss, letters. Three years in the clothes that make you who you are. Nursing VAD Waveney. Occasionally she would imagine what she would wear if she were not serving. Artistic gowns? Cycling suits, as a New Woman? Something practical in jersey? Huge short black petticoats and lace-up boots and the perky cap and Riley's coat? Jasmine oil, and her hair down? What might she have known by now of love, if there had been no war? Her body ached for Riley. But how could she ache for something she had never had?

She came out again at Black Lion Gate. There across the road was Orme Square.

She crossed, and she walked into the special quiet of the lovely white stucco square, past the creamy kid-leather blooms on the magnolia in the little central garden, her feet taking the familiar route of childhood across the York-stone pavement, and she rang Sir Alfred's bell.

Sir Alfred was in, said Mrs Briggs, who was quite pleased to see her. Messalina lolloped up cautiously, and put her forehead against Nadine's waist. Nadine stroked her hard, silky brow, and gently pulled her long ears.

Sir Alfred was working. Nadine skipped up up up the flights of stairs. It had been a long time since she'd been here. A few more casualties of her war: visiting, painting.

Late-afternoon light and the oily lush smell of paint filled the studio. Sir Alfred was at his easel, his back to her. She couldn't see what he was painting. Something small. More medieval romantic stroke-perfect heroes? She rather hoped not. Watching the movements of his arm, waiting for him to turn and notice her, she picked up a brush and stroked it against her face, as she had used to when she was little, loving the silky softness of sable, the tiny shiny chestnut tips, the delicacy, and the roughness of hog-bristle . . . Their different behaviour on canvas and paper, the combinations of combinations of materials and techniques, the inspirations, the opportunities for subtlety and beauty and experiment. Sir Alfred teaching her, calling Riley over to demonstrate a stroke – 'He does it better than me, the little varmint!' How she had liked both Riley's skill and the clarity with which he put it to use. No fuss. One of the first things she'd liked about him. One of the many first things. The remembrance of what she had lost hit her suddenly in the belly.

As if he had heard the blow, Sir Alfred turned around, and broke into smiles at the sight of her. His embrace, beardy and dangerous of stains, was very welcome. She had a rush of her father – the older man looking up from his work, pleased to see you – and a swift lurch that she should not have been so harsh to her mother.

'Dear girl,' Sir Alfred said. 'Dear girl. How very kind.' He wiped his hands, rang for tea, asked for news.

She told him she was at the Chelsea, a nursing VAD now, yes, paid – only half what a trained nurse gets, but there's more respect, and the work is more, um, *direct*, actually with the boys; her father and mother were well, Noel was training recruits in Suffolk, he was well, doing his bit. Yes, conscripted last year, but asthmatic, so . . .

'And do you hear from our friend?' the old man asked.

'He is very grateful,' she began.

'And so are we,' he said. For a moment she sensed the presence of something, a conversation that might be going to be had . . . but it passed. Just as she wanted to reach out for it, it had slipped away and she couldn't get it back – he took it away. Nobody wanted to talk to her about him.

They talked instead of the difficulties in laying your hands on paint and canvas these days – hence the small panel he was painting, which was not a perfect Pre-Raphaelite hero, but – *oh, might as well be* – the Angel of Mons, gleaming and perfect in medieval armour, as if it were 1912. He seemed to recognise her reaction, and said, 'It does all leave one feeling rather useless.'

'Does art feel useless?' she said.

'At the moment, yes,' he said. 'They need the canvas for tents and the chemicals for weapons and the factories and the labour . . . I'm wondering how we can ever come back from war, after so much has been turned over to it . . . That's not something I can paint, though. I don't know what people want. I've always painted what they want, lovely things . . . and I am old, and the young are suffering, and

I can do nothing for them.'

So she kissed him on the cheek, and said, 'For what it's worth, you've cheered me up.'

'Have I? How?'

'By noticing that we need it,' she said.

Later, when she was leaving, somewhere between 'oh dear, it's getting late' in the studio and 'please come again, please do' in the hall, Sir Alfred stopped on the stairs and said suddenly: 'Before the war, I was going to go on a grand tour of Europe. There were all sorts of pictures I wanted to look at again . . . in the Netherlands and Paris and Florence and Rome. I was going to take Riley with me. I read somewhere that one shouldn't take servants to Egypt because they lacked the education which would enable them to appreciate the recompenses for the inconveniences . . . And I thought, Riley is the most appreciative boy I ever knew. Such a passion . . . the way he would swallow books whole . . . He constantly revived me. I cannot tell you how much I miss him, Nadine. Such a clever, passionate boy, and that solid, silent pride he had, and that quicksilver way. Very like you, in some ways. Such a pair, you two, when you were little: like a pair of little curly-haired creatures, always huddled up together, with your secrets and your plans . . .'

'Were we?' she said, blinking. She knew they were. But to have it declared so openly, by an adult, made it real because it had been witnessed. She felt as if a great shaft of sunlight had burst through heavy cloud, picking her out, illuminating her, blessing her.

'A pair of strange lovely little creatures . . .' he said. 'So

– yes, I've decided. I will extend my tour and go to Egypt. I will do it. Whatever happens. And I hope he will want to come with me.' His eyes were bright with intent. He made her smile.

I'm coming too, she thought, and then quickly ran through in her head again the words he had used, storing them, saving them for later sustenance. *Clever. Passionate. Appreciative. Quicksilver. Silent, solid pride. Such a pair, you two, always huddled together. Lovely.*

She was late back, and Matron said Jean and Esther were both down with gastric flu now, 'so get to it, girl,' but she didn't mind because inside she was bathed in light, singing *appreciative quicksilver, lovely, clever, strange, you two, such a pair . . .*

～

The telegram said Tuesday midday. She sat at Victoria station from eleven, propped up, kind of perched on the barrier, the heels of her boots tucked behind the rail, with her skirt sticking out and her cap disrespectfully back. Many of the uniformed men passing up the platforms said things like: 'Darlin'! You made it!' or 'Tell me you're waiting for me – please!' and one said cautiously, 'Edith?' and she had to shake her head quickly, apologetically.

He came straight to her, following an arrow line through the crowd. She saw him coming and the lurch inside nearly cast her off her rail. His case fell to the floor as he snaked his arm round her waist and there was a tiny perfect pause before he kissed and kissed and kissed her.

People around stopped and noticed them. Little smiles of patriotic indulgence, disapproving tuts, piercings of envy, eye-narrowings of vicarious lust, stirrings in trousers.

'Where are we going?' he said, smiling, travel-stained, crop-haired, young, beautiful.

She couldn't speak.

'Cup of tea,' he said. 'I could do with a cup of tea.'

So once again they sat in front of cups of tea, and the clattering world around them fell away. The terror and repression and wrongness lifted like mist, and disappeared. They were completely happy. They couldn't stop smiling at each other, beaming like fools till their cheeks ached and he started laughing. They were laughing when they left the café and got on a bus, and then on a train, and then they walked out of town, and climbed a fence, and climbed a hill, and lay on his coat on a hillside among cowslips and cow parsley and tiny blue cats' eyes.

She didn't say, 'Not here.' Here in the sun in the shelter of the hill and the warmth of the tiny world inside his collar, inside his lining, seemed perfect. 'I won't – don't worry – I won't,' he was muttering. He only blanched a little when she produced Jean's little packet.

'Where the . . .?' he asked.

'Jean,' she whispered, unsure if it was all right. 'Is it all right?'

'If you're sure . . .'

She was sure. She revelled in the battling desires on his face, the intoxication of how much he wanted her and the beauty of his concern for her virtue. She was innocent enough to be horribly afraid the concern might win.

She did say, a little later, entranced and appalled, as he lay shipwrecked on her thighs, 'Is that it?'

To which he replied, gasping, 'No, not at all. That's just the beginning. Sorry. There's much more. Much, much more . . .'

'You said you wouldn't,' she murmured, in his arms.

'For God's sake, woman, how could I not?' he replied. 'It wouldn't be human,' and she laughed, and they did it again, better.

Evening crept up on them, and the chill of the dark earth through the wool. A room in town, they thought, though it seemed worse, somehow, than what they had just done. She couldn't believe she had done it. *I've done it! We have done it!* She felt like a different woman. Something was singing under her skin, and her limbs seemed to fit on her differently. Better. Right.

She turned her ring round on her third finger so it looked like a wedding ring, but the lady at the little hotel looked askance at their youth and the one army-issue bag.

'There's no rooms,' she said, not meeting their eyes, and Riley leant in and said to her kindly, 'Never mind. We'll be all right,' and nothing could blight them. They took the milk train back to London, and walked through the dawn, ending up in a dingy room on Victoria Street near the station where they paid in advance, and once they had each other's clothes off, breeches and petticoat, braces and camisole in piles on the floor, they didn't come out for three days.

Nadine woke with his body curled round her, his face in the back of her neck, his breath on her skin, his arm flung across her, and the momentousness of what they were doing filled her with a great unspeakable joy. *Now I know*, she thought. *Now I know and I am part of it all and part of myself and of him.*

They talked, of love, and food, and their shared memories, their lost world, as if it were a real thing. Occasionally they broached their future – Sir Alfred's grand tour, the adventures to come, the motorcycle and the dog – as if it were perfectly likely. Nadine found herself saying, 'When we . . .' and for a moment stopped herself, knowing that the correct word had to be 'If . . .' and unable to bear saying it. 'If' was a cruel word, 'when' a deluded one. She wanted to say 'When . . .' anyway. She fell silent. He kissed her, and got up, and went out, and came back with pork pies and a bottle of champagne and a bunch of lilies-of-the-valley from the stall in the station, wet from the rain.

They did not talk about the larger present, so circumscribed, so uncontrollable. Their little present was two bodies and a bed, and that was the entirety of time and place: them, there, in the little room, awkward, laughing, happy, warm, tentative, surrendering, overwhelmed, alarmed, astounded, shivering, subsiding, asleep, awake, getting the hang of it, learning, loving, redeemed. Happy.

Chapter Fourteen

London, May 1917

Peter said, in his letters, that he hoped everybody was fine.

Mrs Orris said, in her letters, that Julia was foolish to want to travel during the winter weather; selfish to want to use up the petrol, foolhardy to think of coming by train alone, ridiculous to imagine anyone was available to accompany her, thoughtless in trying to disrupt the routines of the household at Froxfield, ungrateful for the sacrifice her mother had made in taking Tom on, inconsiderate in harping on about visiting all the time, only likely to upset the child by turning up now when she hadn't bothered to come and see him for such a long time . . . The new nurse was splendid, and Mrs Orris very happy to pay for her; of course, there was no room now for Julia to come and stay but that hardly mattered as Tom was perfectly well and didn't miss his mother at all.

Julia wrote: 'I shall come and stay at the Crown.'

Mrs Orris forbade it. What would people think of her?

Julia, always an obedient child, keen to be everything required of her, had never found anyone she could talk to about her mother. Hardly herself, even. Peter had been the only one who had laughed at Mrs Orris, and given Julia the little warm amused glances of support that mean so much to the bullied.

One afternoon Julia went up to London alone. First, she took a cab to the small hotel in Mayfair, and dropped her bag. Then she walked out into the day, bright with the loveliness of London in spring: sun on ornate white stucco, pale green leaves deepening and expanding almost before her eyes, creamy horse-chestnut blossoms standing high. Her heels clicked on the pavement and she felt the brisk purposefulness of being in the city. She turned along Bond Street and looked in shop windows, admiring things. She had money. War was good for business. He could have stayed and worked in the firm and nobody would have thought worse of him. Lots of men did. Look at them – they're all around, prosperous on timber and ball-bearings and biscuits and maps. He could have. Or they could have gone to America. They could have.

So many people. There were couples everywhere. Younger girls than her, pretty and light in the sunshine. She wondered about them. Would they find husbands? Would it finish soon, and would they take their slim young bodies to the Riviera and marry slim young men who had been at school all through the war? Or fat men now in offices, moving iron and cotton from here to there? Or will it not be over till they are my age? And if it is, over which way? Will their children grow up German? Will we all be raped and murdered in our beds? The questions didn't seem real. How could you really imagine that such things could happen?

You can't think about it. You're not allowed to talk about it. Shortage of taxis, yes. Bombed and killed? Not really. Lose the war? Of course not. She clenched her teeth. *Stop it, Julia. That's what he's fighting for. That's why we didn't go away and that's why I must look after things. He is protecting us. All this. He is protecting Trafalgar Square and the Burlington Arcade and the cabbies and the babies and the pigeons and me. It is all so worth protecting. The white terraces and the tall grey elegance and the green squares and the old ladies and the pavement and the King.*

How could these things fail? The Royal Academy, Fortnum & Mason? It was all too prosperous and nice. She let the prosperity soothe her, moving in and out of shops as if pulled along lines of quiet desire: glance, see, draw closer. How pretty the things were. Pretty and safe. She walked and walked. She was nervous. She had told nobody.

It would be all right.

She walked towards Berkeley Square. Her feet hurt. There was a smart little pub on Brook Street, hung with baskets of flowers. It looked awfully attractive.

She had a newspaper in her bag.

Julia laughed to herself, and went into the pub. She had never been in one before. It was warm, cosy, with a manly, tobaccoey smell. She would treat it like a café, she thought, looking round, choosing a table, near the door, sunlit through the window. She caught the eye of a waiter.

'A small sherry, please,' she said. She felt slightly wild. *If my mother could see me!*

She took out her paper. There had been a riot in Paris, after the new Ballets Russes production, and the composer,

Satie – Peter loved Satie – had called a critic something so rude the paper couldn't print it, and the critic had sued, and Satie was to go to prison, and the writer, Monsieur Cocteau, had shouted the rude word in court and had had to be carried out. The costumes had been made of cardboard.

Other people's lives!

She didn't in the least want to be sent to prison for her art, or to dance in a cardboard costume, but, oh, she wanted something . . .

Yes, and she was getting something. She was.

She wondered what the rude word had been.

But it was good to be sitting down. She looked at the stained-glass in the window, the colours the sunlight gave it, greens and reds like church, and the sense of the street outside.

When the man spoke, she didn't think he was addressing her.

'I say,' he said again.

She'd always thought 'I say' a singularly idiotic phrase. *Of course 'you say'. I can hear you saying.*

'I don't suppose I could get you another of those?' He was gesturing to her drink, which was untouched. Smooth, strong hands. Youngish face. Moustache. Lieutenant's uniform, well filled. Hopeful, slightly desperate brown eyes. Slight smile.

She blinked.

'It's just you look a little . . .' He smiled encouragingly.

'A little what?' she said. She didn't want to be discourteous.

'Well, I was rather hoping you looked a little lonely,' he said, grabbing a chair, pulling it over, swinging his leg over it. Her accent had surprised him, she could see it.

'My husband is in France,' she said, alarmed. It came out wrong. She meant it to mean, 'Go away, he's a soldier, have some respect.' It came out (if someone wanted to hear it that way) as, 'Yes, I'm alone, I'm unprotected, I *am* lonely.'

'Good for him,' said the lieutenant. 'Good-oh. All the more reason, really. Dare say he wouldn't mind a fellow officer buying his wife a drink. In solidarity. Let's drink to his health.'

This was awful. Awful. Her heart started going too fast. She could not possibly drink with a strange man in a pub. But she could not refuse to drink to Peter's health.

The waiter was right there. The officer said gaily: 'Same two again, old sport.' She was sitting like a fool, stuck, stupid.

The drinks arrived. The waiter smirked. The officer, who had been leaning back in his chair and staring at her, raised his glass and said: 'To his health, and to the health of his . . . awfully pretty . . . wife . . .'

The way he was looking at her!

He was handsome. She felt a rush of heat. Something was suddenly available and apparent to her that she had never known about before. You could just go to a public place and a man, a total stranger, might come up to you with that look . . .

He leant forward. 'I'm so sorry,' he said. 'You must think me awfully rude. Just approaching you like that. But you are so very pretty, and you do look, if you don't mind me saying so, so very lonely. My name's Raymond Dell.'

He held out his hand, and the implacable force of a lifetime of good manners made her hold hers out too. He took it. His hand was warm and dry. His teeth were white and clean. He didn't hold her hand for too long as men so often did. She was confused. Was he respectable or not? She used to be able to tell. Then she hadn't had to – Peter had been there. Since he'd been away she hadn't gone anywhere where there were men she didn't know. She could feel that she was blushing, staring at him like a cow over a gate, transfixed.

'Tell me,' he said. 'What's troubling you? I'm just back from Flanders myself, and I would love to hear someone else's troubles. Please. Indulge me.' He smiled.

A kind smile. A warm hand. A compliment. A plea for sympathy. Broad shoulders under the khaki. A fully desiring look.

He wants to do with me what Peter and I used to do. He does.

For a tiny flashing moment, she knew it was possible. She could smile and drink and talk and let him take her hand and lead her out into the street under the waiter's smirk and have a little lunch somewhere nice and drink a little wine and they could go together – in the afternoon, why not? – to the little hotel in Mayfair, or to another little hotel, under fake names – one fake name – into an anonymous room and they could do those things, she and this handsome young man.

It was possible.

It was something that people did.

Had she met him at a dance in 1912 she would have danced with him, and asked her mother to let him call, and they would have played tennis.

She was beautiful. She was desired. She was flattered. She was glad. Was she tempted?

It's Peter's fault, he shouldn't neglect me so – even when he's here he neglects me, he neglects me more when he's here because his presence makes the absence of his desire so clear, so cruel . . .

She *was* tempted. She wanted him to kiss her. She felt the dangerous heat rising, a wildness, a flurry of devil-may-care.

She stood up. 'You have mistaken me,' she said carefully. 'Good day.'

She shook her head in the sunshine. She hadn't drunk any of the sherry but she felt intoxicated. The air was cool, clarificatory, on her scalp.

Good Lord! A total stranger. How appalling.

She very much wanted to ring someone up and tell them what had happened. Not that for a split second she had entertained the idea. But that this was something that – that was conceivable.

And who would she talk to? Mrs Bax? Her mother? Rose? All the women she knew thought she was pathetic. She knew that other women were better equipped than her. But, dammit, she was doing what she could.

She shook her head again, briskly, shaking out the foolishness.

My marriage is good, she thought. *I love my husband and my marriage is good. There is nothing I would not do for him. I have turned down temptation for him.*

She marvelled at the wickedness, and gloried in her trouncing of it.

~

Julia had come to London to see Dr Lamer. The plan was, he would drug her and lay her out, then make a series of tiny slices into the smooth white skin beneath her jaw, which, when stitched up, would tighten and remove the slight sag of flesh under her chin that she feared had increased since childbirth and the beginning of the war, thus preventing the dual threats of (1) disappointing Peter by appearing old and ugly and (2) ending up looking like her mother. Her beauty was her strength – everybody had been telling her this for years. It was the only thing anyone had ever valued in her. It was her one weapon. So she must look after it.

But when she went to the clinic the morning after her encounter with Raymond Dell, between the drugging and the laying out, Julia began to flap her hands inexplicably by her sides, and cry out 'No, no, don't do it.' She began to weep, and shout, and stared at Dr Lamer through blue eyes huge with tears. Dr Lamer was compelled to sedate her, out of consideration for the other clients, and if he was annoyed he did not show it.

Later in the afternoon, sitting up in her pleasant bed, still steeped in sedative, Julia was confused. She thought she had had the operation; she was delighted that it did not hurt, and she expected Peter any moment to pick her up and take her home. Before he arrived, would Dr Lamer please give her some advice on her nose.

'There's nothing wrong with your nose, my dear,' he said. 'Your nose is quite perfect.'

'I need to be perfect, you see,' she said. 'My husband deserves a perfect wife.'

'Of course, my dear,' said the gentleman. 'All husbands want a perfect wife.'

'Mine *deserves* it,' Julia explained. 'He's in France, you see, and he's just not the kind of man who should be there. He's really a very peace-loving man, you know. He loves his dog, and reading his history books and music, and it's so terribly important that everything should be perfect for him when he comes back, just the same as it always was . . .'

'I'm sure he likes you just the way you are, Mrs Locke. You're a very beautiful woman.'

'I don't know if he does like me . . . But, oh, God, you're right. I mustn't change my nose. Of course not! I must be just as I was. Oh, I don't know. Should I be just the same as always, or should I be perfect? He always teased me about my nose . . . the little dip . . . You could do it with paraffin wax, couldn't you? Like Gladys Deacon?'

Dr Lamer took her hand, poor creature. 'It is always more difficult to add to the human form than it is to remove from it,' he said. 'And Miss Deacon's experience is not one to emulate, Mrs Locke. It wasn't done in the best way, and there were side effects.'

'Oh, I know,' she said, though she didn't. 'Is it really bad?'

'It was not advisable,' said Dr Lamer. 'Let us discuss these things when you are feeling more yourself.'

'But you must have a better method now, haven't you?' she said. 'Haven't they thought something up? I heard paraffin could be mixed with other things and that it was all right now . . . or . . . There was an article in *Beauty Chat* about featural surgery . . .'

Dr Lamer had considered featural surgery, nose rebuilding. He knew of less principled surgeons who offered hope and little else to saddle-nosed syphilitics. Himself, he did not care for it. It didn't work well. Easier, simpler, and just as profitable to tuck a little loose skin, tattoo an eyebrow, to shave a Jewish nose to match a new gentile name, even to give a little phenol face peel like a lay skinner, a common or garden beautifier. But not *adding*. Adding was too risky and too difficult.

'. . . only he did call it my one imperfection. But he seemed to like it. Perhaps he wouldn't want me to be perfectly perfect, like Mary Pickford . . .'

'Let's talk about it when you're up and about,' said the doctor, as he left her. 'When your mind is clear.'

The nurse, a slightly damp-looking, broad-faced wench called June, said, 'Can I bring you another magazine?'

When she came back with *Vogue* and the *Ladies' Domestic Journal*, June whispered, rather theatrically: 'I read it's slipped. She sits by the fire so the wax warms, and she remoulds it, under the skin. Trying to push it back into place. But I don't believe what I read. But she *has* got sores! Right there!' The girl pointed to the bridge of her own nose. 'A friend of mine saw her going into the Ritz. And then brown stains . . .' She gestured in two lines, down the sides past her nostrils. She pinched her jaw. 'And it's sort of gathered, here. She's looking very heavy-jawed. It's only going to get worse.'

She said it with a low glee, which reminded Julia how very much some people hate beautiful women. Desperate to be beautiful themselves, yet hating women who are. So, trying to make themselves, by their own standards, hateable.

Horrible.

'Would you like a little something to eat now?' asked June. 'Or are you banting?'

When she woke up again, clear-headed, and was told what had happened, Julia was puzzled as to why her drugged self had become hysterical and refused the operation her conscious self had decided on. She wondered if her subconscious self had been reassured by Raymond Dell's desire for her, or if it was just plain old fear. *Coward. You can't even do that for your husband.*

The idea of it being fear annoyed her. She stoked her annoyance into anger, turned that into fuel, and hailed a taxi to Paddington station.

The visit was not a success. Tom stared at her, narrow-eyed, from the arms of the new nurse, who Julia had never even met. When Julia tried to take him, Mrs Orris said 'Don't upset yourself, Julia. You'll make your eyes red and puff up your face.' Julia could find no way to refute this. As a result, she cried all the way back on the train, and all the way she heard her mother's voice telling her off for it.

Chapter Fifteen

West of Zonnebeke, August 1917

Purefoy was walking to the casualty clearing station. Captain Fry saw him up where the duckboards made a crossroads, staring and hustling along past the flooded battlefield grave-yard. Three wooden crosses rose solitary, like a trio of Excaliburs, from strangely smooth water. One was crowned with a jaunty skull. The rest of everything was, and had been for weeks, mud and death.

'Can you walk?' Fry called. Fry was a dental surgeon in reality. 'Good man. *Keep your head forward!*'

Purefoy didn't hear him but it didn't matter. He knew to keep his head forward.

The mud clung to his boots, freighting every step, but his legs were strong and the way was obvious. Follow the duckboards west to the giant charred black tooth-stump which was all that remained of Ypres.

He swung his arms. Inside, his head was very hot, and he was thirsty.

The chaos around him was no worse than the chaos of yesterday or the day before; it was the same chaos. Flat, slimy going. Mud of blood, blood of mud. Oh, yes, we're all poets here. He closed his eyes for a moment but inside his head was noisier even than outside, red and black, shooting.

No one spoke to him.

He spoke to no one.

He didn't know which noises were real.

Trudge on. He wanted to undo his tunic but there was something on it, wet.

Undo his tunic? *Dear God, Captain, what are you thinking? Standards!*

In his tunic pocket were seventeen beautiful letters and Ainsworth's prayer.

There were flies. *I'm not for you yet, boyo.* He wanted to shake them off but his head wouldn't shake. He wanted to wipe his face but his hand wouldn't go there. He wanted to swallow. He wasn't sure who had bandaged him but, oh, the beautiful sky.

Courage for the big things, patience for the small.

Trudge on.

Per ardua ad astra. By effort to the casualty station the station Victoria station Paddington station for Pewsey for the Downs, wild orchids tiny as bees, tiny purple leopardskin bees, lying among the eggs and bacon – no, they're not called eggs and bacon really – and the brain-quenchingly clean air up there, and sheep-cropped grass, mossy and soft. Rabbit pellets. Tiny when you're lying down. Bit damp still, isn't it? Never mind, you can lie on my coat. Tiny little plants. Vetch. Her beautiful flesh and the glory of sliding in.

'Steady on, sir . . .'

'You need a hand there, sir?'

Trudge on.

Something very dreadful happened today – *What, more dreadful than every day?* He'd heard somewhere that self-mockery was a defining symptom of sanity – *Ah, well, I'm still not mad then, something to be grateful for, but I am walking through the Valley of the Shadow of Death.* Don't frighten the horses. Horses wallowing in sinkholes of mud. Half a horse up a tree, head desiccated, legs as it were rearing in empty air, a grisly fairground ride.

And how does a rod and staff comfort me? Isn't a rod a staff? Or will God's butler, God's Barnes, the Barnes of God, God's Mrs Briggs, come and take my coat? Will his housemaids give me tea and say, 'Never mind, Purefoy, sit down, it's not so bad.'

And the others, sweet Jesus, the others, sweet Jesus, the men, the boys, the lads.

Yea, though I trudge.

What had happened? He didn't know. He hadn't died. He might die yet.

Ypres stood before him, craggy, empty, cavernous on its ramparts, shards of remnant masonry pointing to God, accusing fingers, one or two still left, shouting.

～

He stood for a while propped up against the breastworks by the canal, waiting his turn. There was a surprising little burst of clover, just by his nose, growing from between some hulks of indeterminate grey – concrete, solidified sandbag, baked mud, he didn't know which. The metal doors to the dugouts opened and slammed shut again, opened and slammed shut again. A little further along, the gas gong went. The noise seeped into Purefoy's mind and filled in any gaps. The doors slammed. He couldn't turn his head but he could tip it a little. He could see the graveyard, and the ambulance. Graveyard or ambulance, ambulance or graveyard. He heard men shouting. He leant back and looked at the little burst of clover. Leant forward again.

The doors clanged for him. He was propelled in, glanced at, labelled, sent out: ambulance.

I was a soldier. Now I am the walking wounded. I am hardly in pain. You'd think I would be. You never know, do you?

He was glad Nadine was in London. He wouldn't want her nursing him.

~

The bouncing and jouncing of the ambulance made some of the men cry out in pain. Purefoy held on, trying to keep everything still. The driver was a girl. He stared at her. Her face was big and tight, with pink cheeks and pale eyebrows. There was pale down on her cheeks, and her mouth was small. She was smoking and talking to herself firmly under her breath, concentrating. He liked her.

One of the men was saying: 'So he told me he saw a hat, flat on the mud, an Australian one, cavalry, and he didn't have an Australian one, so he reached out to get it, and he could reach it but he couldn't get it, so his mate pulled at it too and they realised, blimey, it's still attached – someone's wearing it, so they got a bit of purchase and they pulled and got the fella's face out, and they wipe his face and he's alive and they say, "Hold on there, mate, we'll get you out," and he says, "It's not just me, boys, I'm still on my horse."'

A young lad was crying.

A dark tattooed man, with gangrene seeping through the mermaid on his forearm, said: 'I heard that before.'

The first man told the story again, exactly the same, word for word.

Purefoy was unloaded and left to stare. There were women in big white hats like windmills. There was mud still but it was dried out and it was not winning. It was being dismissed. He waited. He was propelled into a tent. What a lovely great big canvas. He waited.

∼

Somebody unwrapped the bit of field bandage round Purefoy's face.

He was still young. He still had his shorn black curls, handsome crooked nose, wide flat cheeks, the eyes that girls like. Below them, his tongue flopped out, huge, straight down, untrammelled, unhindered by chin or jaw, to his clavicles. His mouth gaped, cavernous as a house with its front wall bombed off, the interior smashed and open for all to see, his epiglottis dangling like a left-behind light-fitting in the suddenly revealed back room.

Someone photographed him. Above, he looked mad and shocked, a gypsy bargee convict fighting over a dispute at a lock, a fairground man, a boxer, a foreigner. Below, there was this ragged blossoming crater, with its obscene spurting pistil.

They washed it and dressed it and tied up what there was to tie. Someone made a hole in his tongue and threaded through it a wire, with a block of wood hanging on the end. A cardboard label was taken from a drawer and pinned to his uniform: date of wound, destination, and instructions that he be kept sitting up. They injected him with morphine and saline, marked an X on his forehead, and gave him a small card.

He filled in the gaps with a short pencil.

'Nadine'.

'August 21'. He stared at that one. How could he possibly know? The nurse wrote it in for him.

He crossed out 'serious'.

He left the next one blank.

'You're meant to put the truth,' said the nurse, gently.

He glanced up at her from under his hooded eyelids. I dare say, he didn't say.

He signed: Riley Purefoy

Chapter Sixteen

Sidcup, 23 August 1917

Julia was glad that Rose was working at the Queen's Hospital now, but disappointed that she was living in – though from Rose's point of view it was probably lovely: Frognal was a fine house, with that pretty terrace and the little Italian garden. But she would have appreciated the company at Locke Hill. Mrs Bax, irritating though she was, had been company, but now she had retreated to her sister's in York, and Julia was short of things to do. After failing to go through with the surgery, and failing even to ask for Tom's return, she had visited the vicar and failed to persuade him of her need for spiritual guidance: whether or not she felt she was letting Tom down was of no interest to him as there were far more important things at stake. And every day she failed to write to Peter – how could she write to him, when she'd sent six letters asking him if he knew yet when he would be able to come home to see the baby (for that her mother would have to return him!), and had no reply? (*He has his reasons. He must have his reasons.*)

She had hoped that Rose would return home to Locke Hill

to live. She had hoped that Rose would encourage her in good works for the hospital. But, of course, Rose had no time.

'You're doing the vegetables, and that's very valuable,' Rose said. Julia ignored the patronising tone – because, really, how could she not? – and allowed herself a little glow of contribution, putting aside that Harker had done the actual work, digging up the east lawn. It was a wonderful inconvenience, providing a little blush of pride for Julia's cheek as well as good fresh vegetables for Rose's hospital (and for Peter, when at last he came, and he would be proud that Locke Hill parsnips were helping to nourish the poor wounded boys). She sent eggs, too. They have their own chickens, but they practically live on raw egg, Rose said. Because . . . well. You can imagine.

She had seen a poor wounded boy, in the distance, sitting on one of the benches that the parish council had painted hospital blue, like their hospital uniforms. She, like many of the neighbours, had found the blue of the benches a useful sign. Knowing which benches to avoid – *oh, that's not what I mean* – well, to be warned. Apparently they went to the pub too. Of course, some of them weren't that bad after they'd been operated on. Harker, in an unusually chatty moment, had said they were good lads. Not that she doubted it. *Of course they are. They're British Tommies.* But. Most of the local mothers called their children in from play when they heard 'Tipperary' whistled in the street.

Julia preferred to picture fellows in deckchairs on the veranda up there, reading Proust – they'd always meant to but never had the time before. It was nice of the Marsham-Townshends to give the house up for the duration, especially after poor Ferdinand's . . . Such lovely parties there, before the war. Or had the hospital bought the house? She wasn't sure. She did hope they were able to take advantage of the tennis courts. A tiny panic gripped her heart. Should she have given up Locke Hill? As a nursing home or something? Would that be what Peter wanted? Or was the kitchen garden enough?

Oh, don't be silly, Julia.

Was it very selfish of her to wish that she had her husband with her? She was aware of the irony: she only needed him to help with the decisions she was only called upon to make because of what had called him away.

She had meant to invite Major Gillies and the doctors, after she'd met the major at Mrs Bax's, and some of the wounded officers too, if they were well enough. And perhaps do something for the men. Concert party or something. All those poor creatures still there from the battle of the Somme, and now Ypres again. And she had got as far as arranging to visit the wounded men, playing games with them and so on, when something had happened that had made it impossible.

On a very hot afternoon, Julia had sought relief from her massed ranks of failure in the woods beyond the home meadow: a breeze, some shade, something other than her house and the damn furniture. She wanted leaves, preferably ones that would move. The walk had been unsatisfactory: no breeze, just big dark leaves limp with the weight that suggested long use, or slight sweatiness. Coming home, trailing the straw hat that had become oppressive to her, cursing the necessity of footwear, she glimpsed a figure through the narrow trunks of the beeches. Since the interlude in the pub Julia had become terribly, terribly aware of men: how beautiful they were, how hungry, how needful, how – possibly – available. It terrified her. She knew she wouldn't, of *course* she wouldn't, but what if those feelings were stirred up in her again? Even the thought of it was wrong, an insult to Peter.

The sight of a man in the woods both alarmed and thrilled her.

He was facing out towards the road across the sunlit field and hadn't seen her. His shoulders were broad and his suit was blue. It gave her heart a pang, because there was no sign of injury to his limbs.

The position of the brook and the tangled mounds of brambles made it impossible for her to avoid him.

She told herself to be civil. To be kind. To prepare herself. It would be gruesome, but it would be unforgivable to give him pain by her reaction. She prepared herself, breathing carefully. Passing him, as she had to, she would say, 'Good day,' politely, as she had to.

'Good day,' she said.

He turned, suddenly, unsmiling, unspeaking.

His face was perfect. A handsome, healthy-coloured face, regular, unmoving – shocking, actually, in its immobility. Expressionless. A mask.

Dear God, it is a mask – a real mask. Not a face at all.

The surprise of it made her utter a tiny squawk. Her squawk filled her with shame.

The face said nothing. Did nothing. Expressionless, emotionless, made of tin, painted, perfect. Only the eyes looking out. Ordinary blue eyes.

Don't make it worse.

'Oh – I'm sorry,' she said. *Smile.* She smiled. 'I didn't mean to disturb you.' *Can he talk? Am I making it worse?*

He leant forward a little, a sort of bow, a sort of nod. He didn't seem able to speak.

What in heaven's name can I do for this creature? He's not a creature! He's a man. He's just a man. He could be Peter, or Raymond Dell, or anyone.

He lifted his hand, as if to gesture politely that she could pass.

She smiled. She passed. As she passed, she was aware, as she had been with Dell, of his hunger.

'Goodbye!' she called.

Dear God, she thought. *It's not just that I don't know how to look at him without giving him pain – which I don't. It's that looking at me gives him pain. He's seen me. Seen me seeing him. I have hurt him.*

She started crying.

Perhaps he was handsome, before. Of course, beauty is a different thing for a man. But even so . . . to scare people . . . to know that you scare people . . .

~

Rose did not, in general, talk very much to Julia about her work. After the incident in the woods, Julia asked.

'Really?' said Rose. 'Do you really want to know?'

Julia did.

Rose feared the morbid, sentimental response of a woman with not enough to do. She saw that by taking Tom away Mrs Orris had left Julia purposeless, leaping about like a flapping fish. But then . . . knowing might give Julia a better sense of connection with the world. It might make her feel better. So she told her – out of pity, really.

'Well,' she said, 'this week we gave Vicarage a new face. He's a sailor. He was in a massive cordite explosion at Jutland and his face was burnt off.'

Julia was wearing the usual response: pity mixed with disgust and appalled fascination.

'He looked like an overlicked lollipop,' said Rose.

Julia stared.

'Well, he did,' said Rose, brutally. 'He looked melted. He was melted. His nose was a little twist, and his mouth was a hole . . .' *into which I have many times injected egg-flip* '. . . and no chin . . .' *a nothing of a chin: you have to hold a kidney basin underneath for when the egg-flip slops out again, before you clean out the – well, buccal cavity is the phrase, because you really can't call it a mouth* '. . . and his poor eyes . . .' *a pair of bright, lidless eyes in distorted, dragged surrounds, expressing an exemplary and hideous patience* '. . . and no eyelids – so Major Gillies designed him a masonic collar-flap on double pedicles. He measures and fits the flap first in paper and foil over a plaster cast of the face, done by one of the artists . . .'

People did not usually ask. She knew she was getting carried away.

'Pedicles?' said Julia. She pictured something architectural. *Masonic?*

Rose glanced at her. All right, then. 'Flaps of skin,' she said. She waited. 'He cuts the skin for the new face from the patient's chest.'

Julia stared. She hadn't thought for one moment, at all, about how a new face could be built. Or of what. *Dear God*.

'They're serious wounds, Julia,' Rose said, and Julia snapped: 'I know, I know – go on.'

Rose was silent for a moment to punish Julia for snapping. Then she continued: 'The principle is simple,' she said. 'The flap of skin, when it's been lifted and put into place, mustn't die or get infected. Major Gillies uses a technique invented in India two thousand years ago to replace noses. They used to cut a triangle of skin from the forehead, keeping the little section between the eyebrows attached, then twist it round and lay it over a twig or something to support it, and sew it into place.'

Julia found that her finger had wandered to her face, to her uncut jaw and her uninjected nose. 'You don't use a twig,' she said doubtfully.

'Of course not,' said Rose, dismissively, moving on. 'The important thing is that we need to keep the flap of skin that we're moving attached on one side, even by quite a little bit, so it still has blood supply.'

Julia was looking blank.

'You have to take the blood vessels with it. So it doesn't die. What Major Gillies does now is leave the flap attached by a long strip, or more than one, so he can move it quite a long way – from chest to face, for instance. Those strips of skin are the pedicles.'

Rose thrilled a little with superior knowledge and the power to shock. 'The Indian tribesmen who initiated the skin-flap technique,' she went on, 'replaced noses for people who'd had them cut off as a punishment for adultery. The method moved to Italy . . .' *Was she going to tell her this? Yes, she was.* '. . . where people lost their noses to syphilis, or in duels. But they didn't want scarred foreheads, so a new technique was invented where the flap would be taken from the inside of the patient's forearm . . .' Rose gestured to the area on herself '. . . but because this was before the advent of the long pedicle, the patient's arm had to be strapped to his head in a kind of straitjacket, for as long as it took the flap to attach to the face.' She held her own forearm up to her face, smooth internal skin against her nose. 'Try it!' Julia tentatively raised her arm. 'It took months,' said Rose. 'They looked like children pretending to be elephants. Major Gillies has a picture of someone wearing one in the seventeenth century.'

Julia held her arm to her nose. Already her shoulder creaked as she brought her wrist far enough over.

Rose watched her. 'Isn't it clever? What they invent. Did you know Carrel learnt his vascular suture technique from the lacemakers of Valenciennes?'

Julia had not known that. She wasn't entirely sure what a suture was. Or how Rose had become cleverer than her, as well as more useful. How had that happened?

'What happened next?' she asked, lowering her arm. 'To the sailor.'

'All right – where were we? Major Gillies lifted the skin flap from the chest, and turned it, and applied it. It reaches up over his nose, like a bandit's neckerchief in a cowboy picture. Then he split a gap for the mouth, and turned the skin round it out a little, so that the lips will be red and soft, as they should be.' Rose indicated the process on her own face, watching Julia, who was white. 'Enough?' she asked, almost amused. The physical nightmare of it meant very little to her now. You proceed on the understanding that this is how things are, and you make them better. They were all exceptionally good at it, and a vital part of being good at it was never thinking about it. And always in the back of Rose's mind was pervasive gratitude that she wasn't in France, having to be a decent nurse in a tent in the rain under fire, with more casualties arriving and dead boys piling up.

'No,' said Julia, frowning. 'Tell me more.'

'Well. Today he invented something quite new,' Rose said, recalling how the major had swung into surgery, cheerful and relaxed as always, and his team as usual had felt their capacities and their morale and their confidence and their personal virtues rise up in a wave to greet him, as if chorusing 'We *will* be good enough for you!'

'He's never tried to operate on damage like this before – but practically every day, he has to operate on new kinds of damage. Each face may be to the same basic design, but they are all different . . .' *and each wound is its own particular version of chaos. There's no telling what will be required to restore order to a particular chaotic surface, let alone to the damage beneath the surface. Really, he's a genius.* 'And the wounds are different – flesh and bone are perhaps no longer there; perhaps a field surgeon has dragged the remaining skin across to close the hole at any cost, and the features have been pulled around and have adhered, all wrong and twisted. So, the first step of any operation is to undo previous healing, to reconstitute the wound as it initially was.'

222

Julia balked. 'What do you mean?'

'Reconstitute the original wound,' said Rose. 'When they have healed up wrongly.'

Julia stared.

'The soldiers arrive, partly healed,' Rose said, 'and we have to unheal them. Open them up again. Well – we have to wait until they are fully healed, then open the wound up again, then let it heal again, unhindered, and then Major Gillies can start to rebuild.'

'That's appalling,' said Julia. 'They think they're healing, and then . . .'

'Yes,' said Rose.

'It must take for ever.'

'Yes.'

'What about the pain?'

'Well, there're various methods. Today it was rectal ether, on the table,' said Rose. Julia didn't know what that was. Rose smiled – exasperated but amused. Even now, what was everyday in hospitals across Europe could not be mentioned in drawing rooms. 'Up their – you know,' she said, and Julia raised her eyebrows, and said, 'Oh!' Julia, who was married, and had a child, to Rose, who wasn't, and didn't.

'But what about for every day?' Julia asked. 'Are they all completely addicted to morphine?'

'I don't believe Vicarage is,' said Rose, mildly.

Julia was frowning. Rose considered letting her off. It was, of course, all terribly extreme when you weren't used to it.

Am I telling Julia all this to punish her? she thought suddenly. The thought thrilled her. 'So,' she continued, after a pause. 'Major Gillies has a very neat plan: in a couple of months, he's going to apply a second flap like a mask all across the eyes, made from the original pedicles – once they've finished their job supplying blood to the mask on the lower half. But today – this is the exciting bit – today, looking at Vicarage, and his pedicles, he said they reminded him of flying buttresses, and someone said, "Yes, or guy-ropes holding his face in position," and Gillies said, "Or pipes bringing water, an irrigation system," because the edges were rolling inwards, as if the flat strips wanted to be tubes. So that gave him the idea. Tubes. If he stitched them into tubes, the underside, the red interior skin, would be kept inside; the dirt of outside could not reach in; the blood vessels could run through safely, protected. It is brilliant. It was marvellous to see the whole process: first he thought of it, then he did it. He just stitched the pedicles where they rolled into tubes. He said . . .' and Rose gave a little laugh '. . . that Vicarage looked like a banyan from the jungle in Burma.' She was remembering the moment, how she had handed Major Gillies a gauze, and held her breath, and watched him hold his needle aloft, a tiny sword.

Julia was blinking. 'Well, no wonder you're so engrossed!' she said, finally, a little crossly. 'You sound half in love with the whole thing. Major Gillies and all.'

Rose thought about that later. Gillies, and all the other surgeons, and of Morestin, and Valadier in the first years of the war, operating out of a Rolls-Royce behind the lines in France, holding important generals to ransom in his dental chair till they'd give permission for his plans and requirements for facial-injury treatment. Rose could see that it was . . . not exactly fortunate, *opportune*, rather, that such brave, inventive men should coincide with this never-ending supply of patients, who had no other option, so that they could power ahead, with them, in the progress of this new art.

~

It was not so far from Locke Hill back to the hospital, but it was far enough to raise a glow. The stout chestnut horse plodding down the lane in front of Rose's bicycle wore great black leather blinkers, bats' wings steering his big eyes, keeping his attention on the road ahead. His big hairy feet trudged, his driver called to him, and Rose pedalled a little harder, wanting to overtake. She could not go fast enough without indignity so she would have to wait till they reached the Green. The effort was already curling her hair and she could feel her cheeks going pink.

For a moment she thought longingly of pantaloons. When she was in a position of power (and the thought made her laugh) she would transform nurses' uniforms, give them shorter, practical skirts, like the girls in town, neater, more compact headwear, and more pockets on the apron. But she did not believe she would ever be in a position of power, despite her long service, natural aptitude and the kind of ambition that would be frowned on in a woman anywhere else. She parked her bicycle under the oak tree behind the kitchens, nosing it in among papery brown leaves on the hard summer earth, and walked back into her real life. She returned to the ward, which looked more like a cricket pavilion than anything else. The hospital, spread across the gardens of the big house, was like a series of giant interlinked garden sheds, all windows and wooden beams and panels, painted white and connected by covered walkways and ramps among the ancient trees and smooth, desiccated lawns. She read in the paper about how wet it was in Flanders but the weather here had been wonderful. She half expected the smell of linseed oil and liniment, and to be helping with tea for the first eleven and their mothers. Cucumber sandwiches. Grass-stained cricket whites and willow trees. Institutions for boys, after all. The officers at least felt at home here. It was just like the public schools they were at so recently.

Vicarage, a curly-haired youth, freckled, no doubt, originally, had been set up on a plaster prop, to keep his head forward so the neck was flexed, and the flap of skin not too tense. Even so, it was a little tight at the bridge of the nose, its highest point, and it slipped a little, with a risk of gangrene, but no other untoward result occurred. He was sleeping.

The boys were all sleepy. Whatever she had said to Julia, morphia was an issue. (And, along with all the eggs, it put their bowels in a dreadful state.)

She looked in on Private Jamison to say goodnight.

He waved at her, and handed her a note. It read, 'how is sailor vicarage?'

'It went well,' she said. 'Major Gillies stitched his pedicles in a new way, into tubes.' And she wished she hadn't. Jamison's grey eyes shivered like a cat's-paw of wind on a calm sea, a tiny receding, it looked to her, a tiny gesture.

When a man can't speak, other aspects of him become eloquent.

They both knew that if Jamison had lost his jaw at some other battle than the Somme, at some later battle, as much later as possible, then his chances would have been . . . better. Gillies knew it, and minded immensely. Since Jamison, he had done it in more stages: made an initial mandible of vulcanite or celluloid, then replaced that with an organic graft later, when the flaps had healed. Jamison, kind-eyed, unhelpable, was a monument to fallibility.

He scribbled: 'Good.'

Rose smiled at him. Very early on, Jamison had passed her a note:

> So remaineth these three
> faith hope and charity
> and the greatest of these is a sense of humour

which she had pinned up behind the nurses' desk, until Miss Black, having read it and laughed, told her she had to take it down, but not before Major Gillies saw it.

'That's the ticket, Rose,' he had said – the first thing he had ever said directly to her. When she thought about how the boys got by, out there, the trenches, she said to herself, Well, this is it, really, isn't it? Whatever leads Gillies to be like Gillies, and Jamison to be like Jamison, that's how they manage.

～

'Tell me more,' said Julia, the following week

I knew it, thought Rose. *Morbid sentimental reaction.* She didn't want Julia to be interested in her patients. They were hers. But she couldn't resist the rare pleasure of feeling superior to her.

'All right,' she said. 'I'll tell you about Jamison. He came in from the Somme with his jaw shot off. Major Gillies made him a new one from the cartilage and bone of one of his ribs, fixed in place with iron wire, and he brought down a double flap from the top of his head, like the flaps of a Russian hat.'

Julia blinked. 'What happened to him?' she asked.

'The operation took a long time. It was difficult to seal off the junction of the pedicle and the embedded section, and the hair growing made things difficult. The rib started suppurating, and reabsorbing. Actually, there is no new chin any more . . .' There was just an infected double flap, a flaccid skin hammock for the sequestrum, which no longer held it in place, and a wound drain, and a couple of bits of wire and some horsehair stitches, which would have to be removed.

'So what will happen to him?' Julia whispered.

'We have to get rid of the infection, and see what's left, and Major Gillies will think of something. Jamison is a very strong-minded man. Very humorous.'

'But might he die?' Julia asked.

'Yes, Julia, he might.'

'But wouldn't that break your heart?'

Rose could feel her cheekbones tingling. 'Yes, Julia,' she said. 'It would.'

Rose knew why her heart didn't break. Because she was working in an area of construction, and the busier she kept, the less scope there was for fretting, dwelling and despairing at the never-ending flow of smashed-up boys whose reconstructed faces, miracles though they were, would always, one way or another, put them on the blue bench.

~

Julia was hopelessly, passively aware of her hopeless passivity, her passive hopelessness. The magnificence of Rose, of the surgeons, of the wounded men, shamed her. Even Harker, bearing heroic baskets of vegetables, and Mrs Joyce, wielding sheets and doing whatever it was she was doing half the time with the Women's League . . . What? Was she envying the servants?

The day after her conversation with Rose, while drinking tea, a fury descended on Julia, and she summoned Harker to take her to the station. She rode on the train in fury, crossed London in fury, stalked across Paddington station in fury on to the second train. At Newbury she was able – amazed at herself! – to accept a lift in a grubby agricultural wagon going via Froxfield.

She strode, sweating and with bits of straw on her skirt, up the lane to her childhood home.

The fury stalled at the wooden gate. The energy flooded from her limbs. What was she going to do? Declare something? What? *What?*

She was ridiculous, and she had come all this way so that her mother could tell her so. And there was her mother, among the delphiniums.

'Julia? What on earth are you doing here? Why on earth didn't you let us know you were coming? Really, darling

– we could have sent someone to fetch you from the station. You're quite scarlet in the face – you look absurd.'

I am absurd, Julia thought.

Tom would not greet her. When brought from the house, and put on the lawn and instructed to go to his mother because 'Look, Julia, he's crawling now!' he sat lumpily on his padded bottom, and cried.

Julia did not know how to call to him, and make the pretty noises babies like. She remembered the passionate love in his eyes when he had been a few days old; the magical time when they had been the same person.

She pretended not to mind.

Later, she watched as Tom tumbled over, banged his head and tearfully held his arms out to Mrs Orris. She wanted to run to him, but the instinct was warped somehow, and she did not know what to do. Mrs Orris picked him up, cooing and comforting him. Looking over his head, she gave Julia a terrible, piteous, hypocritical smile. Then she said, 'No, Tom, darling, you should go to your mother.' Tom clung to her all the more. He lifted his face and stared balefully at Julia, with a finger in his little mouth.

Julia profoundly desired to slap one and seize the other. But she knew that wasn't right either. It came upon her in that moment that she did hate her mother, she really did, and despite everything she was justified . . . and she shrank inside like the taste of pith. Well. Of course. She'd left it all far too long, and she should never have let it happen. And now it was too late. She smiled boldly at her mother and her son, and blinked.

Chapter Seventeen

London, September 1917

Riley's field card to Nadine arrived at Bayswater Road on a very warm morning. Barnes brought it in to Jacqueline with breakfast.

She read it, of course, then put it down pettishly on her tray. *Why has he sent this to Nadine? Why not to his mother?*

'What's that, darling?' Robert said, from behind his *Daily Chronicle*. He said he read it for the reports from Russia, but Jacqueline thought he was developing sympathies. So far his interest in the war had been limited to annoyance that people didn't want to listen to Schubert, because he was German, when it was obvious to anyone with ears that the Octet was perfect music for cheering everyone up, but lately he had been growing excited. 'Perhaps Communism might be a good thing!' he had said. 'Well, it might!'

'Riley Purefoy's been wounded,' she said.

'Is he all right?' Robert said.

'Well, I shouldn't think so, darling, if he's been wounded, would you?'

Robert said nothing.

'Well, it doesn't say. Only that it's slight. So I suppose it is.'

'Hope he *is* all right,' Robert said. It didn't occur to him to ask why or how the information was reaching his wife, and for that she was glad. She would prefer him to have no opinions on the matter because she had quite enough of her own. So many young girls – and women old enough to know better – were going quite mad, sex-mad. Not Nadine, of course. Though Nadine might have been sex-mad for all Jacqueline knew. Nadine hadn't told her anything for months.

But she was not going to marry Riley Purefoy. A woman's safety is in who she marries: a mother's responsibility was to ensure . . . A memory swept her: the violin-playing man at the bottom of the stairwell at home in Paris. Chantal not being there any more. Their mother's eternal silence. Nobody had ever told Jacqueline what had happened, and now everyone was dead or lost.

Nadine was not going to be a war bride repenting at leisure her wedding to a charismatic nobody. Even a wounded charismatic nobody. Even if it was Riley.

She ate some toast, not even bothering to be sad about the ridiculous smallness of the piece of butter Mrs Barnes had given her, and looked at the paper. All bad. Dreadful. She turned the page.

Damn! If his card has come here, does that mean I'm going to have to write to Mrs Purefoy?

Jacqueline decided to ignore the whole thing. It wasn't a bad wound. It wasn't her business.

'Of course, darling, we all do,' she said.

Subject closed.

~

A week later, a letter arrived from Mrs Purefoy.

Dear Mrs Waveney,

I do not know if you would have heard but Riley has been injured and is at the Queen's Hospital in Sidcup. I am so grateful he is out of the way of further harm but having not seen him yet we don't know how bad it is. I wanted to let you know as you have meant so much to him in earlier years.

Yours faithfully,

Bethan Purefoy

Jacqueline felt a bit churlish. But she still wasn't going to tell Nadine. She hadn't sent on the card, and she wouldn't send on the further news. It was her duty to protect her daughter from a very attractive boy in very dangerous times. The most unlikely girls were getting into trouble. Not everyone could be Isadora Duncan.

However, Barnes had noticed the arrival of the card. He noticed, too, that it was still on Mrs Waveney's bedside table ten days later. He had read it, felt the usual flicker of envy and resentment that Riley provoked in him. He noticed Mrs Purefoy's letter too. His eyesight had not been good enough for the army but there had been nothing wrong with it that day.

Barnes had felt the changing of the times around his dull and steady life. He and Mrs Barnes had had some little

233

conversations about it, discussed some possibilities, some dreams for later on, should circumstances allow, involving savings, the south coast, and a small guesthouse. And he felt quite strongly that these people shouldn't be allowed to get away with thinking they could run other people's lives. On the eleventh day he slipped the card and the letter into his pocket, readdressed them over tea in the kitchen, and slid them into the letterbox on the corner of Queensway.

Chapter Eighteen

Sidcup, September 1917

Captain Purefoy was one of several arrivals that day, all of them underfed, exhausted, stinking and pus-faced. He was unravelled and stripped and cleaned; the general *nettoyage* of the man and the wound. Sluicing and drainage, carbolic soap and clean pyjamas. The starting of the process of putting to rights. Packing, repacking, ligating, temporary splint supports, maxillary and mandibular, to hold him together until impressions could be made for a more accurate appliance. Discussions, plans, surgeons, doctors, nurses, orderlies, VADs. The young man who had been the arrowhead of the system of destruction now became the epicentre of an industry of reconstruction. He who must destroy had become he who must be mended.

∼

He wanted to swallow. He tried to move his turgid tongue. They'd taken the bloody weight off it, thank Christ. But there was new stuff in his mouth. New alien stuff.

It took a little effort to control the line of thought. He made the effort, and failed.

He could hear that he gurgled when he breathed. He started coughing. Kind of coughing. There was always liquid, not saliva exactly, but a combination of whatever it was, and a dried-out antiseptic taste.

It seemed best to go back to sleep.

~

He wanted to swallow.

Coughed and gurgled.

Pain, actually – not much. But the wrongness. A lot of the sense of wrongness. He knew his head was wrong. What about the rest of him?

Itch by his eye – he scratched.

Opened his eyes. Light, white, alarming. Closed again. Hospital, of course.

Did I let them down?

Scratched again. Hands were all right. He opened and closed his fingers, valuing them.

Well. He ran an inventory. Hands, legs, arms, feet. Torso. Dick? He tightened the muscles that could make it bounce. Was it there? *Have I not thought about this before? Is my brain shaken up?*

Yes, it was there. And would it still work?

Ha ha.

Self-mockery. So he was sane. *I've had that thought before.*

What happened?

I don't remember.

What did I do?

I don't remember.

Did I let them down?

~

I didn't die.
I suppose I should open my eyes.
He didn't.

~

His mind and his thoughts were a kind of sucking quagmire. The words emerged and sank again, stretching and pulling away. They meant nothing to him. He closed his eyes: the black and the scarlet, the shooting stars, the sunflowers.

Opened them: the blank white calm, the polite living people, the words muffled in glass.

Closed them again.

'Plenty of rest,' said the doctor. 'Keep him well fed. No visitors.'

This is where I am.

He dreamt of star shells, still looking beautiful, high and silent. Starry starry night. The star shells became the painting, and he was with Sir Alfred at the Grafton Gallery, and everyone was saying, *Oh no, oh no, oh no . . .*

~

A nurse woke him – intelligent-looking, with a dry expression and bony hands.

'Lunch,' she said. 'Lovely egg-flip. Sit up for me, would you?'

He sat up.

She held his head, found the gap in his bandages, irrigated

237

his mouth – *Do I have a mouth?* – with a big steel syringe. She tipped the detritus into a kidney basin, white enamel, white gauze, *I am fucking helpless here,* wiped his – what there was. *What is there?* He couldn't spit. She cleaned him up. Tipped his head back – *I have a neck* – so he stared up at the ceiling, and poured the slop slowly, delicately, as best could be done, from the spout of the cup into the throat.

Why am I being fed like a fucking baby?

He coughed. Kind of.

~

Scraps came back to him. Not the battle, or the getting of the wound, but him on a train, smelling his own infection; tasting his own wound. The taste of his own dying flesh in his own mouth. Throwing up, at a CCS, in ambulances, on trains, on a boat? Delirium with interludes of vomiting. How kindly everyone had tended him. His head wrapped in bandages. The bloody weight hanging from his tongue to stop him swallowing it.

Now he tasted of something drying, alcoholic, stagnant.

'Don't you worry, old fellow,' someone had said. Surgeon? Australian voice, or New Zealand. 'We'll fix you up. You're in the right place, and you'll be all right by the time we've done with you.'

He was all right. He had walked. He had, hadn't he? He had got through the mud, the giant corpse-studded cowpat; he had stayed on the duckboards, past the gaunt dead black burnt wet stalagmite trees . . . a tank upended like a shipwreck, great stern up in the air, like a tufty duck on the Round Pond – tufted duck, Mum said, tufty duck, he insisted, tufty duck, tufty duck. Lovely little tufty ducks, with their bright yellow eyes like the rings you stick on round the holes in a piece of file paper.

All that he remembered. He remembered his name, and three wooden crosses upright in a pool of dirty water.

There was something else. Oh, there was plenty else.

He couldn't remember what had happened. He didn't know how he had been wounded. He didn't seem to be able to talk. Not dumb like shell-shock. (Officers don't get hysterical. They're too dignified – who had said that? Oh, Ainsworth.) It wasn't psychological. He just didn't seem to have the apparatus. Instead, he had a hideous, panicky, creeping claustrophobia.

~

He dreamt he was making mayonnaise with Jacqueline Waveney. She didn't believe any Englishwoman could add the olive oil correctly. Drip, drip, drip, so as not to curdle the egg yolks. The yellowness turned into Sir Alfred's yellow oil paint. The swirl, the oil. And the sunflowers of Van Gogh. Cadmium Naples Zinc Chrome. In the old days they used egg yolks for egg tempera. Country egg yolks for robust complexions; city egg yolks for pale ladies and saints. Botticelli Veronese Piero della Francesca.

She'd let Riley do it. Found it funny that he was interested.

'What are you going to do when you grow up, Riley?'

'Painter like Sir Alfred,' he'd said, and she'd laughed. 'Or a cook?' he'd said.

She'd laughed at that too.

~

Riley stared at the nurse to make her look at him.

She looked. *Handsome eyes,* she thought.

He lifted his arm and moved his hand in a writing motion, like an officer asking for the bill in a Parisian brasserie.

'Pen and paper?' she asked.

He blinked.

She was pleased. He wanted to talk to her.

He wrote:

I assume I'm in hospital.

I must be. I tasted the egg. It was real. And she's still here.

'You are,' she said. 'The Queen's Hospital in Sidcup.'

Blighty!

He wrote:

Will I die?

'Of course, in the end,' she said. 'But not of this.'

He liked her for that. He wrote,

Thanks.

'You're welcome,' said Rose.

He wrote:

How long?

'Since you arrived? A week,' she said, and she smiled, and said: 'I'll get the doctor. He can explain.'

～

A tall, handsome man arrived, clean, healthy, tired. There was something of the midnight oil about him, and that medical coolness off which women's attempts at thanks slip and slide, and against which men's attempts to match up look ridiculous.

'Major Gillies,' he said, introducing himself. 'I'm your surgeon.'

I am here. Hospital. This is the reality. Hold it. Gillies Gillies Gillies – remember that.

'How are you feeling, Captain?'

Riley thought about it. *Not the slightest idea.* He flicked his eyes up.

'Do you know what's happened to you?'

Riley felt a tiny little snort in his nose.

'You've lost quite a lot of your jaw to a gunshot wound, Captain,' Gillies said. 'And we're going to put you back together.'

You'd think you'd remember that, wouldn't you?

He wanted to ask more – *what happened? Did I . . .* But he didn't want to ask as well. And – no one can help being shot. He wanted to know about the others.

Or maybe not.

The tall man was watching for a response. Riley had no response – or no idea how to give it. Gillies continued: 'This is Tonks, and this is Marcus. The first thing we need to do is get a good look at you, see what we're dealing with. Marcus here is going to take some photographs, and later Tonks is going to draw you. Don't worry, he's quite talented. That way, we don't have to disturb you more than we need, so you can heal better. So we're going to take a look at you now . . .'

241

Riley had seen Tonks before. Sir Alfred knew him. Unmistakable man: like an eagle. He was often at exhibitions. He didn't like the Impressionists.

With unutterable tenderness, the major unpinned and unwrapped Riley's face, passing the bandages like streamers to the bony-handed nurse.

I'm so sorry but it's not convenient, thought Riley. *I have an appointment at two thirty in Buenos Aires.*

He lay there while they uncovered his face. Words washed around him: mandible, masseter, ramus, coronoid process. They probed him gently: lifting, turning. Someone set up the great caravan of the camera with its hood, and its lights.

'Because you have had an infection, we have to let it heal up completely,' Gillies was saying, 'before we can get to work remodelling you.'

I am no longer a man who does things, Riley thought. *I am a man who things are done to.*

Major Gillies explained: 'You're going to be here for quite a while, but remember, you're not ill, you're wounded. When you feel up to it, take a stroll. There's a library up at the house. The gardens are nice. Plenty of chaps about.'

Riley saw the gardens when the VAD took him to Tonks's studio to be drawn. Plodding the wooden walkways, he saw the deep green wetness of incipient English autumn, the shrubs dripping in the rain, the moss under the hedge, the collapsed browning stems of the summer flowers, the deserted lawns.

1917, 1917, 1917. 1917.

Tonks didn't show Riley the picture when it was done.

Chapter Nineteen

London, Autumn 1917

The card, when it came; the news it brought – those words that were not his, his words filling in the gaps, the card that he had touched, the fact of him on the same land as her, that he couldn't be hurt any more now, that he was *here*, and she could go to him . . . It filled Nadine with a flooding energy, a magnetic, panicky feeling, and a sense of being hurled towards him: a physical propulsion. Reason left her mind. No thought at all, other than 'be with him'.

Sister recognised it, and granted her leave. One day, in a month's time. Nadine had physically to restrain herself.

'Take it easy,' said Jean.

'Can't,' said Nadine. Her breath was quick and tight all the time, and her knee flickered when she sat. So many still coming in from the Salient. She had only two hours off now on a Sunday. Sidcup and back in two hours? She was filled with mad, fluttering joy. He was safe and everything was possible again.

'He's in the best place,' said Jean. 'He'll be getting better all the time.'

~

Riley, propped up, was staring at Jarvis, opposite him. Jarvis had a recent and well-healing flap over what used to be his nose. The lump of flesh was perhaps twice the size a nose would be, waxy, massive, repulsive. It looked slightly as if he were holding on to his normal nose in a big waxy hammy fist. Every person who stopped by the bed told him that the swelling would go down and the flap settle. At the top, where the bridge would be, where the pedicle from the forehead twisted down, a single tight little horsehair stitch was visible, holding the new flesh in, forming the top point of the triangular nose-to-be. Across the forehead was a wet, naked purple scar marking out where the skin had been taken. Jarvis was repulsive.

Riley did his best not to let that show. He did not want Jarvis to read in his eyes how frightening, how repellent, how ridiculous he looked. Riley kept his gaze steady, unjudgemental. But then Riley had not been here long. To those who had, Jarvis looked pretty good, well on the way, a tidy piece of work.

Riley did not know what he, Riley, looked like. *Headful of bandages, an Egyptian mummy . . .*

And under the bandages?

~

It would be better, Riley thought, *if they just came round with a machine gun and shot us all. We all know that life is*

244

not sacred any more, and hasn't been for a few years now. You can't send us back to the front – we'd scare the horses and Lower Morale. Just fucking shoot us.

He thought: *Fucking fucking bastard bastard war fucking bastard life fucking war fuck fuck fuck.*

Once, he thought *Will I talk? Will I eat? Will I sing? Will I kiss?*

Then, *Don't be ridiculous.*

After a week or two, he started on *Why me?* One of Locke's arias had been haunting his mind, the woman, singing – it was in Italian, of course, and Locke had translated it that night he hadn't wanted to go to the brothel with him . . . I lived for art, I lived for love, I never did harm to a living soul . . . *Oh, but I did . . . we did, didn't we?* . . . in the hour of sorrow, why, oh, Lord, why, why do you pay me back like this?

An eye for an eye, a tooth for a tooth, a face for not even knowing how many men you've killed. And for forgetting what it was those dying Tommies wanted you to say, and to whom. And who they were. And for not reporting Burgess, and not saving Dowland, or Ferdinand, or Couch, Bloom Atkins Wester Green or, dear God, Ainsworth, and for leading them slowly into gunfire, for walking on by as they drowned in craters of mud, for being impatient when the boy wanted water, and for being promoted, and for forgetting, and for leaving home, and for ingratitude, and for squandering love . . .

It may be harder to die here than there but it can probably be done. Burgess, where are you when I need you?

❧

Major Gillies came round again and Riley, more alert, got a better idea of him. He was the boss, the hero, the surgeon. Nice-looking, easy-moving man, cheerful and capable and very busy. He said: 'Captain, you're accustomed to giving orders, and you're accustomed to taking orders. If you put your faith in us, we can help you. If you don't, we'll help you anyway, but it won't succeed as well.'

Riley watched him as he spoke, his mouth moving, the tongue inside, the delicate movements of the lips making the clear, precise words, the characteristic drawl, the idiosyncrasies that made the voice individual and placed the man – educated, intelligent, *au fait,* a touch Anzac, reliable, eloquent, unflappable, warm. The jaw going up and down, up and down. He seemed to be absolutely serious.

Had he had a face to laugh with, Riley would have laughed. *O nice-looking, skilful, kind doctor – what the fuck is the point? Why are you even bothering? Half of my face is missing. You said so yourself. Missing in action . . . still in the filthy mud of Passchendaele . . . Half of my face is dead, doctor, lost without a grave. Known only to God. A jawbone of the Great War. Thank you so much, but – don't make me laugh. I am detritus now. Leave me be.*

The bony-handed nurse, Rose, came to check his dressings. 'Healing up nicely,' she said. 'You'll soon be ready for your first op. You could go for a walk if you like – it's nice out. Take a look at the workshops. They make toys, furniture, all sorts. Embroidery! We've a chicken farm, too. You don't want to lie around all day.'

Riley rolled his head, his eyes, towards her. *Shut up.*

Women's work and chickens. Don't you know all I know how to do is kill?

'If you stay here and brood,' she said, 'you'll make things worse.' She was upset. Everyone was upset. A nineteen-year-old boy had taken off in the night, drunk a bottle of whisky, and thrown himself under a train. They were angry – with him, with themselves. Rose reminded herself all the time that though the staff had grown used to it, the patients could not. And they must not become used to it. *They won't be able to operate in civilian life if they become habituated loafers, dependent on the regime here. They have been so destroyed . . . It is not just their faces.*

'Anyway,' she said. *You can't force it on them. It takes time.* 'Letters,' she said, and she handed over two. He let them drop on the bed.

She looked at him, a *now now* look. 'I'll read them to you if you like,' she said. He glanced up at her. His hooded eyes were a crush of diamonds. *Damn you*, she thought. *Damn you, damn you.*

She tore open the first letter, neatly, forcefully. '"My Dear Son,"' she read. 'It's from your mother!'

Yes, he thought. *I gathered.*

'"I hope this finds you as well as you can be. Your father and I don't understand why you have not written to us but we are sure you have your reasons and we want to say we are thinking of you and hoping for your recovery. We hear that the Queen's Hospital is a very good one and that the surgeons there are doing very good work, there was an article about it in the paper which Susan kept for us. It all sounds very modern with things changing so fast. We had

247

the letter saying you would not be having visitors yet and we were sorry, because whatever happens, dear Riley, we want to visit you. Your father says you must be worried being wounded in the face in case you look a fright, but I told him you know no face of yours could scare us off. I hope I am right. Take care of yourself, my son, and please write and tell us when we can come for a visit the girls send you kisses we have not told them yet it is your face but you know they will always love you something rotten from your old mum.'"

Rose thought: *That's a family who will help if they can. They won't make it harder than it has to be.* And at the same time she thought: *But it's not a letter from an officer's mother.* She looked at Riley again. When a man can't talk, and wears uniform, and bandages, you don't know who he is. She glanced at the postmark: west London. A west London man. She wondered what his voice had been like.

'Do you want to write back to her?' she asked, and he stared at her, his eyes eloquent of something she could not decipher. She handed him the notebook.

He took it, and dropped it on the bed.

She opened the second letter, looked at the first lines, then handed it to him. 'Not sure I should read this one,' she said, with a smile.

He glanced at it. Saw the writing. 'My darling darling . . .'

Tears started from his eyes – no noise, no sobs, just sudden tears.

Rose closed her eyes a second. 'Captain Purefoy . . .' she said.

He picked the notebook up in a sudden swoop and wrote:

My name is Riley.

'All right,' she said.
Then he wrote:

And I would have thought you'd have learnt by now not to pity.

She read it and flinched, and he was already regretting it when she grinned grimly, and said gaily, 'Ninety-nine per cent there. Ninety-nine per cent no feeling at all, you'll be glad to hear, just cheerful efficiency . . .'

He looked up at her. She looked at him. Their eyes met. He wrote:

Sorry.

'Mmm,' she said. 'So am I.' She smiled and made a face – to change the mood, for God's sake, change the mood. 'So,' she said. 'Shall I read it?' She wanted to, now. She was curious.

He gestured a helpless yes with his hand.

Rose read fluently, carefully, more or less without expression: '"My darling darling, Oh my dear, knowing that you are here, so close, and that I cannot come to you – oh god I think this is the cruellest thing of the war so far, such a stupid unnecessary little extra cruelty . . . as if the Chelsea can't do without me, as if there – oh, it's just that nursing these boys I don't know has been enough for me till now, but now I know you are within my reach and need nursing and I am not there to help you – agh! Please dearest Riley let me know when I can come to you. I am going mad here, dropping things, not sleeping, not eating. Mad! Jean says she has never seen a girl so lovesick. It's not just my mind – my body, my heart, my dreams, my digestive system! All shouting Riley, Riley, he's in trouble, go to him . . . I can't shut them up. My poor colleagues here are sick of the sight of me, and of the sound of your name. Apparently I am sleeptalking now! Shouting your name in the night, Jean says. And, she says, rolling over and hugging her!! Which I deny, because I will never ever roll over and hug anyone in the night but you, my darling—"'

A small fine blush rose in Rose

"'But I can't even start to think about that area, and you know why . . . But to be stuck here knowing some other girl will be nursing you . . ."'

Rose smiled and glanced at Riley. "'Say hello to her from me, tell her I say, 'Look after him well, he is so beloved, take care of him.' I hope she isn't pretty . . ."'

Rose grinned.

'. . . Not too pretty anyway – Riley I am imagining what might have happened to your darling face, you said on the card that it wasn't serious, I wrote to your mother but haven't heard back yet – my love you know I don't care about it, don't you? Even if you are going to look like a gargoyle for the rest of your life I don't—"'

Riley touched her arm. He shook his head.

'Are you sure?' asked Rose.

He took the letter from her. Looked at it. Finished reading it.

Folded it.

Very carefully, he tore it in half, and in half again.

'Oh,' said Rose.

He cast her a warning glance.

'Oh,' she said again, very quietly. 'Oh, no.'

He closed his eyes.

Going about her business with her kidney basins and her Lysol, her squares of gauze and her cheerful demeanour, Rose kept thinking about the girl who had written the letter: a nursing VAD like Rose, a girl who was in love, so lively, so funny, so open. Rose hadn't known a love letter might be like that. She'd always thought of a love affair as a matter between two opponents, like Peter and Julia, where poor Julia prances and dances in ever madder circles, desperate for his attention, unable to see that he has none to give, and he, ashamed, tries to hold her off without hurting her, but does . . . Poor Julia, who is no one when she is not desired; who is only beautiful, who has no other woman to be. *I am better off than Julia*, Rose realised, in a glancing shard of illumination. *I really am.*

. . . and so truthful! She had thought that in love truth was a weapon, and subterfuge was the norm, military intelligence in the battle for power, the hunt, resistance and pursuit, and the twisted inverted pursuit that went on before the war in which a girl like her, who nobody pursues, has to trap somebody into wanting her, or fail in her duty of being desired . . . Oh, thank God that was all over. She had never confided in a dance partner or a male friend in her life.

But that letter . . . it was more as if the two of them were on the same side. Two of them in the struggle together, and the rest of the world is the enemy. Not looking into each other's eyes, but looking at the world through the same eyes. And rolling over in the night. Her skin shivered and prickled. *For goodness' sake, Rose!* She shook the image away.

Oh, that poor girl. She could have *no idea* what she was letting herself in for. The families and sweethearts never did. Between pressuring him with hope, drowning him in sorrowful sympathy, suffocating him with help, being angry with him, coddling him, fearing him, avoiding him, proving so inadequate that *he* ends up having to help *them* – Jamison had written once, 'The thing is, Rosy, they seem to think I know what to do about it all. They don't realise I'm as lost as they are.'

Well. That poor girl. Good luck to her.

When Bethan Purefoy turned up, unannounced, Sister and Rose were both elsewhere, distracted by some new arrivals, gangrenous, with the mud of the Salient still on them. Riley's mother slipped alone into the ward, which was silent but for the low, snuffly noises of men who don't breathe as they used to. Standing by the door, looking around for Riley, for her boy, she saw first Jarvis, and his great nose.

That's not right, she thought. *Is that – that's not even real . . .*

But it was, so she started screaming, screaming and screaming, trying to silence herself, appalled at herself even as the sound came bellowing out, but incapable of stopping. Riley, who had been asleep, was woken; he saw his mother standing, shocked, her arms spread against the double doors, and the choked-up parts of the machinery of his voice instinctively, inaudibly, called out to her, a hideous croaky noise, *Mum, Mamma!*

She saw all the men of the ward, scarred, bandaged, swollen, sliced, shattered, festooned with pedicles: staring at her, this interloper, this pair of healthy, well-set eyes from the outside world, come in to tell them the truth – that they were terrifying, pitiable, horrible. She clapped her hand over her mouth, held it in place with the other over the top, but the screaming kept coming out, through her fingers, into their ears as they lay there, helpless.

She fell back through the double doors, still gasping and moaning as she collapsed against the wall in the corridor outside. The orderly was with her. Rose and another nurse came running. It had only taken a few seconds.

'I'm sorry I'm so sorry I'm so sorry,' she was saying. 'I'm sorry I'm so sorry I'm so sorry.' Rose was incandescent with rage. Who had let her in? Who was she? Nobody goes into the wards without preparation, without accompaniment.

Bethan gathered herself. 'I didn't even see him,' she said. 'My son. I can't . . . can I?'

Rose looked at her as if she were mad.

Sister, between tight teeth, said not. It would be . . . disruptive.

Yes, of course. Bethan saw that.

Instead she sat on a chair outside the entrance to the ward, and thought about him. She sat for almost an hour, white with shock. She said nothing. She didn't know which of them was him.

~

Riley grew accustomed to the invisible painful absence, the lumpy lack of rightness that had replaced the lower half of his face. He had had the lecture on what a bad idea it was to grow accustomed to it. He knew all about that already. Hadn't he grown accustomed to the bad before?

He got up. Major Gillies and Rose told him to, so he did. He wandered in the pretty gardens, reading the dark labels on the tree trunks: Judas, Japan, Jacaranda. He looked in on the officers further down the path of healing, reading the newspapers in the Long Gallery of the big house. His capacity for getting on with men had completely deserted him. He stared at their faces: wounds, dressings, scars, stitches. They looked a complete fucking mess. Some of them were chatting, planning a football match. He had a glance at the headlines: heavy fighting continues, Passchendaele, the season, Zonnebeke, push. At night he heard Fokkers overhead.

It's all still going on. His conscious mind, not for the first time, swooped away from him, shrinking as it went into a tiny dot and hid under a clump of Michaelmas daisies.

He went back to the ward and lay in his trousers and shirt on the bed, staring at the ceiling.

Major Gillies came to see him.

'Captain Purefoy,' he said, 'we need you to understand what's going to happen. Can you listen to me now and take things in?' Riley shifted his eyes across. He moved so slowly always. His eyes closed, a tiny sigh, the smallest nod.

'You're ready now for your first operation,' Gillies went on. 'We will reconstitute your wound as it originally was, so we can see how much skin and muscle is actually missing, and to get rid of any adhesions and scar tissue that have built up.'

Was he taking it in?

'Then, we let that heal, scar-free and clean. We'll be able to see what needs to be replaced, and we'll work out a precise design for your specific wounds. It'll probably be a double-pedicled bridge flap. I will take a flap from your scalp,' he said, 'and bring it under the chin on pedicles, which will lie here,' he gestured gently, 'down your cheek, over the healthy skin. I will apply the flap over a reconstructed jawbone to be made of vulcanite, which will be attached with pegs and wire to the sections of jaw that you still have. Then, later, we can replace that with an osteochondral graft – a piece of rib. Or what we might do is grow the bone-graft in place, in two halves under your scalp, and move it all down together. I haven't decided yet. There's plenty of time. Both methods are good.'

Riley listened closely, staring at the ceiling. It was all fascinating. How extraordinary. It seemed physically impossible, unfeasible, inadvisable, revolting, miraculous and a million miles away. *It was fucking mad.*

'This type of flap makes for nice clear, clean healing,' Gillies continued. 'And as it's from your scalp it'll even have hair on. I do my best to make sure it grows in the right direction.'

They're going to open up my wound all over again. They're going to peel my head and wrap the skin around where my chin used to be and slide in a bit of my rib to be my jaw. And, logic says, I should be grateful.

Are they really allowed to do this to people? I suppose they can do what they want. We're half dead anyway. They haven't quite managed to kill us so they'll just chop us to bits instead.

'It's a very good method. You'll get double the blood supply to your graft. It does look a bit like handles, for a while. Well, you've seen how it looks. It'll be like what Lance Corporal Davies had . . .' Gillies tried not to think about Jamison. Poor Jamison.

Riley thought: *It doesn't matter anyway.* He had made his mind up.

Later, Riley handed Rose a note he had written.

~

Major Gillies took it out over lunch.

Dear Major Gillies,
I appreciate everything you and your staff are trying to do for me but I cannot honestly play the role you have given me. For reasons which don't reflect on you, there is no point in undertaking these operations, and I decline them. Thank you, all the same, for your efforts and good intentions.
     Capt. R. Purefoy

Gillies swore, very quietly. He hated it when they did this. It made it so much more difficult. He pushed himself up in his chair and went to see Purefoy.

'Captain,' he said, standing above the bed.

Purefoy looked up, his laconic, hooded look. *Yes, I am down here, and you are up there, and I cannot speak, and you can save me, and you are a hero, and I am a piece of detritus, a leftover, half a man, a piece of turd. An ort, as Ainsworth would have said.*

'You're having the operation. It's an order. Understood?'

Purefoy blinked.

'You are needed in France. You can't go without a jaw. This is a military hospital. Understood?'

Purefoy blinked again.

Gillies knew perfectly well that Captain Purefoy was going nowhere, and certainly not to France.

'And I also order you to put some vim and vigour into your attitude to your recovery, soldier, and none of this lead-swinging.'

Lead-swinging! Here I am with half a face and they still think we're swinging the lead . . . What does a man have to do to be taken seriously?

'You have to put your trust in me,' he said. 'As an officer. What else can you do? Go home and lock yourself in the attic? Would your mother like that?'

Riley felt a very strong urge to punch him. *If I do, I'll be court-martialled. Will they shoot me? Can I pull off suicide by firing squad? You'd think there would be plenty of ways to die in a hospital, but perhaps that would be the cleanest, and no one's fault but my own.*

He stared. *I know what you're trying to do. I'm not falling for it. I can make my own decision about this and you must respect it.*

'Captain Purefoy,' said Gillies. He perched on the edge of the bed beside this blank-eyed man, making an angle of confidentiality and understanding. 'You're taking morphia. It soothes a man's pain, but it also makes him tired and miserable. Don't listen to the morphia.' He leant in, and spoke quietly. 'Yours is a healable condition, if you believe it to be. Men can think themselves into the grave. Please don't do that.'

Riley blinked. *Think himself dead! Now there's a novel method. Perhaps he should try it.*

~

Riley had not found the strength to escape his weakness. He could not imagine that there was any place in the world for him. He could not imagine a world in which there could be any place for what he had become. He was not convinced there would be a world at all.

He accepted egg-flip and morphia.

He did not have the power to resist what they wanted to do to him. They sailed like galleons on the brilliancy of their capabilities. They had power, belief, hope and goodness, generosity, talent, application, determination. He had killed people. They would do what they had to do. He would stare out of the window. Gillies kept talking about trust: mutual trust being a bulwark against disaster. Riley had no conception of trust. He had no choice about anything, and no feelings.

When the time came and they wheeled him in and laid him out, and gave him the ether oil up the backside, he stared into nothing.

Rose watched as the anaesthesia seemed to make no difference to his expression. Previously, she had watched the anaesthetist holding up a mask to a face while it was being cut and stitched, on a man sitting up vertical so as not to suffocate on his tongue and his blood. The two doctors had swapped between anaesthetic and surgery, and she'd seen surgeons half passing out from leaked chloroform vapour, knees giving way. She had seen the insufflation method, which ended up blowing blood all over everyone; there had been a tracheal angle-piece made from a .303 cartridge case, ether blown through a funnel, that green rubber tube they came up with going into the trachea, like a worm going into a hole . . . The methods were getting better.

Rectal ether oil had its problems too: it was too light at the beginning and too heavy at the end; it would probably give him pneumonia, and she would have to clean the oil out of his backside so it didn't continue to absorb, re-anaesthetising him. But at least the surgeon would stay conscious.

They set him up, laid him out, and with their knives released the tangled, lumpen, distorted misplaced healing of his face. Liberated from the scars, his flesh fell away in wings and shards and scraps: they cleaned it and tended it and loosely bound it up again, so it could heal free, and become the fabric for the next stage of the campaign.

Chapter Twenty

Sidcup, November 1917

Nadine walked from the station, trying to control her breath. Turn left, up the hill – there was a bus stop but that would involve waiting and she couldn't do it: her feet wouldn't stop.

The bus came to a halt just by her, and her feet walked themselves on to it.

Why hadn't he written? Why hadn't he told her anything more?

Not serious.

She'd seen so many wounds. Wounded men in their hospital blues walking about; limps, crutches, bandages, slings. She'd seen them arrive at the hospital straight off the train, stinking of infection, emaciated, dirty, blood-stained, temporary splints falling off, bones sticking out.

Her stomach was cramping as she walked up to the entrance to ask after him. She didn't even see the face of the woman she spoke to.

'Purefoy,' she said, 'Purefoy, ah, yes . . . Follow round to the left and down the hill. Ask for Sister.'

It floated over her head.

Down the hill, enquire.

'Captain Purefoy? Yes, one moment, please . . .'

She sat in the corridor, knee jittering. Passing staff observed her uniform and one smiled. She didn't notice. She lit a cigarette. She was so utterly happy.

A youngish woman approached her – tall, dark, same uniform as her, nursing member VAD. 'Can I help you?' she asked, her head craning round a little. She was strong-looking, not pretty, fine eyes, overworked, firm. Good hands, Nadine thought. Good hands for him to be in.

She jumped up. 'I've come to see Captain Purefoy.' Words of joy.

'Miss . . .?' asked the VAD.

'Waveney,' said Nadine.

'I'm Rose Locke. I help look after Captain Purefoy. Um – Miss Waveney . . .'

It was her, Rose thought. *No question.* 'I'm afraid Sister is busy, but I can . . .' She wished Nadine had said she was coming, or that Riley had – oh, she just wished she'd known, so she could have prepared. Well. It wasn't the first time, wouldn't be the last. It might be good for him to have a visitor. *Shake him up a bit.*

'Come this way. Do sit down. Now . . . Captain Purefoy has recently had an operation, the first of several that will be necessary . . . Are you acquainted with the nature of his injuries?' *At least in France you don't have to deal with the relatives,* Rose thought. *Handing out misery like sweeties.*

At the same time, Rose couldn't take her eyes off her. This girl and Riley . . . rolling over in the night . . . *Stop it, Rose.*

Miss Waveney shook her head very quickly.

Ah.

'Miss Waveney,' said Rose.

'Please call me Nadine,' she said. 'I don't know who Miss Waveney is. She's a sort of stranger.'

Rose smiled. Then stopped smiling. Arranged the professional face. 'Captain Purefoy has requested no visitors,' she said.

Nadine was like a jumpy loving dog, wriggling, trying to sit when told, couldn't do it, wriggling while sitting . . . 'Tell him it's me.' She smiled.

You of all people, Rose thought. *You beautiful, odd-looking, yellow-eyed girl, whose letters so leaping with life and love he puts away unread.* 'I'll see,' she said, stood and walked out of the room. She stopped a second, to breathe, and went back to the ward, where Riley was propped, his face newly dismantled, a new mandibular support under his remaining scrap of jaw. 'Captain Purefoy,' she said, 'I know you said no visitors, but there is a young lady here for you who wants to visit you very much.' She always said 'visit'. She never said 'see'.

He looked up at her.

'It's Miss Waveney,' she said.

His eyes froze. His whole body was still. Time paused.

Other people, Rose thought. *Other people and their bloody love.*

Almost imperceptibly within his metal frame, Riley shook his head. Raised his hand. Rose passed him the pen and notebook.

Rose read it, and nodded. 'Probably for the best, for now,' she said.

Riley glanced up at her. He blinked.

'I'm so sorry,' Rose said to Nadine. 'You should really have enquired before coming all this way. I spoke to his surgeon, and Major Gillies says he really isn't fit to be visited at the moment. If you want to write to him, I can find—'

Nadine had slumped down on to the seat. Silent tears were pouring down her face, pouring.

Rose's heart clenched for her. *You never get used to it, you mustn't get used to it.* She was too used to it already. 'Major Gillies is a brilliant surgeon,' she said. 'He's in the very best place. They do really wonderful work here. It takes time but the results are often excellent . . .'

Nadine was weeping, weeping, weeping.

'The first operation was a success,' Rose continued, almost pleadingly. 'We can do a really good job for him. He'll look all right.' *Damn this girl.*

'It's not that!' Nadine said, lifting her head, like a child outraged by an injustice. 'Can't you see? I just want to see him!'

She stared at Rose, and then she gave a split-second sort of apologetic look. Then she leapt up and she ran – she hurled herself – down the way Rose had come.

Rose took off after her, boots slapping the wooden boards of the walkway. 'Miss Waveney! Miss Waveney!'

Oh God, oh God.

An orderly grabbed Nadine's arm, and was swung round

by her impetus. Rose shook her head at him as she careered up.

'Come on, Nadine,' she said. 'Let's go and have a cup of tea.' She was making calming noises, *ssht ssht ssht*, like you might use to a dog, or a horse, or a baby. To something unsocialised and immediate. Nadine, rigid in the orderly's embrace, rolled rigid into Rose's, a sudden shocking intimacy. Rose took her, folded herself round her and enclosed her, holding the flying pieces of her together.

She propelled her to the parlour – a child with a giant doll – and when it came to putting her on a chair, Rose found herself holding on to Nadine's body, hugging her, feeling in its bones and flesh a profound shuddering comfort of her own, so strong that she felt obliged to break away.

'Miss Waveney,' she said, over-compensating with professionalism. She turned to the urn to get tea. Lots of sugar. She would have a cup too. 'You're a necessary part of your hospital, a member of your team. Pull yourself together.'

Nadine had collapsed into the wooden chair, breathing very shallowly. She seemed now half the height and size she had been when she was stiff.

'I really, really, really want to see him,' she said. 'I don't know if you can understand this but the idea that he is – *there*—' she gestured vaguely '—and I can't be with him, is – it's – it's not right. It's very, very wrong. And unlike most of the very, very wrong things,' she said, as if the sense of it were unfolding before her, 'which we are surrounded by, I can make it right – by going to him. I can make it right.

So why are you stopping me?'

'It's my duty,' said Rose. 'What would you do, nurse?'

Nadine smiled. 'Yes yes yes,' she said. 'But you see I'm not here as a nurse. I'm here as a girl. Are you a girl sometimes, Miss . . .?'

'Rose Locke,' said Rose.

'Rose Locke. What a beautiful name. And are you locked? Are you a locked Rose? Oh, God, I'm sorry. Sorry. None of this is your fault. I'll try to be good. I know, I know. Do you have any idea, Miss Locke, Miss Rose, when I will be able to visit my darling?'

'I can't confirm, I'm so sorry,' Rose said, and before she could finish, suggesting phone calls to the front desk, letters perhaps to the patient, and so on, Nadine had said, 'I'll come tomorrow then. Or this afternoon?'

~

Later on that day Rose saw her, walking away from town, wandering, clearly wasting time, in the countryside. She went across a lush field with a few cows in it, carefully climbing the gate on the other side in her long, heavy skirt. Rose had forbidden herself sympathy, as an emotion detrimental to efficiency, but for this girl, the careful way she climbed the gate, weighed down, she felt it, she just did.

~

Riley lay as usual, propped up, eyes shut.

Later, before going to the bathroom, he paused to fossick in his kitbag. He took a small shaving mirror from one of the pockets.

He walked through his ward, seeing the others out of the corners of his eyes. He glanced, in passing, at the other wards off the walkway, and continued up to the big house. A few fellows were sitting about on the flagged terrace in the autumn sun, chatting, reading. As best he could, without causing the particular pain of observation, he looked at the variety of heads he passed, sticking out of the hospital blues of the men, the uniforms of the officers. He imagined what was beneath the bandages, and he made himself look at the various stages of dismantling and reconstruction, of healing and scarring, of swelling and adhesion, of skin pulled this way and that, cut and replaced, puffed up like bacon fat, promising, healing, ugly, terrifying, eyes pulled sideways, noses twisted, the clear, shining skin of burn scars, pedicles dangling, keloids puffing, thick black horsehair stitches, pads and lumps of semi-healed flesh. He looked at the eyes in those heads: moist slits, some of them, crooked, or empty, slack without muscle, a couple of eyelashes stuck in any which way. He considered the souls behind those eyes. As best he could, without being seen to look, because being seen to look would cause pain . . . He didn't know how to look, any more than anyone else did.

People will not know how to look at me . . . Children will scream at the sight of me.

I am angry. I am bewildered. I am scared. I am disgusting. I am embarrassed. I am embarrassing. I can't talk. I can't chew to eat. I will be looked at, judged, rejected, pitied. Pitied.

Pitiable. Self-pitying.

Men, pitying me. My mother, pitying me. Nadine, pitying me. Me, pitying me.

Disgusting.

He ambled delicately back down the wide steps, moving silently into the grounds. In the wooded area beyond the pond, he tried to move his tongue in his mouth. He made the tiny soft snorting noise in the back of his throat: the only noise he could make.

His hands were heavy when he lifted them to unwrap the dressing.

He propped the mirror in the fork of a branch, and carefully, consciously, determinedly, he looked at his face.

He was both ridiculous and grotesque. He didn't look like a face at all. His own wide brow with his hair cropped like a prisoner's, his own grey eyes, with their lashes and folds of skin, their iridic rings and the tiny black holes into the inside of his skull. His own flat cheekbones, his little mole, sitting quietly undisturbed by his left temple where it had been all along. His own strong broken nose, with its pores and its nostrils. His upper lip, shaven, and clean, the dent where, his mother had told him, God had pressed his fingertip to mark him finished, perfect, ready to be born.

The top lip of his mouth, still there, the upper lip Nadine had kissed and sworn was so beautiful to her.

And, underneath, the biggest mess . . . He looked like a scarlet crater rimmed with a half-formed pile of earthworks, a fallen-over pile of dirty sandbags. Grey bruising and purple swelling and black scab, hanging loose over nothing. The metal chin support, like revetting. Seams between pads of flesh running across his face like trenches, swellings like sandbags. A few loose stitches like barbed wire.

I look like fucking no man's land.

~

An orderly found Riley asleep in the woods, his unravelled bandages around him, his face cradled in his arms in the dead birch leaves of the previous year, and the mirror in the fork of the tree staring down at him. He woke him gently, and took him back inside, and when Riley wrote in his notebook that he would like a screen around his bed, Rose spoke to Sister, and Sister spoke to Major Gillies, and Rose, they decided, should keep a special eye on him.

She came to him that night after supper, when everyone had been cleaned up, and the ward was quietening. She handed him the notebook and pencil.

He shook his head, as best he could, rebandaged.

'Please,' she said. 'You can't keep it all locked away inside. We've plenty of experience of this.'

He glanced down, shook his head again, a tiny movement.

'Please, Riley,' she said. 'How can you live in the world if you won't communicate?'

He grabbed the pen and wrote:

How can I live in the world?

'You can,' she said. 'You're loved. Why would you want to die when you're loved?'

Who said I want to die?

'You did. You've made it perfectly clear.'

He was still for a moment. He had had so much time to think about all this.

I was a boy, I knew nothing, I was interested in art, I had a place, I loved a girl.

I became a soldier, trained to live and fight like an animal in circles of Hell.

I was made an officer, leading the animals.

I am a cripple so hideous my own mother screams and can't stay in the room long enough to look at me.

My own mind lies to me and hides things from me.

After who knows how many years of pain, flesh-cutting, other people's generosity, drugs, stuck here, incapable, I am to go back to . . . normality, with a plastered-on face made from my own sliced-up skin, a lying mind, a corrupted soul . . .

Rose was still there.

He wrote:

You met Nadine

'I did. We had a cup of tea. She's lovely and she loves you.'

Still. Then:

tell me if this is cruel enough
and he passed her a letter. She read it quickly.

My Dear

I wanted to tell you, but I have not been able to find a way. We know that war plays strange tricks. Briefly, whatever has passed between us must now be seen as in the past. I have met a girl, and I am in love with her. As soon as my wound is healed, which should be soon, I will return to the front, and when the war is over, if it ever is, and if I survive, I will return to her, in Paris, if it is possible. I do not flatter myself that this will cause you too much pain. We both always knew that if only for family reasons our friendship could not be anything more. However I feel it only fair to clarify matters. So perhaps it is for the best. Will you forgive me, and let it end here? With all good wishes, Riley Purefoy

Is that cruel enough?
Will she believe me?

Rose's hand shook as she put the letter down on the bed. She swallowed. *The . . .*

Instinct number one: the monster. A beautiful living thing thriving in this strange sick world, and he does that to it . . . There are men here who are grasping their futures in two brave bare hands who would kill for the help of a girl's love . . .

Instinct number two: how very much he must love her, to want to protect her at such a cost. How brave to make her hate him, because that's the only way it can be done. How sad, my God, how sad . . .

Back to number one. He doesn't trust her. He thinks she won't be able to cope with it, so he's making the decision

270

for her. Patronising her. Or protecting her. But she is brave and strong, she's been nursing all this time, she's tough, that one . . . She's not some pre-war girlie. He just doesn't want to be nursed, he doesn't want to be weak – he should bloody well fight then! Fight it!

And number two: how brave of him to recognise all that . . .

He wrote:

You see how I spend my time

She said: 'I can't tell you what to do. You'll break her heart, but you know that. I think it's very gentlemanly of you. I think you'll regret it. I think it's the saddest thing. I think you should wait and see how things develop. Of course you look a fright at the moment, but things will get better, and you can always send this later, if you decide you have to . . .'

He wrote:

pity is no basis for marriage

'Pity isn't all there is,' she said. 'Not everyone would pity you . . .'

He wrote:

you pity me

She shook her head. 'No,' she said.

He wrote, and flashed his eyes up at her wryly:

271

should marry you then

And to that, her smile was tight. The jokes people could make – even him! – knowing she was unmarriageable. They didn't make those jokes to pretty girls. With a pretty girl, at this moment, their eyes would meet, and meaning would fill the ward . . . not for her. But she was used to that. 'You made a joke!' she said gamely.

He wrote:

I suppose so

Then,

You're right about everything, Rose

She said, with a little smile: 'Nadine said, was I a locked Rose? Because of my name. Rose Locke.'

Riley looked at her. It fell into place like a mechanism: Locke. Sidcup.

He wrote:

Peter Locke?

'My cousin!' she said.

He wrote nothing.

'Riley?' she said. 'Do you know him?'

Riley thought. Locke. He could feel a pull like thin hot wire through his bloodstream, wire, tweaking you, not leaving you alone, linking you to outside, to Over There, to

them, to it, to all that he did not know how to face. *To face.
Ha ha ha.* He wrote:

My CO

She said, 'Oh, Riley. You were with Peter! Oh!' She was
so glad. It gave a reason, somehow, for the affection she
already had for him. Of course she liked him: he was a
friend of Peter's! He was real. He had a place in the web.
There *was* a web – connections, friendships, society,
contact.

He wrote:

how do you do Miss Locke

'My name is Rose,' she said, smiling so wide. Then: 'Riley,
don't send that letter. Don't. Give it time. Things will
improve and you *will* change your mind.'

He wrote:

Is she still here?

'Yes,' said Rose. 'She's taken a room at the Lamb.'

He wrote:

Give it to her. Please.

Chapter Twenty-one

Sidcup, November 1917

Rose was so angry with Riley. She didn't feel she could discuss it with Matron or anyone else. She didn't want to reveal his private life. But – but, but, but . . .

She was still angry when she called at Locke Hill the following day. She said to Julia, over tea, 'You know the patient I mentioned, Captain Purefoy? The sad good-looking one, with the girlfriend?'

'Mmm,' said Julia.

'Peter was his CO.'

'Goodness!' said Julia.

'They must have been serving together for two years,' Rose went on.

'Peter never mentioned him!' said Julia.

Peter never mentions anything, Rose didn't say.

'Oh, gosh,' said Julia, flustered. 'Gosh. Do you think I should visit him?' She didn't want to. But – would it be right? Was it the CO's wife's duty? He was right there, after all . . . but . . . She remembered the man in the woods. She couldn't inflict that on another man. Or was that an excuse? Goodness, she really should be able by now to look them in the eye and say good morning, like a human being.

'He doesn't want visitors,' said Rose. 'He's – well, the sweetheart, and— Julia, tell me what you think about this. I don't know what I think. It seems so utterly . . .'

Julia listened carefully, as Rose told her about the letter.

'Were they engaged?' Julia asked, when Rose had finished, passing her the plate of buns, and refusing one herself.

'I don't know. He said in the letter that they would never have been able to be together anyway. The girl, Miss Waveney, is well-spoken, but I think he is not a gentleman and that could be part of it . . . but, Julia, he's given me the letter to give her – I just can't bear the idea . . . ' Saying it out loud, her reluctance swept up like tears. She *couldn't* contribute to this.

'I think he's being jolly unselfish and brave,' said Julia. 'I think it's unspeakably good of him. It's for the best. Not just for her – for him. I think it's jolly decent of him to take that responsibility.'

'She loves him,' said Rose.

'Has she seen him?'

'No.'

'And will he talk again?'

'Perhaps.'

A pause, while Julia thought about that. 'How bad is he?' she asked.

'Honestly?' said Rose. 'At the moment, he looks awful. Awful. But with these tremendously handsome eyes, which makes it worse. And he's terribly low. But that's not the point. It's not my decision . . . I just don't want to be the one . . . The poor girl. She's crazy about him . . .'

Julia pictured the girl, the boy, the wound. Could she love Peter if he came back wounded like that? Lie in bed beside him at night, with a warped and snarled face on the pillow beside her? Embrace him? Of course! But he was her husband . . .

And. Well. Best not to think about embraces.

Her mother always said it went against nature to embrace the ugly.

'Is she pretty?' she asked.

'Miss Waveney? Yes – in an odd way. She has yellow eyes, and skin like – sort of like a church candle when it's alight.'

'Sounds like a witch,' said Julia.

'No, she's very healthy, attractive. Mysterious, though. I like her.' For a sweeping moment, she remembered holding Nadine in her arms: the strength of the girl's passion, her narrow body, her bones. 'And I like him. I can't— Why does it have to be like this?' she cried suddenly, piercingly, a curling cry that she controlled almost before she had uttered it. She opened her eyes wide, and put her hands down by her sides.

Julia stared at her. 'I thought you weren't meant to get involved with your patients,' she said.

Rose smiled and shook her head.

~

On the way back to the hospital, cycling by the Green, she heard a voice call her name. 'Miss Locke!'

Miss Waveney.

Well. Rose stopped, and waited for her to come over across the damp grass.

'Hello, Miss Locke.'

'Hello, Miss Waveney.'

'How is he, Miss Locke?'

'There's no change, Miss Waveney. It was only yesterday that you came to the hospital.'

'I wanted to apologise,' she said. 'I was a little hysterical. You understand the situation. Even so, I am sorry to have behaved so . . . passionately.'

'I quite understand, Miss Waveney. Don't worry about it.'

'Thank you,' she said. She tried to smile. 'Did he – did he send any message for me?'

There's no getting out of this. It's not my decision. It's nothing to do with me!

Rose smiled as best she could. 'He did,' she said brightly. 'A letter! Here you are.' She took it from her satchel and held it straight out in front of her, like something on fire. Damn damn damn. She blinked quickly. She understood now why Riley had wanted her to give it, rather than put it in the post. He didn't want Nadine to be alone when she read it. A kind man.

Oh, Lord, the girl looked so happy.

She couldn't let her . . .

There was a bench. A blue one, as it happened. *Well, that's only appropriate.*

'Why not sit here and read it, my dear?' Rose said, stepping irrevocably off her bicycle.

Nadine took the envelope, held it. She was visibly torn between wanting to read it right now, and wanting to take

277

it away to a secret place to treasure it. Rose's face made her sit down.

Rose sat beside her, and gave a very quiet sigh.

After a long moment, Nadine began to moan softly. 'No. No. No. No. No. No . . .' Rose turned to her. She was white, bloodless. Shaking. 'No.' Expressions like wind chasing on water, hands fluttering.

Rose pulled her defences into place around her heart, put her arm around Nadine, and held her as she began to weep. She didn't stop.

They sat there for a while on the wounded men's bench. Rose looked up and down the street, at the two women with their prams, at the old man carrying a basket, at the four small children across the way doing something with sticks. How shameless normality is, the way it just carries on.

'Come on, my dear,' she said. 'Let's go and get some tea. Put your bag in my bicycle basket. Take my arm – I can push one-handed.'

Nadine was docile, weeping, shaking quietly.

The nearest tea was back at Locke Hill.

'Come on, my dear,' Rose murmured softly, over and over, as they trudged.

Julia was in the hall. She took one look and exclaimed: 'Dear God, what's happened to her? Who is she? Was she knocked down?' She called Mrs Joyce to make hot tea with brandy, and sat Nadine down on the sofa, bustling round her. 'My dear,' she said. 'Just sit.'

'I don't know what to do with her,' Rose said quietly in the hall. 'She's Captain Purefoy's friend. I had to give her the letter ... She's in shock, so ... but I have to get back ...'

Julia said: 'Really, don't worry. Leave her with me. Poor girl, it's too dreadful.'

She put her in the blue room, told her to bathe if she wanted, and sent Harker into town for her bags. Bag, as it turned out.

Later, she sent up some broth, and went to check on her. Nadine sat on the bed, dry-eyed and staring, arms wrapped round, hugging herself.

'Do you have what you need?' Julia asked, standing in the doorway.

Nadine seemed unable to talk.

Julia went over to her and put her hand on Nadine's shoulder. 'You can get into bed,' she said. 'You can stay here till you feel a bit better. I'd like you to.'

No response.

'My husband is Captain Purefoy's CO,' Julia said timidly.

At that, Nadine looked up at her: an unreadable look. She moved her hand a little, to touch Julia's where it lay.

Julia sat down on the bed beside her. After a while, she gave Nadine's shoulder a sort of pat, and sighed, and stood, and left the room.

Chapter Twenty-two

Amiens

A tiny round yellow moon, a wretched, shrunken, bitter moon, shone down on Peter Locke, leaning against the wall in an alleyway behind the cathedral. It was a cold, cold night, but he burnt with the artificial heat of brandy. He felt the chill of the stones against his shoulders and buttocks even through his greatcoat. He leant forward. He didn't want to be sick, because he wanted to stay as drunk as he could for as long as possible.

Corporal Burgess stood in front of him. 'Come on, sir, I'll get you back,' he was saying.

'Do you think, Burgess,' said Locke, ignoring that, 'that we took enough ground, in all, since July, to bury all the men that died taking it? Do you think that those few yards we added, round Menin Road, Pilckem Ridge, do you think they would even *fit* those of us who are now . . . horizontal?'

'Don't know, sir,' said Burgess.

'And don't you think it's interesting that actually it almost isn't ground, anyway? As it's below sea-level, it's a few yards of sea-bed. Sea-bed with delusions of grandeur, delusions that it is land . . . Purefoy said, you know, "Flanders, flounders." It's made flounders out of us all, floundering around, and it's made a turbot out of Purefoy . . . and it can't even hold a corpse down anyway, it makes a lousy graveyard, and anyway, some arses had shot it to pieces before we even got there, just a big sinkhole . . .'

'Come on, sir.'

'Oh, yes, that was us . . .'

'Come on, sir . . .'

'Thank you very much, Corporal,' Locke said. 'Thank you very much for your helpful concern, but I have other plans.'

'Be as well to wake up in the billet, sir,' said Burgess.

'Be as well,' said Locke, 'not to wake up at all.'

'Come come, sir,' said Burgess. *Jesus God, sir, shut up.* Burgess was tired. Locke was tired.

'I am going,' said Locke, 'to pay money to sleep in a woman's arms.' He stared at Burgess sadly.

'Well, sir,' said Burgess.

'Would you like to pay money to sleep in a woman's arms, Burgess?' Locke asked.

'No, sir,' said Burgess.

'I would like to pay money for every man out there to sleep in a woman's arms, Burgess,' he said. 'And not in a sinkhole.' His head fell to one side. 'Would you like to pay money to sleep in a *man*'s arms, Burgess?' he said.

Burgess gave the tiniest of smiles. 'No, sir,' he said.

'Would you like to sleep in my arms, Burgess?' Locke said. 'Because I tell you tonight I would sleep in a pig's arms, in a great fat muddy pig's arms, for a touch of human

281

warmth. No hanky-panky. Of course. No chance of hanky-panky. No hanky-panky.'

Burgess had not had an erection since the Somme, since he had felt the power of strength and doing good prickle in his veins like caustic when he had carried Purefoy in; his last moment of any sense of his own power. Since then his impotence had been as complete as Locke's was erratic.

'Come on, sir,' he said.

Locke started to hum, very quietly, through his teeth. *Ta-tumty-tumty-tum-ti-tum* . . . He pushed himself upright, on to Burgess, and for a moment they were locked into the drunkard's dance, the two sets of feet far apart and glued into the ground, tall Locke, short Burgess, the head and shoulders close, embracing so as not to fall. Locke pushed himself away and up, hands on Burgess's shoulders, with a little smile. 'It's the words of love, Burgess,' he said. 'The memory of shining stars, sweet-smelling earth, of a garden gate, a woman arriving. I die in despair, and never have I loved life so much, *non ho amato mai tanto la vita*.'

'Come on, sir, you pissed twat,' said Burgess.

'Good point,' said Locke. They stumbled on together down the alleyway, in the shadow of the cathedral, the great Gothic temple to all that didn't seem to exist any more.

Burgess, fearing for his CO's balance, walked Locke as far as the brothel and went on alone, singing softly:

'O death where is thy stingalingaling, O grave thy victoree . . .
The bells of hell go tingalingaling, for you but not for me . . .'

Chapter Twenty-three

Sidcup and France, winter 1917–July 1918
Nadine appeared again at the hospital the next day, her shirt ironed, her eyes puffy, her demeanour unnaturally calm. Sister was called. Rose stood by, watchful.

'May I see him?' Nadine asked, courteously, very controlled.

'I'm sorry, my dear,' said Sister.

Nadine swallowed. Every movement was an effort. It looked to Rose as if she were having to remind herself to breathe.

'I am a nursing VAD of two years' experience in surgical as well as medical wards. May I make an appointment with Matron to ask permission to apply for a transfer here?' she said formally, but her voice was shaking.

'No, my dear, no,' said Sister. 'Under the circumstances.'

Nadine nodded as if she had expected it.

'Then may I beg you to do everything you can and . . .' She nearly lost her self-control then. Turning to Rose, she said: 'May I ask you, please, to write to me? To let me know?'

Rose glanced at Sister. Sister raised her eyebrows, gave a tiny sigh and nodded.

'Yes,' said Rose. 'If you send your address.'

'I'm going to France,' said Nadine, delicately. 'As soon as I can get a place. I'll send . . . yes. Thank you,' she said. 'Tell him – oh. No. Thank you. Goodbye.'

As she turned away her movements were as stiff as a doll's.

~

'Well, it worked,' said Rose. 'She believed you. She's going to France.'

His eyes flashed up.

'Of course she is,' Rose said cruelly. 'She's not some namby-pamby creature who can't face up to things. Anyway, she has nothing to live for now. She wants to die. Like you.'

Riley stared.

~

A woman came, very blue-eyed, to make a plaster cast of the new gaping face: the gaping face mark two. It was healing well. Everything was going well. Gillies would use the cast to consider and practise the size and shape and position of the flaps of flesh, which he would wrap around the new chin.

They did the cast in Tonks's studio. She and Tonks knew each other from London. He had been her teacher at the Slade, years before. They chatted about art and who was doing what and people they knew. The names trickled before Riley like reflected shadows of sunlight and water on a ceiling, or the underside of a bridge, iridescent glimpses of long ago. Ricketts and Shannon, John Tweed, Gladys, Jimmie, Isadora. The woman, he gathered, had known Rodin – had studied with him in Paris before . . . before. He would have liked to ask about him. He wondered who else she had known. Who she knew. She clearly was not, like him, in the past tense.

Riley stood before them with shirt off and all his wound on display. The bottom of his face hung open, unimpeded, scraps of healed skin hanging loose like pastry waiting to be arranged across the top of a pie. His saliva was in a state of chaos, and he could not always feel when he needed mopping. What should be wet was dry; what should be dry was wet. He had not spoken in five months.

She was very gentle with him.

'You look like a broken statue,' she said. 'Some young god lying around at the Acropolis. Touch my arm if anything is uncomfortable.'

She painted his face with something. Put a little card tube up each nostril, carefully. His splints had been removed for the occasion and he couldn't lie back, so the tubes kept falling out.

She smiled. It was a bit ridiculous. 'You know,' she said, 'Francis Derwent Wood, the painter, is making the most marvellous masks out of tin. They're terribly realistic. It's another option.'

Riley stood, utterly passive. He wondered if she'd met Van Gogh. He wondered if she understood what was going to be done to him. Every thought was a fucking blade through his heart.

He loved her. She was so kind to help him.

She poured the cold stuff over his face in dollops: wet and cold and heavy over his eyes and his cheeks and his nose and the rest of what he had, presumably, but he couldn't really tell because his nerve endings were mashed to bits and his feelings were confused.

The plaster sucked at his face like mud. He felt buried alive.

~

There had been no problem about putting Nursing Member Waveney on the list to go to France. Though a great many of the wounded just drowned in the mudholes of Passchendaele, plenty were still coming through.

She had been sent in midwinter to Le Touquet, to the casino by the sea where Riley had lain with his shoulder wound. No one knew her. She knew no one. She did every-thing she knew how to do. It was surreal but it wasn't uncomfortable. Not uncomfortable enough. She wanted worse. She was thin but she was tough. Given the choice, she took the night-shifts. Daylight upset her. Not that there was much of it. It was a wet, cold, dingy winter.

~

To start with, Rose did not write to her very often. A card: 'Your friend is well; no date has been set yet for his next go of surgery.'

It was difficult for Rose. She had been so thrown by Nadine's plea when she'd agreed to write that she hadn't thought it through. Was she writing to tell the truth? Or to

286

support Riley's lie, that the wound was slight and he was going back to the front?

Nadine wrote back: 'Thank you. We keep horribly busy here. You can imagine.'

~

When she was transferred to the massive metropolis that was Étaples, Nadine hid her face during the journey. She didn't want to see the great tents, the blue sky, the sandhills, the spiky grass and the restless sea beyond, to the north, which was wrong, because sea should be to the south, like Brighton and Lyme Regis and the Riviera. She didn't want to see the Chinese labourers putting up huts, the floods of nurses and wounded, the trains, the horses, the sick and frantic life. There were some trees. She didn't want to see the trees. She didn't want to see the Boulogne to Paris railway running by, a constant reminder that they were in the wrong place. The long huts were ugly, the green and red chintz curtains ridiculous. The ground vibrated constantly with the quiver of drumfire from the front. People all around collapsed with Étaplesitis, puking and crapping. Women were dismissed for running around with men who were not dismissed. Everything was as wrong as she felt. She was glad.

She took all the dirtiest jobs. She didn't complain. She didn't join in. She didn't raise her head all winter. The girls with whom she shared the draughty tent and canvas bunks were half in the same mood as her, the other half respectful of it. They'd seen it before. They liked her, for the simple reason that her headlong misery made her take on all the worst jobs so they didn't have to. They were grateful that she never held back when the gas cases came in, burnt and blistered and sticky, coughing up bits of grey lung. They were grateful, too, that she didn't, like the rest of them, subvert her constant terror into constant nerve-jangling moans about chilblains or tiredness or the weather. They were grateful to her for not throwing hysterics about someone finishing the Bovril or the paltry soup before she had a cup.

She liked only one thing: the patients. The worse their condition, the more she liked them. She liked to sit by them late at night, helping them to move when they couldn't breathe well, adjusting their limbs, scratching where they couldn't reach, talking softly with them. Long, long nights, low lamplight, smells of petrol and Lysol, the roaring guns, far away, the golden glow in the distance. Night and work were her blankets. Best was when convoys came in at night: nights of the full moon or clear weather, when the hits would have been many and direct, and many, many boys would have been saved from the worst fate, survival. She liked meeting the ambulances as they roared and rattled in, careering out of the darkness, their lights off to be invisible to enemy planes, their girl drivers mad-eyed, stiff as wire, crazed with sleeplessness. She liked piling the boys out, the stretcher cases and the walkers, the screamers and the shakers, the blobs, the bleeding, the armless, the legless, Xs on their foreheads where they'd had their shot of morphine, all the characters of the grim tableau.

She knew now exactly what Riley had been talking about when he had said he didn't exist. She knew now the hollow

288

manic energy induced by living at crisis pitch all the time. It left you – well, it never left you: it *rendered* you brutalised, incapable, unthinking, unfeeling, scar tissue all over. No feeling at all. Wild. Everything was terribly remote and she was utterly impenetrable.

Such *marvellous* high spirits, as someone – who? some bloody woman in a hat, in a coat, in a mud-encrusted limousine – had said. Some representative of something. Lady this. Princess that.

~

Another card: 'His spirits are not the best but he has started reading, which must be good news. He got through A Tale of Two Cities in three days.'

Rose might not be able to tell the truth but she was not going to lie.

Replied: 'He took A Tale of Two Cities with him when he first went out in 1914. I suppose he didn't get round to reading it then. He used to enjoy R. L. Stevenson. I don't suppose I would know what he would like now. How is Julia?'

Rose thought, *Sweet girl, to ask about Julia.*

~

She liked washing them, dressing their wounds, being gentle with them, as they would soon be out of this sick, sick world. She didn't like to see them die, the shuddering, the sheet-plucking, the ever-shorter breaths – but she liked it when they were dead. After a while she stopped discouraging it. Death had a happy ending every time. Peace. She liked their poor corpses, safe on their way to a named and numbered grave among their friends, cosy within the system built and created for them. Not lying out there, in the dark, alone.

How lucky for their sweethearts, she thought, *who will not have to deal with any messy aftermath, who will never have to know what 'died of wounds' means. Lucky girls, with just plain grief. Just simple, pure death, and a photo of a hero to weep over and be proud of. Because death was what it was all for, wasn't it? All the bombs, the shells, the snipers, the aerial torpedoes, the submarine torpedoes, the liquid fire, the trench mortars, the artillery, the bayonets, the grenades, the chlorine gas, the mustard gas, the tanks, the planes for dropping bombs from the sky, the tunnelling and laying bombs under the ground . . . endless list . . . well, it is endless . . . all the things that were being invented – were being invented! That* men *were inventing, and women were making – all those things are for killing you. And if they don't kill you they wound you, and when they wound you, you get patched up – by me! – and sent out again until they do kill you.*

The other girls – the bored, the sex-mad, the curious, the sentimental, the power-seekers, the thrill-seekers, the poetry writers, the bovine, those who would do anything to get away from home, even the sanest, sweetest, densest, cleverest, best-adjusted girls, long coats and jerseys, cup-of-tea-and-a-fag girls, even the cheerful, who brayed about the Yanks coming in – Nadine could see that they were all crazy by now.

She did not ask herself what she was doing there. She knew. She was helping. Every lantern in the windswept dark, each phosphorescent gleam, flapping canvas and snapping doors, the rattling of steel and glass in the sterilising room, the galvanised cauldrons boiling day and night, camphor oil, strychnine, caffeine, morphine, saline and yellow soap, temperature pulse and respiration, sweat mud dirt blood sweat piss tears, die now or die in an hour or so. He loved a girl in Paris; he didn't want her; he had done what he swore he would not – he had loved her and left her – and her mother was right and she was betrayed and . . .

Ah, but who cares?

It would be obscene, out here, to care for such trifles.

~

When no one was looking she kissed the dying, their cheeks, their foreheads, their mouths. Sometimes they kissed her back in the dark, in the silence but for groans and calls for Mother. They whispered, 'I love you.'

'I love you too, darling,' she whispered back. Because in the face of death, really, who cares about love?

~

A card: 'Stevenson a great success! It keeps him calm and in decent spirits while waiting for his surgery, which you will be glad to know should come off soon.'

More surgery! Well, Mademoiselle will have something to deal with, won't she?

She had been picturing a pert little Parisienne with tiny feet and fancy knickers, a temptress, a houri, a spy, a snake in the grass with the qualities that not even the best man could be expected to resist, a scented, lipsticked creature with a *moue-moue* mouth and a *moue-moue* accent . . .

Or the peasant girl he'd been with before, some deep, sexual, animal allure that could not be gainsaid . . .

No.

If she hadn't seen it in his own writing . . .

~

Some patients were so impatient that Gillies felt obliged to rush their treatment, lest their frame of mind affect their recovery – but this one was the opposite. The apathy was the danger, but it could be put to good use. They had been able to wait for complete healing. There was no point in trying to race ahead with a graft under the scalp, tempting though the design was. Gillies had decided after all on a vulcanite jawbone. There it sat: ready, beautiful, pink, sterile, made to measure, in a kidney basin. And there lay the ruined face, with its gaping lack, swathed in white sheets like an ancient statue's head half buried in a mossy grove.

Tidy the edges; snipping. Leave enough border to sew on the new. There's a fair bit of muscle remaining – *room for recovery there, with any luck.*

The little jut of surviving ramus, like a misplaced tooth in the red flesh on either side . . . the twists of wire for attaching the vulcanite.

The drill, the forceps, the gauzes.

The poor long-suffering tongue, clipped away to the side for the moment.

The head newly shaved. The iodine and Lysol.

The flap drawn like a sewing pattern on the fine skin, quite far back so he'll look all right with a hat on, *though with hair growth like his he'll be fine, comb it this way or that – shame you can't just stretch skin . . . though you can stretch leather, so why not? Expand hair-bearing skin somehow, fewer follicles per square inch but even so . . . for burns, alopecia . . . have to think about that.*

The scalpel. Cut cut cut, slide underneath with the blade to release: lift. Not much give – good. Slide over forehead, swing down, twist, position under the new jaw. It's so simple – beautiful. The pedicles are already curling in on themselves – tack them, swiftly, carefully, into tubes.

Stitch into place.

Turn the edge for the lower lip.

Clean.

Dress.

Good.

Next . . .

∼

A card:

March 17 1918

In haste – the surgery went off well. The weather is not the best at the moment but that doesn't matter as he cannot move around so very much until he is better healed.

He cannot move around much?
And so Nadine wrote a letter:

293

My dear Rose,

I have hardly time to write a proper letter but I wanted to tell you how very much I appreciate you writing to me about Riley. It makes so much difference to me out here just to know that he is in good hands. But forgive me, I am confused. Why is he still there? He said his wound was not serious. You said his wound was not serious. Has something else developed? When do you expect him to leave? I hope you do not mind me asking these questions but I am haunted by what he wrote to me, torturing myself you may say but there is nothing I can do about it . . .

And in reply came this:

Dear Nadine,

I am so sorry but it seems I am not to write to you about Riley any more. It seems there is a conflict of interests, an invasion of privacy, a – I don't know quite what, but the Powers That Be here deem it inappropriate, for us as VADs, to go into details about a patient's condition and treatment and so on, which of course we must understand, though it seems hard – I'm sorry. It doesn't mean that we can't write though. Just not about one individual patient.

It half relieved Rose to know that she need no longer skate between lying and truth.

It shocked Nadine.

Dear Rose, and whoever else is reading this,
████ individual patients passed through my ward last night;

████ through the hospital. That makes about ████ this month. ████ of them died. It seems a shame that I cannot have news of ████ who I have known since we were ████ years old and who has escaped the final release. ████ tell me their last orders of the day were backs to the wall and fight to the death; ████ tell me they never got those orders because the only leader they have seen out there is Colonel Chaos.

Oh, I am sorry. I know it must be so. 'Things have been very busy here', with the charmingly named Spring Push, i.e. the Germans pushing everybody back through us, and us pushing back like god knows what. I can't write about it. I can't write at all.

The black marks of the censor looked like the mourning stripes for words that cannot be spoken, that may not live.

∼

Fourth year of the war, if not yet four years. It was all hotting up, quite a show: lots and lots of injured men, lots of death. Three weeks of constant shelling. Sunsets lurid and ancient, burning like blood and sugar. Screaming of shells. Lovely little white puffs of anti-aircraft fire. Temperature pulse respiration: keep it up, nurse, good work.

The ghosts of the men killed in 1916 were rising up on the battlefields of the Somme, apparently, side by side, fighting back.

Four years. She would have finished art school long ago.

Six months she had been out here. She would carry on until she exploded, and what form her explosion would take was not her business, not under her control. She would continue, her body jerking and rattling, like a machine out of order. That first letter: *I do not exist . . . be there when I come back out . . .*

The nights were shorter now. More daylight. Sunshine, from time to time. Pale folded leaves on trees. Blossom. She just did as she was told. Physical exhaustion leading to physical pain. Étaples was bombed! Keep scrubbing. Sleepless weeks. In May they ended up spending the sleepless nights in trenches, in the woods. Once, she did sleep, sitting up on a canvas stool, her cheek against soil like a dead woman's. And when she woke that first morning, she saw above her an almond tree in bloom, a twisty branch against a pale, dusty blue sky, waxen white blossoms.

Spring Push.

～

Six weeks after his second operation, Riley was healing. He had a chin, and within it a jaw, of the same hardened rubber as the pink plate of his mother's false teeth. He tapped it, under his peculiar new skin, under his bandages. It was an unlikely, unnerving weight, a strange new sling, under his face. He had, he realised, got used to having no chin.

His scalp, where it had been scalped, itched appallingly beneath the dressing. He could not scratch it. Bare red living skull. As if his head were a very small world and Gillies had carefully cut a strip of turf from it, to be rolled up and used elsewhere in the garden.

He tapped it repeatedly with heavy fingertips, hitting it almost, seeking relief. He scratched his chin instead: it felt as if he were scratching his head. 'Nerve endings,' said Gillies. 'They think they're still on your scalp.'

The chin was the first to be released from the dressings. There it was, the roll, tucked under his face like a pack under a saddle, sliding lipless where his lower lip had once been. Fresh air would help the healing. Riley slid his fingers gently between his pedicles and his cheeks – there was his little mole, hidden away – and fingered the flattened tubes of flesh draped in front of his ears. They felt like very tough pancakes, leathery, spongy, and they stuck out at the side where they were folded down. They seemed to flare back like mad horns, or weird handlebars. *Intestines*, he thought. *Taxi horns.*

They were already sprouting head hair, in a direction not entirely concomitant with a natural beard.

Rose was very gentle when she cleaned his face.

Riley did not look at it; neither did he go among the other men.

~

April

Dear Nadine,

When I think it is four years since I was in France, and that it has all been going on since then, I can hardly bear to think it. But it must end, Nadine, think only of that, it will end, and we will win. We've known that since the Americans came in . . . bit by bit.

I shall write to you whether you write to me or not, because here I am helping to mend and rebuild, and life is much easier than it is for you out there. Stay strong, Nadine.

Rose

April
Dear Rose,
Thank you. I think sometimes I would rather die than ever see a broken boy again.

May
Dear Nadine,
If it helps you at all I wouldn't mind if you wanted to let it out in your letters to me. I know it is almost impossible to talk about such things over there. Write it all to me, I can take it. If there is one thing I have learnt in this place, it is that talking – or writing, when they can't talk – vastly improves a fellow's chances of recovery. Some stay silent and it is like a wound uncleaned, an abscess undrained. There is a girl, Dorothy, who comes up in the afternoons bringing cigarettes for the men: she chats to them, whether they can talk back or not. The same with Mr Scott the barber, and his boy Albert (who also doubles as the men's bookmaker, though I'm not sure I'm meant to know that), always chatting. We always keep the notebooks handy. Sometimes, when someone talks who has not talked before, or picks up a pencil when previously he has looked on it as an enemy, a badge of his disability, it makes me want to laugh and cry and kiss them. Lady Driffield comes by every week now to work with the men writing down their stories. It is so restorative. They have even set up a newspaper! Did I tell you about the Christmas show? Several of the surgeons appeared in it, and some are also on the football team. Of course it is not all good news. Jock Anderson celebrated his fiftieth operation by getting what Major Fry calls Incurably

Cheerful, and breaking every window in the hospital. But then an officer came back to visit who has a two-inch piece of rib in his jaw, and he was breaking brazil nuts for us with his teeth. Sometimes I can hardly believe their courage. Major Gillies inspires them so, and makes it possible for them to believe that they can have a future despite the problems.

Some, of course, still do not want to communicate.

She means Riley. She does. That's her way of telling me he is still there. She would have found a way to tell me if he weren't. He hasn't gone to Paris. I suppose they write to each other. The girl must speak English then – his French wouldn't get them very far. Perhaps she is English. Why wouldn't she be? She's English. They'll marry and have babies and I will see them all strolling down the Broad Walk together on Sunday mornings and I'll have to say hello – STOP IT.

June

Dear Rose,

We are moving up to the front tomorrow, to be closer, to be more use. But I have come to the conclusion that you are braver than I, because you admit the possibility of recovery, and you fight and work for it every day, with your optimism and your cheerfulness. The German armies we are told are falling apart in the champagne cellars of the Marne and the chicken farms, eating and getting drunk and stealing hats and writing home, but there is still a constant supply of boys for me to do no good for. I just roll like a little cog in the machinery. No conscientious objector could do what I do. I am as bad as the Generals of the Somme and Passchendaele. I am as bad as Haig. I am not helping the boys to live.

June

Dear Nadine,

I don't think you have had any leave yet – perhaps you have and I have not heard from you about it. I think you need some. You are getting morbid. At least get a change of scene – go to Paris or somewhere fun. If you do go, look out for my cousin Peter, Major Peter Locke. He's been seconded to an office there after almost three years at the front. If you do, let me know how you find him. We haven't seen him for such a long time and he is one of those types who when he is home says very little about what is really going on, and just wants to go out to jolly places and have fun. Julia worries about him, and to be honest so do I. I dare say he's fine but he hardly writes and we haven't seen him.

Leave?? Has Rose not looked at the papers?

His flap had taken. Clean, alive, good blood supply, no shrinking or shrivelling. His pedicles had been cut, flattened out, and reapplied to the side of his head, halving in one move the area of deforested scalp. And in the jaw, there was some movement. He could eat a little – not chewing, but he had developed a method of mashing soft food against the roof of his mouth. He could swallow. False teeth were talked of.

He could murmur and hum. His tongue had been traumatised for so long that it had forgotten what to do. Rose sat by him. 'Say, la la la.'

He would raise an eyebrow.

'Ba ba ba,' she said. 'You don't need a jaw to talk. It comes from the throat. The Allies are counter-attacking. Did you see the paper? I'll drop it by later.'

He tried it out, *la la la*, late at night, when she wasn't there, when nobody could hear. His tongue lay like a dead thing, but a tiny little noise, creaky, ancient, came out of his tight, immobile mouth. He sounded disgusting and pathetic.

He practised the mashing movement against his palate. Lifting, collapsing. Pushing, letting fall.

≈

A Colonel Masters was wounded. He was to go to Paris. A nurse was to accompany him. It was to be Nadine. 'Why me?' she asked Matron.

'Because you, my child, are the one most likely to collapse on the job here. Don't hurry back. You might try getting a night's sleep, for example.'

≈

She stared at the snoring colonel in the carriage. He didn't need her. The train threw her body around.

By what authority do they do this to us?

≈

Paris. Summer. Oh God, oh God. Leaves. Roses. Little dogs. Pretty hats. Children.

Faint remnants of things she had once been going to do lurched around the back of her memory. Galleries. Van Gogh. Sir Alfred. Papa's friend Lady Scott, the sculptor, who had lived here ten years ago and used to say, 'I'll take you there one day, darling, when you're a bit bigger, and we'll go and have tea with Rodin. We'll take him pomegranates.'

She delivered the colonel to a nursing home. She stayed at the recommended *pension* near the Pont Louis Philippe. She went to look at her mother's childhood neighbourhood near the Place des Vosges, and wondered, looking around, about the past, and why her mother had said so little about it: but she was glad for the moment that if she had any unknown cousins in the neighbourhood they remained unknown. She took her uniform to a laundress. She ate two croissants with jam and drank a bowl of coffee so rich and milky it clagged her mouth. She slept for twenty-four hours in clean sheets, waking every hour or so, sometimes in tears, dreaming about flowers and fires intertwined. She found the number, and rang it, her heart beating strongly, and said: 'May I speak to Major Locke, please?'

He came on the line.

'Hello, Major Locke, my name is Nadine Waveney.'

A pause.

'I am a friend of your cousin Rose.' She liked saying that. They were friends.

'No, you're not,' he said. 'You're Riley Purefoy's girl.'

She dropped the telephone. Almost squawked. The joy, the bittersweet joy, of hearing herself described so.

She picked it up again. 'Hello?' she said.

'Hello,' he said. 'So sorry, that didn't come out quite right. Um. Friend of Rose's?'

'I'm here in Paris,' she said. 'I've been at Étaples. Rose suggested I look you up.'

'Well, find a cab and come over. We'll have lunch – take the cab on. Good,' he said, and hung up.

The brasserie was curled and mirrored, white-linened and clean-glassed. Shining dark wood panels, cool grey marble table-tops. Everything was so solid. The air was drunk with the smell of garlic in melting butter. Waiters burst through doors, pushing them open with a hip, carrying ice-piled platters of oysters and mussels and *crevettes gris* and little langoustines, their frondlike extremities fanned as if they were still underwater. Beautiful women slunk around in fur coats. Officers smoked cigars and drank. Chicken was two francs a plate. There was chicken. Nadine could not quite believe that such parallel universes lived alongside each other, so close, so far.

Major Locke was tall and blond and stooped, gentle, courteous. 'Let's have champagne,' he said. 'You probably deserve it. I'm sure you do.' It was not his first drink of the day.

My God, what a girl. Not obvious in any way, but plenty of SA there.

Nadine drank three beautiful wide glasses of bittersweet champagne, very quickly. So cold. So beautiful.

Locke watched her. 'You look like you need a meal,' he said. 'What will you have?'

'Steak,' she said. 'Rare.'

'And to start?'

'Sole meunière.' At the next table, a group of glamorous people were arguing about classicism and romanticism. An *abbé* was saying, 'What's the fuss? I wake every morning classical, and fall asleep every night romantic!' A wave of laughter crashed up and over. Nadine caught her breath, and gave a tiny hysterical laugh.

'And oysters, I think,' said Major Locke, 'just to get us going.'

She could hardly bear it. It was all so beautiful. Living, extravagant loveliness flooding around her as though Étaples didn't exist.

'I miss him so much,' she said. 'I love him so much. I have hardly seen him – I haven't seen him since July last year. I tried – I went to Sidcup to the hospital but he wouldn't see me. He wrote to me – he said there was a girl in Paris he was in love with and as soon as he was out of hospital he was going to come here to be with her . . .'

Locke's mouth fell open. What the . . . 'Miss Waveney,' he said.

She stopped in mid-flow. 'I'm awfully sorry,' she said.

'Miss Waveney, I was wondering how – indeed, whether – to tell you without embarrassing you that I used to have to read the letters he sent you . . .'

'I know. He used to put little messages to you in them. It made me laugh so much. So you know all my secrets. You know all about me . . .'

'Well, some things . . . I have had to read a lot of letters . . .'

'I know you know,' she said. 'Have you seen him?'

'Not since . . . not since he was wounded.' He remembered Riley's wound. He was thinking. There was no girl in Paris. Riley hadn't even been to Paris. He had not had time to acquire a girl. And he was in love, so in love, with Nadine.

'He said it wasn't serious,' she said. 'His wound.'

'Well, no, it wasn't,' said Major Locke.

'Oh.'

She sighed out of her nose. 'So do you know where he is now? Is he still in hospital?'

'I don't know. Is he?'

'Rose isn't allowed to tell me.'

'Perhaps it is taking a little longer to heal than they expected.'

'Ten months!' she said. 'Or perhaps he has left now. Perhaps he – oh!'

'What?'

The oysters arrived.

'Perhaps he is here.'

'I haven't seen him.'

'He'll be with her. They'll be in bed,' she said boldly.

'Dear girl,' he said.

'And of course you're Julia's husband, aren't you?' she said suddenly. She had so much she wanted to say but all her thoughts, her capacity to think, even, were shattered and rattled by the months of shelling, the gunfire, the fear, the deaths. Her mind was shaking. It had been for months.

She poured an oyster down her throat and looked up at him.

'Yes,' he said.

'She was very kind to me.'

'She is a very kind woman.'

'I stayed at your house! When Riley re-re-re-rejected me. I was upset . . .'

'Well, I hope you come again in happier times,' he said, and lifted his glass, and drained it. It soothed him to have an excuse for getting drunk. A very good excuse, actually.

'Bong jaw, Locke!' said a man passing by, an English officer, with an almost invisible leer at Nadine. 'Who's your pretty friend? Your friends are always so pretty . . .' He stopped at their table, and grinned.

Locke tightened his elbows, holding them in to his sides, resisting the urge to punch the man. He leant back instead.

Nadine glanced at the officer. At Major Locke.

Locke was toying with his glass, looking at it, twirling the stem a little. He looked up at the man. 'She's a nursing member of the VAD,' he said gently, 'stationed at Étaples where she deals daily with our mortally wounded comrades. This is her first leave – and probably her first decent meal – in six months. Her fiancé is in hospital in England, having had his face blown off at Passchendaele. Her father is the conductor Sir Robert Waveney, who raises all that money with the Patriotic Benefit Concerts. Anything else you want to know?'

'Oh, I say,' said the officer. 'I didn't mean . . .'

'Then don't say,' said Locke, staring at his glass. 'If you don't mean, then don't say.'

The officer bolted.

'What do you mean, "had his face blown off"?' Nadine said, as if from an icy suspension.

Locke filled his glass and drained it again. 'I was exaggerating,' he said. 'The man's a twit. Eat up.'

Peter Locke got so drunk that he very nearly made a pass at her. Instead, he took her dancing at Le Crocodillo, and got into a fight because the wrong band was playing. There was a particular saxophone player, an American – 'Mr Sidney Bechet,' he crowed. 'Why is Mr Sidney Bechet not playing here today? Only Mr Sidney Bechet,' he told her quietly, confidingly, 'has the power to SHUT UP the bloody noise in my head. Sorry,' he said. 'For saying bloody.'

'Don't worry,' she said. 'We all get sad. It's only natural to be completely, utterly, fatally sad. Only a very sick person would not be made sick and sad by all this.'

'I get to this stage where I jump in puddles and howl at the moon,' he said.

'It's four in the afternoon,' she said kindly. 'There is no moon.'

'There's always a moon,' he said. 'We may not be able to see it but it's always there.'

This seemed quite profound to them both.

Thrown out of the club, they got another bottle of champagne and went to the Tuileries Gardens, where the gallery was shut and the paintings evacuated, so they sat, and talked, and he was going to read to her but they fell asleep on the grass. A military policeman woke them.

'Excuse me, sir,' he said. 'I know I didn't wake you . . .' he said meaningfully. 'Could you tell me the time?'

They scrambled to their feet and brushed themselves off. Her body was stiff and chill from the grass, and her heart felt a warm strangeness from being with a nice person, an interesting person, a person connected with something that was real, once, even though it wasn't now. *And if the war is ending, what is there left?*

Daddy, she thought. *I'll find my daddy and crawl into his pocket for ever more . . .*

'I'm not going to be able to get away with this much longer,' Peter was saying. 'I seem to have lost all understanding of what I am meant to do.'

'You're meant to resist the Spring Push, sir,' she said.

'They won't let me,' he said sadly. 'I'm unreliable. I'm no bloody good for anything. Oh. Sorry. For saying bloody.'

'You have very nice manners,' she said, as an offering, a suggestion.

'Yes, I do, don't I? There's always that.'

She kissed him goodbye on the cheek, and felt his frisson. 'Take this, anyway,' he said. It was the book he had been going to read to her.

She walked to the station. She didn't know how else to get there.

~

On the train back to Étaples she looked at the book Peter had pressed on her. *Light and Twilight*, Edward Thomas. A story called 'The Stile'. The words fell clear and strong before her eyes. A man was trying to say goodbye to a friend after a walk, standing in English countryside, understanding the nature of being. It was the most beautiful thing she had ever read.

She read: '. . . something not to be separated from the dark earth and the light sky; a strong citizen of infinity and eternity . . . I knew that I could not do without the Infinite, nor the Infinite without me.'

She read it over and over.

When she got back, she wrote a letter.

21 July, Étaples

Dear Riley,

I don't know for certain if you are still at the Queen's Hospital, or if you will get this. I am well. I went to Paris and met your Major Locke. At every corner I expected to see you with your arm around your new girl, and I spent the entire leave in expectation of being sick.

I hope you are well.

I have cut all my hair off. It was bad enough in London but out here it was just not possible. All fleas and lice, and impossible to comb. My life has been just iodoform, rubber boots, enamel dishes, squares of gauze. Little things fluttering round the gates of hell. Tomorrow they are moving us up closer to the front, ready for the big push. Already our boys die to the lullaby of guns. They ask me for permission to die, and I give it to them. They are afraid the doctor will be angry with them, or that they will be seen as cowards. They are so nice about it.

Riley, who led us into this blind alley lined with mud and corpses? Why do they talk of the sanctity of life when what I see before me is life squandered and trodden underfoot in the mud and pouring off the edge of the table, leaking and turning to slime? Surely what is precious is treated as precious? So how can life be precious when it is at every moment destroyed ignored humiliated neglected and left to seep away? We see before us that life is not precious to the big who, what, whatever it is that let this happen. That didn't prevent it from happening. Was it wickedness or was it ignorance? It It It . . .

You probably know that I am killing my heart here. I cannot stand the pain it feels. I cannot do what has to be done here, with that pain going on. Sometimes a scrap of the woman I was before comes to me, the pull of a voice, the scent of a hyacinth, trees whispering – I die of it. It is impossible to be a woman here and not die of it.

I cannot bear to end this letter, to break this small contact with you.

I think of you all the time.

Nadine

When he read it, in a deckchair on the handsome York stone terrace at Queen's, under the first blooming of heavy pink roses, his voice came. He was roaring, inarticulate, roaring. Nurses came running.

Riley wrote Rose a note:

Rose I had a letter. Please, write and tell her I have left here.

'Oh – no,' she said.

He wrote:

tell her no forwarding address

He added,

please

'Oh, God,' she said.
His eyes urged her.
She had seen a notice in a magazine:

Lady, fiancé killed, will gladly
marry officer totally blinded or
otherwise incapacitated by the war. . .

And she still had the scrap of paper where he had written
'should marry you then'. She had kept it, like a schoolgirl,
because it was, she felt, the closest she would ever get.

'Riley,' she said. 'You could give her the chance. She might
want to. You could give her the choice.'

His eyes were very articulate. As loud and as clear and
as desperate as could be desired. No.

∼

Dear Nadine,
In haste – I should let you know that Captain Purefoy has
now left Queen's Hospital. His surgery was successful and
he left no forwarding address. Affect, Rose

∼

That night Riley lay awake. He could hear the guns across the Channel.

He had done the right thing.

She needed someone stronger than him. He could not help her. He was, now, only to be helped – and not the way she would want to help. She would want to drag him back to the life and the light that he did not want. He could not gratify her in that. He had nothing to give. The only decent response left to him was to admit it.

He had to protect himself from her and her bloody love.

Chapter Twenty-four

Sidcup and London, September 1918
A letter came for Rose, from Peter:

France,
September 1918
Dear Rose, Old girl,

Well I know I should have written before, I should always have written before, but there we go I didn't, and I'm sorry. Anyway I'm writing now to tell you that I've been told I'm to go back to England. My position here will soon be closing, and I am held to be too 'tired' to go back to the Front, despite the fact that it is still all go out there and every Englishman in Christendom is going to be needed. Well. Every Englishman but me. I am to take leave, and that's an order, and they'll see about me in a month. I can't say I'm happy about it.

They say I am to come home and rest. I don't know exactly when. I'll send a telegram when I've got my times. Could you tell Julia?

Your loving old Pete

Oh, thank God. Oh, thank God, he has escaped it, he has come through. It will be too late, surely, for them to send him back afterwards. Surely, surely, it will be over soon now. Surely.

But why hasn't he written to Julia?

Julia was in London again. Rose rang her at the hotel she used.

'Oh,' she said. 'Oh . . . ' a sort of swoony gasp '. . . did he say when?'

'He'll send a telegram,' Rose said.

'Then I must – oh.' Her breath was feathery and odd.

'Julia? What's the matter?'

'Nothing! Nothing at all. Let me know when the cable comes.'

'Well, it'll go to Locke Hill, and I won't be there . . .'

'Harker can bring it to you. Ring up and tell him.'

Why can't you ring up and tell him? It's your husband, your house, your servant. And I do have other things to do, you know, unlike you with your lunches and your matinées and your . . .

'Julia, why can't you get back?'

'I've got a few things to do here,' Julia said. 'I'll be back in good time.' Rose could almost hear her speedy heartbeat.

I suppose, thought Rose, with asperity, *that anything's better than tuning the cello twice a day. I suppose.*

Everyone was annoying Rose. Peter, assuming she would deal with Julia. Julia, assuming she would deal with Peter. Mrs Orris, setting herself up with Tom and never mind the effect on Julia, who should be looking after the poor little thing instead of going shopping and having massages all the time. Nadine, still banging on about Riley. Riley, still lying around like a week of wet Tuesdays.

Oh, come on. Who doesn't annoy you?

Only Gillies. She envied him so much the ease with which he seemed able to deal with the human tragedy around him, his capacity to think about the science of what he was doing, to move smoothly on through the never-ending self-replenishing sea of pain and confusion without being side-tracked or capsized. And not only that he had these qualities but that he spread them, brought them out in those around him. Rose had thought, a year ago, that she was developing that medical knack. Jamison (*don't mention Jamison. Don't think about Jamison*) had caused it moments of instability, but overall she had been proud of it – until Riley capsized her. Riley with his eloquent eyes and his utter silence, his beautiful girl, his noble act, his enigmatic notes. None of the others who had come and gone, or come and stayed, had got to her. Just God rest Jamison's soul, and don't tell Riley. There was a reason they had always been on different wards.

Clenching her teeth, Rose sat down to her correspondence:

Dearest Pete,

I am so so happy to hear that you are coming back at last. We have been hoping ever since the Americans joined in that men like you who have been out so long would have a chance of some time at home. It has been so long we almost thought that perhaps you weren't going to be getting any leave at all. Julia is delighted of course, and didn't even

315

ask why you had not written to her yourself. We're all ready for you, and longing to see you.

   With love from Rose

She liked the word 'longing'. It sounded rather racy.

~

In a smart little London hotel room, Julia sat motionless for a while, thinking, trying to breathe steadily, wondering how much to say. As little as possible. It was so close to the end, it had to be . . . Everyone said it must be over soon. Dared she hope that Peter would not have to go away again? Dared she?

   She had not written or spoken to her mother since the last disastrous trip to Froxfield. Every week she had sent cards or pretty toys to Tom, and every night her body had craved his presence. Her fury with her mother was immense, and her hand quivered as she wrote, carefully, politely, formally:

Dear Mother,
I am writing to let you know the good news that Peter will be returning from France any day now. Please arrange for Tom to be returned within the week. I know Peter would be very disappointed not to find his son at Locke Hill when he comes home from the Front.
   With best wishes,
   Julia

Before leaving town, she gave the letter personally to the porter, and asked that he make sure it went right away.

Back at Locke Hill, she stared. Time to take stock. It wasn't the mirror. It wasn't the light. It wasn't the colour of her dress. It wasn't the time of the month. It wasn't because she hadn't been regular. It was because she was getting older, and showing the stress, and that was all there was to it, and it had to be dealt with *now* – now! – *because he's coming back!* And she knew what to do. Not surgery – not after the last fiasco – but there were other things a girl could do. The problem was that until she knew *when* Peter was coming, she couldn't know if there was time. A week, they said, at least, for it to settle down afterwards. She'd been terribly sensible, asking about how it worked. Madame Louise just said 'special formula', but Julia had pushed, and discovered the ingredients – phenol and glycerine and croton oil (croton! A very ugly plant, she'd always thought, but you can't blame it for that) – and Gladys Deacon had had it done, as had many of the beauties. Mostly it was for older ladies to get rid of wrinkles, but younger women would have it for the clarity and tightness it gave, and the pallor. Julia thought of the Boldoni portrait of Gladys, how she glowed like a lily, like moonlight, like snow. No sign of the scars and droops the nurse had mentioned. *I wish I could see her in the flesh, and ask her . . .*

A week later, there was no news from her mother, and no news from Peter. She realised she had landed herself in a position of desperation without the possibility of action, entirely dependent on the responses – unforthcoming – of others. *I could have had it over and done with by now! And when the telegram does come, it might say he'll be here the next day . . .* A moment of boldness seized her as she read the newspaper. No one ever achieved anything by hesitation! Did the men hesitate when going over the top? Did the generals hesitate in making those difficult decisions? If the Americans had not hesitated for so long after the sinking of the *Lusitania*, wouldn't everything have gone quicker and better?

She fired off another letter to her mother; exactly the same wording. Perhaps it had been lost in the post. She was nervous to have been so straightforward with her mother. She clung to it.

Then she rang the salon, and arranged to go up the next day. *Serve bloody Peter right if I'm not there to greet him. After all, haven't I been waiting for ever? And holding on to very little? And aren't I doing it for him anyway?*

Oh, God, he's coming back, he's coming back – dear God, I know you're busy but please please let him love me the way he used to please let him love me let me make him happy . . .

The frontage of the little salon was familiar to her now. Welcoming, with its pleasant memories of massages and facials and her pretty eyebrows, pedicures and manicures, loving attentions from Madame Louise and June, the silly young nurse with the very deft hands.

Lying on her back on the narrow white bed, consciousness fading, the gust of the smell of Lysol and chloroform was somehow promising to her, like a spring breeze. She was sad, as she went under, that she wouldn't be present to witness, properly to experience, the melting of the crystals, the mixing with the oil, the coating of the solution on to her ready face, the layer of plaster to be painted on top. She was glad, though, that she knew what Madame would be doing while she slept, while the chemicals worked away under the mask, tightening and drying the surface layer of her tired skin into little flakes, which would then rub off and fall with the crumbling flakes of the drying plaster, revealing a naked layer of new young skin. *A chemical assault on the ravages of time* . . . She felt again the bravery and sacrifice, the modernity, the joy of it . . . *I am doing this for you, my darling. I will be everything you could want* . . .

. . . She came round, staring through the tiny eyeholes of her plaster mask. It hurt, but not much. Phenol was itself an anaesthetic, Madame had told her.

The next week, the week of salves and balms and staying in, was maddening. At least there was no word from Rose about the telegram. Her face was red and burnt-looking, and as it calmed down, each day, it looked better. At least, it looked better than red and burnt. It did not look better than before the peel. She checked every day, every few hours, in between chapters of Marie Corelli, which made her feel as if she were eating entire boxes of chocolates at a sitting, but she couldn't stop.

'It's made no difference,' she said to Madame, on the telephone, and went round to show her.

'Oh, but it has, madam,' said Madame. 'See, here at the brow, around the eyes, and those little freckles you had . . .'
I had no freckles!

319

It's made no difference.

'I think we're going to have to do it again,' Julia said.

'That is not advisable, madam,' said Madame. 'Certainly not for some while. The complexion must be allowed to recover.'

'But you can do me before Christmas?' she said hopefully, thinking, *before my birthday. He'll be back by my birthday.* She had decided that a while ago.

'Oh, no, madam. Not till perhaps February at the earliest.'

Tears started in Julia's eyes. February was far too late! Could she explain to Madame Louise? Would she understand, if Julia truly opened her heart to her? She looked at her, trying to judge whether there would be any understanding there of the situation in which Julia found herself. She feared not. Madame Louise was a working woman, with a role to play. Julia was beginning to see, intellectually, that her own role – pretty, useless, adorable – had been rendered valueless by the war. She half knew it. She half knew that other women found her pathetic, banal . . . She had felt the ground she was bred for slipping from beneath her feet during the course of the war, and she had seen other women finding new kinds of women to be – women who had not, before the war, been so totally bred for the altar of adorability and marriage. *I could have gone off with Raymond Dell, and been that kind of new woman; I could have driven ambulances, if Rose hadn't so entirely scorned the idea; I could be a decent mother; I could, I could . . .*

There was nobody to say to Julia, 'It's not your fault. You didn't invent marriage and the traditional roles of women;

you didn't start the war; you didn't choose to be valued only for your beauty, and prepared for nothing more useful than displaying it.'

'Please,' was all she managed to say to Madame Louise. 'There's nothing else . . .' But Madame Louise was not to be persuaded, and found Julia tiresome, and went into the other room.

~

Julia went home in a new dress, looking wonderful, slender, elegant, with unshed tears and a sense of profound personal irrelevance rising within her. *Still* no sign of Peter or his telegram. Still no letter from her mother. Knowing it was neurotic, she plumped all the cushions in the house, tuned the cello and went back to London.

She came home in another new dress, ashamed of it, unable to stop despite how ludicrous it had become. *I'm a clockwork figure, rattling round and round in circles. I'm absurd.* No sign of her husband; no sign of her son.

She couldn't believe the war wasn't over. It must be over. She read in the newspaper that Guatemala had declared war on Germany. *Well, if even Guatemala thinks it's safe to get involved, it really must be finished.*

Everyone was on edge. *Perhaps I'll go to Paris. I could go to Paris and fetch him! We could have a marvellous reunion . . .*

She went back up to London.

Mrs Joyce thought she would sour the milk at this rate.

She came back again. She told Mrs Joyce she was going to bed, and wanted no visitors, 'but call me if Rose rings up'.

Mrs Joyce hoped it wasn't this flu.

'Of course not,' said Julia.

She too hoped it wasn't the flu. The flu was killing people faster than the war. She felt . . . strange.

'It's really nearly over now, isn't it, mum?' said Mrs Joyce.

'Yes – I . . .' Julia realised she didn't know what to think.

'And the major coming home, mum,' said Mrs Joyce.

'Yes,' said Julia, almost hysterically. *If he'd only deign to tell us when.*

'And Mrs Orris called, mum. She said to say she'd be bringing the little one on Saturday week.'

'What?'

'Master Tom, mum, she'll be bringing him on Saturday week.'

'Yes,' said Julia. Tom. Peter. Christmas. Peace. The appalling potential of the situation made her almost swoon. What was a woman meant to do with so much normality?

She went upstairs and turned on her bath, and started the ritual, staring at herself in the mirror: from the front, from the side, from the other side. Waist: slender. Bust: elegant yet alluring. Hair: still long. Peter preferred it that way. *I should have been a better kind of woman for him. I should have loved him better. I am pathetic – they're right about me.*

Tom!

Close-up: on the body, on the face. Left side, right side. Her jaw was all right for now. Her nose was charming with its little imperfection. Eyes vast and blue.

A thought skittered across the surface of her mind, like a water boatman across a pool, brittle, delicate, alarming: *IT DOESN'T BLOODY WELL MATTER!*

322

For a moment, her beautiful eyes showed absolute fear. Gone.

Of course it matters. Something has to matter. It has always mattered. If it didn't matter, then what, after all, was the point of her? *It's the only thing I have.*

~

Rose popped in. She'd had a note from Peter.

Julia jumped up. 'Any firmer news on when he's coming? Or where he is?'

'I don't know, Julia,' Rose replied. 'He didn't say exactly.' The phrase lay on the air softly, drifting, unfinished.

Well, thought Julia. *That's good. It could be good. He'll turn up when he's ready. For goodness' sake, what difference does it make after all this time? It's not a problem.* 'Well,' she said smartly, 'it's not as if we haven't got plenty to do without him.' She hadn't breathed properly in days. Little brittle panting breaths. No wonder everyone hated her.

She half didn't even want to see him. And Tom! She was terrified.

Chapter Twenty-five

Sidcup and Wigan, November 1918

The war, after dragging its tail around for weeks like a dying serpent, crawled into the armistice, and was, if you could muster faith in that, over. For those not closely involved, felicity was unconfined. The maroons went off. The lights came on. The bells rang out. The bunting went up. The champagne went down. There was talk of who was coming home, and when. Talk, once again, of being home for Christmas. For the rest, felicity was complicated by disbelief, bereavement, unhealed wounds, location, unspent contracts, logistics of travel, and the vast immobility of the vast body of the machine and bureaucracy of war.

At Sidcup, the news brought much laughing and cheering and clapping each other on the back, and sudden inclinations to be best friends. Though the patients were all stuck there as long as they were stuck there, they were at least released now from the War Office's requirement that they stay there all the time between operations.

Riley thought: *But there's no reason to believe it won't start up again at any moment. It's only an armistice. And even if it is real, lovely for some people but so what for us? It's rather uncouth of us to be such living reminders that, over though the war may be – um, what was the right word? – aspects of the war are not over at all and never will be.*

Someone said, *Come, come, lad, it's over!*

Riley had had more than a year to forget all the things he couldn't forget, and to get used to the things he was going to have to get used to. But so far the outside world, a world of peace, the new world, whatever it was going to be, had not been part of that. It was not something he cared to ponder. Riley thought: *Before, while it was still on, I was Captain Purefoy, wounded soldier. Who am I to be now? Mr Purefoy, disabled ex-serviceman?* His age rang through his head like the tolling of a bell. Twenty-two, twenty-two, twenty-two. There was an awfully long time ahead of him.

On the day the armistice was announced, he was remembering Jack Ainsworth (over). He had taken his Small Book (over) out of his officer's valise (over) two days before, and Ainsworth's scrap of paper had fallen out. Riley, who knew off by heart the words on it, nevertheless read it again, where it fell on his white sheet. (Whitesheet, Plugstreet, Zonnebeke and Pop . . .) (Over.)

> *Courage for the big troubles in life, patience for the small. And when you have laboriously finished your day's efforts, go to sleep in peace.*
>
> *(Be of good cheer. God is awake.)*

It wasn't Jack's writing. It was Sybil's. Riley knew because he had censored enough of Jack's letters (over): long, fond letters, missing her, missing the children, sending love (over) to so many people, by name. Admitting he was bored. No mention of the fear and the horror (over). Longing, longing for home (over). Finding it in him to say, 'The smell of the apple trees is lovely here.'

Riley was not of good cheer. He didn't know what good cheer was. Was finding the smell of the apple trees lovely good cheer?

He glanced out of the window. There were trees outside. They were not burnt and sharp and black. (Over.)

Courage. Patience. Efforts. Laboriously. Good cheer. Peace.

Jack Ainsworth's voice: *You could give it a go, lad.*

Ainsworth, Couch, Ferdinand, Dowland and many more (over). And the smell: over. And the noise. Over.

For the next few days he watched the other patients. *Patience.* He was looking for good cheer among them. How did they bear it? *How could they bear it?* This was not a rhetorical question. He wanted to know how the others bore it, what they actually did to bear it, because he could not bear it. And he could not suddenly start to bear it just because *It* was over. No one ever wins a war, and wars are never over.

He had dreamt he'd sent a telegram to Ainsworth saying, 'Please come back and bring the boys,' and Ainsworth had replied, 'All right see you on Saturday.'

Over.

That afternoon, in the garden, a young gunner, a Welshman, with no nose, turned to him, and said: 'Captain, you've been staring at us for months. You never come out, and when you do you stare at us. Give it a rest, now, would you? You're giving me the willies.'

Riley stared. Another man clapped his shoulder, and said: 'Never mind him, old man. He's just a bit upset. He lost his nose, you know.' And they all started laughing, except the Welshman, who looked as if he were about to hit someone.

I'm making it worse for them, Riley thought.

He was so, so bored. Bored of misery, of anger, of why-me, of poor-me, of what's-the-point, of self-deception and of stoicism and of waiting for a miracle; bored of his mother's letters saying how brave he is, bored of his cruelty in not replying to her – what could he say? *No, mother, bravery implies a choice, a cowardly alternative, and, mother, if there had been an alternative I would have taken it, really I would.* He was bored of egg; of his misery in his speechlessness, of debating with himself whether suicide was the brave or the cowardly choice. Bored of being unable to discuss this, or anything else, with anyone. Bored of inflicting his misery on other people.

But if you don't die, you have to live.

You have to live.

In which case, what?

Be of good cheer?

～

When Rose came, Riley gave her a letter:

Dear Major Gillies,
Having been here for over a year, under orders, I would like

to apply for leave. Four or five days should do. Could you let me know how to go about it, under the circumstances? I think I will need one of Archie Lane's masks, which I understand could take a little while to organise.

Yours sincerely
Capt. R. Purefoy

He gestured to Rose that she could read it.

∾

Gillies called him in. 'Why d'you want a mask?' he said. 'Nasty things. Hot, uncomfortable, and an admission of my failure. Be patient, Purefoy, and you'll be presentable in the end. To be honest, though I'm glad you want to go out, I'm not sure you're ready. Have you been to the village at all? To the pub, walks?'

Riley shook his head.

'What will you do about communicating?'

Riley lifted his notebook.

'But it's not just a physical thing, old man – you're out of practice. I know you talk to Rose . . .'

Riley liked his loose use of the word 'talk'.

'. . . but you're not exactly the chatty type.' Gillies cocked an eyebrow at him, waiting for a response.

Riley blinked, and wrote:

I haven't had very much to say. I wouldn't have had anyway. But there is someone I want to talk to. I need to visit them, and don't want to scare them. Then I'll come back.

Gillies read it. 'What about food?' he asked. 'It's very easy to become malnourished, and that would be very bad news. I've worked hard on you, Purefoy, and we have more to do. I would like you to be a success. Are you motivated enough to feed yourself properly?'

Riley wrote:

soup

and Gillies said, 'How are you going to get it down?' Riley wrote:

by embarrassing slurping in private

A little shot of joy ran through Gillies. Sign of a sense of humour. The best possible sign.

Because of Riley's quiet insistence, Lane and young Mickey Shirlaw, the miner from Motherwell who'd arrived as a patient and was well on the way to being a dental technician, made him a mask. It was as unpleasant to wear as Gillies had said it would be, and in the end Riley didn't take it with him when he went.

~

Jarvis was back, to have his great ham-nose restyled a little. Mrs Jarvis had complained of his snoring, and he even woke himself up. Major Gillies had been happy to oblige.

'Glad you're going out, Purefoy,' Jarvis said. 'Here – have this.' He was brandishing a slender metal tube about eighteen inches long. 'I made it for Jamison, in the workshop, from a bit of shell casing. Brass. From Hill 62.'

Rose passed it over. It was beautiful. Jarvis had chased a pattern in spirals round and round its length.

Purefoy nodded his thanks.

Jarvis said, 'You're welcome.'

Have they always been kind? Riley wondered. He drank his egg-flip through the brass straw that night, and used it to rinse his mouth in the bathroom afterwards. *Don't forget the sulcus. You have a sulcus now. It's the gap between the flesh of the lower lip and the mandible. Keep it clean.*

∽

One of the anaesthetists was going up to London in his motor-car, and dropped Riley at Euston station. 'Good luck, Captain,' he said, and Riley nodded.

He had his wound stripes, his pips and a scarf. He wound it high.

He glanced around. City streets. Crowd. Jesus Christ, what a racket. What a mob. Jesus.

He put himself with his back to the wall and breathed carefully. Here is the world. Here is London. Here are the people. The war is over. He knew absolutely nothing about it. *You're twenty-two years old, Riley, and it all starts here, like this.*

Only as the train pulled into Wigan North Western did Riley think he should have written to her. He'd scare the daylights out of her. Even if he looked all right, just turning up out of the blue would give her a shock . . . Damn. He should write now, deliver the letter, stay somewhere, wait till he heard from her . . .

The town was busy. He came out into the street: men, women, wagons, girls, children. Mill chimneys loomed beyond, and the air was metallic. He'd never been in the north before, but the accent he knew well: the great troops of scrawny tough boys in big caps, with dirty jokes and big hands, railwaymen and miners and factory hands. Ainsworth's voice had been something between the Manchesters and the Liverpool Irish.

'La la la la ba ba ba,' Riley murmured, behind his scarf, and crossed the road to the Swan and Railway. Beautiful stained-glass panels: a swan, almost embracing a steam train in its snowy wings. *Like Leda and Zeus*, he thought. *Now who was that by . . . Burne Jones? And that one at the British Museum* . . . It was a strange, surreal pairing. He liked it. He breathed deeply as he entered the fuggy room, and went up to the bar. He took out his notebook – a new one – and wrote:

Brown ale please. Do you have rooms?

He tore out the page and passed it across to the waiter, who was polishing a glass. The waiter glanced down at it, then at Riley, and said: 'What's the matter? Cat got your tongue?'

Riley stared at him. A feeling of cold rose up his body. He leant forward, putting his elbows on the bar, and resting his precious chin carefully on his hands, the scarf wrapped round it. The cuffs of his sleeves, with their assorted pips and stripes – his promotions, his wounds, his years overseas, his pre-1915 – were right there for the fellow's information. *Does he not know there's been a war?*

The man was grinning at him.

'Well, do you want a drink or not?' he said.

Riley glanced down at the note, and back at him.

'I can't read,' the man said, with a smirk, eyeballing. 'You'll need to take that scarf off and talk, like a human being.'

It was all Riley needed. His arm snaked out across the bar and punched the little squit in the face.

Warmth flooded him.

Concentric circles.

The man reeled.

Stop.

Riley stood back suddenly, holding his arm as if to restrain it. He was breathless. He wanted to say sorry. He felt a light come into his eyes, and an unaccustomed feeling across his cheekbones, which he identified as a smile.

'Right,' said the waiter. 'Get out.' He touched his jaw. 'Piss off.' He had picked up a glass, cowering, aggressive.

It's not his fault; he doesn't know, Riley thought. Then: *He ought to be able to tell.*

Riley felt his eyes smiling, his cheeks stretching. *Sorry*, he thought. *But you asked for it. And now I will know the truth.* He took off his hat, and put it on the bar. His hair was a little longer than the army would normally prefer, but the curls didn't hide the shining scarred stripe over the back. He unwrapped his scarf, keeping his eyes steady on the waiter.

As the scarf dropped, the man gasped. His hands fell suddenly, heavily, to the bar. The glass bounced and shattered on the wooden floor. He was saying, 'Jesus Christ, Jesus fucking Christ.' With one finger, Riley pushed the note towards him, then went and sat down at a small table at the front of the room. He dug in his bag, and pulled out his straw. He played with it between his fingers, and he felt like a twat. *Well done there, Riley. Good work. Just the ticket.*

A few minutes later a different man brought over the beer; older, barrel-chested. The landlord, at a guess.

'Sorry about that,' he said. 'Flat feet. Never went. 'Asn't a clue. Anything I can do for you, sir, just say. Will you be all right with that?'

Riley gave a little twirl of his straw in his fingers, like a sergeant major's baton in parade. *I'm the fucking Phantom of the Opera. I shouldn't be allowed out. I have to speak again. I cannot be out here in the world and not speak.*

Riley gestured to the man to sit, and nodded thanks to him, looking him in the eye. This was going to be exhausting. At Sidcup, everyone knew what to do. The routine bore them along. He had been ricocheting between routine and crisis for years. Here, there was neither.

He wrote:

If you could direct me to Poolstock Lodge, Poolstock

The landlord, having read the note, put his hand briefly to his mouth, and said: 'Is it Sybil Ainsworth you're after, lad?'

Riley nodded.

'Does she know you're coming?'

Riley shook his head.

The man was thinking.

'Were you alongside Jack Ainsworth?' he asked.

Riley nodded.

After a moment the man said, 'If you can wait till closing, I'll take you over myself. Likely she'll offer you a room there. If she can't there's a bed for you here, on the house, as long as you're staying.'

Riley looked for a moment as if he might demur, but the landlord said gently, 'Don't be too proud, lad.'

Riley nodded.

~

Sybil was broad-faced, full-figured, small-waisted, strong. The house was clean and comfortable within its means. The landlord had gone in first.

'Come in, Captain,' she said. 'You'll take us as you find us. Please sit down.' She took his greatcoat. The scarf was tucked into his tunic. Two studio photos of Jack stood on the mantelpiece: one in uniform, hat on, standing beside Sybil as she sat, a curtain behind them, formal. The other, clearly taken at the same time, Jack hatless, standing alone, a cloudy backdrop behind him, looking very handsome, and just like himself. His big ears.

He wanted to say, 'Mrs Ainsworth, your husband . . .'

He took off his hat, sat on the edge of the little armchair she offered him, and pulled out his notebook.

He couldn't even think what he wanted to say because he had to write it, and it was different: it was formal; it was permanent; it had no tone of voice to carry it over its own inconsistencies; it had . . . He had to learn to talk again. Or to write. *So much to learn.*

334

'Would a cup of tea be nice?' she asked. 'Mr Sutton's told me about your face – if you want to keep it covered that's all right with me, but if you'd like tea I can look the other way, or you can do whatever you need to do. I wouldn't mind the sight of you, if you're concerned about that. But perhaps when the children come in from school . . .'

There was so much he could say to that. He wrote:

A cup of tea, thank you. I drink through a straw, it's tidier and not too frightening I don't think. I'll be gone before the children come.

'You will not, if you don't mind,' she said. 'Jack wrote very highly of you, Captain, and the children would like to see you . . .' She stumbled for a second over 'see'. 'They'd like to meet you. Arthur and little Sybil hardly knew their dad. Alice and Annie remember him better. They'd be sad if I let you go.'

She hadn't sat down. She went next door to make the tea. Riley could hear her moving about. She could have come back into the front room, the company room, but she didn't.

He went across to the little desk opposite the fireplace, and started to write her a letter.

Dear Mrs Ainsworth,
It's easier to write to you now, having seen your face. My previous letter written from France was full I know of all the weaknesses that such a letter always must have. I have come now because I want to tell you how Jack died, but

335

more importantly how he lived, and how much he meant to me.

He died bravely – they always say this but it is true. He was blown up by a shell near Hébuterne; well, he was sent flying, and he died of a head wound that day. They were able to bury him in the village cemetery, where in times of peace I am told daisies grow. Prayers were said, and the CO read the prayer of yours that he carried with him always.

He lived, as a soldier, with kindness, odd though that may sound. He was kind. He was older than many of us, and his kindness meant a great deal to a great many of

Riley had to stop a moment, his memory sabotaged.

Sybil came back in, carrying a tin tray, flower-patterned, with two cups of tea. 'Sugar?' she said, and he nodded, and handed her the letter he was halfway through.

She read it, and nodded a couple of times, and she folded it and put it in her pocket. As she did so, Riley reached into his inner pocket and took out his Small Book, and from it, her prayer. He passed it to her, and she took it, and read it as if she had never seen it before. She stood a few seconds in silence, holding it. 'Did he give it you?' she said, finally.

Riley nodded, and scribbled:

Indirectly. It came on to me in hospital.

'I wondered what had happened to it,' she said. Then there was a moment of embarrassed confusion as she tried to give it back to him, and he wanted to say, 'No, no, it's yours,' but she said: 'He gave it you. It's yours.'

He put it back in his book, back in his pocket, and he wrote:

Thank you.

And then he wrote,

Mrs Ainsworth, what is good cheer?

She smiled then. 'Remembering that things will change,' she said, 'and maybe for the better.'

He wrote:

Look on the bright side?

She curled her lip. 'I know,' she said, 'some think that sounds like claptrap from a simpleton. And you know what the war's done to me and my children. But bitterness never helped anyone and that's God's truth.'

'Na,' he said. The scarf was loose around his face.

'You, for example,' she said. 'Will you talk again?'

He shrugged.

'Likely you will if you want to,' she said. 'Who do you want to talk to? And don't say Jack.'

He smiled. 'Ya,' he said.

'Me?' she said. 'All right.'

She didn't know it was his first word.

~

Mr Sutton from the Swan joined them for supper, and told stories of Jack's boyhood, and their times together at the railway coachbuilder's. Sybil gave Riley his food beforehand, on his own, and he thanked her for the courtesy. The children stared. They warmed up after Riley sketched each of them in his notebook, and tore the pictures out to give to them. Young Annie was very like her father.

'It's very good,' she said. 'It looks just like me.' She looked at him. 'But I can't see what you look like. Why've you yer scarf on at supper?'

Sybil didn't tell her to hush, though Alice did. Riley put his finger up, to ask them to wait a moment, and scribbled her a note. She read it out loud. '"I was hurt badly at the battle of Pass-, Passchen-, Passchendaele" – oh, yes, I know that one – "and now my face is very frightening so I cover it up."' She stared over at him. 'Is it really, really frightening?'

He nodded.

'Is that why you don't talk?'

He nodded.

'Have you not got a mouth any more?'

He kind of shrugged.

'Can I see?'

'Annie!' cried Alice. Arthur stared, agog with appalled hope. Sybil was still silent, watching. Mr Sutton said, 'Oh, dear God, child.'

Annie turned and said, 'Don't swear, Uncle.' Then: '*Can I see?*' she asked again. Her face was kind and curious.

Riley looked at Sybil.

'It's up to you,' she said. 'You can't shelter the little ones too much.'

He looked pensively at Annie. Eight years old, her father's daughter. Then he wrote:

If it gives you nightmares, you can come and kick me in the morning. And remember, I have a very pretty heart.

She read it out, and laughed, and settled down to stare at him. The others were motionless, except for Mr Sutton who started refilling his pipe. Alice looked at the table.

Riley unwrapped his face.

Silence of anticipation.

There.

My half-healed face naked in a room of strangers.

Such handsome eyes, thought Sybil. The expression in those eyes, the fear, the apologetic concern for the feelings of those looking, the expectation of revulsion, filled her with tenderness towards him. The eyes transfixed her before she saw the rail of scars, the crooked, still swollen jawline, the strange rebuilt mouth.

Poor lad, thought Mr Sutton. *Dear God, no wonder Bert dropped a glass.*

'Eyurrgh,' cried Arthur, fascinated, and only six. Alice shushed him, and would not look. Little Sybil's mouth was wobbling. Riley glanced at her sadly, and Alice smiled at him with a tiny gulp and took her out into the kitchen. They could hear as she started to howl.

'That is quite scary,' said Annie, in an observational tone. She squinted at it, and moved round to look at it from the side. 'I quite like it, though. Can I touch it?'

Riley felt the tightness across his cheekbones again: a

little snort of utterly unexpected laughter, trying to find a place to go. He nodded, and watched her until she went out of focus as she came up close and carefully prodded different places on his face.

'But you have got a mouth,' she said. 'I bet you could talk.'

He said, 'Ad da da.'

She grinned. 'See?' she cried. 'You must take honey and hot water, and whisky, for your throat.'

He reached round her for the notebook. She passed it to him.

He wrote:

The surgeon at the hospital made me a new jawbone out of rubber, and brought the skin from my head to cover it. They are going to get me teeth. They say I might be able to chew and eat again. I think I'll always be a messy eater, though.

'Arthur was a messy eater,' she said kindly. 'He grew out of it. He practised eating tidily because Mam said to. Did they cut you and stitch you?'

yes

'Do you remember, Mam, they did that to Jean's dad after the fire in the engine house?'

Arthur and Mr Sutton were still staring. Sybil said, 'They did that, Annie.'

'It's clever how they can do that,' Annie said. 'And it's not

340

that frightening, you know. I suppose because your eyes are kind.'

His pupils shrank away, tiny, black in the grey fields. He blinked several times. Then he groped for his notebook. Sybil passed it. Riley wrote:

Thank you. What you have said makes me feel much better about my face.

She read it, smiled at him, jumped up and patted his cheek. 'Best do the dishes now,' she said.

~

Riley lay flat on his back in Arthur's little bed, opening and shutting his mouth. Opening and shutting, opening and shutting. He held his nose, and tried to breathe through his mouth. 'Nga, nga, nga,' he said. 'Na da da la la la na na na dee nadee nadine.'

He fell asleep weeping.

Sybil heard him. Lying beside her, so did Alice. Each wished there was some way under God's sun that she could go next door and comfort him.

Chapter Twenty-six

London, December 1918

Peter was at the Forty-Four, trying to locate relief in his body. His booth was by the tiny dim dance-floor, lit with the pink twinkling gleam of gas lamps. On his small table were a dark, glowing whisky and an ashtray, semi-full. The club was almost empty except that on the bandstand Mr Sidney Bechet, the new saxophonist from the Southern Syncopated Orchestra, was doing a cocktail-hour turn.

Peter's long torso was curled around a cigarette, and the line and swirl of the smoke rising from it looked to him like the line and swirl of the saxophone line that encircled him. He felt the smoke inside his lungs, moving and sighing. This was one of the joys he was counting in his mind. The feel of the smoke in his lungs. The fact that nobody was going to interrupt this cigarette. The thrill of the vestige of whisky on his lip. The beautiful pure clean liquid-honey sound of this glorious instrument. The smooth dryness of his socks. The soft clean wool of his vest. His face, still fresh from this morning's excellent shave: hot towels, essence of Jamaican lime, only a small attack of the shakes when the barber opened the cut-throat razor to strop it. He hadn't drunk very much tonight and he wasn't going to. Things were pretty good, really. He was doing all right today. When he felt all right enough, he was going to go home to Julia.

The sounds inside his head had been very, very bad but you wouldn't know it to look at him. A tightness in the hollow under his cheekbone, perhaps. The saxophone was unravelling it.

A woman sidled up to him, sweaty green satin dress, poor choice of lipstick colour. '*Quelquechose à boire?*' she said, with a powdery smile. Her eyes were made up huge and round, and looked like pansies.

He shook his head quickly. This was his third whisky. He didn't want more. More didn't work any more. No doubt he would try more again, and it wouldn't work again – but not today. Today had been all right.

'*Quelquechose à boire pour moi?*' she said, a little louder over the music.

He wondered why she was speaking French to him when she was so clearly, from her atrocious accent, English. The answer came on the heels of the thought – *Oh, God, of course . . . She's assuming I have acquired a taste for the French, over there.* It seemed to him strangely pathetic: this English whore pretending to be a French *pute . . . As pathetic as the fact that she can't conceive of any other reason why a man would be in a place like this alone, unless he was looking for one of her type.*

Woman, it's over. It's changing. Let go, for God's sake. Go back to a decent life.

But then she probably doesn't have a decent life to go back to.

He wasn't going to look up at her. If you look at them they never leave you alone. As if, once you looked up, let alone anything more, they tattooed you with a secret sign, and then they and their sisters knew, they always knew, and they would always find you. Or perhaps they could smell it.

'No,' he said. She was spoiling his moment.

Suit yourself, her shrug said. She perched at the next table and scanned the elegantly seedy room for newcomers. It was too early. She smiled at Peter again, and lowered her eyes. He looked the type to like demure. Nothing else to do, anyway.

Peter rubbed the back of his neck where it was stiff, stretched his arms out. The sound went through him like a filament along the veins, silver. So pure! And yet it knew everything. Mercury. And fire. It could clean you out.

It was the only thing that cut through the still-roaring barrage.

A rather exquisite Chinese man lounged two tables along, wearing a white scarf of the type that used to be called a cataract, held by a diamond pin. He glanced at Peter, offered a little nod suggesting the compliments of the evening, and an exploratory stare. Peter looked away to the bandstand, just as the American girl came on.

Ah, the American girl. Her name was Mabel. When she wasn't singing she kept the bar at the Turquoisine. Her skin was deep brown and her hair was shining black, plastered to her round head, her eyes were huge and her lashes lay on her cheeks. She was nothing like anything he had known in France and Flanders, and Peter loved her as he loved Mr

344

Sidney Bechet's saxophone, because she was so utterly new and strange and beautiful. She greeted him with a little wave, and moved on up the stage with a smile for the sax-player. After a few bars, she started to sing: 'How you gonna keep 'em down on the farm, after they've seen Paree?' Then a song of her own, one of her long slow numbers, 'I Saw You Yesterday', her voice as sweet and harsh as the sax was pure.

The Chinese man closed his eyes. The prostitute smiled lazily. Peter lit another cigarette, and felt the barrage subside a fraction, and relief emerged, finally, sending out a few tendrils as the music wrapped and washed and purified each drop of his battered mind.

More people started to arrive. The Original Dixieland Band lot came crowding in, gradually filling the place up, like champagne in a glass, rising, bubbling: a noisy, glittery, laughing splashy mob of officers, swells, the odd dowager, and bobbed-hair upper-class girls, flashing eyes, wet-lipped, short-skirted – the longer the war went on the shorter the skirts became . . . *Lucky for the sake of public decency it's over. It's over.*

They were ready to be hysterical, raucous, drunk and las-civious. Peter smiled, and drew himself together against them, their glare, their mania, the great surge of pity that flooded his heart at the sight of them, the shards of hatred for those who had sat out the war . . . *To pity or to hate. What a choice.*

Mabel was leaving the stage, going on to her next engage-ment. Mr Bechet had disappeared, and with him the fire-pure mood. In its place came the new band, in top hats spelling out 'DIXIE', clashing saucepan lids, squawking blind gaiety, and fun fun fun. Peter listened to the first two numbers, watched the mad energy and wild dancing they provoked, bare knees swinging, legs flashing, and then he moved out, against the tide. A feather boa snagged on his jacket collar for a moment, purple, light and clinging, and a sharp waft of patchouli, cut with potassium permanganate, caught in his throat. The smell of brothel. The boa's owner turned and twitched it off him, leaving a little clingy scrap of purple ostrich fluff on his shoulder. She caught his eye, hers heavily lined with black, shining. She didn't stop talking to the man in front of her, but her eyes and her long, painted, chattering smile lingered.

Outside on the street, Peter leaned on the wall for a while, breathing, closing his eyes. He had in his mind – running alongside the barrage, as if the barrage were a soundtrack – images of then and now, then and now. The girl with the boa, before. What had she been? A tart already? Or a farmer's daughter? A vicar's daughter? A schoolgirl? A girl in long skirts, a clean face, an early bedtime, an exchange of glances after church and perhaps a walk, if he'd met her father . . .

When did the girls all start wearing cosmetics? On his third leave, Julia had greeted him with blackened lashes and a reddened mouth, like any *pute* in Étaples or Amiens, and she had cried because he had not thought it beautiful, and he had felt himself a boor. Again. He closed his eyes, opened them, and moved on towards Greek Street.

The girl in the green dress followed him.

'Come on,' she said. 'You want to go somewhere? You got nowhere to go . . .'

He looked back at her. 'Dear girl,' he said. 'How about you? Don't you have somewhere better you could be?'

346

'Wherever you want, love,' she said. 'I'll look after you. I can see your wife don't understand you.'

'On the contrary,' said Peter. 'My wife is perfect.' He stared at the girl – nothing to lose now. Thin blonde hair, short like they all had it, thin little knees, a yellow tinge to her skin, eyes painted huge. 'Were you in munitions?' he asked.

She made a saucy face.

'Got used to the money?' he said. 'Lost your job?'

'Piss off,' she said. 'You don't look like a do-gooder. I'm all right.'

'I'm not a do-gooder,' he said. 'Far from it.'

'All the better,' she said. 'Come and tell me about it.'

'No,' he said. 'I have an appointment.'

'Oh, suit yourself,' she said, bored suddenly, and turned on her narrow silver heel, her little bottom in the green dress twitching.

Guttersnipe princess, he thought. Phew.

Women no longer kept Bloom's corpse from his arms. Nothing did. There was no point in trying. All that was over. It was over. It was all different now and he was going to be a good man.

Over. The terrifyingly lovely word. Over.

And what now?

The aftermath.

Now there's an interesting word.

He came to the door of a Georgian house of smoke-blackened brick, and pushed his way up the narrow flights of stairs that led to the one crooked room that was the Turquoisine. A very different crowd: drunks, foreigners of all sorts, some Yanks, black men, only one or two slumming

347

aristocrats, on the arms – or in the arms – of unsuitable lovers.

'Welcome to the Turquoisine,' purred Mabel, already on stage, unpinning her hat, smiling a beautiful big broad smile. 'By my watch,' and she held up her elegant wrist where a pretty jewelled bracelet watch glittered, 'it's December eighteenth, and that, my friends, means happy one month of the Armistice to y'all!'

Peter winced as if he had been slapped.

Today was Julia's birthday. *Oh damn, oh damn.*

Is there no end to the ways I let her down?

He breathed gently. His hands on the edge of the table were quite white. *It's too late anyway – it makes no difference now.*

He pushed himself off his chair, and went to the bar. 'Could I trouble you for some champagne?' he said wearily, courteously.

The barmaid – a new girl – blinked at him, like a little cartoon lady. 'It's after hours, sir,' she said sweetly.

'Then perhaps you would ring up Eustace for me, Mr Eustace Hoey, on Rupert Street, and have him deliver me a bottle. Moët,' he murmured. 'The 1909, if he has any left. I may have drunk it all. And a bottle of whisky. That Islay he keeps. To my table – I believe it is table nine. Major Locke. Thank you so much.' He lurched a tiny bit on his way back to his table. It was as if his body, anticipating drunkenness, launched itself prematurely into the familiarity of the movements, the manners, the quiet danger, the elaborate courtesy.

I don't deserve to be anything better than a drunk, he thought. *I deserve all the shit that I cause.*

Chapter Twenty-seven

Sidcup and London, towards Christmas, 1918
Returning to Sidcup, Riley went straight up to Gillies's office in the big house. He banged on the door. Gillies answered impatiently.

Riley said: 'Gi-lee.'

A curious, tender look appeared on Gillies's face.

Riley took a breath, and said carefully: 'See. S-pee . . .' He had trouble with the *p*, so he did something with his tongue behind his upper teeth to approximate it. It sounded as if goblins were pulling it in different directions, and a couple more were hanging off the end of his tongue.

'Yes?' said Gillies.

'Ke,' said Riley. *Can he understand me?*

'Well,' said Gillies. 'Evidently! Well done, Riley, well done.' He had not expected this. He had expected that the muscle loss, and more particularly the attitude, would conspire against. (He had been thinking about muscles – whether it would be possible to move the masseter, split it perhaps, form a sling of some kind that might allow movement and control, proper closing of the mouth, less droop, re-creating

349

the oral sphincter even, where the lower lip had been lost . . .) 'Did you talk to your friend in the north?'

'No,' said Riley. And his cheeks lifted, and his eyes elongated . . . *He's smiling*, Gillies thought. *Well, thank God for that.*

'I a' o' good chee,' Riley said. *Ch*, he noticed, came out more *t*-based.

'I'm so sorry, Captain, you are doing awfully well but I simply couldn't quite make that out,' Gillies said kindly and briskly.

Riley stretched his cheeks again.

He wanted to throw away his notebook, to be brutally demanding of himself, but Rose persuaded him against it. 'I still want to be able to understand you quickly,' she said. 'Long sentences. You know. For practical purposes.' He grunted. Grunting seemed like good exercise for little-used throat muscles.

Riley dreamed he was laughing.

He said to Rose: 'Locke?'

She hadn't known he knew Peter was due.

'Eeta?' he said. 'Is he not here?' He'd wanted to say, 'Not coming?' but the *m*, like the *p*, the *f*, the *v*, the *w* – anything using the bottom lip – was just not available to him. Yet.

'No, he's not here,' she said. Riley watched her.

'I don't know,' she said, to his unasked question. 'He's due. He was due weeks ago. We don't know where he is.'

Riley grabbed his notebook.

Rose how can you be embarrassed in front of me after everything? You know where he is.

'No, I don't,' she said, shocked.
Riley wrote:

he's drunk. The only question is, where is he drunk? answer – somewhere you can't go. So I will go.

'What?' she said. 'No!'
He wrote:

He and I shared trenches for three years. You've been feeding me and washing my face for fifteen months. No secret shame now Rose. No secrets. I'll go and find him. London? Or Paris?

Rose said, giving in, 'Well, I assumed London.'

On Christmas Eve Riley wrapped his coat around him and got an early train. He'd developed a way of wrapping his scarf loosely inside his turned-up coat collar so that the bottom of his face was concealed but he was not muffled, and if he chose to speak, his words were not hindered by it.

The frames of countryside and backyard rattled by: muddy remains of vegetables, stark trees, unidentifiable outdoor kit draped in worn grey tarpaulins. Riley thought about hibernation: spiders in their funnels like puffs of solid white smoke, in the folds of tarpaulins; furry creatures in piles in burrows, cold-blooded things in icy ditches, waiting, semi-conscious. It was an unlikely time of year for a hibernator to wake up. Was it just because It was Over? Was that all it took to send his mind trundling off again in a new direction, believing in possibilities?

He didn't think so. He could have remained in the misery. He could have remained there for ever. The misery wasn't far away – look, it's just over there, lurking next to the idea that this armistice is just a pause, and that the war will start up again any day (because if it's really over, why are so many men still Over There?).

Over.

There.

The misery is always going to exist. Lethargy, misery, nightmare and shame. The thought shook him to his bones. But – knowing it was there made it easier to avoid. He was safer in the knowledge of his enemy's location. *And I will be miserable again. Oh, I will. We all will. This relief is no more permanent than anything else, but the misery will be easier to bear knowing that this other feeling is possible too.*

I can't be alone in this, he thought – and the smile sensation came to him again as he realised the ambiguity of the thought: *(1) there must be others feeling the way I do, and for similar reasons, and (2) it is necessary that I find company. I will make friends*, he thought, *and rediscover friends, and look after friends. Well, that's what I'm doing.*

Bit by bit.

Two voices from the seats behind him emerged into his consciousness. Women.

'Lost a leg, and he's blinded,' one was saying. 'Well, I don't know. Would you want to live?'

He wanted to say— He wrote a note, tore it off the pad, laughed at himself, and leant over the back of the seat to pass it. 'Dear Madam, Forgive me, I overheard your conversation. I was badly wounded in the face at Passchendaele, have had some operations, and am trying to learn to talk again. I do not know about your acquaintance [He had almost written 'I cannot speak for your acquaintance'] but I for one have never loved life more.'

When they looked back, he put kind, accepting reassurance into his eyes, as best he could, and tried out a shrug, with an upturned palm, friendly, helpless, non-threatening.

Well! The women practically kissed him.

It was interesting to him how much better he felt for having written it down.

~

On Victoria Street, he caught sight of himself in a shop window. He stopped a moment to look. Still broad-shouldered, still strong. *I look like a man and a soldier*, he thought. *I am a man and a soldier. I am twenty-two years old with a pretty heart and a brave mind and a horrible past and a face that – a face that – a face that is fucking horrible. Half horrible.*

'*Not that frightening.*'

I am a man and a soldier.

Now I just have to behave like one.

And then I have to learn how to be a man without being a soldier.

The shop was a gentleman's outfitter. He stepped inside. Blue leapt out at him. Blue like the summer sky, like hospital blues, his mother's eyes. He chose two long scarves, one silk, one wool, one azurite egg-tempera Renaissance Madonna blue, one paler Pre-Raphaelite Alma Tadema blue. He paid, and he left, and he looked up, and his feet stopped themselves, and his eyes rose higher.

Across the road was the hotel where he had holed up with Nadine in the spring of 1917. It looked unbearably shabby. He could see the window of their room. He was standing in what had been their view. A profound shudder shook him from head to feet, a sickening wave, a punch, and his ribcage gaped within him. He didn't even know where she was. He had cast her off. He had deserted her and betrayed her, out of fear. He had not trusted her. It was nearly two years since he had seen her, and he did not even know where she was.

The little girl had patted his cheek.

Yes, but the other one had cried at the sight of him.

Yes, but Annie had patted his cheek and said, 'It's not that frightening'.

Well, Nadine would hate him now anyway. She would be over him. Two years! She would have found people to love her everywhere she went. *She will be fine. Beautiful girls are always all right. It's girls like Rose who suffer.* He should marry Rose.

He remembered, with a little pang, that he had said that to her once. Which had perhaps not been kind.

Who's talking of marriage? He would never be able to ask any woman to take him on.

Wounded Captain Purefoy, with the not-so-frightening face . . . That's neither a husband to offer nor a job for life. Who am I now? What am I meant to do now?

A wave of panic was right there.

He stepped aside – physically, on the street. *One thing at a time. Bit by bit. I'm meant to visit my mother, and I'm meant to find Locke. That's what I'm meant to do now.*

His mother was after work. Locke was after dark.

What do I love?

He turned into town, and walked towards Trafalgar Square and the National Gallery. He wanted to look at Sebastiano del Piombo's *Raising of Lazarus*.

~

Bethan, when she saw him, wept and gabbled in the doorway of the little house. He had to hug her close to shut her up, to muffle her against his chest. She pulled him inside, pulled his coat off him, wheeled him into the parlour, winter-dim. She lit the lamp and the fire and he noticed: *My mother is living without a fire unless there is company, in December.* The girls and Dad were out.

He stood away from the window to unwrap his scarf, to show her. Held his hand up to her in gentle warning. It should have been a momentous moment, revealing to his mother the visible mess that history had made of her son's face, but it was no more to him than something he had to do, a job required of him.

Bethan, when she saw his damage, said quietly, 'Oh, Riley, oh, my boy . . .' and she started to weep, and he let her, and soaked her up, contained her as a glass would melting ice. He would have to tell her how to be with him. That was his job.

He wrote her a note.

Mother. It's going to be all right. I promise.

'But how?' she wept, and he silenced her again against his tunic, and then wrote:

Weep as much as you like mother I am and it is going to be all right

'But your lovely face . . .'

new face now mother plug-ugly like dad

She giggled. Howled. 'But you can't talk . . .'
He said, fairly clearly despite the goblins, 'Actually, I can talk.'

She howled.
He hugged her. *I can do this.*
'You come back and live at home when they've finished with you,' she said, later.
No, mother.
'You'll stay here tonight, at least.'
He wrote:

I've things to do mother. Sorry. I'll be back soon and I'll write to you.

He didn't know where he would be spending the night.

'But it's nearly Christmas, Riley,' she said. She had thought he was back for Christmas. That the war was over and her son was back for Christmas. Her disappointment flooded and eddied over her previous confused joy. There were too many feelings for one face, but Riley could hardly see beyond his own relief and gratitude. She'd seen it, she still loved him. Had he doubted she would? It didn't matter.

Not demobbed yet,

he wrote.
'I suppose,' she said.
He wrote,

bit by bit eh mum? You know I'm safe anyway.

His smile was almost comfortable.
'You're smiling.'
Yes, mother.
'You look almost happy.'
Working on it, mother.

~

I have to learn to look at people looking at me, to see what they need from me, and to give it to them. My face gives an outlet for everything else – the fear and the loneliness and the long years apart; it gives a visible focus for it. I am always going to remind them of the war, and they will thus always remind me, and I am never going to be able to forget anything.

~

It was a cold evening, dreary. The glowing glass roof of the station stood out like a gigantic beetle against the purple sky. Shop lights smeared and dissolved, golden and gassy white in the watery air. The pavement was greasy, the street quiet. No horse-drawn cabs – no cabs at all. Riley hesitated a moment before ducking into the station, pulling his scarf round his face as he entered the underground world, hiding himself from it and it from him. The corridors were tiled and lit up. *It's nothing like the trenches*, he told himself. *Completely different. Nothing to worry about.*

His mother had tired him. Travelling had tired him. Seeing the hotel in Victoria had tired him. The National Gallery had put him in a state of shock. Botticelli's *Venus and Mars* – the beautiful creamy girl, the naked sleeping soldier – had given him an erection, which had amazed and confused him. Heart and soul, body and feet, he was tired.

Not the tiredest you've ever been, though, eh?

Walking up behind Regent Street he stopped a moment to look in the window of a small gallery, showing photographs: stark, extreme images of moonlight and flowers, racks of trees, drops of rain, yet as far from the usual look of these things as the war was from a pink sugar mouse: an extremity of richness in the metallic black and luminous white that reminded him, shockingly, of nights on the fire-step, and which yet were profoundly peaceful. He noted the photographer's name, Steichen, and stared at them for a long time. Inside, there were portraits: Matisse, concentrating on a serpentine figurine he was modelling; Bernard Shaw laughing behind his hand. The pictures glowed, and their dark radiance burnt the Botticelli out of his mind.

He had wanted to visit Sir Alfred, for Christmas, for the symbolism of it. He wanted to give everyone the present of the news: that though his face had been massacred his soul had not. He was not going to indulge a fatuous *faux*-modesty: he knew that it would make everyone happy to see him survive this. They'd be happy to see anyone survive it. It wasn't personal. Except where it was, and then so much the better.

But he was tired. He would write to Sir Alfred, give him notice of the situation, visit him later. As he made the decision, he felt a pang for the warm handshake, the manly embrace, the cry of matronly concern from Mrs Briggs, the weight of Messalina's dear heavy head on his knee, that he would not, after all, be having that evening.

His own words to his mother came back to him. *Bit by bit, eh?*

And: *Things to do.* It was likely to be a long night. He had prepared a few notes to hand out as required. He would not be trying out his tender new speech on strangers in public places.

Sitting on the tube, he raised his hat and stroked his scalp with his fingertips, ruffling the hair, feeling the granulated scar of the bald strip like a road sliced roughly through a jungle. *I'm glad I'm not dead.* He got off at Piccadilly Circus, and rose again to the surface, to the world. He stopped a moment at the entrance to the station and breathed carefully. World. People. Streets. City. Light. Dark. Drunks. Buses. Women. Music. Festivities. Traffic. Christmas. Laughter. Chat. Shouting. Men.

He breathed.

I have killed. I have saved. Normality does not care. Now I must walk city streets, push through a door, push through a crowd.

He went first to the Trocadero. Approached the ticket booth. Wanted to smile. Attempted to put some kind of courteous smile in the angle of his shoulders as he approached out of the dark wet night in a greatcoat with a scarf wrapped round his face. He felt like a bank robber in a silent movie as he handed over his note.

I am sorry, I cannot speak to you directly as I am injured.
Do you know if a jazz saxophonist called Sidney Bechet
is playing tonight? And if so, where? And if not, do you
know of anyone who might know? Thank you.

The girl, young, pretty, knowing, glanced at the note and said, with a tut of sympathy and a nasal curl, 'Aaoow,' as if to a kitten with a hurt paw. Then she called behind her, 'Billy!' and a man appeared.

'Sidney Bechet?' he said, pronouncing it 'Betchit', rather than the French way Locke used. 'Coloured feller? I'd try the Forty-Four, Eduardo's, the Turquoisine, if you know it . . .'

It was early for the clubs, so Riley first quartered the area. He dodged away from the more crowded streets, leant in doorways when necessary, pacing himself in the face of so much humanity. A square mile of pubs lay before him, any one of which Locke might or might not be in. The John Snow, the King's Arms, the Nellie Dean, the Admiral

Duncan, the Pillars of Hercules, the Sun and 13 Cantons, the Intrepid Fox, the Blue Posts, the Carlisle, the Coach and Horses, the Dog and Duck, the Element, the Red Lion, the other Red Lion, the Angel and the White Horse . . . It was a long time since he'd been in a pub; a long, long time since his mum used to send him on this round looking for his dad.

He had to prepare for the mere fact of a room full of people. Pausing before the first door – how would it be? Full or empty? Loose women or nancy boys? Army or students? Quiet and staring, or raucous and celebratory? Happy sad angry upforapunchup fucking suicidal or all of the above?

Breathe. Push. Flinch – regroup.

It was, above all, crowded: a wave, a huge almost physical barrier of noise and warmth and breath, laughter, social cacophony, bodies, clattering, smoke, light. The sheer force of human emotion in a confined space, of crazy glee, of triumphalism, of drunkenness, mad relief, desperate loss, bereavement, wild happiness, this night of all nights, Christmas 1918. He should have thought it through. He was in no condition to trail through the pubs in the heart of London on this night of all nights. This was a stupid night to do it. And Peter could be anywhere.

He forced himself to slide in. He gazed round, and he had to leave. He developed a technique: in through one door, manoeuvre through, looking, looking, out of the other, lean on the wall, breathe.

He'd said he'd do it, so he did it, for Peter and for Rose. *You've killed, you can save.* In the quieter pubs he handed over another note: 'I don't suppose you know Peter Locke? Tall, blond, a major, thirty or so?'

Several knew him. He'd been in the Star and Garter earlier.

So Riley had to continue.

At closing time, he went straight to the Turquoisine. He couldn't afford the Forty-Four and he couldn't stand in the street outside – he'd fall over, he was so cold and tired. Billy at the Trocadero had told him the address. He climbed the unlikely stairs, almost staggered in, sat at the bar. The room was crowded, the music low. He looked at no one, just wrote a new note. 'Brandy. Please.'

The barmaid – black-skinned, fine-eyed – laughed at him. 'Honey, I surely cain't read this in this dim light.'

Riley turned his eyes to her. She was beautiful. He had never seen a black woman before. (Men, yes, in France – and Williams the Nigerian, at Sidcup.) He had never met an American woman. He would have loved to talk to her.

He made a vague gesture around his face, his mouth, a floating movement followed by a cut-throat slice, a shrug, and the half-smile, the eye smile, which was all he could offer.

'Cain't talk?' she said. 'Well, hell, honey, why didn't ya say so?' Then came the gasping laugh of appalled embarrassment at what she had said, her realisation that he had forgiven her even before she said it, his realisation that his forgiveness (as opposed to the punch in the mouth the barman in Wigan had had) was based not only on her beauty but on the fact of a smile. With the pointing at the brandy bottle, and the working out of what he wanted, a friendly atmosphere arose between them. Riley pulled out his metal straw, and slid it between the folds of his scarf.

The girl eyed him. 'That baid, huh?' she said. He gave her a palms-up gesture of futility. He wanted to tell her that he would chat with her if he could . . . *vicious circle.* She eyed him a moment more, then leant over and looked at him closely, taking in the scarf, the heavy-laden cuffs, the cheekbones, the grey diamond eyes. She lowered her long lashes, and raised them again, very close to him. He could smell soap and warmth and something sweet. Quite seriously, she said to him: 'You still cute.'

His straw was still in his mouth, and he sipped his brandy, and he felt the coldness circling his heart, which might at any time descend on him again to protect him from all this stuff, this human stuff, which hurt you and . . . *What's the opposite of 'hurts you'? Not 'comforts you' . . . 'Pleasures you' sounds like it gives you a hand-job . . . Why isn't there a word for 'makes you happy'? 'Brings you joy'?* He sighed, lingering on the fact that this moment had *the opposite of* hurt him.

In the doorway a lean Chinese man in a white suit was standing, smiling. A voice came from behind him: 'For Christ's sake, Mr Chang, move on in, would you, so we can get some bloody service?'

The man moved aside, and Riley looked up, and there was Peter.

The very sight of him softened Riley. *Look, there he is. Alive, here, now. Like a ghost.* The ghosts of the others danced across his mind, but he watched Peter, as he carefully approached the bar, calling out, mildly, elegantly: 'My usual,

Mabel darling, my darling Mabel.' He brushed past Riley as he moved to the bar, next to him. He was very drunk.

Mabel glanced up at Riley, her eyes kind, apologetic – for Peter's condition, perhaps, or for the end of their little moment – as she poured a glass of whisky.

Riley watched him a little longer. He found he was smiling. He leant on the bar, scribbled a note, and passed it to Mabel.

Say to him, Peter, look, here's Riley Purefoy come to take you home.

She took it into the light to read, then looked up and said, in the unsurprised, unsurprisable tone of the barkeeper in the face of other people's drama: 'He won't want ta go home.'

Riley heard a touch of resignation in it too. Well. That was not his business.

He wrote:

he hasn't been home since coming back from France wife and child Christmas future perhaps even. please

The girl rolled her eyes up to the ceiling and stared at it for a while, as if trying to keep something in. She stared, and after a while she swallowed. Then: 'Hey, Peter,' she said. 'Sweetheart? Look, here's Riley Purefoy. Look.'

Peter turned.

'He's goin' ta take you home now, honey. You're goin' ta go home and have a good rest, and I'll see you later.'

Peter stared at her. 'But I want to hear you sing,' he said. 'And I rather hope Mr Chang, Mr Brilliant Chang, has a little something for me . . .' He swayed slightly as he looked around.

'I ain't singing tonight,' Mabel said gently. 'And Mr Chang has left. You go on with Riley. Go on now.'

'Riley?' said Peter. He turned, and his drunk eyes saw. 'Jesus Christ, Riley. Riley. Jesus Christ, Riley, how are you? Oh, God, I heard. I'm awfully sorry, Riley – not – I— Oh, God. Mabel, this is Riley. We were . . .' He paused on 'were', giving it full weight. We were. We were. 'Over there,' he said finally.

'He cain't talk to you,' Mabel said. 'His face is hurt. But he's goin' ta take you home. Go on now. Don't worry – go on home.'

'Oh,' said Peter, mildly, and Riley touched the woman's hand for a moment, before taking Peter's arm.

She passed over his hat. 'Bye, honey,' she said, as they moved away, in a voice that made Riley glance back. Then they were out of the club and down the stairs and in the street. At the doorway Riley looked round for a cab, and Peter suddenly, like a broken scarecrow lurching in a high wind, flapping perilously down the darkness, made a bid for escape.

Riley caught him up easily, and clutched at his coat. Peter was flailing, long skinny limbs everywhere. Riley feared hurting him, as one would a daddy-long-legs. It seemed Peter's legs might just snap off.

In Riley's moment of concern, Peter swerved, and made to hurtle off again. Quickly, Riley came round in front and, with a 'sorry about this' under his breath, punched him. As Peter spiralled down, Riley caught him, held him, then hitched him over his shoulder, awkward and heavy. *Where's the stretcher-bearers when you need them?*

Four cabs didn't stop for him before one did. 'He's injured, not 'runk,' Riley said to the driver – but the man clearly thought Riley was drunk too. Riley registered that this was going to be another fucking issue, but he was not interested in resenting it now. He dumped Peter in the back, dug into his pocket and found a soft, expensive, sign-of-real-officer-class wallet containing money and – aha – visiting cards. Riley handed one to the driver, who sniffed and held it out to catch the light of the lamp.

'Sidcup!' he yelped. 'I ain't driving to blimming Sidcup . . .'

Riley proffered a five-pound note.

'Well,' said the cabbie.

Peter, despite the rattling and shaking, slept. Riley stared across at him. *Look at us. Jesus Christ, just look at us. And we're the lucky ones.*

Then he lay back and thought: *I did it. I did something. I did it.*

Chapter Twenty-eight

Locke Hill, Christmas Eve, 1918

All afternoon rain had streaked heavily against the dark glass of the French windows, hurtling off the flagstones on the terrace, furrowing into the lawn, battering the huge withered burnt-orange rosehips that bobbed wildly in the sharp wind. The world had turned, and the seasons, and now it was Christmas Eve, and the child was to be born, again, who was given by his father for the redemption of sin, if you care for all that, which of course some people still did, though Rose didn't. It seemed to Rose that religious faith, which had previously been shared out equally, now desperately swamped half the world while the rest wondered, sadly, bitterly, or with bereft bewilderment, how the notion of God could ever have offered them any comfort. Riley had given Rose an answer to the religion question that made sense. Clearing around his bed, right at the beginning, she had picked up his notebook; it had fallen open, and her eye had been caught:

Ainsworth and Burgess that night talking about God: Christian nations slaughtering each other across the world,

Love Thy Neighbour, how can he allow all this to go on, etc etc. Ainsworth insisting on hope as the only hope; Burgess cynical. Answer is simple. Man made in God's image, men stupid violent murderous destructive, ergo God stupid violent murderous destructive

When she'd read that, Rose had stopped short and had had to sit down for a moment. *If that's how he was thinking, my God* (she noted that she still needed him to swear by), *were they all?*

Rose just knew that there had been enough giving of sons. The idea of rebirth and a new season, on top of everything, was exhausting. Of course she was *happy*: the war was over. She'd half thought she wanted to stay at the hospital, to be with everybody, but in fact she was glad to have a little leave, and to be at Locke Hill tonight. If nothing else, she'd get a quiet evening and a rest. And if Riley did find Peter . . . Well, there were plenty of ifs. She wasn't expecting anything.

In town everybody seemed mad with joy. All the singing and dancing and the vicar in tears, Mrs Bax going on about cracking open her champagne from 1908, the young people quite hysterical, and the expectation, the absolute palpitations, because the boys would be *coming back*! And some of them *were* back. One or two looked very well.

But the war was over. And Tom was home, though things were not . . . well . . . *instinct will carry them through, won't it? Given time? Everything must get better now.* Actually, Rose had been quietly impressed by the news, via Mrs Joyce, that Julia had not even invited her mother to stay the night: had just given her a cup of tea, and sent her back to the station.

She'd drawn the curtains across against the weather, and built up the fire. Peter's cello, propped up by the window, glowed softly. The narcissi blossomed in their Chinese bowl, white and heavenly like tiny angels' wings. The good firewood burned slowly in the grate: seasoned apple from the orchard, which Julia had saved for when Peter was here, or expected, which meant a certain amount had been wasted, but not even Julia would suggest that was inconsiderate of him.

So everything was nice.

Rose had made soup for supper. *He never wants a big dinner when he's been in town. Lord, even I am talking as if I know what he's feeling . . . and as if he's coming.*

Good that there's a chicken for tomorrow – quite a coup—

The telephone rang, and Rose started.

It wasn't Peter, or Riley.

'Rose?'

The sound of a human voice shook her.

'Hello . . .' she said.

'It's Nadine.'

Rose's lassitude fell off her.

'Oh, Rose, I'm in Dover. I'm . . . I just got off the boat. Look – can I come? There's a train in ten minutes. I'm meant to be going home but I can't face it.'

The cold damp metallic air of travel and outside and railway soot blew clear as a draught down the line through the rainy night into the golden lamplit drawing room.

'Of course,' said Rose. She remembered her first night back in Blighty, after her stint, years ago.

'I'll walk from the station,' said Nadine. 'Don't bother Harker, even if you have fuel. *Thank you.*' The line went dead and the cold disappeared again. Rose replaced the earpiece, and noticed that she didn't mind being taken for granted by Nadine. Because Nadine took nothing else for granted, it was a compliment.

Rose went to find Harker, to send him down to meet the Dover train. It was a filthy night.

It was only then that she thought, *If Riley does go looking for Peter, if he finds him, if he brings him here . . .*

Oh.

❧

Nadine blew in two hours later, cold, still in uniform, a kitbag that hardly counted slung over her narrow shoulder. Her face, always sallow, was waxen. She still looked like a tomboy Lillian Gish. She placed her bag in the hall, and hugged Rose carefully, dripping. Her body was strung tight as a wire.

'Gosh, your hair!' said Rose.

Nadine smiled. She didn't seem able to talk. The rooms were huge and extraordinary to her.

'We have hot water,' Rose said. 'Running water,' and they both smiled hugely.

'Running water!' said Nadine.

'Julia had it done.'

Nadine made a 'My *dear*!' face, and took off her heavy overcoat.

'Well, yes,' Rose continued, conspiratorial, apologetic. 'She has a way . . . Life goes on, you know . . .'

Nadine flinched, a tiny flinch, like the movement of a leaf on a still day.

Rose gave a little breath through her nose. 'Still no Millie, though,' she went on. 'She's staying on at Elliman's. They're converting to motor-cars.' *Why am I saying that? Am I trying to demonstrate the household's suffering to Nadine? Offering credentials?*

Rose would bring the bag. Nadine would go on up. 'You're in the blue room,' Rose said. 'Help yourself to the bath salts.'

The room was the same. The deep turquoise walls, the gleaming pink-hearted seashell from the Bosphorus on the mantel, the pale quilted bedspread. Nadine gazed at its clean softness. She had not been in England for a year. She had not been in this room since the autumn of 1917. Since . . .

'Since' was not a good word. Don't let 'since' in.

Her bag had precious little in it, but Rose had laid out a nightdress, a dressing-gown and slippers, God bless her. Slippers!

Folded on the quilt was a great soft bath sheet. Nadine stared at it, took its soft pile between her fingers. She had very often thought about this. At the start of many short nights in damp mal-framed canvas beds, still wearing eight-days-on-the-trot underwear, with the cold gnawing the small of her back and the fleas dancing gung-ho, or when faced again with a jug of cold water and a whistle calling her to duty, she had rehearsed the joy-to-come of a hot bath. The discarding of dirty stinking clothes. The sound: rushing water, lots of it, the clanking of plumbing, the roar of the pipes hurtling to her comfort, the hiss of steam and creak of great big taps. The luxurious smell, the choice: lily-of-the-valley? Lemon? Rose geranium? Now, she found herself staring at them, bemused. The cold tiles of the bathroom floor; the rubber underfoot of the mat. The hard echo of a tiled room with a high ceiling. The slow descent of the body into the water. The flood of blood to the skin, and the tingling, flickering, shivering release from the flesh of the deepest cold, the tightest tension, rising off the skin like bubbles, bubbling, gone . . . The promise of a big towel, warm from the rail, of a big fire.

She unpeeled herself, dropped her war and travel-stained carapace, and stepped into the large enamelled tub. She was amazed. How extraordinarily strong a physical pleasure could be.

She slid below the surface. Her hair lifted and floated. *I'll just stay here*, she thought, opening her long eyes under water, a naked Ophelia, shivering. *This is perfect.*

Her lungs wouldn't take the water. Unlike the bodies of many of the men, her body was still sane.

She washed her white legs, her cropped wild black hair, her thin arms and every other part. Between her toes, behind her ears, pushing back her cuticles with her thumbpads, rubbing her feet with the pumice-stone. How absolutely extraordinary to look at her own body so, to have so much time to pay it so much attention. There it was. Flesh. Undamaged. How absolutely extraordinary to clean and tend an undamaged body. A female body.

She flexed her feet, rolled her shoulders, bent her knees, lifted her arms. No wrong bends, no patent holes, no leaking. Nothing missing. Nothing shattered. Nothing rotten.

Wrapped in the big towel, she called gently from the doorway: 'Is Major Locke here?'

'No!' called Rose. 'You can come down in your dressing-gown!'

Nadine brought the towel, and rubbed her hair in front of the fire. Rose had poured two small glasses of golden sherry, and lit the little candles on the Christmas tree. What luxury! They reflected in the gilt mirrors at the back of the room, twinkling. For a mad instant, Nadine expected a tiny crack and a boom, the sound of tiny shells to accompany their tiny light, and felt a tiny twinge of adrenalin, an after-shock of the bitter metallic sweaty layer that had shivered her limbs, destroyed her nights, coated her mouth, lined her existence for the past year.

It's over, it's over.

'I can always scarper upstairs if anyone comes,' she said. 'But where is Julia?'

'She hasn't been very well,' Rose said.

'Poor dear!' said Nadine. 'Not this flu?' she said, with sudden concern. 'Rose?'

'She's gone to bed,' Rose said. 'You'll see her tomorrow.'

'Well, she's in good hands with you,' Nadine said.

Rose smiled.

~

Julia's burnt-orange curtains hung heavy and overlong to the floor, a second layer over the windows with their closed box shutters. The room was stuffy and miasmic. One lamp burnt low on the table by the fireplace, and the corners of the room were dim and lost to her. She slithered a little on her sheet, her legs moving as if under water. It was not clean enough – seamy, somehow. Slippery. She felt her negligée moving against it, and didn't like the feeling. Her mind was a mist to her. Like swimming through icing sugar.

She heard Rose and Nadine downstairs. She couldn't sleep. She hadn't been able to get rid of the little edge of tension she had built up in making sure she remembered to do Tom's stocking – sweet little sleeping Tom – *Peter, come and see how dear he is. We can start again, the three of us. I could have another, a little sister for him* . . . Her mind gagged on the words. Not by a man who didn't love her, who didn't find her attractive, who kept away from her, shaming her by his absence, in front of Rose and the servants and the neighbourhood, didn't even write to her, didn't even come to see his child . . .

She dragged herself up and looked at her watch on the bedside table. *Well, he won't be coming tonight.* As the familiar phrase passed through her mind she slipped automatically, yet again, into the familiar spirals of resentment and fear: *broken limbs, other women, motor accidents, shellshock* . . . those loyal ghouls lining up again at the end of her bed, conscientious, hideous, pulling strings in her belly, polluting. A new one had joined the rank: at least when he had been in the trenches it had been something outside keeping them apart – but now he was doing it all by himself.

Damn him – *no! Don't damn him. He has suffered and must be allowed for, whatever it takes, whatever it takes. Don't give up now. Peace has come! Now is the time to be strong.*

Round and round.

Hold on, be strong, he has suffered, don't blame him. (Blame yourself, came the echo).

Lines from a poem were haunting her – 'We have years and years in which we will still be young,' or something. What were they talking about? Nonsense. Young was for – the others. Those creatures who had been at school all this time, those buds bursting into flower only now, fresh, happy, innocent little things untouched by the war. Peter should go off with one of them – forget all his harsh grief, all their resentments. A young girl could dilute his sorrow with her innocence. Maybe that's what was happening right now . . .

NO! Everything will be all right now. He'll be back soon and everything will go back to normal. We can make it right.

She was cold.

A dark anger lurched inside her. Surely things had been going to be different when the war was over. She threw back the covers, crossed the room to poke and prod the fire, feeling the heat on her cheeks. Cold back, hot face. She could almost feel the capillaries bursting. More damage . . .

As long as she was beautiful she would be loved. As long as she did her bit. Took on her responsibility. There had been nothing she could do for so long except wait, and be pretty. It was so unfair that the last treatment hadn't worked. *SO* unfair. *Bloody Madame Louise and her bloody useless treatments. 'Bring back the bloom' – oh, the liar.*

And now the waiting was nearly over – *Oh, you look dreadful, old and tired and dreadful* – and she had waited so long that she was . . . *Miss Havisham . . .*

And where is he? Where is he? Where is he? Weeks since his letter, years since . . .

Not for the first time she thought of Penelope, weaving and unweaving her tapestry for Odysseus. Europe must be full of Penelopes, failing, one way or another, to cope. *Oh, Rose, of course I wanted to be more like you!* Meanwhile, the open-ended, eternal absence continued. And what would he be when he finally came? And what would he find?

She straightened up. The dressing-table mirror flashed the fire back at her, and the three glass bottles she had stolen from Madame Louise twinkled.

As she moved towards the dressing-table, she felt the little click of helplessness in her head – like the one she felt when she walked into a shop, knowing she was going to buy something she didn't need, following the lines of desire that pulled her immutably along, when no one was watching . . . *no one is watching so I can do this thing I shouldn't do* . . . As she had known that she shouldn't steal the bottles in the first place, shouldn't have bought half the clothes she had bought recently, shouldn't have carried on with half the things she had had done to her face, shouldn't have let Rose's mockery discourage her, shouldn't have let her mother take Tom away.

She sat at her dressing-table and hated herself.

Her skin looked so dull, even in this light. She stared at herself, trying not to cry, not to make her eyes red.

How could you be so shallow and so wicked?

The loss of her youth, the golden years they should have had that the war had taken from her, the past, no past, no present, what future?

Thirty. Thirty thirty thirty thirty thirty. Horrid word. Between thirsty and dirty and flirty. Thirty.

She knew she should leave the bottles alone.

She knew she had never been going to.

~

Rose and Nadine ate the soup at ten o'clock. Nadine hadn't eaten since a roll on the train at breakfast. Peter didn't arrive.

'He's very taken with London at the moment,' Rose said. 'Very busy. Probably he got the offer of a lift down tomorrow. You can't always get through on the telephone.' *Who am I protecting?* she thought. *Nadine can read between the lines, anyway.*

Nadine noticed, but she didn't say anything. There had been too much that she couldn't do anything about. Too much, for too long. She couldn't think what to say.

So, 'And how are you, Rose, my dear?' she said instead – and immediately damned herself for letting that impossible unforgivable question slip out, that tiny little question, the question no decent guest or friend could avoid asking, that simplest, most treacherous little question that leads only into the mire. There was only one honest answer, one she'd had often enough from the Tommies: 'Not a flippin' clue, darlin'.' Or as one sweet boy had said thoughtfully, moments before dying, 'I don't know. It's a very complex question.'

Here, now, to Rose, 'How's work?' had to follow, and that would lead on . . . Well, she might as well say it. It was there, said or not. Her stomach lurched a little. *You can forget, you can think you've forgotten, you can stay away, you can blot out, you can drown your mind with things that are far, far more important, but some things do not go away.*

Nadine had found it fairly easy to acknowledge that she couldn't go home because it was not possible to change, at one leap, from being what she had become, in France, to being something she could allow her parents to see. And home was the past: unbearable now. Possibilities. Might have beens.

Be straight, Nadine. Before – before the war, and before Riley's betrayal, there had been – *God! The significance of it all, so trite!* – notions of innocence and the possibility of happiness and . . . Before the war was Riley. But it was all Riley. Riley was everywhere. Before the war, during the war, in France, in the field hospitals, in the stations, in the letters, in the absence of letters, in the shouts of the men, in the mist, in the angle of the kitbag on the shoulder of the stranger on the street, in London, in Paris, in the park, in the *estaminets*, in the Lyons tea rooms, in the mud, in every bloodstained bandage, on the trains, on the road, in the dark, in her dreams, in the night, in the dawn. And here . . . yes, Riley was here. Of *course* Riley was here.

Wherever he might actually be, in reality.

'Busy,' said Rose, a little briskly. 'A constant supply still, as they're starting to get people back over here. It may be *over* but . . .'

Nadine gave a pale smile. She knew about that. So many men, wounded or not, alive or not, who would not be home for Christmas. Such an echo of 1914, that phrase. She wasn't going to ask. 'So tired,' she murmured instead.

'Of course,' said Rose.

'Think I'll turn in. Such luxury! Clean bed!'

'Your hair's still damp,' said Rose. It didn't matter. 'Well, I'll see you in the morning.'

'See you in the morning,' said Nadine. 'Happy Christmas!'

In bed she lay and thought of Riley's face and Riley's arms and Riley's warmth and every part of Riley, and she cried herself to sleep.

Rose sat by the fire, and blinked slowly, in time with her breath. In, shut; out, open.

Rose's muscles were strung too tight and sharp for sleep. Four females and a child under one roof. Herself, sleepless. Nadine, as mad and taut with unspoken distress as any wounded soldier. Julia, who had been so odd for so long, impossible, moody, self-blaming and miserable. Mrs Joyce, so calm, so unchanging throughout everything that Rose could only assume she was half-witted. And Tom, the silent, obedient, big-eyed child, two years old now, whom Rose for one had never seen do anything but stare, as if in bemused horror – *which might make him the sanest of the lot of us.* She thought about the stocking Julia had done for him: a chocolate coin, a silver sixpence, a little piggybank to put it in, a twirly red and white sugar cane. Daft, for a child so small. But sweet. A sweet, good, generous thing. It will take time; it will all take time. Mrs Joyce was so happy to have him here . . . God, this house needed family in it again, needed everything to pull back together. Needed peace for the damage to settle, and to heal, and to pass. Needed sleep. Needed the men back – the man. They only had the one between them all.

379

It seemed to Rose that she had been good for a long, long time. Could she go off duty now? Could she have a breakdown? Get drunk? Sleep? Disappear? Be carried away, elsewhere, to safety, to where she was no longer expected to carry anyone else? Anaesthesia, a hospital bed, the swift release of responsibility to somebody else, or to nobody, just not on her?

She'd carried them all in her time.

A breakdown, perhaps? A nervous collapse? That would be nice.

She was not aware that the storm had died down until she heard the sound of the engine outside. Her brain cried, *Emergency!* and she was standing in the silent midnight hall, her heart a-batter, before she was even fully awake. The floor was cold beneath her feet, and the night shadows strange. From the drawing room she heard the little shifts of the embers of the dying fire.

Through the glass panels of the front door the car was sleek and dark. The rain had stopped and the moon raced on high in the wind that had blown the storm away. Black twigs and branches were silhouetted around the drive. Rose could see it all clearly but found that she did not know what to do.

She saw three figures. One was drooping, a limp doll figure – injured?

Was this tableau outside something to be admitted to the house? Or something to hide from? Her judgement had fled; her decisiveness bolted.

The doll was tall, swooping, stumbling. Drunk.

Peter.

The front door was locked. Of course, she had locked it. Where were the keys? Where had she put them? She didn't know where she had put them. The tableau was unfolding. She couldn't open the door to it. She felt very strongly that if she let the men in, chaos would come too, and either the house would subsume it, or it would subsume the house. But there was chaos already within. Decorous repressed chaos for ladies. This was male chaos.

Of course – there they were, tucked up on the little shelf by the grandfather clock. Same as always. Open the door. She struggled with it, pulling, rattling. It came open.

Two men were half carrying Peter, his arms around their necks, lolling like Christ crucified, or a wounded man coming in. One of them was Riley, and her heart was glad.

'Is he all right?' she said. Another figure appeared – Harker, in his nightshirt, down from his room over the garage, with a blunderbuss. Rose was disconcerted by all the sudden masculinity in the house.

'He hit his head,' said Riley. 'When I knocked him down.'

She looked at Peter's eyes, and took his pulse. He didn't look entirely all right. Even for a falling-down drunk. 'Bring him,' said Rose, and they followed her through into the kitchen.

'Ring for Dr Tayle, Harker,' she said. Better safe than sorry.

Peter removed himself suddenly from one of his supports, and hung in the kitchen doorway, head slung forward, swaying on elastic arms.

She put on the kettle. 'Keep him upright,' she said

381

unsteadily. 'Riley, can you walk him round?' She didn't move. Riley went over, saying 'Come on, sir,' but Peter launched himself on to a chair. The cabbie looked embarrassed.

Peter wouldn't stand up, so Riley made the tea, and Rose said to him, 'You might as well unwrap,' and then she started crying.

Riley unwrapped his scarf, took his straw from his pocket, and stirred his tea with it.

Rose wiped her nose, poured the rest of the hot water into a basin and started carefully to part Peter's hair, looking for damage.

She found it. It wasn't bad. She washed it. She dressed it. Smell of Lysol. Smell of fresh blood.

Riley swallowed. *I can swallow*, he thought.

Peter was staring at him.

Oh, yes. He hasn't seen the full glory of the face before. Time to make it all right for the person looking at me.

He said: 'Ello, Beter.'

'Hello, Riley,' said Peter, puzzled.

'Hello, Peter,' said Rose, and Peter said: 'Oh, Jesus, Rose.'

'How many fingers am I holding up?' she said.

'Seven,' he said, as if it were a joke.

Their expressions evidently still meant something to him. 'Oh. Awfully sorry. Four.'

After a while Rose and Riley steered Peter into the study, and made him flop on the divan there. She couldn't welcome him or comfort him. There was nothing to give. Running on empty. No patience, no tolerance, no sympathy, no strength – no love no words no time no breath almost. All she could say was 'Go to sleep'. She sat on the side of the divan, her hand on his arm. She sat for quite a long time.

~

The cabbie said, 'I'll be off then, I suppose.'

Riley would have said, *Stay a little, have a rest, before you start back.* He would have said, *Thank you.*

He shook the man's hand, and nodded, and the cabbie went out, alone.

Riley sat at the table and thought: *We have been outside humanity, beyond the moral universe, where there is no reason and no ground beneath your feet. We have been in a parallel reality. We're going to have to come back.*

He wrote it down:

> Talk about it. I want to talk about it. I can't. I wish I could. I've seen the shock cases who can't talk because their brain won't let them, because of their shock, and I've seen the unwounded blokes who can't because talking about it makes it real and speaking about the unspeakable makes it as if it weren't unspeakable at all. Although it is. It's a paradox. I want to talk to someone. I'll talk to any of you here – Rose? Peter?
>
> Talking is what you do with who you trust.
> Talking is human.
> Humans talk to each other.
> The truth, the whole truth, nothing but the truth
> You can all talk please talk
> please trust
> please love

> I want to feel at home in the world again
> We thought our lives were ours
> and they have not been after all
> isn't this true? Can we all admit it?

He folded the piece of paper and put it in his pocket and felt suddenly very, very tired. He sat, rolled a cigarette. He stood, walked up and down. He filled the kettle again. He looked out into the hall. When he saw the shape of the doctor at the door, he withdrew into what turned out to be the drawing room. Leave them to it. Nothing he could do anyway.

∼

When Dr Tayle let himself in, summoned by Harker and forgotten by Rose, he found no one but a very small boy in flannel pyjamas, staring, and asking was he Father Christmas? He said, no, he was afraid he wasn't, and then Miss Rose Locke hurtled down the staircase into the hall, pale as anything, saying, through a throat constricted with fear, 'Don't worry about him for the moment, doctor, you'd better come upstairs. Tom, go back to bed.'

He heard the low moans coming from the master bedroom.

'I just looked in,' Rose said blankly. 'I'd been sitting with Peter. I heard a noise.'

Julia was on the floor in the dim orange light, collapsed, in a silken kimono strewn with vomit. A kind of turban wrapped her head, and her chest was heaving and fluttering.

'Good Lord,' said the doctor.

Her face was a ghostly, ghastly mask of flaking white.

'Poisoning,' he said. 'What's that on her face? Wash it off. Call for a servant.' He turned back Julia's lower lip: the flesh there was grey and sick-looking. He had one skinny hand at her pulse, the other fumbling to open his bag.

'She's in shock,' he said. Rose snapped his bag open for him, and ran to the ewer for water. As she picked it up, the smell hit her, familiar, retch-inducing, and she gasped.

'Carbolic!' she squawked. 'Doctor, the ewer's got carbolic acid in it!' She ran from the room – 'Mrs Joyce!' – and into the bathroom where she filled a pitcher with clean water and grabbed towels. Back in the bedroom, she threw herself on the floor. She didn't seem to be a nurse at all: she was a friend, she was family – *oh, Julia, what have you done, you stupid, stupid—*

She swallowed and stopped herself. Calm. CALM. 'Julia, my dear,' she said. CALM. Professionalism was reasserting itself.

'Julia – something bad has happened,' she said, to quiet herself as much as Julia. 'We're going to make it all right, now, it's going to be all right. The doctor is here. I'm just washing this off your face, just washing your face . . .' Mrs Joyce came up, flustered, bundled in a dressing-gown. Rose was murmuring all the while, soaking off the plaster scales, bathing, bathing, bathing the skin beneath, pouring water, fetching water, flooding the floor around her, almost hysterical in her calmness. The doctor was unrolling a rubber tube, preparing olive oil and charcoal.

'I don't think she's swallowed it,' said Rose. 'She's plastered it all over her face.'

'Why?' the doctor said. 'Bathe her eyes, keep at it.'

Rose was finding it hard to tell what was skin and what was plaster. Unnatural white patches had appeared, dead-looking among the grey. Julia's heart was still racing, and she shook as a creature does when you try to rescue it.

'Get her off this wet floor.'

They lifted her carefully on to the bed. Rose's voice continued like a nun's at prayer. Mrs Joyce brought soap. The women washed her, washed her, washed her. They put a pillow under her feet, built up the fire, spread blankets to warm her. Mrs Joyce made hot-water bottles and suggested brandy. The doctor said no: water, and lots of it. He gave her olive oil and charcoal anyway. He could not believe, Rose realised, that Julia had covered her face with carbolic acid.

The jars were there on her dressing-table, labelled: phenol crystals, croton oil, glycerine.

'Croton oil!' he said disgustedly. 'Where did she get this stuff? What in the name of sanity was she trying to do?'

Rose was staring at her. She had no idea. She had no idea about what Julia had been doing, what she thought, what she minded, how she had tried to deal with it all. It was as if she hadn't credited her with having a war of her own.

～

Mrs Joyce was with Julia. In the kitchen Rose sat down suddenly, very heavily, and the doctor said, 'She'll be all right, you know. She won't die.'

Rose raised her eyebrows, shook her head. 'Well, good!' she said. 'Would you . . .' She gestured loosely towards the door to Peter's study, across the hall. 'He hit his head. I dressed it, but I wasn't sure . . . Good Lord! Everybody suddenly – just falling over, and . . . ' *They should all lie down. Everybody. It isn't safe.*

Dr Tayle went in, and came out again a few moments later. 'He's, er . . .' he said.

'He's just back from France, doctor,' she murmured.

'Well, he's asleep. Breathing's all right, pulse is all right. Colour's all right.'

The doctor poured two small tots of brandy, and they drank, and felt the ripples run off their shoulders. 'If there's any kind of . . .' he said delicately. 'I can look in tomorrow and . . .'

'Thank you,' she said. 'That's a good . . . We seem to be rather . . .' Her eyes were closed.

All in due course. All in due course. If the drink is really a problem, well, there are places . . . And the cause of the problem is over . . . She took another sip of brandy. 'Happy Christmas, doctor,' she said.

And Tom's back . . . She put her head on her arms, on the table. *Four mad females, two broken men, and a child. I'd better keep them all here for a while, for as long as it takes. Perhaps we could take it in turns to be all right. Just till we get an idea.*

She forgot for a moment that she had a job elsewhere. 'It's fine,' she said. 'It will all be fine.'

Chapter Twenty-nine

Locke Hill, Christmas Eve, 1918

Riley was standing in his coat in the middle of the drawing room, exhausted, wondering where he could clean his tired mouth out, and whether he could just sit here, or lie down here, drop off here. He could walk back through the night to the hospital but he'd rather not and they'd be locked up; he didn't want to bother Rose or get in the way; there was no point in talking to Peter; he didn't know the house . . .

He put a log on the fire, and was just eyeing the largest sofa when Nadine, quiet in her borrowed nightie, poked her head round the door.

Riley turned, saw her. She was already asking a question when she saw it was him, and the words stopped in her throat.

His hand had already grabbed at his scarf to cover himself. It gave an impression of guilt.

His first thought: *God, look at her, just look at her, her face, her look.*

'Don't you dare,' she said quickly – because it appeared to her like a movement of leaving: a man indoors in his coat, lifting his scarf. And, whatever he was doing here, he was not to leave. She stared at him, seeing only him and the fact that it was him. She revelled in the sight of him. He'd let the scarf drop, and stood before her, help-less, his scarf and his hands hanging by his side, his coat open. Bare-throated, bare-headed. His eyes! Diamond-crush eyes – *what are they full of?* She couldn't tell. The tender area at his temples, the flare of his eyebrows, his high forehead with the touch of widow's peak, the shorn curls a little longer again. The little hollow under his cheekbones. The shoulders, the angle of his standing, the cut of his jib, the fact of him, the lurch he induced, the fear and the tenderness. She didn't, for some moments, notice his scars.

Then she did. Her eyes flicked: upper face, lower face. Upper face, lower face. Perfect, mangled. Perfect, mangled.

She realised then what his expression was. *He's waiting. He's waiting for me to flinch, to cry out in horror.*

She stared, straight, confused. *His wound was slight. Why the scars? What did they do to him in there? And why is he here? The girl in Paris – Rose?*

She didn't know what to do. None of it made sense.

His scars were too fresh. The damage too much – but that wasn't damage. It was the facial rebuilding . . .

It became apparent that he had lied to her.

Look at him. He stood there, hardened. He was expecting pity, and he was armoured to reject it.

She walked up very close to him. She leaned in, so close she could smell the soap-and-man-and-greatcoat smell of him, which made her catch her breath. She put her face next to his, and she whispered in his ear, close against his warm white flesh: 'You lying faithless bastard.'

His heart lifted and filled, a slow swelling, a huge joy. As she turned he took her wrist, grabbed it, held it tight. 'Come back,' he said, in his swollen lumpy voice.

'No,' she said. 'Bastard.'

'Please,' he said.

'Why?' she said. 'Liar.'

He lifted his head and the words felt like balm. She yanked her arm away and shook off his hand. She said: 'What are you so pleased about?'

'Truth,' he said.

'What?'

'You're telling the truth,' he said, but she couldn't understand him, so he took out his notebook and scribbled it. The method was second nature to him now, but it made her stare.

'Well, you're not,' she retorted. 'Why aren't you in Paris with your girl? What are you doing here? You and your slight wound.'

He felt the ground sway slightly as he said, quite clearly, 'No girl. No Paris.'

'What – did she drop you?' Nadine said, her voice clear and true and cruel, and she winced even as the words left her mouth, and at the narrowing of his eyes, and she wished it unsaid, but he swallowed, and he took it.

'There was no girl in Paris,' he said. Slowly, lumpily.

That stopped her. She stared at a few points around the room: the orange-glowing lampshades, the brass coal scuttle, the big glass paperweight on the mantelpiece reflecting the light of the remains of the fire. All was shadow and glow.

'No girl,' she said.

'No girl,' he said. He was about to say, 'only you', but the look in her eye stopped him.

'Oh,' she said, taking her time, as everything changed and realisation slipped in. 'You thought I'd drop you so you dropped me first.'

'Stop saying "drop",' he said. 'This isn't some social acquaintance.' The phrase came out mangled but she understood it.

'Oh, no,' she said, very fast, 'of course it isn't. It's – how did you put it? Not that I remember every word of your letter – oh, yes: "We both always knew our friendship could not be anything more." That's what we both knew. That's it. Our *friendship*. Which could not be anything more.' She stared at him, hard-faced.

He said: 'I didn't think you'd drop me. I thought you would stay with me. Out of pity. And that would have been unfair on you. And unbearable to me.' He closed his eyes. *I sound like a drunken, lisping, brain-damaged idiot.*

'Unbearable to you?' she said, in a nasty little singsong way. 'Oh dear, what a pity, poor little—' and he said very faintly, 'Stop,' and she did, ashamed but furious, and not ashamed of fury. A fire of anger and frustration and resentment was burning inside her, building and burning. She could not, she would not – more to the point, she *did* not – feel sorry for him. After what he had done? Was he to be forgiven everything, for ever, because of the bloody war and his bloody wounds? Were none of them ever to be straight with each other again? Were they all to be grateful and noble and gentle and discreet and stiff-upper-lipped for ever more, and never release what was inside? What about truth? What about her, and what she had suffered? What about what she was losing, right here, again, before her eyes? The patronising, arrogant, presumptuous, lying, deceitful bastard.

She turned on him and roared: 'What if I had wanted to stay with you out of love?'

He gazed at her, steady.

'And should it not have been *my* decision?' she cried.

'It should,' he said.

'There's little enough any of us can do to have any control. Over anything. And you decided that you were the one to make that decision for me.'

'I was wrong and stupid and mad,' he said, as clearly as he could. 'About lots of things. There are reasons, but there's no excuse. I'm sorry.'

The 'sorry' was a beautiful word. Tears sprang to her eyes. 'Did Rose tell you I came to the hospital?' she asked at last.

'Yes.'

'Did she tell you how I was that day?'

He flinched. But he was glad, a mighty clean gladness, which stayed with him and upheld him, because they were not lying, and she was not pitying him. 'I misjudged,' he said. 'I was . . . in a crisis. I'm not any more.' Though the words in his mouth were strapped and entangled, his statement was clear, and it flew.

'You're not,' she said.

'Not so much.'

A log fell sideways in the fire, making a tiny noise.

'Did you tell Rose to lie to me?' Nadine asked.

'Yes.'

Her body was caught in the tension between the force that dragged her to him and the force that forbade it. She was swaying. Furious, still.

They stared at each other for quite a while. She started to take in his face: the laboured movements of his mouth, the careful scars where the flaps had been sewn, his own beautiful upper lip lying familiar across the top of the re-upholstered one. The shape of his actual jaw was the same, but there was a padded quality to the flesh, a sense of things at the wrong angle, on the wrong plane. Though a lot of work had been done, clearly, the natural harmony was not there. She was wondering what it had looked like before. What had it looked like when she had tried to visit? What was the initial wound? It had taken so long . . . When had this been done? Was it fully healed? It looked swollen to her, tender.

How had it happened?

He said miserably: 'I'll go in the morning.'

She had the field postcard he had sent her still in her pocket, in her papers, where she always carried it. She rummaged for it now, found it, looked at it.

There. 'Slight'. She thought of him sitting in the clearing station, or the dressing station, filling it in, his face falling off.

The reality of him was such a shock in so many ways. She was still shaking.

When she looked up, the question 'How did it happen?' on her lips, he wasn't there.

She found him outside, by the burning glow of his cigarette in the pearly blackness, sitting on a tarpaulin-covered garden bench under the shivering stars, and went to him, in someone else's overcoat and borrowed gumboots.

'Tell me one thing,' she said, pulling the coat round her, breath hanging on the air.

'What?'

She could hear the emotional pain tangling in the physical distortion of his voice. She sat down by him. 'Anything. Just one thing. To start with.'

The silence deepened around them.

After a small eternity, he said, 'I killed.'

After another, she said: 'I let them die.'

They were both surprisingly unaffected by their confessions. Each had a sense of 'Of course. Is that all?' Each was aware that this could not be called morally normal. Each knew that they couldn't help it. Each knew that the other knew it, and each felt the tendrils of tenderness rising. So when he put his hand out, she gave him hers. When he kissed it and fell to his knees at her feet in the dark on the black muddy lawn, she said: 'I think we should get married now, before anyone has a chance to think about it. Then, whatever else, we'll be safe together.'

He didn't say, 'Are you sure?' It was the only thing they were sure of.

Chapter Thirty

Locke Hill, Christmas Day, 1918

Julia was up first the next morning. She half woke from fitful sedated sleep unaware of what had happened. Only when she tried to open her half-paralysed eyelids, and touched her cheek and felt dressings, did she lurch from her bed to look in the mirror. A horrified elation seized her. What was underneath the slathered ointment and the draped and taped gauze? Dared she look? She didn't need to. She could feel burning and aching, a toxic, insubstantial shredding. Nothing that felt like that could be anything but ugly. Her mind was far from clear, but what was clear to her was that everything she had been was over. No more beautiful face.

After a moment she gave a little laugh. *Well!* The word 'over' was the one that stayed in her mind.

Determined not to hide in bed, and misjudging her physical strength, she went downstairs. She looked into the morning room, saw that Mrs Joyce had laid for breakfast the night before, and then went to the kitchen, where she took out bread and tea and milk, and put the kettle on the range, before her knees gave way and she sat down, feeling very weak and odd. She was sitting at the kitchen table when Tom pottered in, dragging his stocking behind him, looking for someone to witness its glory.

'What have you got there?' Julia asked carefully, through her burnt lips.

Tom was frowning at the sight of her.

'I hurt my face,' said Julia, observing him. His hair was sticking up, like a little duck's tail. 'Don't be frightened.' *The doctor must have given me something – I feel quite light-headed. This is awful, to let Tom see this.*

'Poor Mummy,' said Tom.

When Peter came in, looking for water, shambolic and seedy in last night's clothes, hangover dripping from him like slime, he stopped dead at the sight of his wife crying through her dressings, and the little boy sitting with her, patting her shoulder, saying, 'Poor Mummy.'

Julia looked up at him. Amazement stopped her tears. She hadn't known that he was here. 'You look dreadful,' she said.

'You too,' he said. 'But I think I smell worse.'

'You can bathe,' she said.

'I will,' he said. 'Um . . .'

'I did something stupid,' she said. 'To my face. I may be ugly now. I don't know.'

It was too much for him. He blinked. Her eyes were blue and clear. That he saw.

'Mummy,' said Tom, in an explanatory way, to Peter.

'Yes,' he said. His son's eyes were just like Julia's. Four great big blue eyes. 'I am most awfully sorry,' he said.

There was a pause.

'Tom, this is your father,' Julia said. She was holding the little boy's hand.

Tom stared, disbelieving. 'Daddy,' he murmured experimentally, not convinced.

''Fraid so, old chap,' Peter said. He folded himself down from his great height to squat by him, and put his hand over his own mouth.

Tom hid his face in Julia's shoulder. (Her heart swelled at this, and the clean smell of his hair.) He peeked out again.

Peter was watching him, smiling a little. 'Mummy and Daddy,' he said ruefully.

'Poor Daddy,' Tom said, and came over to him, and patted his shoulder too. *How does he know?* Peter thought. He put his arms round the boy. Tiny.

'Pooh,' Tom said. 'Smelly.'

He was holding their child in his arms. 'I am most awfully sorry,' he said again.

'So am I,' said Julia. 'I suppose I've ruined everything, really . . .'

'Oh, I don't think it was you,' Peter said.

'But everything is ruined, isn't it?'

He was rubbing his forehead with his long white hand. 'Could I perhaps be allowed a bath and a shave, do you suppose, before we . . . before you . . .'

'What?'

'Discuss things . . .'

'Do we have to?' she murmured miserably.

'I suppose we . . . I'd rather like, if . . . Well, perhaps we don't. I just had an idea about, um . . .'

Julia's shoulders were hunched up around her neck. She said: 'I don't know if I'll be up to much.'

'I don't suppose, um,' he said. 'I mean, nobody, really . . . none of us is at our best.'

Mrs Joyce was next in: bustling, shocked at Julia's being up, shooing and cuddling Tom, almost fainting at the sight of Peter. She made them all go into the morning room and sit, and be brought their breakfast, and made Julia promise to go straight back up to bed afterwards. *They look like ghosts, the pair of them.*

'Bath and a shave first,' Peter said. 'Will you wait for me?' His eyes were still on his wife. He couldn't remove them from her.

'Don't stare at me . . .' she said, ashamed.

'I'm glad to see you,' he said. 'That's all.'

'Oh,' she said. That was what it came down to. He was glad to see her. 'Well,' she said. 'I'd better . . .' The nervous hysterical laughter was still lurking. *Better not laugh. Too mad. Oh, God. Peter, this really isn't what I . . .*

'Yes,' he said. 'Yes . . .'

They were both completely incapable.

～

Rose ran into Peter on the landing outside his bedroom as he emerged, clean and pale, in strangely fitting civvies from before the war.

'Oh, gosh, hello,' he said.

She threw her arms round him. 'Oh, my dear, my dear,' she said. 'Oh, my dear.'

He was pleased. He had been so very scared of the reception he would get.

~

Nadine appeared during breakfast.

'Good Lord!' Peter blinked.

'Hello,' she said, shy with him now, remembering Paris, lying drunk as lords on the lawn of the Tuileries.

'She's staying,' Rose said. 'I thought you wouldn't mind.'

'How could I?' said Peter, gallantly.

Nadine had turned to Julia, and gasped.

Julia, who had been quietly watching Peter, following his every move, disbelieving, almost, in his physical actuality, rose to the occasion. 'I've burned my face,' she said calmly, through her tight lips. 'Stupidly. My own fault.' Looking around, looking at Peter – *Look! Peter! The real man! He's as real as Tom, and here, they're here* – veils were lifting. As a pattern becomes recognisable at a distance, as monsters disappear when the curtains are pulled wide, it was beginning to become clear to her what folly she had been immersed in. But now . . . now . . . *what made me mad is over. Peter needs me sane more than he needs me beautiful. How could I not have known that? If he needs me at all . . . Oh, look at him, look at his shoulders, his hands. He needs . . . he needs everything.*

'Oh! Well—' Nadine was saying.

'But of course you must stay,' Julia said. 'Please.' She felt like a queen. She could look up, look out. She could show concern for others. Now she could start to be what she should have been. Wife and mother. 'Excuse me,' she said.

399

'I must . . .' and as she rose, her legs gave way, and Peter
and Mrs Joyce took her back upstairs.

$\approx$

After a while, Rose saw Riley through the French windows,
walking up the garden. Quickly, she said: 'Nadine, there's
something I must—' *Oh dear, there's quite a lot—*

   'I've already seen him,' Nadine said, and as she said it,
huge joy rose like a balloon inside her, and a radiant smile
burst on to her face, a smile she couldn't help, that made
Tom blink and laugh, and Peter, returning, say, 'What?
What's going on?'

$\approx$

The day developed strange and pure and outside time; a
pause between the late chaos and the approaching future.
Peter took Tom out to run around the gardens and play
with Max. Lunch was the chicken, which Mrs Joyce
roasted. Harker produced some leeks. When Peter reached
for the decanter, Rose said nothing. Afterwards Peter and
Tom played Poor Man's Patience on the floor of Julia's
room, very quietly, and when Mrs Joyce brought up a
pot of tea, Julia roused a little and fed Tom some sugar
biscuit dipped in milk, because she wanted to say how
much she wanted now to look after them, both of them,
properly, but she couldn't say it. Peter was unable to help
her out, but late in the afternoon, before falling asleep
in her chair with Tom on his knee, he called her 'my
dear', and that seemed all right. 'Plenty of time,' he murmured, every now and again. Not until Mrs Joyce took

Tom to bed, and Julia was sleeping, did Peter start on the whisky.

Nadine and Riley spent all day in the drawing room, by the fire, among the plump silk cushions on the chintz sofa, their feet tucked under each other's legs. She fell asleep, over and over. He sketched small parts of her – an ear, a wrist, a foot – letting her rest. Thoughts – *her parents, my parents, Sir Alfred* – drifted across his mind, gulls mewing, high in the distance. Riley had realised, looking around at the others, that though he was not very far along, he was further along than the rest of them. He thought about Mickey Shirlaw: a mess when he had arrived at Sidcup, a useful member of the medical team now.

Rose looked in. 'Stay,' Riley murmured, so she did, even though there shone around him and Nadine a glow, a dazzle, that repelled outsiders. Towards dusk, a log fell in the fire and Nadine, woken by the sound, looked up and laid her hand on Riley's tender, swollen, misshapen jaw. 'Is this it, then?' she asked gently, with the frown of waking. 'Is it fully healed now?'

Rose answered. She said, 'Well, the worst of it's over, but very deep bruising can take forever to come through,' and Riley felt the tight stretch of a small, dark smile over his cheekbones.

Nobody expected anybody to leave, or converse much, or anything. Nobody talked about the terrible things they had all seen and done and had done to them, or of the vast and treacherous swamp of recovery and practicality that lay ahead of them. There was an air in the house of disbelief, of shock; a silence too great and mysterious to be broken by more than the quietest courtesies. 'Will you have some tea?' 'Here, let me pass that.' The silence seemed to have crept out across the drenched lawn and dead roses, the wet garden, the village, out over the ancient sleeping Downs, with grief and realisation hanging in it like rain in clouds. It covered England, under the grey and silver wintry air, and the sleeping heavy Channel. It lay all across France, and Belgium, and Germany, Poland and Russia; all over the great heart of Europe, her fields and rivers, grass and stones and black wet earth, and it rose up through the layers of cloud racked against the wide and empty sky, and the dusk descending. In due course it would become for some a great and unbreakable dumbness, from which reconciling truth would never be able to break free; for others, a healing silence from which some peace might be redeemed.

Historical note

This novel is fiction with aspects of fact. The history and medicine are as accurate as I have been able to make them. Frognal House and the Queen's Hospital are real; the house belonged to the Marsham-Townshend family, whose son Ferdinand was killed in 1915. The characters are fictional, apart from Major Gillies, Major Fry, Vicarage, Sir James Barrie, Archie Lane, Mickey Shirlaw, Mr Scott the barber and Albert his boy, Miss Black, Henry Tonks, Williams the Nigerian, Brilliant Chang, Sir James Barrie, and Lady Scott, who was my grandmother, and my introduction to the miracles performed at Sidcup.

There were patients called Jamison and Jarvis, but they are not the characters for whom I have borrowed their names. Jack Ainsworth from Wigan did die of wounds at Hebuterne in 1916; his daughter Annie, Granny Annie, as I knew of her, carried Sybil's prayer in her purse, and passed it on to her grandson who showed it to me. And Jock Anderson really did break every window in the unit to celebrate his fiftieth operation. I intend my use of these men's names to honour all the patients at Sidcup, and the staff: in particular I think often of Corporal Riley, number 139 in Harold Gillies's book *Plastic Surgery of the Face* (1920).

Three other books I raided rather shamelessly are *The Great War and Modern Memory*, by Paul Fussell (1975); *Sexual Life during the World War*, by HC Fischer and Dr EX Dubois (1937) and *King's Nurse, Beggar's Nurse*, by Catherine Black (1939).

Any mistakes in what I have attempted to make an accurate historical context for a fictional story are my own.

Acknowledgements

I would like to thank Dr Andrew Bamji FRCP, curator of the Gillies Archive at Sidcup, very much, for the kind and useful help he gave me when busy with far more important things; the Wellcome for first exhibiting the field postcard which inspired me, and then letting me use it in this book; Robert Lockhart for the melody which is now irretrievably entwined with this story; my agents Derek Johns, Linda Shaughnessy, Rob Kraitt and Sylvie Rabineau; my editor Katie Espiner; my former co-author Isabel Adomakoh Young; my literate and generous friends Susan Swift Flusfeder and Charlotte Horton, and Robert Lockhart (again) and my cousins-in-law-to-be Diane Haselden and Denise Grundy for lending me the photograph of their great-grandfather Jack Ainsworth, and letting me transform him into an invention of my own.

And, in memoriam, John and Kath Lockhart, and Wayland Young.

Reading Group
Guide

Author Q&A

What inspired you to write My Dear, I Wanted to Tell You?

My grandmother, Kathleen Scott, was a sculptor, and during World War One she worked briefly casting the faces of wounded men, to help surgeons who were trying to rebuild their damaged faces. I wrote her biography years ago, and came across photographs, drawings and diagrams of those early years of maxillofacial surgery which have never left me. The courage of the doctors on one side and the damaged young men on the other seemed to me quite extraordinary, and yet, in wartime, in a war on that scale, it was not extraordinary, it was quite everyday. So how do human beings cope with that? How do we deal with what is unbearable? Also, like most people, I am secretly fascinated by the strange line where the miraculous and the disgusting meet.

Can you tell us a little bit about your creative process?

I read a lot, I try to write, sometimes I succeed. I tend not to know why. I may write nothing for weeks on end, and get more and more frustrated, and then I remember that this is part of the process, and write like a mad thing for a few months. I do dream of writerly solitude, and love it when I achieve it, but then I get lonely.

Are there any authors or prominent figures who influence your work?

Everyone I've ever read. Or nobody. It depends on my mood. I can't name particular people though. It always suggests you're comparing yourself to them, which can make you sound a bit of a prat.

Where did you come across the field postcard from which the book takes its title?

I saw it in an exhibition at the Wellcome Collection in London. When a soldier was injured, it might take a while for news to get home, either via the official telegram, or in a letter which would have to go through the censors. These pre-printed tick-the-box multiple-choice postcards were available at field hospitals and could go directly. I saw it in the display case, and found it touching, sitting there, pristine, nearly a hundred years later. I felt sorry for it, that its purpose had never been fulfilled – but then its purpose would have been a sad one. It seemed to hold an untold story – what story? I imagined having to fill in a card like this – the circumstances under which it would come about – and that became the first scene that I wrote: Riley at the casualty clearing station. I thought: you'd lie. Of course you would. What are you going to say? 'My Dear Mum, I have been badly wounded in the balls'? Of course not...

Also, it echoed what everyone always says about their soldier dad or granddad or uncle or brother: 'Oh, he never talked about it, after the war was over.' I bet they wanted to, some of them. They must have wanted to. The men in the photographs from the Queen's Hospital seemed to me to be desperate to talk.

What kind of research did you undertake when coming up with the plot? Are any of the events based on a true story?

I read everything in sight, and stole all kinds of true things for this story. My grandmother appears, Major Gillies is real, and the Queen's Hospital at Sidcup, its barber and the cigarette girl, the houses on Bayswater Road (I grew up in one of them). And there was a patient who did what Riley Purefoy does to Nadine, though we're not told what became of them in the long run. I've tried to keep the history accurate.

Many people are profoundly moved when reading the novel. Which part was the hardest to write?

None. It came naturally. I did make myself cry quite often. I don't find that hard though.

Do you have any personal connection to the events depicted?

Yes, a great deal.

What does the future hold for Louisa Young?
I'm writing a sequel now, about Riley, Nadine, Rose, Julia
and Peter in their forties, and their children, and the
coming of World War Two. It brings in Nadine's family
across Europe. The book is doing what it wants, which I
like. The characters are real to me now; they do what they
do, and I don't have to push them around. It's much easier.
They generate their own chaos, and their own patterns
within it.

There's going to be some more books after these two.
1918 is done, 1938 I'm working on, and I foresee 1943,
1952, 1965, 1976 – then I'll regret not having written 1928,
1936, 1948, 1959 . . . I think I may be writing the twentieth
century, through these families. Or at least these families
through the twentieth century.

Discussion Points

- -

Class

'Riley was neither shy nor ashamed to be there. He did not
feel that he was in the wrong place.' (page 15)

'Not good enough for their girl, only fit to be used by
their boy.' (page 43)

To what extent does Riley's class influence his behaviour,
and the behaviour of others, throughout the novel?

War

'Length of service: one year or duration of war? Duration of war of course. He didn't want to spend a whole year in the army.' (page 46)

How does Riley's attitude to the war change as the novel progresses?

Do you think the actions of Riley and his reasons for going to war were good ones and do you think society has learnt lessons from the atrocities that occurred, or is it still happening today?

Do you think society's attitude to going to war today differs from the attitude at the time of World War One?

Beauty

'Julia had learnt to love her own beauty, because beauty was her currency, and other people valued it so highly.' (page 83)

Discuss how this view of Julia's influences her behaviour throughout the novel.

Compare her experiences of plastic surgery with those of Riley's. Is feeling ugly on the inside really that different to looking ugly on the outside?

The Role of Women

'A girl needs a good reputation, these days more than ever. Art school is for times of peace and plenty, not for unmarried girls in wartime.' (page 93)

Consider this advice that Nadine's mother gives her. How does this symbolise society's attitude to women, and does the war change this view in the novel?

Communication
'*My Dear, I Wanted to Tell You*'

The title of the novel is taken from a standard-issue field postcard that soldiers had to fill in during the war – Riley fills in one such field postcard on page 216.

Consider the ways we communicated with our loved ones then compared to now.

If you liked My Dear, I Wanted to Tell You *you might enjoy:*

The Night Watch by Sarah Waters
The Very Thought of You by Rosie Alison
The Regeneration Trilogy by Pat Barker
Birdsong & *Charlotte Gray* by Sebastian Faulks
Hotel on the Corner of Bitter and Sweet by Jamie Ford
The Outcast & *Small Wars* by Sadie Jones
Atonement by Ian McEwan
The Still Point by Amy Sackville